From distant regions of the galaxy to the offices of the world's most advanced corporation a war rages between good and evil. Caught in the middle, a young woman fights to save those she loves while struggling with her own terror. The Robot's Daughter is a stand alone novel although it is the second book in the Shaman Gene series. It is a nominee for the 2015 Global Ebook Awards

.

THE ROBOT'S DAUGHTER

by
W. Blake Heitzman

2015 Global Ebook Award Nominee

Arched Gate Books

Acknowledgements

This book has been a team effort. Many thanks to Pauline Nolet for patiently working through many drafts and offering suggestions that brought the story to life. More about Pauline can be found at her website: http://www.paulinenolet.com/.

Thanks to Aidana WillowRaven for creating a fantastic cover that conveys a sense of the supernatural and the mystery of the story. Many thanks to my critique partners: Cindy Harris, Shannon Brown, Patricia Boyle, Elena Manzo, and Tanda Clauson, for keeping me on track and writing clearly.

Dedication:

To my loving wife, for her support and understanding during the grueling process of birthing this story.

Table of Contents

Chapter 1: Near Earth

Yanitur, the youngest captain in the Associated Galactic Societies (AGS) Navy, was commissioned to *Quantum*, an Ajax-class cruiser powered by generation III dark-matter drives. Assigned to the frontier of the Second Galactic Leg, Yanitur pushed the engines hard and arrived at his patrol sector four years ahead of schedule, to the good fortune of Earth and the Amazonian child.

**

March 26th, 1954, in space near Earth

The observation deck was deserted and as dark as the void above it. Yanitur sipped his drink and gazed into blackness speckled by infrequent stars, their sparkle lost in the emptiness of the galactic fringe.

He thought of the Nirvanian home sky, its night thick with stars: blues, reds, yellows, and whites strung like lights overhead, declaring a perpetual raucous party. Home in another galactic leg, so distant its cornucopia of stars was a wisp as ephemeral as a morning haze hanging low, shifting, thinning, disappearing; the disbelieving eye wondering if it were there at all. Home, a haze so remote it might no longer exist.

Yanitur downed his drink in one long swallow and lowered the glass to the table with a loud clang.

The intercom beeped, followed by First Officer Kale's voice. "Captain, we've picked up an interesting signal."

7

Yanitur laughed. "Yesterday, we all thought this tour would be fifty years of boredom."

"I wouldn't say we were all that wrong, yet." Despite Kale's proviso, he sounded excited.

Yanitur's curiosity heightened. "Signal? You do mean communication from a sentient being, right?"

"More like was a sentient being. It's archaic." Kale couldn't restrain his enthusiasm further. "It's AGS."

The single known possibility flashed in Yanitur's mind. He coughed and slammed the top of his fist against his chest. "Say again."

"It appears to be an old AGS beacon. It's been shredded by gamma, but the computers reconstructed a few segments. It contains two occurrences of the name 'Gimish.'"

Naomi broke in near Kale, "Captain, wouldn't it be crazy if we're the ones who found Gimish?"

Her sexy, upbeat voice delighted Yanitur. It left no doubt why Uriel had used every chip ever owed him to get her on *Quantum*'s maiden mission.

"I gather," Yanitur said, "that my officers have briefed you on the legend of Gimish."

"The Gimish Paradox is a topic in the social ethics curriculum at the academy. Gimish, the first Nirvanian to reach the Second Galactic Leg, became stranded on a planet called Earth for three thousand years, then was rescued and time transported back to his original era."

"Yes, and the paradox is?" Yanitur asked.

"History verifies that Gimish returned to his historical period; however, as of yet no AGS ship has found him. So he is both found and yet unfound, hence the paradox. Frankly, Captain, we cadets thought it was a myth made up to encourage us to persevere regardless of how dire our situation became."

Yanitur chuckled. "You wouldn't be the first class to think that."

Uriel, also near Kale, solicited Naomi, "And what else is Gimish famous for?"

Yanitur flipped on the holographic screen and watched her eyes lavish Uriel with adulation. "He developed cell bonding, which allowed him to configure his intellectual seraph into the form of a humanoid, whom he named Herman Rothe. Legend says, he left—or

8

will leave—Rothe on Earth to guide its inhabitants into the AGS fold."

"Well," Kale interrupted, "if I can redirect the conversation back to our current situation. Of significance, we have inventoried a star with habitable planets about 2.34 light-years from here."

"Have you pinpointed the 'Gimish' beacon?" Yanitur asked.

Uriel spoke up. "We'll have to execute a search pattern to home in on it."

"Okay," Yanitur said, "let's survey the habitable solar system then come back to find the beacon. Deploy a marker here."

Yanitur signed off. In the background, he could hear Uriel and Naomi talking excitedly about how, as rescuers of Gimish, they would both be immortalized in history.

Yanitur swirled the ice in his glass and shook his head. He thought a moment then flipped the intercom back on. "Hey, Kale, it's going to take a couple of hours to get to that habitable solar system. Can you cut loose for a game?"

Kale's sigh roared in the microphone. "Cube ball? Yeah, I owe you one."

"Good luck with that. Uriel, please relieve the first officer so I can give him a cube schooling." Yanitur started for the ball court.

Only five decades separated them, with both in their prime, but Yanitur's long body and limbs gave him the advantage at cube ball. The captain never challenged the first officer to stick sparring, a sport where Kale's compact mass held the edge. When the crew kidded Kale about being a patsy, he shook it off, saying, "You wouldn't want to ride with a captain who jumps into situations he can't win."

**

Two hours later

The ball smacked off three cube walls in a rat-tat-tat. Kale somersaulted off the ceiling and extended his glove to deflect it.

"Gentlemen." Uriel's voice boomed over the men's heavy breathing and ball's collisions with the walls.

For once Kale had gained position. Yanitur yanked the first officer's ankle back. The ball tipped Kale's mitt and deflected to the ceiling.

"Gentlemen," Uriel repeated with school-master ire.

"To be continued," Kale said, then twisted his foot from Yanitur's grip.

9

Yanitur's chest quivered with silent laughter. Kale flipped his mitt at Yanitur's head then pushed himself toward the gravity control panel.

"May I speak?" Uriel asked.

"Just a second," Kale replied. "You ready?" he asked Yanitur. Yanitur nodded and Kale counted down to the restoration of gravity, "Three, two, one, gravity initialized." Instantly, they both slumped. Their legs wobbled while they regained their balance.

Yanitur placed a palm against the wall. "No matter how many times you've done it, you're still never quite ready."

"Gentlemen."

"Yes, Uriel," Yanitur said.

"The third planet in this solar system is in the early Nuclear Age."

"A prospective AGS customer," Kale wisecracked.

"Yeah, maybe in a thousand years." Uriel spoke in a deadpan comedian tone. "And we've already got a competitor." He let the humanoids absorb his words. "There's a spook dogging the planet."

A rush shot through Yanitur's body. "Yesterday, we thought we faced fifty years of mental petrifaction. Now, we have a twofer, Gimish's artifact and a snooper."

The crew, at least the live ones, and maybe the new model seraphim, felt the same. He could hear it in the timbre of Uriel's voice and the chatter coming from the bridge.

"What can you tell me about this spook?" Yanitur asked.

"We can't get an ion read, yet," Uriel replied.

"Move into analysis range, but stay hidden." Yanitur had reason to be confident. In 19,000 years of galactic exploration the Nirvanians had never met a superior force.

"Shall we wait for you on the bridge?" Uriel asked.

Yanitur looked at Kale. Every contour of Kale's body showed through the sweat-soaked cube suit.

Kale grimaced and hugged himself like a swimmer emerging from cold water. "The observation deck is closer, and warmer."

"We'll holograph in from the observation deck," Yanitur said.

While the captain and first officer moved to the observation deck, *Quantum* glided into the solar system and hovered near the moon of a large ringed planet.

**

Uriel's hazy holographic image grinned at the officers when they entered the room. "I've got a particulate signature."

They approached him. The ghostly forms of the bridge and its staff filled in around them.

Uriel pointed to the alien craft's image on a monitor. "It's a class A freighter."

"Verg?" Kale's forehead wrinkled in disbelief.

Yanitur's lips curled up in a half snarl. "Their modus operandi, but how are they here?"

The Vergish empire, broken by AGS over five millennia earlier, existed today as ragged bands of pirates that preyed on underdeveloped cultures beyond the borders of AGS control, cultures like the early Nuclear Age planet here.

"We've got a good trace on him now. From the pattern, it's certain he's monitoring the inhabited planet," Uriel said.

Yanitur clicked his tongue against the inside of his cheek, making a popping noise. Scattered chuckles broke out across the bridge, relieving the tension.

Yanitur cleared his throat. "Okay, folks, it's our job to protect this sector of the galaxy. Let's shake him down.

"Feed the view of the solar system to the screen here."

The dark void above the observation deck burst with pulsing reds and oranges that winced Yanitur's eyes into slits.

"Geez, Uriel," Kale said, raising his palm to shade his eyes. "You could have phased that in."

Uriel groaned. "Sorry, guys, forgot about your biological frailties."

"Lock him." Yanitur referred to the Verg transport.

"Locked." The holographic image of Uriel's face turned to Yanitur. "He's beaconless."

"Put him on the screen," Yanitur said.

The blinding sun vanished and the view shifted to the white and blue swirled globe of the third planet.

Yanitur studied the scene. "If he spots us, he'll raise the insignia of a harmless merchant."

"There's an eighty-three percent probability he's running slaves," Uriel said. "Either he has them on board now, or he's planning to take some from that planet."

"Or both." Kale spat his words, emphasizing his disgust.

"Or both?" Uriel knotted his eyebrows in reprimand, a pedantic assertion that the branches of an "or" statement are not exclusive.

Kale ignored him.

"Argus, energize your weapons," Yanitur told his armaments seraph. "If he runs, destroy his generators."

"Captain Yanitur, I am operational now." Across the observation deck, Argus coupled himself to the ship's battle stations, linking his internal computers to the ship's sensors and weapons.

Uriel maneuvered *Quantum* into the shadow of the third planet and waited.

The alien ship drifted from behind the far side of the moon. An archetypal class A transport, with antennas and sensors protruding from its hull like spines, it looked like an inflated blowfish.

"They've retrofitted it with ion dynamic thrusters and a battery of mid-range sonic pulse weapons," Uriel reported. "Statistically, they have a dozen combat träger robots on board. The standard deviation is two. The capacity of the hold, crammed inhumanely full, is about two thousand slaves."

When the ship was close and vulnerable, Yanitur opened every communication channel, including short-range pulses that would resonate in the freighter's hull. "Flagless transport, you are in violation of AGS naval code. Hold for an inspection boarding."

The Verg ship accelerated in an attempt to put the moon between the ships. That action, among the thousands of data points flowing to Argus's decision matrix, was the one he needed, and when the transport lunged, he struck its main generator, sending the vessel wobbling.

The Verg ship's response was seamless. Regaining control while bringing auxiliary power online, it continued to run for cover.

If nothing else, Yanitur thought, *Vergs are excellent pilots*. When he considered it, there was nothing else good about them.

"Pursue," Yanitur ordered. *Quantum* surged, but not fast enough. The Verg disappeared behind the curve of the moon.

As if locked in time, everyone froze and stared at the screen. They all knew what was next. With the moon as a shield, the pirates would shove their slaves into garbage bins and blast them into the sun.

***

The Slave Ship

Months ago, Katiri knew the Verg pirates would take Viekki, her thirteen-year-old daughter, during the orgies of Saint Eros. Days before *Quantum* attacked the slave ship, Katiri gathered her two children into the corner of their living space, no more than a cargo crate, one of many that lined the corridor of Slave Block 31A. Each had only enough space for sleeping mats and a stack of meager possessions: bowls, a water basin, and a few clothes.

Katiri told Viekki it was necessary for her to accommodate their Verg captors. Viekki, daughter of a warrior, protested. "We should have died. We should never have surrendered to them.

"When they come for me, I will pluck out their eyes and rip their ears from the sides of their heads. They will kill me and I will die a warrior, not a slave." Her narrow face knotted, squishing her eyes into angry slits.

Meirri, Viekki's four-year-old sister, sat on a mat and rubbed the soles of her feet together, a sign that the argument between sis and Mom distressed her.

For a moment Katiri disengaged from Viekki and sifted her fingers through Meirri's long raven hair, letting it slide from her palm and down the side of her daughter's head.

Meirri grabbed her ankles and held them still. She grinned, her coal black eyes twinkling at Katiri as if to say that squalor and subjugation, enslavement, and rape were just a game like the ones they used to play when they wore fine robes, vibrant in color and geometry. This game was the penalty round levied against them for being ill-prepared.

Had we been unprepared? Meirri's feet began to slide against each other.

Katiri's face turned stone hard. She locked eyes with the youngster.

Meirri stilled her legs again.

Katiri whirled about. Her arm shot out, fingers clamping on Viekki's purplish-red hair, the same color as her own. She yanked the teenager's face close and hissed, "These walls are thin. Make no more threats against the pirates. Hear me?"

Viekki's teeth locked, trapping her words within. Her eyes steamed hatred at her mother.

Meirri's fingers strained white to hold her feet motionless.

13

Viekki grasped Katiri's wrist and shoved. Katiri gripped harder, her fingers knotting the hair and pulling against its roots.

They stood like that, frozen in tension. A silent tear dripped from the corner of Viekki's eye and slid down the side of her nose. Her hand softened but remained against her mother's wrist.

As suddenly as she had assailed Viekki, Katiri released her and pulled her close. She caressed her child's cheek, then combed her fingers through Viekki's hair, straightening and untangling the knots she'd caused.

"Daughter, be brave for our people and our family: Meirri, your mother, you, and me. Since you were young you have heard: When arms fail, minds shall rule, thus Amazonia shall prevail. We are here because the call to battle has passed from the military to the Katameiri.

"Go with the scum and buy us a few more days. Soon we shall commandeer this old dirigible and warn our people of the new enemy."

She took Viekki by the shoulders and held her at arm's length. "When we take the ship, you can kill the ones who abused you."

Viekki clenched her fists until her fingernails dug into her palms. She looked to the ceiling and through gritted teeth she said, "I will pull their intestines out…"

Katiri held her finger to her lips. "Shush," she warned, then smiled. "Just a bit longer. The Katameiri have learned how to run this ship. A little more time and the slaves will take it."

She turned to Meirri and sang out, "Isn't that so, my little Katameirini?"

Meirri pointed to three pluses carved into her inner wrist, the mark of the Katameiri, the eight percent of the Amazonian race born with eidetic minds capable of mapping and understanding things of great complexity. Even at four years, Meirri's head was full of numbers, pictures, and diagrams regarding the operation of the Verg spaceship, all compiled from bits and pieces of information delivered to the Katameiri by slaves working throughout the vessel. Today, any Katameiri could operate the ship. They only waited for the slave revolt.

That was the goal, but if the revolt failed, then everyone, Vergs and slaves, would be killed. Killed in such a way as to warn their sisters and allies of the new threat.

14

Viekki glared at her little sister's arm. Meirri dropped her wrist, hiding the scars against her inner thigh. Viekki repressed her envy of Miekki's status and smiled. Meirri laughed, but kept her wrist against her leg.

Katiri pinched Viekki's cheek and shook it gently. "When we get back to the people, your mother will be proud of you."

**

It was the custom of the pirates to draw lots, letting a few have the young virgins the day before the entire crew used them. The morning the lucky ones were to take Viekki, Balo wandered into Slave Block 31A, the home of fifty-some slaves, both Amazonian and Nirvanian.

Meirri, sitting in the doorway, saw him approach. She poked her head inside and said, "Mama, Balo."

Working a hypnotic spell on her older daughter, Katiri pushed her palms toward Viekki and intoned, "D-e-e-e-s-p-a-a-a-c-i-oooo." She stared at Meirri and blinked as if coming out of a trance herself.

"Balo," Mierri repeated louder.

"Sleep," Katiri said to Viekki. The teenager's eyelids closed. Katiri jumped to her feet and hurried to the doorway. Her back against the wall, she raised her left foot under her thigh, causing her slave smock to barely cover her vulva.

Balo leaned toward her in a lustful ogle.

"You got somethin' to trade?" Katiri snapped then leered back at him.

"Fresh algae cake."

"Let me see," Katiri demanded.

Balo fumbled in his pants pocket then held out a bundle wrapped in crumpled paper.

"I need to see the cake, not your nasty old paper." Katiri made rapid unwrapping motions with her hands.

He hurried to her, opening the paper, leaf by leaf, as if it held jewels. They spoke in hushed whispers.

"At breakfast, officers said Piddling Cluster Station marked a G cruiser banging our way two days ago. If it latches, they're going to wipe."

Meirri knew the lingo. It meant that an AGS patrol was in the region, and if it got too close, the pirates would push the slaves into the garbage modules and blast them into the sun.

15

The paper lay open on his hand, revealing four cubes of algae cake. "One or two?" He fixed his eyes on the cakes.

"Have you news from Kalininni?"

Meirri bent toward them and tried to focus on his half-hidden lips.

His answer was so heavy with implications that he had to pry it from his throat. It came out with a croak. "No."

Meirri's heart jumped. The child of four hadn't been told the takeover plan, but a child with the mind of a Katameiri didn't need to be told.

Now Katiri took extra time. She paused and flashed a quick glance to Meirri. Then she extended two fingers and pressed them onto the top of a blue cake. "Rotten," she said then whispered, "Luck."

The spicy odor of the pirates' aftershave wafted into the hall.

"Mommy, Vergs."

Katiri laughed at Meirri's attempted stealth.

Her mirth sank into quick sobriety. "If Kalininni has the locks to the bridge, then she can change my decision. Now go! Out the back! The Vergs are here for Viekki."

Balo dipped his head. "Yes, my Queen."

It was nice, under the circumstances, that her AGS attaché still called her his queen.

The pirates' footsteps rang down the hall while Balo slipped out the back alley. Katiri yanked one sleeve from her shoulder down to the crick of her elbow, tearing the cloth and exposing one breast when she did. She slapped her face several times, bringing a rosy blush to her cheeks.

"Awake, Viekki, awaken," she said.

Eyes flinging wide, Viekki panted, "Are they done with me?"

The Vergs' jovial voices became louder.

"No. I need you alert—both of you." Katiri clapped her cupped hands, causing a loud pop. Viekki's face blossomed with its first joyous smile in months. At the same instant two pirates stepped across the threshold of their cargo crate.

"No need for applause. I'm Curly," a boney-faced Verg said. He made a mock bow, causing his stringy yellow hair to flip in ropey clumps over his face. His partner, a wide-shouldered dark man, contorted his cheeks into a disapproving frown.

Giggling lustfully, Katiri rushed to the blond and took his hand to her breast. Like a barroom wench, she clipped endings from

words and added sounds to others while slurring the entire mess together. "Takes me too. I ain't been funning for many a turn."

She cupped her hand between his legs and squeezed slightly while grinning at the dark one, who did not grin back. "I'll show the younging whats ya likes. Make her hot at the groaning and moaning. She'll be begging ya to takes her." Katiri winked at Viekki, who stared back, petrified, in a perfect mixture of horror and bewilderment.

Curly raised his eyebrows at the dark one, who tried to suppress a smile while he shook his head no.

"Eh," Curly said. "It's fucking Eros. Everyone should be funnin', even the old hag." Curly looked her up and down. "She be lookin' good yet. Won't last forever. Shame to waste it."

Face stone cold, Dark One jerked his head toward the door and grunted, "Bring 'er."

Katiri took Meirri's hand and dragged her to her feet.

"Leaves the little one," Curly ordered. His brows furrowed into threatening knots. "She'll just whine when things get going. Takes the flavor outta it."

"She ain't no whiner." Katiri held Meirri's hand for them to see the scars on her wrist.

The Dark One recoiled in disgust. "These people be barbarians, carvin' with knives on chillins."

"You do that?" Curly growled through his teeth.

Katiri wobbled her head with sudden terror and stuttered, "It show she be one wit' our people." She rubbed her thumb over the scars. "But I cain't left her wit' dem utters. No tellin' what da men folks doed wit' her."

"Bring 'er," the Dark One huffed, "But keeps her mout' shut when funnin' starts."

**

The five of them stood before the pirates' playroom door. Curly, his face flushed with arousal, laid his thigh over Katiri's hip like a dog. He cocked his head to his accomplice and said, "We ought work her over good first, so's da virgin gets warmed to the idea."

Dark One squinted at Katiri, who winked and pushed her chin down on her naked shoulder. His head bobbing in agitation, he said, "You oughts be sayin' ya wants it, thinks ya so? Or want ya the

17

little missy bein' all scared and makin' fits. Gets herselfs hurt maybe. Thinks ya on that, eh?"

Katiri's eyes flashed while she licked her lips. In short hot breaths, she said, "Oh, yeah, me first would be pleasin'." She turned to Viekki. "So's ya sees what be funs for 'em."

Curly leaned toward his darker companion and whispered, "What thinks we makes the tiny one sit outside while we be funnin'?"

The dark one smiled wolfishly. "Me thinks it good fer the young one to learn, so when her day come, it ain't no surprise."

Curly wrinkled his nose into a snarl. "Surprise be good. Makes 'em frantic not knowin' what be next."

That was when *Quantum* torpedoed the slave ship's engines.

Even with auto-adjusting gravity, the floor lurched and they all staggered to regain balance. A speaker crackled in the corridor, "Man stations—man stations—wipe down—wipe down— commence full wipe down." A siren wailed and drowned the broadcast, which continued to drone on.

"Damn!" Curly looked wistfully from the females to his partner.

From end to end, the ship rumbled with a deep hollow groan. The pirates' faces went from lust to terror. They muddled about in mindless little steps while their lips twitched indecisive words back and forth. Their eyes flicked from the game-room door to the main corridor, where the distant rumble of panicked voices increased in volume.

"Perhaps it be a slug; all this commotion be for naught," Curly said. Their eyes turned hopeful.

Viekki took Meirri's hand. They watched their mother's face and waited.

The escape chute, Meirri thought. Katiri had taught her the map of the ship. She knew an escape module was ten steps ahead and to the left. Katiri widened her eyes and glanced toward it.

She wants us to go there. Meirri tugged Viekki's thumb.

The siren began to cycle in short then long pulses.

"No gamin'," Dark One said. "We got to be wipin'."

The pirates stood still, frozen between lust and duty.

"We might have time." Curly spoke more to himself than to his partner.

The lights blinked, turned dim, then went flat dark. With a heavy click, the pistons of auxiliary units began to vibrate against their eardrums. Emergency lighting filled the space with a ghostly haze.

Curly jutted his chin toward the garbage dump.

Dark One shook his palm, signaling to wait longer. Curly nodded his concurrence. Sour-faced, they watched the lights.

Katiri's feet slid toward the pirates. Her index finger twitched toward the escape chute. Again Meirri tugged. Now Viekki drifted with her.

A mechanic's wagon raced up the corridor toward them. A loud staccato of crackles sparked in the air and the space again went pitch black.

The wagon slowed. Its headlights came on. Katiri stood next to it. She pulled a wrench from the wagon's tool tray. The driver turned toward the scraping sound. The wrench blurred in an arc and crashed against his skull. He was flung across the seat and onto the vehicle's floorboard. His foot hung out the side and twitched.

The cart rolled on.

Unaware of the driver's fate, Curly pointed to the escape module and urged, "Let's go."

They pushed past the girls and ran to the chute. The Dark One held a light. Curly's fingers fumbled over the keypad while Dark One read the access code from a tattoo on his inner arm.

Wrench still in hand, Katiri stood behind them. In the distance, the driverless wagon slammed into a wall, throwing a shower of sparks that illuminated the wrench as it shattered Curly's skull. Dark One jumped sideways at the sound of the thud. An upward swing drove the wrench through his jaw and into the roof of his mouth. His body fell backward. Gurgling, he pressed against the floor to right himself. She kicked his arm away. His face smacked to the deck.

Katiri grabbed his broken jaw and yanked it toward her. His mouth lengthened grotesquely. His dazed eyes flickered in confusion.

Her thumb latched over his teeth, she spoke into his face. "You should have learned from your ancestors. Never attack an Amazonian." She released his mouth and slammed the wrench squarely into the center of his forehead.

The sparks from the cart faded and darkness blanketed them. With a mind that simulated reality better than most beings saw it, Katiri punched the code into the escape module controller.

The hatch sprang open. Meirri guided Viekki in. Locking her fingers with Katiri's, she said, "Mummy, come with us."

"There's only enough air for you two. I'll take the one further on."

"But I'm afraid."

The mother caressed the child held between her arms and bosom. "Meirri, sissy will keep you safe."

Then she held Viekki and said, "The planet below is inhabited; it's a good chance. The ride will be rough, but that's the atmosphere you will soon breathe."

"Do I warn them down there?" Viekki asked.

"No. They wouldn't understand. The beast is locked on the bridge. She'll suffocate along with the Vergs. The AGS Marines will find her body. We've completed our mission."

Suffocate? Miekki knew everyone on board would suffocate.

The portal squeaked then clicked shut. Meirri banged her little fist against it and screamed, "Hurry, Mommy! Hurry!"

***

The Message

The girls were gone.

Katiri, in a sprinter's stance, pictured her way through the inky blackness to the next escape module. The pirates' order to wipe clean should have triggered a slave revolt and, with it, the Katameiri's doomsday plan.

Blood pounding in her temples, she listened for the whoosh that would suck the air from her lungs and drag her soul into the eternity of space.

Not yet.

She inhaled, cherishing the breath of life, then leaped forward, her footfalls fast and light. Her right foot landed and launched her body long and high into the blackness. She breathed again. One more time, her lungs filled with life-giving air.

From behind her came a whisper, a rustle like a mouse's scurry.

The wheels spinning on the crashed cart.

Her left foot landed. She bounded again, her ears now intent on the sound that followed her.

It came again, clear and decisive. In midair her hope to join her children ended. A plasma slug sizzled into her right kidney, burning its way out through her abdomen. Flung by the slug's momentum, she crumpled against the wall and slid to the floor.

Cheek flat on cold metal, she pumped her legs, her mind still urging her to run. Her body rotated in a slow circle that painted the floor with her blood.

A beam of light cut through the corridor and slithered over her. Her eyes saw it swirl and twist, then drain into sepia, darkening until she saw only blackness.

Far away, a voice echoed as if down a long hollow pipe. "I couldn't let you take the escape pod without me. Oh, what fun I would have had with you on the way down. Must hurry off now."

She recognized the voice, though it sounded tinny to her blood-starved ears.

The beast stepped over her and toward the next chute.

Katiri's blood poured out. Her body shuddered.

Warn them, she thought.

She forced her trembling fingers into her belly, bending them together to hold her blood like a quill pen. She brought her hand out and traced a symbol on the floor. She dipped her hand back into her cavity. Then like an angel, the hiss of the vacuum came and pulled the air from her lungs, giving her soul to the universe.

***

Chapter 2: The Arrival

Like a runaway sled, the escape module careened through the atmosphere, missing Muddy Peak in southern Nevada by only fifty yards, then slamming to a stop over a narrow canyon. Wobbling slightly against the night sky, it floated down and disappeared between the stone walls.

When the module settled, Viekki opened the hatch and helped Meirri to the ground. Naked except for the slave smocks that hung like gunnysacks from their shoulders, they stared at the cliffs, gray and surreal in the pale starlight.

A planet. I'm on a planet, Meirri thought. "Viekki, we are on a planet, aren't we?"

Viekki pulled her sister tight and kissed the top of her head. "Yes, we are. Yes, we are."

Meirri extended her hands downward. Viekki kneeled by her and together they pressed their palms onto the sand as if they expected an earth spirit to rise up and embrace them.

An explosive roar shattered the air overhead. A whistle from the north grew louder. The canyon rim brightened then glowed like fire while the noise elevated to an ear-piercing shriek. A blinding ball of light shot over the cliffs and disappeared beyond the opposite rim.

"That's Mommy," Viekki said, watching the glow fade.

"Why didn't she land next to us?" Meirri asked.

"I doubt there are controls for that."

"But there are," Meirri insisted. "I see them inside my head."

"They're probably broken. The lazy Vergs probably didn't maintain them." Viekki took Meirri by the shoulders and turned her toward the canyon mouth. Far off, twinkling lights glided back and forth on a shimmering strip. "Let's go there. It's different than other things around here. She'll look for us there."

At dawn they wandered into the rest stop at the intersection of Highways 93 and 169, east of Las Vegas.

***

Derek Runningbird

The sun's early rays cast the hills in hazy silhouette, leaving the valley with its gash blanketed in the puddles of night.

Three days of fasting left Derek Runningbird weak. He laid his fire drill by the kindling and stopped to rest. The first rays of early dawn warmed his cheeks, breaking the night's chill.

Best do it now, he thought, *before the Sun's light strikes the Earth's wound.*

To the north, the morning rays lit Toad Mountain, the place of the sacred canyon, home of his guardian spirit, Panther Woman.

A hum, a chanted prayer, gathered in his throat and rolled off his lips to the cadence of an imaginary drum and hardened his determination to combat the monstrosity.

He turned his head fast, skimming unfocused over the terrible slash, and brought his eyes to rest on a nearby canyon.

Last night, a miracle, the descent of two star children, one into the canyon, another farther off.

Tears filled his eyes. He raised his hand. Too weak to extend it, he pointed just one finger, as if to assure his dazed mind that he had seen objects descend during the night. His head slumped. His own voice buzzed in his ears. "Other side, Highway 169."

He took a deep breath and pressed his hands out against the canvas of the landscape, one palm kissing the canyon; the other, the hills where the second star had fallen.

He forced air through his throat. His vocal cords resonated against the sky, calling for the help of hidden spirits.

Star children!

The thought fed his will. He rubbed the fire drill between his palms while pressing it hard against the anvil. Its twirl became a blur before his eyes.

23

Old way—must be old way, must be pure, he thought over and over. The fire had to be going and the blessing finished before the sun touched the terrible gash in the earth's flesh.

An ember glowed. He dropped the drill and pulled the tinder bundle close to his mouth. Gently, like the breeze from a butterfly wing, he whispered life into it. It brightened. He blew harder. Flames rose between his palms. With sudden focus, he laid the burning tinder below a teepee of twigs then lowered his face to the ground and gave it two more strong breaths. The tiny stems smoked then burst into flame.

He pushed his hand into his pouch. His fist, tight with sage leaves, opened over the fire. Fragrant smoke billowed around him, and, at that instant, a beam of light jumped over the distant hills and into the valley, illuminating the quarter-mile-wide cut in the earth that slashed from horizon to horizon, straight as a ruler's edge, brush, cacti, and all that lived among them piled in broken heaps beside its course.

As if awakened by the light, bulldozers eager to destroy life coughed and belched purple fumes into the air.

Derek groaned and fell backward. His eyes closed. The spirits did not neutralize the earth-murdering machines. His quest to stop Interstate 15 had failed.

The peyote glow from the previous night was gone. He didn't like peyote. He didn't believe in it; he thought it clouded visions rather than enabling them. But he had used it.

"The star children are real," he assured himself. He relived what he had seen in the night sky. One came, streaking like a meteor from the north, growing from a prick of light to a pulsing luminous ball.

Then stood still in midair over the canyon.

He opened his eyes and pondered the valley to the east of him.

Not far, I could walk there.

He sighed and shook his head.

Between the fasting and the peyote, I'll be lucky to get to my truck.

In his mind, he saw the second star child arc over the same path as the first, but it went beyond the ridgeline and out of sight. He pushed himself up onto his knees. His ceremonial fire sputtered then died. Below him the bulldozers snarled, diesel fumes exploded into the air, and the steel jaws ripped into the earth.

He shook the loose embers from his fire drill then laid it in his pouch. His head dizzied when he stood. He bent over, hands on his knees. He wanted to lie back in the shade and nap, but feared that because of his dehydration, he would never rise again.

He forced himself upright. An annoying honk came from the rest stop at the intersection of Highways 93 and 169. Closer, somewhere on 93, another car beeped in reply.

Derek took one final look at the evil scar.

Startled, he froze and stared.

Barely visible, a panther weaved through the brush just a hundred yards from the earth movers.

His heart filled with joy.

Panther Woman has come.

Then he lost her. He cast a frantic search over the dunes, but she was gone. Had she even been there?

Peyote, he thought in disgust.

His shoulders slumped. His thoughts turned to the food and water in his pickup, but his eyes stayed on the brush, scanning.

Huh? His heart jumped in his chest.

Below, a white woman stood where he had seen the panther.

He considered slapping his own face to knock the drugs out of his system, but he watched, expecting her to dissolve into the air.

She stood, hand over her eyes, her head turning back and forth. Another horn came from the distant rest stop, and she looked toward it. Then she ran, bounding over the dune, toward the sound. Up and down over the dunes she went, flinging her body through thorny mesquite, her feet pumping against the heavy sand. He watched her until she was lost beyond the brush and the rolling dunes.

Materialized from air? Chills flowed over his back.

Food. Need food.

He stumbled down the hill. The world around him rocked like a boat in a storm.

***

25

Chapter 3: Ghost Ship

The Verg trägers were ancient, no match for the warrior seraphim. It took only minutes for the AGS Marines to secure the slave ship. However, their report saddened Yanitur. During the conflict, a group of slaves slipped through air ducts to the compressors and vented the atmosphere to space, suffocating everyone, slaves and pirates alike—except for those who boarded two escape modules and jettisoned to the nearby planet.

Yanitur, Kale, and Uriel entered the slave ship through one of the emptied escape hatches. The beams of light from their helmets crisscrossing in front of them, they clanked heavy-footed down the empty corridor.

"A body here." Yanitur's spotlight locked on the figure of a woman cut in half at the abdomen and lying in a pool of blood. "Our assault team didn't mention slaves being killed by weapon fire." He adjusted his spacesuit microphone.

Uriel kneeled by the body. "They haven't submitted a detailed after-action report yet, but clearly, this one was killed by a plasma slug." He lifted her blood-caked hand and held it in midair then bent his face downward to study something.

Kale peered over his shoulder. He turned to Yanitur. "We may have a big problem."

"What?" Yanitur moved closer to look.

"Amazonian." Uriel laid her hand gently on the floor. "Their symbol for the mythological beast that rules hell. She wrote it with her own blood."

"Wow," Kale said.

Yanitur's breath hissed rhythmically through his respirator. "What's an Amazonian doing on a Verg slave ship?"

"She's wearing slave garments," Uriel said.

Yanitur rolled his eyes beneath the glass of his helmet and groaned in aggravation. "Okay, let me be more specific: How did an Amazonian become a slave on a Verg ship?"

"My thoughts exactly," Uriel replied.

"I should kick you," Yanitur sniped. "Please think in analyst mode but filter your conversation through your humanoid filter. It's frustrating as hell to communicate with someone who requires absolute precision."

"Sure." Uriel chuckled.

"Maybe she's something else and just knew a few Amazonian symbols," Kale suggested.

"We'll do a DNA test," Yanitur said. "But I can tell you right now she's Amazonian. Only one of them has the steel to be cut in half and still scribble a message—in her own blood."

Kale nodded his head and sighed. "Probably right about that."

"Not a message, a warning." Uriel pressed a tube into her ear. Information flowed from it to his database. A second later he said, "Yes, she is Amazonian. I'll run her through the genealogical pool to see if we have her record."

They formed a silent crescent around the body.

Yanitur cleared his throat. "You're going to have to take the DNA of everyone on this ship, even the fucking Vergs."

"Of course," Uriel replied.

"Another problem." Yanitur raised the bulky arm of his spacesuit and uncurled a finger toward the chute they had entered through. His voice crackling with agitation, he said, "Whoever killed her took a plasma launcher to the Nuclear Age planet. We were supposed to prevent that."

"Yeah, that's sticky." Kale shined his light farther down the hall. "Hey, more bodies." He bounded toward the corpses. While the other two approached, his voice came into their headsets. "Two Verg pirates, heads crushed to pulp, and a bloody wrench—victims and weapon. I suppose we know who did it.

"Dumbass Vergs, didn't they figure out why we allowed the Amazonians to have independent rule?"

Yanitur's stomach contracted. He opened the unspeakable topic. "When did Vergs ever raid Amazonia?"

Uriel began answering before Yanitur finished. "Never. Even at the height of the Vergish empire they didn't take on Amazonia."

"They must have captured a transport or warship—sometime?" Yanitur suggested.

"Maybe," Kale said. "But the Amazonians would never admit it."

Uriel looked at Kale in a "what the hell are you talking about" manner. "Our intelligence is pretty good. It has been centuries since any Amazonian ship has been taken by a Verg. In no case were Amazonians taken alive. It's their code to never be taken alive."

"So they say," Kale said skeptically.

Uriel shook his head at Kale. "There is no evidence to the contrary."

Yanitur raised his palm to stop the argument. "When was the last significant military encounter with the Vergs?"

Kale paused then guessed. "Roughly three thousand years ago we destroyed their last stronghold."

"Yes." Yanitur spoke slowly. "We were taught that in school. We shattered their military. All that remained were inconsequential bands led by petty warlords. But what if that is wrong? What if they escaped to the Second Galactic Leg and got here three thousand years before we did?"

"The threat of annihilation is certainly a motivator." Kale raised his palms to the others. "Let's quit beating around the bush. The Vergs have attacked our colony, here, in the Second Leg."

"Let's not speculate," Uriel interrupted. "The DNA study will tell us."

"Captain." A voice crackled in Yanitur's earpiece.

"Go ahead, Throdin." Yanitur patched Kale and Uriel in so they could hear.

"Sir, the forensic unit just arrived on the Verg bridge. You'll want to come over."

Yanitur clicked his routing device on. He signaled the others to follow then took off at a trot. "Did you recover their master data banks?" he asked Throdin. His words came between heavy breaths.

"No, sir. They were wiped clean."

A commotion broke out near Throdin. Seraphim shouted angry commands like police during a drug raid. "Hands on your head! Down on the floor! Now!"

"What the fuck is going on?" Kale struggled to keep up with Yanitur.

"Sounds like we need to hurry." Uriel ran up beside both of them. "Mind?" he asked.

Kale and Yanitur looked at each other. "Go ahead."

Uriel held his palms out, forming seats for them to sit on. They did and he raced forward at sixty kilometers per hour.

***

The Librarian

A chrome gorilla squatted on the floor, hands clasped behind its neck. Its red eyes stared straight ahead.

Yanitur came through the door. "Captain," Sergeant Throdin announced loudly. His platoon, six marine seraphim, snapped to attention.

The chrome gorilla eyed Yanitur. "Kong not fighter. Kong too old for fight."

"What the hell is it?" Kale jerked his chin toward Kong.

"Early form träger," Yanitur said.

Uriel went straight to Naomi, who was on the Verg bridge as part of the CSI team. She squatted next to the body of the dead Verg captain, taking his DNA and other data. She gazed moon-eyed at Uriel. He lightly massaged the back of her neck. They talked in a low private hum.

Everyone knew about their affair, one of the first between a humanoid and an emotionalized seraph.

"Uriel," Yanitur snapped, "how long since they used this class of träger?"

"Them or us?"

Yanitur squinted one eye in a peeved look. "If you paid attention, you wouldn't have to ask. Us, obviously they still use them."

Naomi blushed and pushed Uriel away.

"Five thousand years, other than museum pieces—"

The träger interrupted, sounding desperate, "Kong no junk. Kong librarian."

"Captain, there's something over here—" Kale started.

29

Yanitur held out his palm, shushing him. "Librarian? What the hell does that mean?"

"Kong know things. Kong helpful. Kong want to be helpful."

Yanitur turned to Throdin. "Take full control of his mechanical systems then move him over to *Quantum* for interrogation."

Yanitur tilted his head to Kale in a questioning gesture. "You were about to say?"

Kale pointed to the bodies of the Verg staff scattered over the bridge.

Throdin was lifting Kong to his feet when the träger pulled free and stepped toward Uriel. In an instant, three marines had Kong locked in their steely grasps.

"Kong helpful now," the antique träger pleaded. "Kong saw thing."

Yanitur thought a moment then acquiesced. "You can stay, but let Throdin take control of your motor center. You can't yank away from him, or they may decide you're dangerous and melt you into a steaming ingot."

Kong pointed to his chest plate. "Kong tell how to disable."

Throdin opened the plate and followed Kong's directions, which were passed between the two by means of a data stream that sounded like short bursts of whistling.

Uriel pointed to the bodies of the bridge crew. "These officers and the Amazon near the escape modules were all killed by a plasma device."

"So you think someone killed the bridge officers then escaped to the planet?" Kale asked.

"Kong see—"

"Speak when spoken to," Uriel snapped.

Kong ground his jaws together and huffed through his nose.

"That's my assessment," Uriel said. "Someone killed everyone here then ran for the escape module. The Amazon must have gotten in his way, so he killed her too."

"Two escape modules were taken. Maybe several were involved in these killings." Kale studied the bodies.

Kong cleared his throat.

Yanitur forced a bemused smile. "Okay, tell us what you know."

"Advisor kill everyone. She do all killing. No one help her."

"Advisor?" Yanitur asked.

30

"Ally send military advisor to guide Verg mission."

"Ally? What ally?" Uriel asked.

"Kong know only advisor. That enough for Kong."

"Kong is not very helpful." Yanitur laced his voice with disappointment. "Does Kong know where this ally came from? The Third Galactic Leg? This galactic leg?"

"Not here," Kong answered.

"Then the third?" Yanitur suggested.

"Not here."

Yanitur emptied his lungs in a rush of exasperation. He rolled his eyes at Uriel. "Do you understand him? Because if you don't, we'll have to review his memory line by line."

Uriel shrugged his shoulders. "I think it's a language problem. It's likely the Vergs taught him limited Nirvanian."

"Try Vergish, then."

Uriel looked into Kong's eyes and smiled pleasantly. "*Vas meank du, nik dorm? Vorm koemen dim ally uf?*" Uriel said.

"*Ally koem vorm en odter galacen.*"

"*En odter galacen? Dim ik nik poslich.*" Uriel's tone was condescending, as if he were speaking to a child.

Kong responded in Vergish, saying, "I'm not dumb. I know exactly what I said, and yes, the Vergs claim this ally came from another galaxy."

"Maybe you aren't stupid. Maybe the Vergs are," Uriel retorted. "Or maybe you misunderstood them the way you misunderstood our captain. It's most likely these allies came from the third leg of our galaxy."

Kong's chrome jaws bit together and locked hard while he listened to Uriel. He remained silent for a few extra moments then spoke slowly, enunciating his words, "You said 'men.' Everywhere in our galaxy, sentient beings are manlike: Nirvanians, Vergs, Amazonians, and all the others, manlike. They all come from the same genetic forefather.

"The advisor was not manlike, at least not at first."

Yanitur and Kale waited while the two androids conversed.

Uriel pondered Kong's words. "What did it look like?"

"A human," Kong said.

"Don't play games. I'll take your memory and junk the rest of you." Uriel was shouting. Everyone else stared at him then at the ancient Kong.

31

Kong laughed. "There, you said it. You can have my memory and not me. Same with these allies. They suck fluid from men's bodies and after a while they begin to look like men. The last time I saw the advisor, she looked almost human. Even so, she was very scary."

"Why didn't she blast you with the plasma gun?" Uriel asked.

"I was in the computer vault."

"Very well, you and I will speak again on my ship, *Quantum*," Uriel said. Then he told Thorin, "We have a lot of forensic work to do in a hurry. I'll need the help of this entire squad. Call in some other combat marines to escort Kong to *Quantum*."

When Kong was gone, Uriel told Yanitur and Kale what the träger had said.

"You think the Vergs left him to misdirect us?" Yanitur asked.

Uriel grimaced. "We'll have to peruse his memory to authenticate his claim. Of course, if he is a plant, then they will have falsified that too."

Kale shook his head. "Sounds like a hobble-goblin children's story. No fucking way it's true."

"Yeah." Yanitur spoke in a whisper. "It doesn't add up, but a lot on this ship doesn't add up. We need to make a detailed record of everything then blast it into the sun. We can't leave it floating here to be found by the humanoids on that planet, or by other Vergs."

"What are you thinking?" Kale asked.

Yanitur didn't answer.

***

The souvenir

Yanitur signaled Kale to come. "Let's go back and take another look around those escape chutes. Uriel will finish this work."

Yanitur stopped at the entrance of the bridge. He ran his fingers over the frame where the seraphim had cut their way through its locked door.

"If the captain locked the bridge, how did the alien advisor get out?"

A forensic officer taking pictures looked up. "We think the slaves locked the bridge, sir. Found some notes written on the inside of an air duct. Described a battle strategy of sorts. Step one, lock the bridge. Step two, bleed the atmosphere and kill everyone.

32

"They left a note to us: Check the bodies on the bridge for unknown DNA. They knew a lot about this ship."

"Katameiri," Kale said.

"What?" the officer asked.

"Amazonian Katameiri," Kale explained. "They can deconstruct anything in their heads. Break it into basic parts, like you would scatter puzzle pieces on a coffee table. Then they put it together again, all in their head."

"They wanted to get captured," Yanitur said. "There was something on this ship they wanted to uncover; then they killed themselves so that we would learn about it."

"Unfortunately, the advisor seems to have escaped," Kale said.

Yanitur called Uriel on his headset. "Uriel, tell Naomi to do an extensive DNA sweep of the bridge."

Yanitur and Kale walked on toward the two dead pirates.

Kale spoke under his breath. "I don't know if emotionalizing the seraphim was such a good idea."

"Afraid of the competition?" Yanitur stopped and studied the pirates, their heads unrecognizable, their bodies crumpled like limp rags. "The Amazonian was here with them for some reason," he mused.

"Geez," Kale said, "it looks like a 500-kilogram ursus ripped into them."

"Two chutes are gone," Yanitur said, thinking out loud.

Kale offered no comment.

"Given the slaves' battle plan, I don't think any Vergs made it to those chutes," Yanitur said.

Kale nodded thoughtfully. "So a slave took one chute and the alien took the other one?"

"Why not? The Amazonians nearly had command of the entire ship when they decided to suffocate everyone."

"Fuck," Kale said. "I don't know what's worse, having them on your side or against you."

Yanitur cocked his head toward the two dead Vergs. "Against you is worse."

Kale ignored the comment. "So there is one of these alien pseudo-humanoids on that planet, and probably one Amazonian, too. Maybe we should send a patrol down and retrieve them both."

Without commenting, Yanitur walked to the dead Amazonian. One of his crewmen was about to wrap the AGS flag around her body in preparation for her cremation.

"Hold on." Yanitur kneeled by her. He lifted her hands, checked her wrists, then her neck and chest. "Any rings, bracelets, tattoos—anything personal?"

"No, we think the Vergs took all their personal items when they were captured," the crewman said.

Yanitur nodded. His face went dead solemn, almost fearful. He grasped Katiri's red hair and yanked her head up by it. A razor-edged bayonet sprang from his wrist. He gritted his teeth and slashed a clump of scalp from the left side of her skull.

The officer's mouth fell open. He panted in shallow breaths while watching Yanitur place the scalp in a sealable pouch.

Then Yanitur gripped her ear.

"What the fuck!" Kale turned his head just as Yanitur sliced.

Yanitur guided the ear into another sealable pouch; then his face shot red with anger. "You assholes ever take a cultural anthropology class?"

"Yeah, but good God, just because they do it doesn't mean you have to…" Kale left his sentence hanging and pressed his hand against his stomach.

Yanitur nestled the two pouches in his cargo pocket then reverently repositioned the flag. He mumbled softly, "Someone on that planet down there may want these someday."

***

Kong

Kong lay on a metal table. All his physical functions were shut down except he could speak. Rainbow waves of light danced on Uriel's face as he bent forward to guide a probe through the tangled strings of light within Kong's belly.

Kale leaned in from the opposite side. He peered into the träger's abdomen. "I'm surprised you could find anything on the mechanics of one this old." Kale took a sip from an Emerald Lightning drink he had just gotten out of the dispenser in the corner of the room. Lightning had slight revitalizing properties.

"Didn't," Uriel said. "I mean, the actual manuals aren't around anymore. The principles don't change, though. This system was easy to deconstruct."

Kale peered down at the twisting maze of thousands upon thousands of light channels, all weaving among each other. "Easy, right."

Uriel continued his exposé. "Interesting, these old technologies. They could run forever, I suppose. Too bad we scrapped them except for the museum pieces. The Vergs don't junk anything."

"Yeah, well, they don't have much choice, do they? They don't have heavy industries anymore—at least in our leg of the galaxy." Kale took a swig of his green soda.

Uriel shrugged his shoulders. "Well, they make ingenious alterations. Often they install microswitches, circuits that can turn the träger on or off, hidden behind an eye, in the ear, inside a fingernail. Sometimes they're three and four deep, like a puzzle. If you shut one down and don't find the rest, the träger will just pop back up and attack you again."

"That's why you put a plasma slug right through its guts." Kale glanced around the room as if looking for something to smash Kong's innards with.

"In his case, it's not a problem. They removed all his combat functions, along with the secret switches. I guess they didn't want him to trip into warrior mode while he was on their bridge."

Kale laughed. "He does look brutal."

"Mind holding this a second?" Uriel said. "I need a free hand."

Kale tensed his muscles to hold the probe steady. To his chagrin, it undulated back and forth through hundreds of light strings. "God, I'm making a mess of it."

"Don't worry." Uriel put a light cable into his own ear. There was a slight click. "The probe tip is vectored to my target. Long as you don't lift the rod completely out of the belly, it will maintain the coupling."

"Pretty humbling," Kale said. "Your hand didn't waver a micron."

The connection complete, Uriel smiled and took the device from Kale. "I've uploaded his data to my memory. I'll copy it to the *Quantum*'s data storage later."

Yanitur entered the room.

"Captain." Uriel and Kale saluted simultaneously.

"Captain." Kong cued off them, only he couldn't salute.

"Are we ready?" Yanitur asked.

35

"Yes, sir," Uriel said, "I've downloaded his data banks."

"Kong, I'm sure Uriel has informed you that if any subroutines attempt to interfere with your responses to my questions, Uriel will disable them. Eventually you will tell me the truth."

"Right out of the gate, Kong no lie."

"Okay then, let's start at exactly one minute before *Quantum* fired on your ship. Were you on the bridge?"

"Kong in computer room. Door closed."

"But you told me this advisor killed everyone on the bridge. How do you know if you were behind a door?"

"Kong know many ways. Kong know who on bridge when Kong go into computer room. Kong know bridge locked. No one else come in. Kong hear good. Kong hear everyone. Kong—"

"Okay, good enough. Don't the Vergs forbid weapons on the bridge? How could this advisor have a blaster on the bridge?"

"Advisor have blaster in pocket. Look like Uriel's probe. No one realize it is weapon."

"Is this blaster from the alien society?"

"Kong think yes."

"Obviously the ally didn't share these blasters with the Vergs. Were other alien technologies given to the Vergs?"

"Vergs complain ally not share technologies."

Kale glanced at Yanitur and nodded.

"What does the ballistics report say?" Yanitur asked Kale.

"The gun used against the Amazonian in the corridor was the one used on the bridge staff."

"So, there is no doubt that the Vergs' alien carried a blaster down to that planet?" Yanitur looked to Uriel.

"Someone, something, predatory is down there with a plasma blaster," Uriel said.

Kale walked over to the drink dispenser. "Emerald or orange," he called back to Yanitur.

Yanitur thrust his palm toward Kale, shushing him.

"Kong," Yanitur said, "your story about the advisor's society is confused. You said it came from another galaxy. We know that is impossible."

"Can Kong talk now?"

"Yes, please do."

"Vergs been all over this galaxy. Never see creature like ally. Vergs take DNA from ally. Never seen DNA like that."

"The ally stood still and let them take its DNA?"

"No. Vergs smart, get DNA secret."

Yanitur lifted Kale's empty cup. "So the Vergs took a sample from a cup that the ally drank from, or something like that."

"It drink blood. No use cup."

"Lovely." Kale returned from the dispenser with two orange elixirs in his hands.

"So it's like the mythical vampire, sucks blood from the neck," Yanitur said.

"Sounds suspiciously like a campfire tale." Kale handed one drink to Yanitur.

"No. Cut vein. Drain blood into bucket then drink," Kong said.

"Original." Kale wrinkled his nose in disgust.

"True?" Yanitur asked Uriel.

Uriel smirked. "He couldn't make that one up. To answer your question, no subroutines overrode his response. I've tried to make a visual of this alien from his memory. It's garbled, too mixed up to be helpful."

"Thing drink human blood, soon look like human."

"Did you feed it slaves' blood?" Yanitur asked.

Kale hovered over Kong, glaring furiously at him. "You—" he started.

"No!" Yanitur broke in and waved Kale away.

In a huff, Kale marched all the way back to the dispensing machine. Shifting his weight from foot to foot like a boxer, he punched its buttons hard with his index finger.

"Kong no feed," Kong said. "Kong only librarian. Vergs gather blood from dead."

Yanitur lowered his head. Finally he asked, "Which dead?"

"Vergs feed own dead not slaves' dead."

Kale spun about. The muscles tensing in his jaws, he shouted, "Liar!"

"No more outbursts, or you leave." Yanitur glared at Kale.

"Why their dead and not ours?" Yanitur asked.

"They say great honor. Warrior live on forever in body of ally. Go to Warrior Heaven."

"Really?" Kale said. "Wonder if they would consider group suicide and take the fast track to Warrior Heaven."

Yanitur hissed at Kale then continued with his interrogation. "Where did those Nirvanian and Amazonian slaves come from?"

37

"May I?" Kale asked in a huff.

Yanitur shook his head. "No. You may not."

Kale crossed his arms. "You tell him, then," he told Uriel.

Yanitur's eyes shot to Uriel.

The seraph mollified his words. "We don't have a full set of our colonists' DNA, but there are several matches with the dead on the slave ship. The probability is over ninety-nine percent that our colony at Nueva Alpha was attacked. The Amazonians, as usual, never gave AGS Headquarters any of their records, but I patchworked from genetic heritage lines. I can say with seventy-eight percent certainty that these women came from their colony in the Nueva formation—"

Kale interrupted, "It's fishy. Everyone is dead on that ship except this character and he's loaded with sensitive data." He stared at Uriel.

Uriel raised his eyebrows. "The DNA doesn't lie."

Yanitur glared down at Kong. "You went too far. We might have let bygones be bygones and let your pathetic culture coexist with ours, but your he-man blood-crazy warriors just had to attack our colonies."

Yanitur kicked a chair screeching across the floor. It banged into a wall and spun onto its side. "This time we're going to burn you to the ground. There won't be a scrap of DNA left to clone a Verg for a museum."

His voice distressed, Kong said, "Kong no warrior. Kong only librarian."

Kale smiled.

Uriel frowned like a disapproving parent.

Yanitur jutted his chin toward Kong then asked Uriel, "You got everything he has?"

"Yep." Uriel removed the probe and began to reassemble Kong. "Sit up," Uriel ordered. The träger swung his feet over the edge of the table and sat like a gorilla on a branch.

"Take him back to the Verg ship…" Kale started.

Yanitur's face knotted with rage.

Kale stopped with his mouth half open.

"Kong not attack AGS. Kong help AGS," the träger begged.

Yanitur stared at Kong. Finally he asked, "Could he be useful?"

"Yep," Uriel replied. "He's full of information about their operations. He has the route to the Verg outpost where they first took our people."

"You don't need him. You have all of his data," Kale protested.

"I've made him completely honest," Uriel said. "He can interface with you directly, setting me free to attend to other things."

Yanitur lowered his head. After a long pause, he looked up at Kale. "Commence the cremation of the slave ship. Leave Kong here."

Kale stiffened. "There's the issue of the monster on the planet. It eats people's blood then assimilates their DNA until it looks like them."

Yanitur thought about it.

Uriel and Kale waited.

Yanitur took a sip of his drink then looked to Uriel. "Launch a pulse signal to AGS Central. *Quantum* vacating mission to investigate unknown military threat. Send replacement."

Kale widened his eyes. "That's ballsy."

"We're supposed to take the initiative." Yanitur winked. "And our new mission will be less boring.

Kale saluted. "Sir, what about those people down there?"

"That's our replacement's problem," Yanitur replied.

***

Chapter 4: Button Visions

Derek was almost to the valley floor when three shots popped in the distance. He ducked down, making himself small and close to the earth, a wise precaution anytime bullets are loose. It took a moment for him to realize they had been fired from the rest stop, the place of the obnoxious horn honking, the place the white woman had run to. He thought about her speed of travel, weaving through and over dunes. He didn't need to think hard. The shots came after she got there.

His heartbeat skipped.

Panther Woman had shown her to him. He had to help her. He thought of his Winchester in the pickup.

He stood. His head spun from the effort. It was a bad time for all of this to happen. He placed his hands on his thighs, steadying himself. The gyrations lessened to a wobble.

What the hell can I do in this state?

Someone revved an engine at the rest stop. Tires squealed. With each gear shift, the car grew louder. It was coming toward him.

Back at the rest area, another two shots rang out. They were muffled, as if fired in the opposite direction. He hunched down and hurried to his truck.

The pitch of the approaching car suddenly turned from a high whine to a low drone when it passed him on the road above. Light glistened off the rear window while it headed up the Highway 93 grade.

40

A second car accelerated out of the rest area. It went in the opposite direction. Its motor dissipated into the breeze that sifted back and forth and occasionally brought the rumble of the distant bulldozers.

Derek reached the pickup and leaned against its rust-splattered hood. Breathing heavily, he edged to the passenger door and opened it. He dragged his ancient Winchester from behind the seat and cranked a round into the chamber. The effort exhausted him. Every step exhausted him. He laid the gun over his shoulder and trudged around the hood to the driver's side.

He crumpled into the seat and laid the Winchester beside him. He turned the ignition key—halfway.

The world spun and rocked. He dropped his hand to the edge of the seat and groaned. He closed his eyes and laid his head back. The world still spun.

"I can't do this." His right hand fumbled to raise the lid of the ice chest that sat on the floorboard. Like a miniature oasis, coolness caressed his fingers. He wanted to leave them there, part of him in paradise, most of him in hell. He let it last only a few moments then latched onto the canteen and dragged it across the seat. Now all of him was in hell again.

After two long swallows, he put the canteen between his legs and sent his hand back into the chest in search of food. He found the foil-wrapped burrito. It was cool.

Therefore not spoiled?

He tore through the foil and nibbled on the tortilla. As if a bystander, he watched his hand crank the window the way a medieval man would turn a wheel to raise a drawbridge. Notch by notch, the window opened. The cab cooled, a little.

Cross breeze. He looked at the passenger-side window, there at the far end of the seat, in some distant kingdom with its own drawbridge. He was too tired to send his little man over to crank that drawbridge.

Three days of fasting caused his stomach to buck on the beans and send bile up his esophagus.

He looked toward the rest stop. *All quiet over there now. What has happened has happened.*

It meant he could do nothing to help. The dead were dead.

He needed to sleep.

What if she's bleeding to death?

41

One hand pressed against his belly to subdue the gastric storm. He used the other hand to drive. Minutes later, he took his foot off the gas and coasted into the rest area.

I hate peyote.

But this wasn't a peyote dream. He just wished it was.

Derek stopped the pickup in front of the cinderblock restrooms. Its shadow cast over a man curled in the road. The blood pooling under him had begun to dry into burgundy tar. Flies crawled over his face. A few lay fluttering with their wings coated with blood.

Derek left the truck blocking the hot sun from the body. The women's toilet door stood ajar. With the Winchester laid over his shoulder, he inched toward it.

He took a deep breath and, with a mighty surge, used the gun barrel to push the door wide. He aimed the barrel into the darkness and listened for movement. His ears buzzed with an eerie, dead silence.

His eyes adjusted, separating dark from gray within. His mind struggled to mold the shades into recognizable forms. His eyes settled on a long pale object lying on the sink countertop. His knees buckled. He caught the door frame to steady himself. A wail burst from deep in his chest. A chill raced through his bones.

His legs struggling to stay standing, he stumbled to her. His instinct was to drop the gun and carry her outside. He stared into her face, hoping to see life. Instead of dropping the gun, he clung to it. The facts didn't fit. The body on the counter was too small.

A child, not the woman.

The size told him. Her battered face couldn't. He laced his fingers on the top of his head and groaned. Thunder erupted in his belly. It threw him to his knees. He lurched and sent beans splattering across the concrete floor. He moaned then cried in shame.

His lungs heaving to pump oxygen to his brain, he wiped the bile from his mouth and stared at the floor. A breeze filtered over his face.

He looked up and tightened his grip on the gun. Something dark lay blocking the back door open.

Derek rose to his knees.

Another dead man.

He pushed himself to his feet and leaned against the wall. Not wanting to face her, he looked at the dead girl askance. Someone had tended to her. Her arms were crossed over her chest. Her ankles were crossed, and the ugly gray skirt she wore had been pulled down and wrapped neatly under her knees. She didn't look Indian, or white, or black or anything he knew.

A star child! They killed a star child.

His skin chilled to gooseflesh. He backed out the door to seek the warmth of the sun. But it didn't drive the cold away. He got in the pickup. It was warmer. After a while he could turn the ignition key without his hands trembling.

He had to get away from there. His head woozy, he couldn't drive far, so he went back to his hideaway near the construction site. This time he drove past the end of the trail. Mesquite branches scraping the sides of the pickup, he forced it deep into their midst. When he was as far as he could drive, as far from mankind as he could get, he passed out.

***

Child of Light

While he slipped into sleep, Derek reminded himself not to rest long; he needed to contact the law, probably Officer Lightfoot of the Paiute Police.

His mind flashed through the things he had seen: The star children, luminous bodies descending to Earth in the dark of night, the panther that drew his eyes to the brush just when a woman appeared and raced toward the rest stop, and lastly, the dead star child.

His body lurched at the memory of the girl. He tried to dream that he had gotten there before the men attacked her. He tried to dream that he shot them with his Winchester and the girl was alive and she threw her arms around him. "You saved me. You saved a star child. I love you. The star people love you." He heard heavenly choirs singing—but then he saw her dead again, so he restarted the dream, trying to get there in time to save her. He never could.

Since he couldn't help her he ran away, but everywhere he went, her body was there. So he changed her. She became Janie Henderson, six years old and dead from radiation sickness. He saw Thor Henderson and Sally Longwalk, Janie's father and mother, standing by her grave. Next he saw Thor's grave, and then Sally's grave, and all of their children's graves. Their stones all stood in the tall grass below the cabin Thor had built with pitchblende stones

43

from his uranium mine. Chas Stagskull, the shaman, said Thor's mine killed them.

Proof! Andreas Henderson, Chas, and other men from the tribe knocked Thor's cabin down and threw all the stones back into the mine. Andreas dynamited it shut.

Derek dreamed he was seeing it, although at the time he had been a baby. In a moment of cognitive continence he wondered if he had been there as a baby and was remembering it after all.

Derek's dreams dove back and forth like swallows. Thor's mine, with its poison and death, required something good for the cosmos to balance against it. Andreas Henderson's silver mine never killed anyone, but it wasn't much good and it didn't belong to the tribe anymore. Some dumb clerk in Vegas deeded the property to Andreas when the tribe only wanted to lease it to him.

Derek saw a stern little clerk, bald head poking out of a green visor, his face red and shouting, "No! No! Henderson owns it now! It's no longer part of the reservation!" The clerk wore a black and white striped vest, and you could see his forehead through the green visor. The clerk vanished into images that fluttered and flashed like butterfly wings under the sun.

Suddenly Derek was in the sacred canyon again, flat on his back, with Panther Woman's fangs dripping saliva onto his face.

He knew where this dream was headed.

"I've done everything you asked." He struggled like a cartoon character tied to a train track.

"You must keep the valley of the silver sacred," she demanded.

He started to protest, "It doesn't belong to the tribe—"

"Don't argue. Listen. The star children bring a new beginning and a new queen. When she arrives, bring my daughter to me."

The girl dead on the restroom counter flashed in his mind.

Stupidly, he said, "She's dead."

The panther's fanged jaws lunged for his throat.

His mouth opened, but someone near his pickup screamed before he could.

***

Creature of Darkness

He slid up in his seat and peeked out. Grains of sand and scratches on his windshield sent needles of light knifing in all directions, fragmenting the world like a shattered mirror. The scream

44

that had awakened him ended. He listened. Mesquite leaves and grasses fluttered softly.

Was it the dream?

He peered through one clear spot in the corner of his windshield.

Who screamed?

He slid gently to the passenger side and peeked through the side window. He looked out at every angle, but the mesquite disrupted his view.

At last, he leaned his head back against the top of the seat and took a long deep breath. At least his stomach felt better. The nightmare had ended. His thinking seemed clear now. He started to exhale a long groan.

Beyond the mesquite bramble came a shallow gasp. Derek closed his mouth and slid his body down in the seat. Several more gasps came in rapid succession. The hair on his neck tingled.

An animal dying—something dying.

He turned his head in tiny increments toward the sound. The mesquite branches swayed in the breeze, allowing an occasional view. The sparkle of chrome broke through and then disappeared again. The branches parted. A sky blue fender showed through.

Now he heard gurgling, like water sloshing out of a canteen.

Someone drinking?

Now a human shape dressed in black showed, here and there, between the branches while it moved back and forth beside the blue car.

The trunk lid popped. Noisy tossing and clunking followed.

He took advantage of the noise and carefully cranked the window open a crack so he could see around the edge of the glass.

Clearer now, another form was in front of the car's rear window. Something was wrong with it. It didn't move. It hung there.

Hanging like a deer carcass waiting to be gutted.

He studied it, piecing together the incongruent image. He clapped his hand over his mouth to keep from gasping.

A man!

A man hung upside down, the rear window tightened up hard against his knees, locking him in place.

Heavy plops of dripping came from near the body.

Derek took the window crank in both hands and, holding his breath, turned it as slowly as he could. He dared move it only half an inch.

45

The man's head hung at a crazy angle to his body.

Throat cut.

A big blob of blood fell from the victim's jugular. It splashed noisily into something below the man's head. Grunting like a wild pig, the person dressed in black came around the car again.

Derek extended his hand and clutched the stock of his Winchester. His hand trembled, causing the gun to rattle against the seat cover. He let go and clasped his hands together to hold them still.

The man in black kneeled by the victim. Far off, the bulldozers burst out a long loud grumble. The killer cast a furtive glance toward the machinery.

Through the branches, Derek saw the face. It wasn't human. Worse—it wasn't fully human. Though Derek's hands clung desperately together, he could no longer stop them from shaking. He needed the gun. Without it he would die. With it, he might live.

He pried his hands apart and willed his right one to creep across the Winchester until his finger lay on the trigger guard. There it rested like a vibrating insect.

He raised his eyes to look out again. The thing spun about and looked toward him. He saw the face of a creature from *The Island of Doctor Moreau*, human features set in the skull of a predator. He could see that its eyes looked to his right; then they panned toward the left, taking forever to pass over him.

Did it see me?

If it attacked, he would get only one shot, one chance to live.

Is there a round in the chamber? Do I need to pump a shell into the chamber?

If he did, the thing would hear it. The noisy earthmovers belched and the creature spun about to face them again.

Derek slid the rifle stock onto his lap. The creature lost interest in the machinery. It hunkered down and disappeared from view below the victim's head.

Derek glanced down at the rifle. The hair stood on his neck.

Wrong time to look down.

He glanced into the mirror and peered everywhere he could without moving his head even a fraction.

The creature bounded up beside its victim. It brought a jug to its mouth. Red rivulets ran from the corners of its lips and splattered onto its black clothing.

Derek's stomach yanked against his esophagus. He wanted to cover his mouth, but dared not move.

The beast tossed the emptied jug toward the noisy machinery, then stood in a humanlike posture and wiped its mouth. It studied the victim, then raised its hand. Its fingers curled as if around an invisible handle.

Derek blinked his eyes and saw a faint shimmer, like light reflecting from steel above the beast's fist. In a flash, it yanked the victim's arm out straight and slashed downward through the shoulder. Suddenly the raw flesh of an arm joint was against its mouth. The sound of sucking twisted Derek's intestines.

A quick flip sent the arm with a thud into the open trunk. The beast raised its shimmering translucent blade again.

Derek wanted to throw the door open and run, firing his Winchester over his shoulder as he went, but he sat still as a slab of granite. Piece by piece, the man went into the trunk. Then the lid slammed shut.

The creature sauntered to the front of the car and opened a suitcase onto the hood. It rummaged through the contents, setting aside a skirt and a blouse.

It killed a man and a woman?

Derek was thankful he didn't know. He would be more thankful if its murderous spree ended with the dismembered man.

The beast repacked the suitcase, folding everything with care, then put on the dress and blouse and drove onto the highway in an easterly direction.

Derek waited until the car engine faded into the distance. Then he threw the pickup into reverse. Branches scraped along the truck's sides with ear-piercing screeches. He stopped and stared at the pile of black clothes in the middle of the trail.

Would it come back for them?

He raced the engine. His tires spun. The pickup shot sand out behind him. His eyes locked onto the heap of black. He gripped the steering wheel and watched the black clothes vanish underneath him. He didn't look back to see if they were still in the trail, or if they had caught on his undercarriage to be dragged everywhere he went.

He turned west on the highway. Wheels smoking, he floorboarded it.

End of Part 1

Part Two
Twenty-Two Years Later

Chapter 5: August 12th, 1976

1:04 a.m. : Quantum's *replacement cruiser, having traced Gimish to Earth, launches a shuttle craft to rescue him from near the Henderson Mine in southern Nevada. Millennia after his death, his rescuers are now known and the Gimish Paradox is solved.*

**

Minutes after the AGS shuttle craft was launched, Wendell Lee Boyd eased his pickup, which wasn't really his, off the pavement and back into the brush. The pickup belonged to Haines Companies, and he should've turned it in when he got fired, but nobody came for it, so he kept it, along with the Haines camcorder and their .38 Special revolver.

"Wendell, we're gonna get stuck." Lorelei sat up straight despite her pot-induced stupor.

Wendell gave his neck a quarter turn to look at her. Dropping all the word endings, while adding a few random sounds, he said, "Don't worry, hun. This, what we're driving on, is called caliche by desert folks, and it's hard as concrete."

"How can you tell in the dark?" She was loaded and slurring her words.

"I told you, me and Bobby Hendricks learned all these secret spots when we was outlands security for Haines. We been here drinking beers once'd when we was working."

"Wendell, you come out here with crazy-assed Bobby Hendricks and drinked beer? No wonder you got fired. I don't want to be here."

"Lorelei, if you get in the mood, we don't want no cop or motorcycle gang checking us out. Back here, we're hidden from all them."

"Hell, Wendell, ain't no one gonna see us out here. It's after midnight."

"Well, it's done." Wendell turned the engine off.

Lorelei pressed her forehead against the side window. In the dark she formed a black silhouette against the glass. Faint starlight sparkled on the lip of the bong resting between her legs.

Wendell embraced the silence of the desert for a moment then spoke, keeping his voice soft and reassuring like a father to a child. "Lorelei, don't speak bad of the dead. Hendricks was a dumbass, we all know'd that, but he was my partner. Besides, you know I weren't fired for drinkin'. You know Miss Stephanie Noble got me and Carr fired for that time we detained her in a small room at the Black Lava Hotel."

The name Carr choked in his throat, causing his words to jumble. *God, that man is scary.* Prickles like a centipede ran down his spine.

Lorelei's shadow shifted. She looked upward. Her face turned gray in the starlight. "Carr got himself fired and you along with him."

Wendell hissed as if injured. "Don't you say that, Lorelei. Don't you never say nothing against Carr."

"It's true," she said.

Wendell gulped loudly. "Yeah, it is, but when you say such, it sounds like you're bad-mouthing Carr. Don't never do that. I cain't get crosswise with him. Neither you either."

"You're afraid of him," Lorelei said.

She was right, and it wasn't anything to be ashamed of. Anyone in their right mind would be afraid of Carr.

"You know that ain't so. Carr done good by me, hiring me on his personal staff after Haines fired me. Carr'll be on top again once'd those directors force Herman to take him back on the board. It's a matter of time. In more time still, he'll put me in some manager job. You watch."

Wendell slapped the seat with his hand. "Look here, I'm drivin' this Haines' truck still. Ain't like Haines Companies to let an ex-employee keep a pencil let alone a pickup truck. Carr had to made them leave me keep it."

Her face glowed under the starlight. "Since Horace Haines died, there prob'ly ain't no one who knows how many pencils Haines Companies got any more."

"No matter," Wendell said. "Point is we don't want nothing bad you say about Carr finding its way back to him. Right?"

Lorelei laid her head against the side window. "Yeah," she whispered. "Tell that to Bobby Hendricks and that man Abernathy."

"You shut up about all that. You hear me?" Wendell spoke louder than he had intended. He crossed his arms and stared out the windshield into the desert night. He stayed like that until the vast universe sucked the anger out of him.

Lorelei faced forward again. From the side of his eye, he saw her hand grip the neck of the bong.

"Here." He took the pipe and emptied the ash out the window. He lit a fresh bud. She filled her lungs and held it.

"Hey, you know I met Horace Haines once? Right over this hill, at the ol' Henderson Mine." He pointed left to a dark ridge outlined against the stars. "He was all dressed up like a miner. Him and a big, flatfooted Indian was hauling shit into that run-down mine. Can you imagine that, the richest man in the world out in the middle of the desert carrying shit into an abandoned old hole? With an Injun?" He chuckled to himself.

"The stars is sure pretty," Lorelei said.

Wendell laid his hand high on her thigh and sucked her earlobe. "What say we go sit on the hood and look for falling stars?"

She turned toward him, half of her face in shadow, half in starlight. The lit half smiled. She wrapped her arms around his neck and kissed his lips, pushing her tongue, which tasted like tar, into his mouth. "But there's snakes and scorpions out there."

"They cain't climb up on the car, hon." He buried his face in her lap while he reached under the seat for his flashlight.

Minutes later, Lorelei scooted onto the hood. Her skirt pushed up, leaving her bare bottom flat on the metal. She tried to whisk her dress underneath herself, but lost her balance and tipped back onto the windshield. There she lay, gazing into space.

Holding her hand, Wendell looked up at the sky. "It sure is amazing, all these stars. Some folks says hundreds got people on 'em."

51

Lorelei pointed. "That cloud of 'em that glistens like diamonds, that's the Milky Way." She placed his hand right where her legs came together and giggled.

Far off an owl hooted.

Wendell kicked off his pants and hung them over the side mirror, high above the scorpions and snakes.

He slid back on the hood and positioned himself over her, belly to belly, keeping his weight on his knees and hands, which was painful on the hard metal. Her chuckles metamorphosed into gasps. Gasps and groans became a duet. He pressed his head against the side of hers and breathed into her ear.

Her moaning rose to a crescendo. "The whole world is throbbing with us. The stars is throbbing with us."

She passed out just when Wendell spent himself.

He rolled off of her and gasped one last contented time then looked her over. She was as limp as a bag of potatoes.

How was he going to get her back inside?

He reached for his pants. When he did, he saw a bright purple light reflect off the windshield.

Goddamned cop.

He knew that wasn't right. Cops didn't have purple lights.

He looked around and, for the first time, saw that the truck, the desert, and the hillside were all coated in a faint purple haze.

Wendell looked skyward. He stiffened. A boomerang-shaped object with a huge purple light on its bottom descended toward him. The light grew bigger and brighter until everything around him, including Lorelei, glowed bright purple.

In a panic, he nudged Lorelei. "Come on!" He shoved his legs into his pants, which somehow twisted at the knees so that he couldn't push a foot through.

"Fuck, fuck, fuck," he mumbled and kicked his legs in the air to make the pants straighten out. Finally they did.

He shook Lorelei again and shouted her name. "We got to go!"

He glanced about for a place to hide. Just as quickly as the hillside had brightened, it went black again, except for a tiny purple aura that came from the Henderson Mine side of the ridge.

"Lorelei! Lorelei! Did you see that? Lorelei!"

She snored.

Cursing her and his back, he heaved her over his shoulder and lowered her onto the car seat.

He finished dressing then grabbed the Haines Companies' camcorder and his flashlight. He had an idea: God had sent him his winning lotto ticket, in the form of a flying-saucer video. He just had to take a walk over the ridge to cash in.

Lorelie's eyes were shut and her mouth hung open. He locked her in the cab.

He scanned the ground, checking for rattlesnakes and scorpions while he trekked up the hill.

They show fake videos of flying saucers on TV all the time. A real one got to be worth a million.

He stopped dead in his tracks. It was quiet: no coyote yelps, no owl hoots, nothing. For the first time he questioned whether climbing that hill was worth a million dollars.

Million dollars is a lot of money. Wonder if it's enough to disappear— like really get unfindable—even by Carr?

It's best to make this video.

He started up again.

The alternative was working for Carr until Carr didn't need him anymore. When Wendell thought about Carr, he felt like someone was standing behind him with a gun.

When you look over your shoulder, the man slides to the side so you can't see him. When you look over the other shoulder, he slides back. You never see him, but he's always behind you, and he's always got that gun.

Wendell's hair stood up. He looked back to make sure a man with a gun wasn't there.

I ain't gonna end up like Hendricks and Abernathy. I need getaway money. Fuck the goddamned snakes and Martians.

At the top, he hunched close to the bushes and crept down toward the Henderson Mine. He dove behind a small boulder. His nose just above the sand, he listened. Through the ground, he could hear his heart banging. It was so loud, he could hear nothing else.

His heart slowed some. He pushed himself up to glance about. His arms trembled so badly he thought they might give way.

But they didn't.

Through the brush, the top of the spacecraft glimmered like solid glass. Below it, the purple light spread over the valley floor and splashed up the sides of the distant hills.

He hung the camcorder strap over his shoulder and crept down to a thicket of willows. He could see the underbelly now, with its big pulsing purple light. He peered through the camcorder viewfinder. He watched the purple pulses emit from the center of the craft and flow in waves, one after the other. He slinked deeper into the shadows to keep the purple from touching his skin.

Far off, a manlike thing approached the UFO. Then a second figure came from the Henderson Mine. He zoomed in on the figures. The two humanoids came together under the bright underbelly of the spacecraft.

Feeling secure in the shadows, Wendell began to think about maximizing the impact of his film.

I should zoom in on the aliens.

His finger hit the wrong key. Everything blurred.

"Shit," he said in a near soundless whisper then grabbed the lens to focus it by hand. The men-things were hundreds of yards away, but when he made them clear again, one was staring right at him.

Wendell wanted to whimper, but he didn't even gurgle. He thought to run for it. But he didn't move. The alien didn't move. Wendell didn't dare breathe, for fear it would hear him.

Finally the alien turned away. At the same moment, Wendell rolled onto his hands and toes. With the camcorder bouncing against his back, he loped off, spraying sand out from all four appendages. When he reached better cover, he pushed up onto his feet and ran, zigzagging through the brush. At the crest of the hill, the ground dropped away and he somersaulted head over heels, sending sand down his neck and into his ears and hair. He rolled uncontrolled until he banged against a dead yucca.

A layer of sand stuck to his sweaty skin and shirt. It had piled up inside his underwear and shoes. He wobbled to his feet. He patted the camera, making sure he still had it, and he ran straight through the brush and cacti, pumping his knees high to make the rattlesnakes miss. He hit the pickup at full speed.

Lorelei jumped, banging her head against the roof.

"Where you been?" she screamed.

"Shush." Wendell shook the sand out of his hair. He flopped into the driver's seat and twisted the key. The starter ground. He gassed it. The engine roared. The tires spun. The truck hurled through the brush.

"Hold up, baby," Lorelei pleaded. "I got to pee."

Wendell's head jutting forward over the steering wheel, he said, "Piss in the truck." The pickup squealed onto the pavement and fishtailed down the road.

Daybreak

Last night, Matt Krause, descendent of the great shaman Ahmose, came to the Henderson Mine with Stephanie Noble and the Africa Sufi, Emil, to search for the ancient alien, Gimish. While the others slept, Matt wandered, without a flashlight, through the pitch-black tunnels, believing that his shaman abilities would lead him to Gimish. Indeed they did.

Impressed by Matt's clairvoyance, Gimish tested Matt's shaman ability by having him use crude templates to create a synthetic atom known as 268.

The atoms formed. Convinced that human shamanism could be restored through Matt and his descendents, Gimish left Herman Rothe, his intellectual seraph, behind to manage the regeneration process. Herman was also the acting CEO of Haines Companies, the premier technology conglomerate on the planet.

**

At daybreak, Matt gazed south from the entrance of the Henderson Mine. Last night's events made him wonder if he were delirious. Proof that he wasn't stood beside him in the form of Herman Rothe.

Stephanie and Emil had already left the mine and were far down the slope near Matt's battered World War Two jeep. Since they had slept through the night, they knew nothing of Matt's encounter with Gimish, or of Herman's true nature.

"When will you tell them the truth?" Herman asked.

"A wise man," Matt replied, "once said, tell them what they need to know only when they need to know it. My shaman sense will tell me when they need to know."

Down below, Stephanie leaned her tall body against the jeep's hood. Face hidden in the shadow of her scruffy cowboy hat, she adjusted the band in her long blonde ponytail.

"She knows something isn't right," Herman said. "You need to think this through."

Matt touched Herman's shoulder. "I have. Let me handle her."

Herman slapped dust from his pants. "Let's go to my place, the Black Lava, and get some food. You should live there so we can work together. It's safer too."

"Safer?"

"Carr may still be after Stephanie," Herman replied.

55

Stephanie had a splitting headache and was a bit nauseous. Neither was normal for her. She blamed it on spending the night on dusty wooden boxes just inside the mine entrance.

Earlier this morning, Matt and Herman had awakened her and Emil from an unusually sound sleep. Matt informed them that he had found no sign of Gimish. He even suggested Gimish had died centuries earlier.

Now, with the bright light stabbing her eyes, Stephanie tilted her cowboy hat down to block the sun while peering up at Matt and Herman.

She grimaced and clamped the skin of her forehead between her thumb and fingers. Despite her mind-numbing headache, she realized it was strange, even for an eccentric like Herman, to visit a deserted mine in the middle of the night.

I should have asked him why he came, she thought then leaned back against the jeep's fender.

"Do you have a headache?" she asked Emil.

He raised his eyebrows and rolled his head, indicating it was a bad one.

"Me too." She also had an odd sense of disorientation, which as a nurse, she normally associated with anesthesia.

"Well, who knows what molds and chemicals are floating around in that hole."

"What?" Emil asked.

"It didn't seem to bother them." She raised her finger toward Matt and Herman.

"We were in the entrance for a lot longer than they were," Emil said.

"Yes, lying with our heads in the dust for hours." That might explain it. Still, Matt and Herman standing together back at the mine gave the impression they were sharing something secretive. She was too groggy to sort it out at the moment. Maybe after some food and a shower, she could.

Now Matt hurried down toward her. He slowed the last five steps then pointed his thumb at Herman, who was far behind. "Can you believe he had his staff drive him out here in the middle of the night?"

She scoffed. "I guess as acting CEO of Haines Companies, he can order his staff to do anything he wants."

Matt wrapped his arm around her, then slid his hand from the small of her back to her neck. His fingers massaged her there. "It's an odd choice, the CEO coming to inspect a deserted silver mine in the middle of the night."

She played along. "Yeah, well, Herman's odd."

Herman started down. When he was within hearing distance, she pointed to Matt's jeep, indicating that it was the only vehicle nearby. "Hey, Herman, how'd you get here, anyway?"

Matt's fingers on her neck stopped. He blurted, "Ah..."

"When I saw Matt's jeep," Herman said while approaching them, "I had my staff drop me off. I thought I could ride back to the Black Lava with him. I didn't expect there to be so many of us." He glanced at Emil and shrugged.

"Why," Stephanie asked, "come to a deserted mine in the middle of the night?"

"Security reported a jeep out here. I assumed it was Matt and I wanted to talk to him."

Stephanie persisted. "Don't your executive duties at Haines Companies fill all your time?"

"Yes." Herman rocked heel to toe nervously. "Of course, that's why I came in the middle of the night. It's the only time I can get free." He pointed to the mine. "Horace willed this and the Black Lava Hotel to me. Everything else belongs to the corporation. This mine is a therapeutic diversion for me, much as it was for Horace, I believe."

Matt's fingers began to massage her neck again. "It's been a long night," he said. "Let's get out of here."

Because of Herman's large size, Stephanie and Emil conceded the jeep's front seat to him.

Matt glanced back over his shoulder and started the engine. "I'll try to get us to the Black Lava before it gets too uncomfortable back there."

Stephanie's shoulders tensed. "The Black Lava, why there?"

Herman cranked around to speak. "We need to eat. I have a gourmet chef, and I'd really like to show the place to you. It's now Haines Companies World Headquarters. As such, it is no longer open to the public. It's very secure. I venture to say the seventh floor, where I live—where you would live—is safer than the White House."

"Why would I live there?" During her last visit to the Black Lava, Stephanie encountered Carr Ferguson and his female

57

companion, Kit. Kit possessed a purse that Stephanie claimed had once belonged to her friend Janet Schlest. Weeks before, Janet had been found dead in the trunk of an abandoned Cadillac.

Matt watched through the mirror. "Stephanie, with Kit at large, I think we'll need the security Herman offers."

Stephanie gripped the roll bar to steady herself. "Okay, Herman, tell me about that security of yours."

"Tell you?" Herman chuckled with delight. "I'll have Marie, my head of security, show you."

**

Matt's jeep entered the Black Lava grounds through a traffic-control queue worthy of Langley. Atop the high outer walls, security cameras followed their movement. Once parked, they walked through another guard station and entered the ground floor, where an area called the Commons provided restaurants and activity centers for Haines Companies staff at no cost.

Herman led them to the kitchen, where gourmet chef Piero Rosi and his staff began preparing gourmet breakfasts for each of them. Matt headed for the cafeteria buffet, saying he was too hungry to wait.

Herman touched Emil and Stephanie on their shoulders. "You two go ahead; I'll keep Matt company."

"Nothing to eat, Herman?" Stephanie asked.

Pausing in the door, he looked to his chef. "Piero knows what I want."

Piero nodded.

Stephanie fiddled with her hair and watched Matt and Herman through the portal in the chrome kitchen door. Her headache had lessened, but she felt dense, like a hangover.

She bit her lip in frustration. Both she and Emil had failed at their duties last night. Emil was supposed to meditate and send his spiritual vector to protect Matt from Gimish. She, in turn, was to protect Emil's body from physical harm. Both were overcome by the sudden need to sleep.

Nothing eventful happened.

Watching Matt and Herman with their heads huddled together, she reconsidered.

When Piero handed the breakfast to her, she tugged Emil's elbow. "Hey, I'm going out to sit with them."

He smiled and signaled her to go.

58

Matt pulled a chair out when she approached. She offered a sterile, "Thanks."

One thing at a time. Right now, food would help. She shoveled down three forkfuls of hash browns and eggs then downed half a glass of orange juice. Setting the glass aside, she locked eyes on Herman. "You and Matt are up to something. When are you going to tell me about it?"

"Stephanie!" Matt looked appalled and he sounded hurt.

Herman stared at Matt. "I think you need to be forthcoming."

Matt looked down as if ashamed, then smiled. "Okay. We believe Horace Haines had a good reason for spending so much time at the Henderson."

Stephanie held her palms up in a "what the hell" expression. "You think there may be a back door to the SAM? You could have told me that from the start." She gave them both forgiving smiles.

Emil walked up with his tray of kosher food. "Yeah, SAM, that is the couch Matt lay on to see the life of the prophet Ahmose, right?"

Everyone nodded and Matt explained. "Yes, when I lay on it, it played a holographic record of Gimish's encounters with Ahmose, the greatest shaman of all time."

"Didn't Haines hide this SAM in the Shotwell Mine, the one that caved in?" Emil asked. He was reiterating things that had been explained to him before.

"Actually," Stephanie said. "We believe Gimish dug the tunnels long before either mine was excavated. Horace probably kept the SAM right where he found it."

Emil forked a piece of turkey sausage and held it in the air while he thought. He took a bite and said, "I don't think this Haines would lose a thing as valuable as the SAM."

"That is exactly right." Matt tapped the table for emphasis. "Horace Haines always had a back door."

Stephanie pointed to Herman and Matt. "They think the back door to the SAM is somewhere underneath the Henderson mine. Herman wants us to help find it. That's probably why he invited us to live here." She looked at Herman for confirmation.

He nodded.

"Okay," she said, "I suppose you have room for Emil to live on the seventh floor, too."

"Of course," Herman said. "You each can have an apartment built to your specifications: scenic views, Jacuzzi, gourmet kitchen, whatever you want." He frowned at Emil. "But you came to find Gimish, and since he's not here, I assumed you would want to go back to your home in Africa."

Stephanie patted Emil's arm. "I think you should stay. I know you want to see the SAM." She glanced back at the kitchen as if she wanted more to eat.

"Go ahead," Herman urged. "If you live here, Piero will fix you gourmet meals every day, all day long. He serves my guests and me. His other cooks handle the rest of the staff."

As he said that, a tall, muscular woman stopped in front of the kitchen and spoke to Piero, who pointed toward their table. She smiled and strode toward them. Her raven hair flashed burnishes of purple when she passed through the filtered light.

"Oh, there's Marie, my security chief." Herman beamed proudly at her. "Marie, why don't you take Stephanie around and explain our layers of security, then show her an apartment on the seventh floor. I would like them to move in."

Stephanie blushed. She held up her blouse sleeve. "I'm filthy. At the moment, I'd rather take a shower and get some rest."

Marie's eyes sparkled with amusement. "We can take care of that too." She tilted her head in the direction of a corridor. "Come with me." She turned her eyes to the men. "Let them yammer. I'll give you the real scoop."

"Why don't you check it out?" Matt said. "I think it would be good for us to consider Herman's offer."

Stephanie exhaled through her nose. She slid out of her seat and without enthusiasm said, "Show away, then."

Marie put her hand on the small of Stephanie's back. "So Herman offered you an apartment on the seventh floor? That's a great opportunity. There is so much to do here, and you can have anything you want." Her hand applied slight pressure to Stephanie's back when she said that.

***

Chained to the Devil

They walked into another corridor. The noise and traffic of the Commons dissipated.

A stream meandered down the hall beside them, cascading over beds of tiles and clusters of geometric ceramics, their surfaces glistening in sheens of bronze, emerald, lavender, and gold. The water cut across the women's path and they traversed over it on a flat slab of gray marble. Stephanie stopped on the bridge and studied the manmade brook.

"You like it?" Marie asked.

"The colors and sound of the water are comforting," Stephanie admitted.

"It came from a dream." Marie gazed at the shimmering geometric shapes. "Herman let me design it. He said working on it might be psychologically beneficial."

Ahead, the hall ended in an area where a small waterfall flowed into a pool that never filled. On one side were two elevator doors; across the pool, one.

Marie pointed at the two doors. "Executive areas, fourth floor and sixth floor. Security control room, fifth floor, and over here"—she swung her arm toward the single door—"all alone, in a completely isolated shaft, is the elevator to the seventh floor."

Marie pointed out redundant security cameras that monitored the elevators on a twenty-four-seven schedule. She explained that a code was needed to open the elevator door, another to activate it.

Marie punched the keypad. "At the moment only Herman and I have access." They entered and went up.

**

The elevator opened into an entry reminiscent of a nineteenth-century villa. Marble pillars flanked an eight-foot-high wrought-iron gate. Rows of dwarf fruit trees lined a path that led between the pillars to a marble fountain complete with koi and a white marble statue of Mercury. An ornate floor tiled in mosaics of gods and mythical beasts stretched down the hall.

Stephanie studied the floor while they walked. "This looks Roman."

"Etruscan," Marie corrected.

Marie pointed to doorways. "That's Herman's place. That's the library." She stopped in front of one. "This is an apartment." She punched a numbered keypad and explained, "You can personalize it with your own code."

61

She opened the door. "It's elegantly furnished and stocked with towels, plates, everything you need. It'll hold you until you can have a flat made the way you want it."

Stephanie stepped onto its cherry-wood floor. Before her, the kitchen with black granite counters flowed into the dining and living areas forming one large open space in front of a wall of glass that overlooked the city. Two bedrooms flanked the living area, each with a walk-in closet and a full bath.

Marie dropped onto a couch. Her calf flexed sexily. "Piero will cook for you, but you also have kitchen stuff here too, top quality."

Marie adjusted her skirt around her thigh, then jumped to her feet and walked toward the master bedroom. "Hey, you said you wanted to clean up. There are towels and robes in the bathroom. Toss me your clothes. They'll be washed by the time you've showered."

Stephanie felt her face flush. "Aren't they expecting us?"

Marie wrinkled her nose. "Men, they'll just jabber about their plans for the mine, not that Dad doesn't have more important things to worry about."

Stephanie stopped halfway to the bathroom. "What did you just say?"

Marie frowned in an amused way. "Not sure what you're after. Herman has more important things to worry about, maybe?"

"No, you said dad."

Marie let her breath out with a gush. "You've got to be kidding. He didn't tell you?" Her cheek muscle knotted. "Most people would say, 'Oh, this is my daughter, Marie,' and maybe touch my hand or put an arm around my waist and smile. But he says, 'Meet my head of security.' He's such a lug head."

She pointed her finger toward the bathroom and commanded like a sergeant, "Go on, take your shower. Leave the clothes by the door. I promise I won't watch."

Great, Stephanie thought, then did exactly what she was told.

**

Stephanie cinched the robe then poked her head out the door. Her clothes weren't there.

Oh crap. I don't have time for this.

The plush queen bed did look delightful. Her whole body sighed at the thought of crawling in and letting the world go to hell.

62

"Clothes are almost ready," Marie called out, then stepped into the room, holding two cups of tea. "May as well come out and enjoy the view."

Stephanie rolled her eyes, then tagged along. They pulled bar stools close to the window and took in the panorama of the city and the mountains beyond it.

Stephanie started with small talk. "This is really nice."

"Yeah," Marie said. "It's in the style of the European elite."

Stephanie took a sip. "I can't believe..." She began to stumble over her words. "I can't imagine Herman—married. I mean—"

Marie burst into laughter. "Adopted," she said. "I'm adopted. Herman married? God, I can't imagine it either."

"And your real mom?"

"Never met her." Marie sipped her tea and shifted agitatedly. A bell tinkled.

"Your clothes just came on the dumbwaiter." Marie jumped up and retrieved them. She glanced at her watch and grimaced. "Well, my break's over. I've got interviews with some ex-Green Berets to fill some of our security positions. I want to get them on board before Carr is back in the building."

"What?" Stephanie lurched, spilling tea on her robe.

"Oops, I thought you knew." Marie seemed confused.

Stephanie clamped her cup in a white-knuckled grip. "Carr," she snapped, "should be in jail. What the hell is he doing here? Why the hell would you ask me to live in the same building with him? That's like being chained to the devil." Stephanie felt her face become hot.

"To answer your first question, Herman and Carr came to an agreement. Carr was to end his takeover bid; in return Herman gave him a seat on the board."

"He's a murderer." Stephanie sat her teacup on the table next to her clothes. "I saw Kit with Janet Schlest's purse. She killed Janet, and I'm sure he helped."

Marie shook her head. "I wish we could prove it, but Kit has disappeared. As far as we know, she's dead too. Without her, nothing connects Carr to Schlest."

Marie checked her watch again. "To answer your second question, Carr only comes here for meetings, and when he does, I have eyes and ears on him every second. That makes this the safest place you can be. Now excuse me while I go hire some more people to help me do that."

***

Chapter 6: Primary Axioms

Stephanie lay on a bed of memory foam, the material that kept the astronauts comfy during their long space flights. Light danced softly on the walls and ceiling above her while she indulged herself with two more minutes of cramp-free rest. Then she stood. Her feet cool and moist on the cherry-wood floor, she tiptoed to the big picture window and gazed out.

Below, people flowed like water through the streets. In the distance, the mountains, timeless sentries, stood still and silent.

The Black Lava sits like a luxury liner on a sea of desert, food flown from France, textiles and ceramics from Italy, and art...

"Possibly from Mars," she said to herself, reflecting on Marie's quaint indoor stream. Of it all, the astronaut foam bed was the best. But after two weeks of living in the Black Lava, it was time to get free from its smothering security.

Her eyes went to the gun safe mounted by her bed. A week ago, Marie had come, pushing her cart loaded with boxes, one with a thumbprint-sensitive safe, one with a .38 Special, one with ammo, and others with other things. Raven hair combed wet and dripping with fragrance, pink lip gloss thick enough to wipe your finger across and eat like frosting, she was hot enough to melt steel.

Clearly braless. All smiles and gushing compliments about my suntan, Stephanie recalled.

Still staring at the safe, Stephanie crossed her arms under her breasts.

Oh yeah, and there was the standing offer to coach me in the basement shooting range.

65

Stephanie had said she preferred to do it the old-fashioned way: girl, boy, jeep, guns and clean desert air. Marie winked and went on her way.

Since then she's kept her distance, not even eye contact.

"Perfect excuse," Stephanie said. She dressed and grabbed a croissant Piero had sent up the dumbwaiter. Her purse slung over her shoulder, she headed down the seventh-floor corridor to find Matt and goad him into a showdown with a gang of cans near the old Henderson Mine.

"...before Marie comes back with another offer."

She knew Matt would be in the seventh-floor library with Herman. Herman was fixated on working Matt into Haines Companies' corporate activity in some high-level position. Herman needed someone with charisma to sell his ideas to the board. According to Herman, Matt learned charisma from one of the best, Ahmose, while Matt sat in the SAM and relived the holographic record of Gimish's encounters with the shaman.

Maybe so, but from the start, Stephanie knew it didn't matter who Matt learned from. When Matt's fickle curiosity wasn't sparked by an activity, then he moved on to something more adventurous.

On the other hand, she knew it would not be difficult to lure him out to ambush a bunch of tin cans, although she would have a twinge of guilt for sabotaging Herman.

Matt would better serve Herman by exploring the Henderson Mine for a passage to the SAM. That activity would get Matt's attention.

The SAM, loaded with alien technologies, would be a valuable asset to Haines Companies. Its recovery should be at the top of Herman's list.

"Wonder why it isn't," she said out loud.

Satori, zen realization, flashed in her mind. Herman, the most efficient person she knew, and Horace, the most paranoid person she had ever known, would never lose something as valuable as the SAM.

Herman isn't looking for it because he knows exactly where it is.

A door opened. She turned to see Emil, his pool-cue case hanging off his left shoulder. He propped up a lifeless smile.

"Hi, Stephanie." It sounded perfunctory.

"You going downtown to play pool?" She felt guilty.

He played pool alone a lot. They'd neglected him. Clearly, they all would be more comfortable if he just when home. That made her hurt inside.

66

"No, I'm going downstairs to play pool." His face brightened a bit.

"Your poolroom is finished?" A week before she had seen a dirty boot print on the side of Emil's cue case. It sent her into a storm. She caught Herman in the library and demanded that he build Emil a poolroom where the little African would be safe from the hoodlums that hung out at pool joints.

Herman offered a private room on the sixth floor. She then demanded, "And one on the first floor so he can play with staff and meet some people."

How ironic, she had caged Emil in the Black Lava to protect him from thugs.

Emil's plastered smile cracked a bit. "See you for dinner?"

"Yes, yes," she said, then turned toward the library. She spun back to him. He stood facing the elevator, his shoulders slouched a bit.

"Hey, Emil," she called out. "I'm going to talk Matt into driving out to the Henderson. You know, just to get out, shoot guns, explore. Want to go?"

"Yeah, that would be good. You let me know." He sounded unconvinced.

"Come on, don't you really, really want to get out of this stinking place. I mean out there in the wide-open desert?"

His face filled with an honest smile. "Yeah, yeah, I would." The elevator opened. He waved, still smiling.

**

Emil was attracted to billiards from the first time he saw it played. In North Africa, when his Sufi master, Kalid, sent him to town for supplies, he always spent a few hours at the local bar, where he played pool with the occasional foreigner who foolishly included El Nejid in the travel itinerary.

However, pool became obsessive after that night they spent in the Henderson Mine. Now he was addicted, and he was disgraced.

Those were his thoughts when he stepped into the elevator, smiled big, and gave Stephanie a wave.

The doors shut; then he slumped forward with a sad sigh.

That night at the mine, Emil was supposed to meditate and form a psychic shield to protect Matt from the alien Gimish. Instead, while Matt wandered the tunnels, Emil fell asleep, failing his duty sinfully. Instead of protecting Matt, his head filled with a dream about a strange form of pool that involved dozens of balls, some as big as basketballs, others as tiny as grains of sand. The objective was to slam them so that they stuck together, like a big popcorn ball. When he did it right, the number 268 would flash in his mind.

More disturbing, his billiards skills leaped skyward after that night. The day before, he was average; the day after, damn near a pro.

Emil wrinkled his nose and nodded at his hazy image on the polished brass door.

Better than a pro—the damned best.

He meant damned too, though the back of his mind always had a spark of dread regarding profanity, whether thought or verbalized. He heaved his breath out in disgust.

Gimish wasn't even there. Kalid is a clown. What kind of Sufi master sends his apprentice to find something that's not there?

The elevator descended.

Emil exited on the first floor. Staff, there early, hustled through the halls, their briefcases swinging to the rapid beat of their feet.

"Hey, Emil," an engineer named Jerry called out. Then over his shoulder, he asked, "You good for a game about 4:30 today?"

"Yeah, sure, I'll be there." The warm glow of confidence filled Emil's chest.

He looked into the cafeteria, its tables packed with early risers downing the free Haines Companies gourmet breakfasts. Nearby, in the poolroom, Dick, one of the night security guys, was warming up.

"Emil, you want to go back home?" Herman had asked him shortly after the night at the Henderson.

"I'll give it a try here," Emil had replied.

Now he entered the poolroom and opened his cue case.

"Waiting on you," Dick said. "I got an hour before my old lady wakes up and wonders where the hell I am."

Emil screwed the cue together. "Okay, then. You break."

I'm not going back to North Africa. Now I live next to the richest man in the world and play pool while I watch and wait.

**

In the pre-morning dark, Herman sat in his apartment looking like a statue of a pharaoh or Abe Lincoln, facing straight ahead with forearms on rests parallel to the earth. He was every bit as motionless and just as much a statue, pragmatically speaking.

Only his mind moved, and what it did would baffle scientists. Much of his technology hadn't been discovered on Earth yet.

He ran dozens of models at once, things more complex than Monte Carlo simulations and decision trees with variables and relationships changing on the fly, but it took Marie to enlighten him.

"Dad," she said, "listen to this."

She had managed to bug Carr Ferguson's attaché case. And though the man didn't always carry it, he did when he set out to blackmail a loyal Haines board member, Doc Watson. Whatever Carr pulled out of the briefcase got the doctor's attention.

"That reduces your majority to two votes," Marie said. "One of those is your own."

"Are other board members compromised?" he asked.

Marie shrugged her shoulders. "We didn't think Doc was."

Marie realized Herman wasn't human about the time she turned six. He hadn't bothered to display emotions to her since. "I'll talk to Watson," he said. "I'll remind him that Haines Companies can make a lot of problems go away."

"Talking won't win him back," she said.

"That's silly, I control the company, not Carr."

"Dad, humans don't think that way. They want to be on the winning side."

Herman frowned as if confused. "I am the winner."

Marie swallowed. Tears filled her eyes. "For now, but they see Carr as the one with the vision for the future."

"I know," Herman said. "My plan is to paint him as a fool, then Matt will step forward and, like Ahmose, lead the board to the Promised Land."

"Will he?"

"He saw Ahmose do it."

"But will he do it?" she asked again.

Herman's face turned contemplative and he said as if telling himself, "Matt has the wind in his sails, but I fear he may be rudderless."

Marie walked away with tears rolling down her cheeks.

***

Statistics

Minutes before Stephanie talked to Emil in the hall, Herman entered the seventh-floor library, which looked like it belonged in an eighteenth-century palace. In fact, Herman had designed it like the Austrian National Library. In fact, some of the pieces in it had come from that collection.

Across the room, at one of the many mahogany project tables, Matt sat, head down, with leather-bound books fanned out in front of him. His pen scurried in a frenzied dance over a notepad.

Herman recognized those books; they were ancient French tomes. They were not the packet he had urged Matt to study for the Thursday Haines Companies board meeting.

If Herman were human, he would have been frustrated. *Would it motivate Matt if I acted upset?* He filled his lungs and blew out a loud mournful gasp.

Matt didn't notice.

And that demonstrates humans' ability to wipe away reality and focus on the trivial.

His noisy gush failing, Herman approached Matt, clattering chairs and tables with increasing ferocity in a loose experiment to measure the threshold at which Matt's concentration would break. Herman hadn't reached that limit when he stopped behind Matt.

Herman boomed out obnoxiously, "Henri Fourth of France again, I see."

Matt's finger drifted down the page and marked his place. "I've read this several times. It's very odd."

Herman contorted his face into an expression of benign disapproval. His head, hands, and hips moved in agitated motion. "Henri has been dead quite a while now. Haines Companies and the Shaman Project aren't quite dead yet, but might be, if next Thursday, we can't convince the board that you are the young charismatic genius with the vision to guide Haines Companies to stellar heights. I mean that figuratively, of course.

"We damned well can't..." Herman paused, replaying his words to measure their timbre. It sounded right, so he went on, flinging each word out with a jerk of his head. "Yes, damned well can't do that if you don't have a complete grasp of the financials I gave you to study."

"I have time to get it," Matt assured him.

Now that is charisma, confidence in the face of the impossible, Herman thought.

"Matt, the board members will arrive on Tuesday. That's when I need to introduce you, and you must overwhelm each with your brilliance. That's one week from today."

Matt closed the ancient volume with a dramatic swing. The thud reverberated through the room. He marched to the end of the table and lifted a binder from the stack of Haines reports and opened it to a page marked with a yellow sticky. "I've got it figured out, except for this hocus-pocus."

Matt laid his finger on the first of Herman's three key actions to reposition the Haines airline business in the face of fuel shortages and rising costs. Herman had purposefully obfuscated the material to lure Carr Ferguson into stubborn resistance, and thereby present an opportunity for Matt to be the Messiah while making Carr appear myopic and dull-witted.

"I've never seen this type of analysis. Are you sure humans have done this before?" Matt asked.

"Hi. So what's up?" Stephanie stepped through the door.

Another diversion, Herman thought.

Despite Herman's cold demeanor, Stephanie kept her smile. "Matt, I want to go camping out by the mine. Maybe you could help me practice with my new pistol, or we could check for tunnels." She stared straight at Herman. "Maybe we can find one to the SAM."

Matt raised the Haines binder to eye level and spoke in the Texas accent he reverted to when flustered. "Herman wants me to present his convoluted plan to his board next week. I'm sure his work is correct. The problem is no normal human understands this statistical crap."

He slapped his hand to his mouth as if to take back his insult.

Herman watched Stephanie's smile turn into glee.

"Statistics! What are you trying to do?" She yanked at the binder in Matt's hand.

Matt pulled back as if to stop her from touching something dangerous. His voice wavering and doubtful, he said, "It's a bunch of probabilities and stats about markets, production, industrial advances, every damn thing that influences the airline business, all chained together to formulate the optimal decision for the future of Haines Trans-Air."

He tugged again on the binder. She held firm, giving him no choice but to let her have it.

"How," Herman asked, "does a nurse know more about statistics than an engineer? Unless he wasn't paying attention in class." He gave Matt a pedantic stare.

Stephanie paged through the report. "I was a math major. My emphasis was stat."

71

The men waited in anticipation. Her face sparkling with enthusiasm, she shut the binder on her finger. "Wow! Things are moving fast in decision theory! Phillips at Cornell proposed this about nine months ago. I didn't think he'd published it yet."

Herman cocked his head and shifted his eyes. *It's so straightforward.* Then he said, "Yeah, I guess I read it somewhere."

She giggled. "Just like you, Herman. Remember the math, forget the source."

Matt narrowed his eyes. "Steph, who is Phillips? You sound like you know him."

"I do."

"I wish you'd told me. I've wasted a week when you could have been helping me." Matt flung his arms up in frustration.

"Really? Do you listen?" Her voice had a dagger's edge, yet her eyes dripped a tear on her cheek. Her voice quivering, she said, "I've told you this more than once."

Matt widened his eyes with a mimed "aha" expression. It was so faked that she sneered at him.

She turned to Herman. "I used to work in the University of California San Francisco Medical Center's research department." She pursed her lips then added, "Advisor to Greg Jacobson, the director."

Matt sighed.

She ignored him. "I was better at stat than most of their staff, so they had me do the math for their professional papers. When money tightened, the board needed to limit projects to those with the greatest potential. They sent me to study under Professor Howe at Stanford. He's one of the pioneers in decision analysis. Eventually, I was promoted to assistant director of research. I couldn't be director because I didn't have a PhD. Just the same, I was the one who did the analysis and presented the recommendations to their board."

She lifted the binder. "Pretty much like this."

Matt glowered at Herman. "Maybe she should be teaching me this instead of you."

Herman focused on Stephanie. "Can you learn this material in time to present it to our board by next Thursday?"

She opened the binder to her finger and nodded. "I'm used to presenting to men who aren't that mathematical. If they're like the UCSF board, it will take about two days to break it into increments they can digest.

"I'd rather not use Robert's—Dr. Phillips' method; it's not well vetted. I can make these arguments using more conventional techniques."

Then her eyes lit up. "I should call Bob and congratulate him!"

Herman buzzed his lips. "I really don't know where I got it. It would be rather awkward if you congratulated him and one of his competitors actually published it. There are so many things we must do between now and the meeting. Could you give me a contact at UCSF? I'd like them to provide a recommendation based on your work there."

"Greg and I parted on not-so-amicable terms, but yeah, it's pretty much a matter of record what I did. He'd back it up. He'll have to."

Matt sat straight in his chair. "Herman, wait a second." He sounded like he was giving an order. "I don't know if that will work. I think Stephanie should teach me the material."

Herman didn't hesitate. "Matt, time has run out. Stephanie understands this stuff. She has the résumé, and she has experience. She's the one who should do this."

In a consolatory tone, Herman added, "It'll free time for your study of Henri Fourth and the fifteen hundreds."

"Those events are truly important," Matt said. "And I will need my resources, all of my resources." He sounded threatening.

Herman groaned. "Of course, Matt, you'll still have your resources. Thank you for understanding, Matt. I believe Stephanie offers us the best chance with the board."

Herman turned to Stephanie. "I assume you're willing to help marginalize Carr Ferguson."

Stephanie's fists clinched. "Marginalize? I'd hang him, if I could."

Matt opened his book but didn't look at it. "Very well then," he said.

"Yes, very well," Herman repeated. "Stephanie, why don't you and I take these reports into one of the isolation booths and go over the plan."

Matt watched while they shut the door and spread the binders across a worktable. They were well focused when he began to flip distractedly through his notebook. His fist pressed against his cheek, he stared at them again. After a few minutes, he found his place in the text and began to scribble.

A bit after six in the evening, Herman and Stephanie emerged, carrying plates with leftovers from sandwiches Piero had sent earlier in the day.

Matt looked up from his ancient leather volume. "How's it going?" He still sounded hurt.

Stephanie grinned wearily. "I think I've got it. Now I'll have to design my presentation and polish it."

Herman came behind her. "How about dinner at my place for all of us?" His voice mimicked her tired cadence.

Clutching a pool cue, Emil rushed into the room. "You have a TV here?" He pointed to one across the room and took a step toward it. "You have the control thingy?"

"Not now," Matt groaned.

"Yes! Now!" Emil hurried toward the TV. "You need to see this! It's about Mr. Herman's mine. The one we were in!"

***

Hello Mindy

"Hello, Mindy?" a light-skinned, suave Hispanic cooed into his microphone.

A slight breeze ruffled his shirt. Beside him, but out of focus, stood another man. Both were decked out in heavy cowboy attire: boots, jeans, shirt, hat, the big belt bucket—the whole enchilada.

"Yes, Roberto, we hear you," Mindy replied with urgency, signaling to the audience that something profound was about to be revealed.

"Mindy, as you see, the sun is hanging low in the sky. Evening approaches. Right now I am standing on the very spot where the UFO landed, and beside me is Wendell Lee Boyd, the man who filmed it."

The camera panned to the sun standing over a nearby butte.

Matt's eyes zoomed to the TV. "Ah, shit!" he blurted.

Then Stephanie realized too. "It's near the Henderson!"

"Yeah, hold on, let's listen." Matt signed silence with a swish of his hand.

A hiss vibrated through Stephanie's bared teeth.

"Wendell, a few minutes ago you told me how you were on patrol for Haines Companies a few weeks back and saw an odd

74

glow." Roberto raised the microphone to Wendell. "Could you tell our viewers about that?"

On cue, Wendell Lee raised his finger and pointed to a low ridge. The camera followed his gesture in sympathetic response.

"Yeah, Roberto, like I was sayin', it was just after midnight, and I seen this purple glow from behind the ridge over yonder. I thought it must of been RV campers, like a Winnebago trespassin' on the Haines properties, so I grab my camcorder—it got night vision—and I walk up to the top of that ridge there to investigate."

Unable to yield the limelight for more than a few minutes, Roberto cut in. "And instead of trespassers you saw…"

A splice of Wendell's video played for the fifth time during that news segment. Though blurred, several humanoid figures could be seen walking in purple light near a large boomerang-shaped vessel of unworldly design.

Roberto leaned toward Wendell, and they both faced the camera. "Well, that must have been quite a shock. You were expecting trespassers, but you never expected—extraterrestrial trespassers." Robert chuckled spookily.

Wendell joined in, his voice a bit high pitched and hysterical.

Roberto clamped his hand on Wendell's shoulder and pushed it back and forth in a reassuring tough-guy way.

Roberto stared deep into Wendell's eyes. "Wendell, High Five News has confirmed that your film is the only ever to show aliens on the ground. You got pretty close to them too, didn't you?"

On cue, Wendell responded, "Yes, Roberto, I got so close my hands was shakin'. It caused the film to blur. It's still good enough." He nodded, confirming his statement to himself.

"Wendell, I'm sure anyone's hands would have been shaking. Most wouldn't have stayed to make that video. You did, for a full five minutes. It's one of the longest UFO films ever. Wendell, you've made history. How do you feel about that?"

Roberto suddenly cocked his head to one side, indicating to the audience that information was flowing into his earpiece. He smiled into the camera and gave Wendell another shoulder shake. "You filmed for five minutes and twenty-five seconds to be exact." He released Wendell's shoulder.

"Well, Roberto, that five minutes sure seemed like forever. God knows what they'da done if they seen me."

"Wendell, you told me that you stopped filming because you thought they did see you."

"Yeah, Roberto, just before I stopped, I heared some movement in the brush, and I feared that maybe they seen me and come to abduct me. This film might never been seen by no one if I hadn't run right then."

"Mindy, Mindy?" The camera panned to Roberto. He held his hand over his ear as if to block out distracting noise. "We have breaking news. Look over my right shoulder at the mine entrance."

The camera panned to the entrance of the Henderson Mine. "Our lab technicians just enhanced Wendell's film. It appears that an alien came out of that mine."

The broadcast switched to the studio. Mindy stared into the TV, with hands clasped rigidly on the desk in front of her. Voice full of desperation, as if Roberto had just been abducted, she said, "Roberto? We are playing the enhanced film now."

The film replayed for the sixth time. Now it had little blue circles on each of the humanoid figures. One circle circumscribed a distant figure. The screen zoomed to that figure. Mindy's voice, fading in the background, said, "Yes, Roberto, the film shows an alien emerging from the mine."

The broadcast jumped back to Roberto. "Mindy, just a few minutes ago a Paiute chief, Jim Runningbird, came down off the hill behind us to see what we're doing. He has a very interesting story to tell."

The camera panned to Roberto's right, and there stood Jim.

"*Yahaite*, Jim," Roberto said.

"I'm Paiute," Jim replied, but Roberto didn't catch on. Jim glanced at Wendell instead of looking into the camera like he was supposed to. "Yeah, I was explaining that the mine over there is forbidden."

Roberto interrupted, "You said that your grandfather, a Native American medicine man, called it a devil place. How long have the Native Americans believed that a devil inhabits that cave?"

Jim looked stupefied then became catatonic. Roberto's eyes grew desperate and flicked to someone to his right.

Finally Jim spoke. "Yeah, my grandpappa told me when I was a little boy. For a long time that place has been bad."

Roberto started to interrupt, but Jim kept going. "No one can go into that place and live very long unless they have protection from Panther Woman."

This was not the line which Roberto and Jim had agreed upon, so rather than let the interview deviate further, Roberto

76

announced, "Very mysterious. This is Roberto Rodriquez reporting for High Five, numero uno in the news. We uncover so that you can discover. Back to you, Mindy."

Mindy, her voice burdened with the significance of the broadcast, said, "Earlier, Chief Runningbird told Roberto that the mine has been cursed for several hundred years. Runningbird told Roberto that, protected by the Panther Woman spirit, he once accompanied an old prospector into the mine. That prospector recently died under strange circumstances, possibly from radiation sickness."

After that, she swiveled her chair toward an associate. "What do you think, Tom? Could the devil spirit have something to do with these aliens?"

Tom, a gringo with perfect gray hair and wearing a blue pinstripe suit, faced Mindy, who crossed her legs, showing a lot of thigh. He said as if in a side conversation, "Mindy, it does make you wonder if there is some connection between the UFO and the Navajo legend."

Tom turned his well-chiseled tan face to the camera. "We have learned that the mine belongs to Haines Companies. Mr. Carr Ferguson, a Haines executive board member, has given us permission to enter the mine. Our High Five crew, including staff scientist David Levin, will penetrate the mine within the hour.

"High Five, numero uno in the news. Tune in tomorrow, High Five at five, and see what our team finds. We uncover so that you can discover."

Then the camera panned out, and Tom turned to Mindy, whose fading voice said, "Aliens may have visited long before Europeans—" Their lips kept moving, but nothing more was heard.

**

Stephanie squinted at the TV. "What the hell was that? It was so blurred it could have been anything, but I'm sure I've never seen anything like it before."

Matt's eyes grew wild.

Herman glanced around the room, then leapt to his feet. He threw his arms wide. "It's my hovercraft, and no one has seen it except my crew and the scientists working on it. I wanted to test it, so I had the crew fly me to the mine that night."

He flopped his arms to his sides. "It works damned well. It can land on a dime."

Stephanie glared at him. "Herman, why is Wendell still working for Haines Security?"

Herman threw his arms up again. "He doesn't. He probably never turned in his equipment. Hell, I bet he used a Haines Companies camcorder to film a Haines top-secret aircraft, then splattered it all over the news for the world to see."

Stephanie jerked her head in surprise. "Herman, you told me your staff drove you out to the mine."

In every way Herman froze, face, hands, body, all statuesque. It lasted a fraction of a second; then he said, "I meant my staff brought me out there. But drive, brought, or flew"—he flipped his palm toward the TV—"that is what I meant."

Stephanie's face went ashen. "Herman, you can't let a TV crew go into that mine. They may find the SAM."

Matt, in a tongue-tied state of excitement, faced Stephanie, then Herman, his head nodding to each in nervous confirmation.

Herman moved like a sprinter. Phone to his ear, he ordered the helicopter on the roof to prepare for immediate departure. The call took seconds. He clicked the phone down and headed for the door. "Matt, let's go!" he said over his shoulder.

"I'm going too," Stephanie said.

Hurrying, Herman shouted back to her, "No reason to risk all of us in one helicopter. Besides, you need to focus on the board meeting."

"The helicopter risk is miniscule. I'm going," Stephanie yelled.

"Me too," Emil said.

Inside the elevator, Herman turned to Stephanie. "You're right about Gimish's artifacts. Horace left me the mine so I could locate them. Of course, outsiders cannot be allowed in there."

The vibration of the helicopter penetrated the walls and the floor. The door opened, and the noise became deafening. Herman bent into the wind and ran toward it. Everyone followed.

The pulsing blades drowned all sound. Matt could not hear his own words when he muttered, "On a need-to-know only basis, Herman."

Herman, fifteen feet ahead, turned to Matt and nodded while he thought, *That's what I'm doing.*

***

78

Chapter 7: High Five News

The retreating sunlight shimmered orange on the Haines helicopter and the faces of distant buttes. Below, the violet fingers of night advanced into Henderson Valley.

Roberto's High Five helicopter sat at the end of the road. A second High Five helicopter circled low near the mine, stirring dust that engulfed the aircraft. It then pulled up and, ignoring Roberto's furious shouts and gestures, set down in the middle of the alleged UFO landing site.

Herman nudged his pilot's arm and pointed to the High Five staging area. "The High Five team seems in disarray, and it's going to get worse."

Jaw clenched, the pilot descended upon the film crew. Several cameramen waved their arms and shouted. The gust from the rotor swept the ground, flinging sand and pebbles at them and their cameras. They buried their faces into the elbows of their jackets and hurried off.

Shrieks of approval reverberated from Herman's entourage.

Herman turned to Stephanie. "Stay here. I don't want you tarnished by the squabble I'm about to start. Emil, you stay too. The fewer of us who become involved in this, the better."

Matt signaled a frantic *no!* He grasped the back of Herman's seat. "Herman, you need to avoid negative public perception. Let me, your engineering archeologist, handle this."

Herman snorted. "I own the land. Carr Ferguson can't give them permission to trespass on my property."

"Yes." Matt drew the word out. "But High Five made promises to their audience. Maybe I can help them save face while denying them access to the mine. A win-win."

"Yeah," Stephanie chipped in. "You mustn't vilify youself with cameras rolling."

Herman squinted as if in thought, then acquiesced. "We'll listen on the distance microphone." He adjusted a long tube toward the knot of High Five staff. "Once you've calmed them down, I'll join you."

Matt leaped down. With his back bent against the pressure of the whirling rotor, he ran after the High Five group, who were walking toward the mine.

"Sir," he shouted out to the leader, "may I ask what is going on here?"

They all glanced back. The leader, a dwarflike man with a plate-sized black beard and a bald head, raised his hand to hail Matt. "I suppose you're from Haines." He pointed to the Haines emblem on Herman's helicopter. "It's so good of you to give us permission to explore the mine. I'm sure this whole thing will turn out to be a hoax, but right now the public is interested in Wendell's video."

Matt caught up and shook his head. "I'm sorry. You can't go in there."

Running up behind Matt, Roberto called out, "But Carr Ferguson gave us permission." Red faced, Roberto heaved for breath. The High Five group spread into a crescent around Matt.

As if Matt, who had just disembarked from the Haines helicopter, wouldn't know, Roberto added, "Ferguson is on the Haines board of directors."

The cameras' dull cyclopean eyes swung toward Matt.

Matt forced a smile. "This mine is the private property of Herman Rothe. Ferguson has no authority here."

"I'll radio my executive producer and have full authorization in fifteen minutes." Roberto squinted at the falling sun, then threw his hands up in exasperation. "Who the hell are you anyway?"

Matt stuck out his hand. "Matt Krause. I'm Mr. Herman Rothe's engineering archeologist."

Roberto cocked his head imperiously. "Herman Rothe, the acting CEO of Haines Companies? I'm sure he'll give us permission; it's just an old deserted mine, for Christ's sake!"

Matt grimaced, then rolled his head side to side in long emphatic "no" cycles. "It has nothing to do with you. Ferguson and

80

Herman hate each other. Ferguson illegally gave you permission, so Herman will stand firm on denying it."

Realization filled Roberto's eyes. He crimped his nose into a snarl and glared at Wendell.

Wendell looked down.

"You didn't know that, Boyd?" Roberto's eyes cut into Wendell's skull.

The bearded dwarf, a geologist named David Levin, flicked his eyes back and forth between Matt and Roberto, then looked toward the mine. "He's bluffing. I'm not going to let some personal feud between two fuddy-duddies ruin this broadcast."

David was retained by High Five to provide expert analysis on science issues. They would pay him five hundred dollars to do this field report. He took off for the mine. His cameramen hurried after him.

"There are a couple of reasons why you shouldn't do that," Matt yelled.

Levin stopped. "What the fuck might they be?"

"For one, your helicopter just stirred up a bunch of dust. Some of that stuff is about seven microns in diameter, and you're risking a bad case of silicosis if you go up there right now."

Speaking directly to the camera crew, Matt explained, "Same thing as black lung disease. Even this far away we're breathing some of it."

The cameramen looked at Levin. David studied the hill. The setting sun exaggerated the intensity of the airborne dust. "It's not that bad."

The crew turned to Roberto for confirmation.

Roberto swung his arms up in disgust and shook his head. "We might as well get everything worked out with Rothe then come back tomorrow morning."

"You just committed to a 5 p.m. broadcast for tomorrow," Levin said. "The dust will settle in an hour or so. We'd better do it tonight."

"There's a second issue," Matt said, "radiation."

"Radiation?" The word gurgled as if it caught in Roberto's throat.

"Yeah," Matt replied. "The Henderson was a uranium mine, pitchblende. Old man Henderson built a cabin out of it, even used it to build a wall around his vegetable garden. Everyone in his family got cancer and died. I'm sure that's why the Indians call it a 'devil' place."

Roberto rolled his eyes. "Why the hell isn't it fenced off with warning signs?"

"To answer your question, there's a padlocked iron gate just inside the mouth of the mine. The potential hazards are posted on it."

"That ain't true!" Wendell whined. "I caught ol' Spruce and Runningdog up there 'bout six months back. If it got radiation, they'd be sick."

"Runningbird," Matt corrected.

Everyone turned to Jim, who stared at Wendell. After a minute of Jim's sustained silence, the camera crew shifted their gaze to Wendell, who finally blurted, "How the hell was I suppose to know?"

A voice came from nearby. Herman, his tie blown over his shoulder, waved and hurried forward. When he reached them, he pulled his tie down and buttoned his coat. "So, Mr. Rodriquez, you may now understand that there are good reasons for not letting you film my mine. Once you show it on TV, every teenager and yahoo in the region will be sneaking up there to find the alien. Then they'll sue me for endangering them. I'm sure High Five doesn't want to be party to those lawsuits as well."

"I'm Herman Rothe." He extended his hand to Roberto.

Roberto plastered on his best smile and took Herman's hand.

Herman demonstrated improving social skill by saying, "Mr. Rodriquez, I would know you anywhere. My executive staff and I break every evening to watch your broadcast."

Roberto kept his handshake firm and his grin glowing.

Herman continued. "I know you promised your audience to get to the bottom of this UFO thing. I can help you keep that promise in a much more impressive fashion than poking around that dirty old hole over there."

Roberto finally let go of Herman's hand. He pressed his arms against his sides and glanced from Matt to Herman. "It gets damned cold out here at night."

"It can." Matt wrapped his arms around his chest in demonstrative agreement.

"May I explain?" Herman said. "Most of these flying-saucer things are cases of mistaken identity. In this instance, Wendell filmed

82

a top-secret Haines hovercraft that we were testing. That will be clear when you see it."

Roberto stepped back as if he hadn't heard correctly. "You just said that you'll let us see a classified aircraft?"

"Film it. We planned to declassify it this year anyway. Since this all came up, I figured we may as well let you do an exclusive. My staff agreed."

Then Herman's face hardened, and he spun toward Wendell. "By the way, I have a strong suspicion that your film was taken with a Haines Companies' camcorder. If so, then the film and the recorder are Haines's property, and you should turn them over immediately."

Wendell set his jaw in defiance.

The cameras locked their cyclopean eyes on him.

Roberto's neck bulged red against his shirt collar. "You dumbass. Please tell me you didn't do that."

"Ah shit, man, Roberto." Wendell crab-stepped away from the High Five anchor. "What the fuck, man? I used what I had…"

Roberto finished for him, "And it just happened to be Haines Companies property."

"Eh, yeah," Wendell said as if it were irrefutably logical.

Roberto pressed his lips into an angry line. His eyes went to Herman. He shook his head. "Mr. Rothe, I am embarrassed in the extreme. Believe me, I speak for the entire High Five Corporation when I say this video will be retracted and the tape delivered to you. Regrettably, we failed to vet this source thoroughly."

Matt whistled through his teeth.

Herman crossed his arms and turned his back on Wendell. "I understand. No foul, no harm. Neither I, nor Haines Companies, will hold you, or High Five, accountable for the misfeasance of others." He glanced over his shoulder toward Wendell, then back to Roberto. "And my offer still stands."

Wendell's head jerked with sudden realization. "Hey! I've got real live aliens walking around. It don't make no shit whose camcorder I done it with."

Roberto spat on the ground. "Wendell, start walking, because it's a long fucking way back to Vegas."

Herman laughed. "Ah, Roberto, we don't have room to take him back with us, and I'm sure we both don't want one of those other stations broadcasting that we left him out here to die. Please take him back to Vegas for both our sakes."

Roberto grinned. "Just indulging myself in a few moments of fantasy. Of course we'll take the dumbass back with us." His tone said he would prefer not to.

Herman touched Roberto's elbow. "Tomorrow is Wednesday. What if we give you some preliminary photos for that broadcast? Maybe you could tantalize your audience to wait for a Thursday revelation? We'll get you into the shed Thursday morning. I'd do it sooner, but I have to twist some government arms. Literally takes an act of Congress to get them to move on anything."

"Yeah, we can stall, but in the end, it has to be worth the wait. We can't make our audience feel like chumps," Roberto said.

"It'll be good, real good." Herman shook Roberto's hand.

***

Stephanie's Inquiry

The camera crew packed their equipment into their helicopter. Levin stood paralyzed, except for his eyes, which jumped from the mine to Rodriquez, to Herman, and then to Matt. He stepped toward Matt. "Hey, you got any sources on that uranium mine?" His voice was filled with amicability.

Matt answered in a tone of reconciliation. "Yeah, back at my office. Anything in particular you're interested in?"

Levin moved away from Rodriquez's hearing. "This UFO gig isn't going anywhere. Thought I would offer Roberto a science supplemental on the old mine."

Matt frowned. "You mean like how ol' man Henderson's whole family died from radiation poisoning and it had nothing to do with aliens?"

Levin ran his hand over his bald head like he was combing imaginary hair. "Yeah, that's it. Let me get back to you. I need to get Roberto on board." Levin left at a trot.

**

"Excuse me," Stephanie said. The fading sunlight glowed golden on her face and on the fuselage of the High Five helicopter.

The cameraman pushed a case into the hold and shut the hatch. He smiled at her.

"Are you the crew foreman?" she asked.

84

"Lead." He smacked the side of his pants. An expanding cloud of dust billowed from his leg. He nodded to her. "With Haines, right?"

"Yeah." She held out her hand. "I'm Stephanie Noble."

"Terry Braunson." He shook her hand. "What a mess. Of course, we always knew it had to be a misidentification or a hoax. I mean, UFOs always are, but the public is gaga over them. We thought it would be a nice piece. No one thought that klutz Wendell would use Haines property to film a top-secret Haines aircraft."

"Unfortunate," she said.

Terry dusted his pants again. "We are so lucky that Herman is giving us an out."

"I wasn't up there." Her voice grasped for more information.

His face brightened. He launched into a long-winded ramble about the events on the hill. She rolled her eyes when he told her of Wendell's duplicity. His hands gyrated and his face contorted in exaggerated expressions while he spoke. His narrative took on the form of a mating ritual. That was not lost on her.

The sun sat against the horizon. Its golden rays cast long purple shadows through the brush. A grayish form slinked through the undergrowth several hundred yards down the valley. Stephanie's eyes caught it. She disconnected from Terry's soliloquy to see if it would reemerge.

Terry's voice rose to pull her attention back to him. "Wow, we should get out of this hellhole."

Her eyes remained distant a moment longer; then she returned to him.

"Well," he said. His mouth half opened. It seemed his words would flee away unsaid; then he blurted, "So we owe you one. Anytime I can help, you give me a call." He pulled a worn wallet from his back pocket and flipped it open.

Worn strips of paper, notes scribbled on them, hung out. He fingered about and withdrew a card, also worn on the edges. His face uncertain, he pushed it forward, letting their fingers kiss.

She took the card. "There is something you might help me with right now."

"Shoot."

"Wendell's flying-saucer video, is it time-stamped?"

He arched his eyebrows. "I'm sure it is. They probably didn't show it in the broadcast, did they? They usually don't."

85

"Not during the part I saw."

"I do know I've seen it somewhere." He angled his eyes up and to the right as if he would find it in the sky. Then he snapped his fingers. "Here!" He opened the passenger door and thrust his hand behind one of the seats. He brought out a red binder.

"It's in the script notes." He let the door light fall on the pages while he thumbed through them. "So what do you do for Haines? Lawyer?"

Stephanie didn't respond. He looked up from his papers. The title of her last job, with "assistant" removed, jumped into her mind. "CRO, chief research officer." It would have to be that if she were going to report to the board.

"Sounds important." His voice was unsure. "But it's new to me. I've heard of CEOs, CFOs, COOs, but never a CRO. What does a CRO do?"

She laughed. "Well, Haines is a conglomerate with many divisions. We can't fund every idea that comes along, so I decide which ones are worth pursuing and which aren't."

His eyes widened. "Wow! That is impressive! You kind of decide the future of civilization."

"No, only Haines Companies."

"Like I said, civilization."

She beamed at his flattery. She jutted her chin toward the binder. "So, find anything?"

"1:32 a.m. on the 12th, Wednesday morning, very early." He frowned again. "They never mentioned the date in the broadcast?"

"Maybe. I didn't see the very start." She extended her hand.

He took hers with both of his and held it sensuously, shamelessly begging for the relationship to escalate.

She smiled without pulling away.

"You think you'll be at the demonstration of the hovercraft?" Terry asked.

"I'll get loose. Wouldn't miss it." Her hand fell to her side. His lingered in the air, like a lover's last look before parting.

She stopped in front of the Haines helicopter and watched the last bit of the sun press into the horizon. She tried to find the form in the brush again.

The cool evening desert air prickled her skin. The ridgeline darkened against the sky, and the land lay in ghostly patches among expanded blocks of blackness. Her eye caught the pale form gliding from a distant patch of light to a pool of darkness. Then it came back into the light again. Before her eyes it faded into darkness one last time and was gone. Its shape was never clear, but it was large and moved like a cat.

**

Jim stared at Wendell's feet while hiccupping a silent chuckle. "Damn it, Wendell, you're sure good at getting yourself on the wrong side of things."

Wendell's eyes filled with sadness; then anger rushed in. He spun and walked away, trailing his middle finger behind him. He never slowed, nor glanced back, but Jim was sure the man's ears were listening for fast heavy footsteps.

When Jim looked down, he gave Wendell an out. He'd intended that, not wanting to kill Wendell, at least not that evening with all those people around. No doubt Wendell had thought to kill him too, but Jim figured it would take some time for the bandito wannabe to figure out a chicken-shit way to do it. Most likely, before that, Wendell would find another target, and with luck, someone else would kill the little asshole.

Watching Wendell stomp off, Jim caught a shadowy movement in the distant brush, just like Stephanie had, except he knew who was up there, crouched and slinking bush to bush. He figured she must have been there all along, amusing herself with the interactions of humans, possibly wanting to relearn their behaviors after centuries of self-imposed isolation.

Then his attention shifted to the Haines helicopter. From the way the fading light shone on her face, he could tell Stephanie had seen Panther Woman too. Not believing it, he blinked his eyes to be sure Stephanie was watching the same spot. He followed her gaze, hoping to see a sandstone butte or other formation that had fooled him into believing Panther Woman had been there. But no, he saw the spirit one last time, standing in the ghostly light, staring back at Stephanie.

From deep within his chest, a chill poured out over his arms and up the sides of his skull.

Panther Woman had come for Stephanie, a white woman.

He shivered. The legend of the twins was true. He stared catatonically into space and grappled with a new problem: how to explain it to Derek.

"Hey, you play billiards?"

Jim jumped.

87

His fists clenched. His eyes flung wide. He gasped at the little fellow Matt and Stephanie had brought from Africa.

"Yeah, I play. You always sneak up on people like that?"

"You were looking at something. I didn't want to be rude and disturb you." Emil couldn't cover the hurt he felt from Jim's rebuke.

"Yeah, well, you'd better not go sneakin' up on Injuns like that." Jim softened his words while he collected his wits.

"I saw you and thought you might want to play billiards. I got my own billiards room at our house in Vegas."

Jim nodded his head. "You scared the shit out of me. Ain't many can do that."

"Sorry."

"No bother. My mind was somewhere else. You say you have a house in Vegas?"

"Yeah, we all share it, Herman, me, Matt, and Stephanie. It's called the Black Lava."

"You all live in the Black Lava? Rented rooms or something?"

"No, we own the whole thing, at least Herman does, but he gives us whatever we want. I have two billiards rooms: a big one on the main floor that I share with all the workers, and a small one all my own on the sixth floor.

"Want to come play? You can fly back with us. I could use the company of another Bedouin."

The two High Five copters revved their engines. Jim waited for the first one to lift off, then shouted into Emil's ear, "I can't now. I have to stay here a while. I'll come in a day or two. How do I find you?"

The second helicopter was away when Emil yelled, "I'm Emil, just ask for me." They shook hands; then Emil hurried to the Haines copter.

Bedouins? I guess we are, Jim thought. *We both have brown skins.*

**

The engine racing for liftoff, Herman said, "I asked Stephanie and Emil to stay in the helicopter, and you both went out." It wasn't a reprimand, just a statement of disappointment.

Stephanie's face flushed. Anger boiled at the back of her head. "I needed information from the camera crew. By the way, you have to make me your chief research officer."

88

"The board has to vote on all chiefs," Herman said. "I'll suggest it—if your presentation overwhelms them—"

"Make it happen. I'll do my part," she snapped.

"What?" Matt muttered in confusion.

She whipped around in her seat. "What, what? You want to say something?"

He leaned away, but her eyes demanded an answer. "No," he whispered and stared out at the darkening landscape.

"You had your chance." She sank back into her seat. Her dust-covered sneaker tapped against the floorboard at a machine-gun pace.

The helicopter was lifting off when Emil said into his headset, "I invited Jim to fly back with us, but he said he has work to do here. It doesn't seem right; everyone flying in, everyone flying out, but he has to walk."

"We're full," the pilot announced. "He must have gotten here somehow. He can get out the same way."

Matt added, "Emil, you offered him a ride, and he said no. This is his land. If he needed a ride, he would say so."

"How can it be his land?" Emil shoved both hands to the right. "Here is Haines's land." Then he pushed his hand left. "Here is Herman's land. Where is Jim's land?"

"All of it is his. We're just a temporary smudge on it," Matt said.

Stephanie, her voice still agitated, said, "Matt, you were quick with the uranium mine story. What are you going to do when Levin discovers it's a lie?"

He explained, "There was a Henderson uranium mine. Thor Henderson did build his cabin out of pitchblende and so on, just like I told Levin. However, this is Andreas Henderson's silver mine. The uranium mine was about thirty miles northeast of here."

Matt smiled slyly. "I'm betting Levin does minimal follow-up and just assumes there was only one mine. Anyway, once he calls it a uranium mine on TV, he'll never admit he was wrong."

"Great," Stephanie said under her breath. "Yet another bomb waiting to explode."

"Not an issue," Matt said. "The most important thing tonight is that there was no gate on the mine, and tomorrow morning there will be."

Stephanie dug her fingernails into the triceps of her crossed arms and thought, *That is not the most important thing that happened tonight.*

***

Chapter 8: Lies and Obfuscations

Against the wall by the elevator, David Levin's cubicle had barely enough space for a desk, a chair, and a file cabinet. Reports scattered over his table shone like sand under the glare of his lamp. Outside his cubicle, the floor was dark and silent.

He touched his coffee mug handle, cold as ice, and peered over the rim, then swished it. The tan liquid sloshed about, giving off the odor of cigarette butts. It was midnight. He told himself he shouldn't drink coffee that late. Then he sipped it.

He had spent an eighteen-hour day forming a science snippet from the sources provided by the engineering archeologist, Matt Krause. David knew his production would captivate the High Five audience, particularly those moneyed people from the East who sought authentic Western lore.

His fingers closed on the cup handle while he skimmed over his notes. He would earn two hundred dollars for the studio show, less than half what the site investigation would have paid, but he wouldn't have to crawl around a radiation-laden mine either.

He arched his back against the top of the chair and stretched his arms. Then he slumped forward and took another swig of coffee.

"Brrr, nasty!" he said in a near whisper. He stood and surveyed the gray cubicle world that extended beyond the glow of his light.

He vibrated his lips, "Br-r-r-r-r-r-r," then glanced back and forth as if he expected someone to jump out.

91

"Nasty! Fucking nasty!" he shouted, then pushed the cup to the far edge of his desk.

He flopped back into his swivel chair, laced his fingers behind his head, and leaned back. He closed his eyes and hung his jaw open to emit a long, "Ahhhh." Sleep deprivation amped up on bad coffee gave him a sense of accomplishment, similar, he imagined, to what a farmer felt when he turned a bag of cow shit into fertilizer, but that was delirium speaking from inside his head.

He had a flash of inspiration. He sat up and pushed through his papers.

Photos of Henderson with his Paiute wife and kids would be great, particularly with them in front of the cabin or working in their garden—naïvely unaware that the walls they had erected were killing them.

The majestic native seduced by the allure of civilization, or tragically caught in its onslaught, deserting his Garden of Paradise to reap the bounty of technology, only to be poisoned by the toxins released through man's assault on the natural world—or some poppycock like that.

The Easterners would figure his point and explain it better than he could, even if he never really had a point.

The hazy image of a faded sepia of the cabin tried to materialize in his mind. It fluttered just out of reach but had enough substance to assure him he had seen it. An old-time photographer wouldn't break his sacrum riding a bumpy buckboard all the way from town to take just one photo; there must be more. Surely the mixed marriage of a Norwegian and an Indian warranted a family photo, or several.

Thinking his vague memory of the photo had originated in Matt's papers, he tossed through them again. Twenty minutes of shuffling pages, one by ever-loving one, yielded nothing. With a bitter groan, he laid his head on his desk.

It must be in the archives of the county library. He wanted it. "But damn, I have a 7 a.m. golf meet with the editor."

Maybe he'd skip the photo and mesmerize his audience with his charming voice and intense eyes.

He placed his face between the palms of his hands. His half-opened eyes stared at the strata of paper tilting and spilling across his desk; then with prospector's acuity, he spied a familiar piece.

A minute later, he had it thoroughly scrutinized.

Like the prospector, he had struck pay dirt. He picked up the heavy black phone.

Call Matt at midnight? No, that would be uncouth. Let the smartass have his beauty sleep. He'll need it to dig himself out of this.

David clicked the phone back onto its receiver, then heaved an uproarious laugh that reverberated through the black alleyways of empty cubicles. This job would pay a hell of a lot more than two hundred dollars, maybe ten times that much.

**

Wrapped in a heavy pile robe and sipping her coffee, Stephanie stood barefoot before the huge plate window that stretched from floor to ceiling. Dawn's light formed a haloed crown over the distant peaks. People and cars, as busy as beetles, swarmed the streets below.

On the table next to her were a carafe of Kona coffee, another of orange juice, and a plate each of hash browns and scrambled eggs.

Lately Matt had been eating her leftovers and Piero had begun to double the orders to accommodate him.

Beyond the bedroom door, Matt lay tangled in the sheets, his face turned to the opposite wall. Seeing him snooze firmed her resolve to have her own apartment, one where two gigantic windows came together in a corner. She could stand in its vertex and float above the city.

The northwest corner. It has the best view of the mountains.

Those plans were for later. Now, she stepped back from the window and put on her navy blue Parisian suit, with a wide black belt and white ruched-collar blouse.

She turned sideways and studied herself in the full-length mirror by the bedroom door. She looked like she was headed to an executive meeting. She wondered about her heels.

"They make me about six three. Well, most men go gaga over tall women."

She poured herself another cup of coffee, then emptied the rest into the sink. The orange juice followed the coffee. She tipped the extra food into the disposal; then with her coffee cup in tow, she carried the tray to the dumbwaiter. She kneed the apartment door shut with a loud bang.

Through her teeth, she hissed, "Enjoy your sleep, asshole."

Cutting through the central atrium, she deposited her empty cup on a stone outcropping above a pool where tropical fish darted.

93

She rang Herman's doorbell while raising her watch high. *Alarm on bed stand to go off at full volume in fifteen minutes.*

Now it was time to deal with Herman, alias Butthead II. She suspected he would be up and about at this early hour, mainly because he never slept, at least not the way people did.

Light filtered under the library door, and she decided to check there first.

She loved the library. When she crossed the threshold, she blinked her eyes and made believe she had been transported back to the time and place where knowledge was the ultimate aphrodisiac.

Books, from floor to ceiling, wrapped the walls and alcoves. Along them an occasional roller ladder rested, waiting to serve in a search for the arcane. If she wanted, she could sit at a long mahogany table and read under the gaze of Sir Isaac Newton, Socrates, or Descartes. Their marble busts stood on stands here and there throughout the room.

Herman was in the corner, wearing a fresh suit and poring over documents, or asleep, or both, or neither. She took a quiet step toward him. He looked up, faked a stretch, and smiled.

"Up early, Stephanie?"

"Herman, can we go to your flat and talk? I don't want Matt to interrupt us."

Herman acted as if he had anticipated her request, and they went.

She and Matt had been inside Herman's apartment several times. It was spacious with an upscale kitchen and entertainment area, somewhat puzzling since outsiders were banned from the floor.

Herman waved her toward a comfortable chair and then seated himself.

"Hum," he said, wrinkling his forehead with concern, "you seem to be upset with Matt."

"Yeah, that and other things. I'm not too sure where to begin."

"Take your time. You know you don't have to live with him. You can have your own space built exactly to your specifications."

She nodded. "Yeah, I do want that, for sure. For starters, I called Robert last night, and I congratulated him on the publication of his new work in decision analysis."

She waited for Herman's response. He sat quietly. She expected that.

She went on. "He said he hadn't published the stuff I described. So I asked him who had, and he said no one. So..." She paused, giving Herman a chance to explain.

He threw his hands up and shrugged his shoulders. "You know me, I do numbers. I was sure I read it somewhere, but maybe I just fell into it on my own." He pointed to his head. "Mind plays tricks sometimes, you know."

"Maybe. You remember last night when I left the helicopter?"

"Yes, against my advice. It's okay. Everything worked out fine."

"Not yet." She couldn't restrain the disdain that colored her voice.

His face showed alarm.

"I talked to the film crew chief." She wondered if he had figured out where she was going. If he did, he hid it well.

"The guy said Wendell filmed the UFO at 1:32 a.m. The camcorder time-stamped it. Do you remember when you first came to Emil and me that night?"

He started to answer.

She cut him off. "I know you do. It was around 11:45 p.m. I'm sure you know where I'm going, but I'll be explicit: The hovercraft didn't bring you to the mine. You were already in the mine when we arrived."

Herman shrugged. "Wendell is such an ass. Maybe he never set the camcorder clock right."

"Hum." She loaded her voice with contempt, then waited for him to react.

He didn't budge.

"Oh." She made herself sound disappointed. Her eyes twinkled with amusement. "Okay then, if you insist. When Matt descended into the tunnels to find Gimish, Emil went into a trance. I was wide awake, nervous, and not the least bit sleepy. A sudden and inexplicable drowsiness came over me. Just before I passed out you came to us. You came from inside the mine, not from the outside."

Herman stared blank-faced as if baffled. "Well, when one is about to fall asleep, the mind drifts between reality and dreams—"

She interrupted. "Herman, let me tell you something: When my appendix was removed, just before I went under, I had an allergic reaction to the antibiotic. The surgical nurse drew lines, one per minute, marking the progress of welts while they moved up my arm.

95

Even though I was drugged, I fought to control the histaminic response. Only after I succeeded in stopping it did I allow myself to succumb to the anesthesia."

"Your point?" he asked.

She expelled a deep breath. "Herman, when I tell you that I remember you being there, you need to understand that I remember everything I saw before the anesthesia you pumped into the air put me to sleep."

He remained silent.

She continued. "Who are you? Are you Gimish? If so, why did your people leave you here after coming this far to rescue you?"

Herman beamed with the kind of delight a parent showers on a child, along with pats and hugs, when the offspring crosses a pivotal threshold in life. He gushed his praise. "Amazing deductions on your part. I am pleased that you shared this."

He stood and walked into his kitchen. "Have you had breakfast yet?" He pulled a butcher knife from the block.

"I've already eaten." Her hands pressed against the arms of the chair. Her legs tensed.

She stared at the knife tilting back and forth in his hand.

***

Revelation

Herman grinned. "I've learned to make Southwest omelets, with chopped chilies, onions, and tomatoes. Come over some morning instead of ordering from Piero. I want your opinion."

She tried to relax, but her tendons cut like steel cables into her neck.

Why didn't I just leave it alone?

Herman laid the knife on the counter and returned to his chair. "No, I'm not Gimish; he did indeed leave. I'm his intellectual seraph. I'm sure Matt told you about the seraphim, right?"

"Yeah." Her head spun. Her lungs couldn't draw air fast enough.

Herman studied her then smiled reassuringly. "Calm down. You're breathing too fast. Would you like a paper bag to breathe into? I read it helps reduce anxiety."

"No." She balled her hands into fists at her sides.

"Really, Stephanie, it's early, but you're welcome to have a shot. I have the best Glenlivet Scotch."

96

She shook her head, then giggled nervously. "I'm that bad, huh?"

"If you wish, we can do this some other time, but we do need to do it," Herman said.

She crossed her arms and arched her back against her chair. "Go on. I'll just get more nervous if we put it off."

"Okay," Herman said. "I stayed behind to mentor Matt, his offspring, and theirs, and so on for a thousand years. I'm here to see the project through."

"What?" The word jumped out. She coughed and punched her chest with the side of her fist. "Which project?"

Herman explained, "Gimish and Horace wanted to cultivate the human shaman gene. You were sent to North Africa to connect with Emil's tribe. It is one of the last places on Earth where the gene still survives, howbeit in a very recessive form."

She sighed and leaned her elbows on her knees. "Horace Haines and Gimish, the alien, worked together—"

"For decades," Herman interrupted. "They built Haines Companies, the world's most advanced technology corporation, using Nirvanian technology—a bit at a time, of course, but always on the cutting edge of human knowledge."

"All to resurrect the human shaman gene?"

Herman chuckled and waved his hand in a don't-be-silly fashion. "Oh, no, rather it was to become advanced enough so that Gimish could send a distress signal to AGS. The shaman thing was an afterthought. Actually it was Horace's idea."

Stephanie sighed. "Well, I guess the rescue signal worked."

Herman rolled his eyes. "In any case, AGS did rescue him, and I was left here to help rebuild human shaman capabilities. That brings this conversation back to you and me."

"First," she said. "I need to know when Horace told Matt the truth about this."

"Gimish told Matt that night at the mine."

Stephanie's mouth dropped open in disbelief. "Matt lied about Gimish, too?"

Herman grimaced. "Matt said he would tell you when the time was right."

Stephanie's words came out in a volcanic surge. "That's him, and he's a fool. But why didn't you tell me?"

Herman sat back as if startled. "Because Gimish ordered me to assist Matt. Telling you would have sabotaged Matt."

"What?" Stephanie was shaking with anger. "Oh, I forget, I'm talking to a robot. You don't have any feelings, do you?"

He looked too human, and although she knew he was a robot, she regretted her words. She waited for him to muster up a hurt expression, but he didn't. She felt worse.

Herman explained, "Being a statistician, you'll understand that all of my emotions are just displays of statistically relevant responses. For now, I've turned it off. I know you don't want to be lied to, either with words or false expressions. I can keep it off for you, if you wish. Of course, when others are around, I must engage it."

She wanted to vomit. His words shouted that she had reduced him from a man to a machine. She had committed murder.

"Just be yourself," she whispered. "Okay, you couldn't tell me this before because of your orders. What changed?"

Herman shifted back in his chair and laced his fingers together in front of his chest. He smiled, but now it seemed so artificial that she wondered how she ever believed he was human.

People see what they expect to see, she thought, *and no one expects to see an android.*

"I've considered telling you," Herman said, "ever since you showed your math abilities. I planned to approach you today, in fact."

"You still haven't answered me." Stephanie studied his face. Perhaps he was better at manipulating her emotions than she thought.

"Gimish put Matt in charge of Project Shaman. I was to assist him. Matt's decisions, beginning with his failure to be truthful to you, have not been in the best interest of the project. He fritters his time with historical trivia and neglects the financial health of Haines Companies."

Herman held his hand out toward her. "It is my good fortune that you are so qualified."

She scoffed. "I suppose you'll make me Haines chief research officer just to assure that Haines Companies continues to support your secret project?"

"Not quite." Herman paused in a dramatic move that reminded her of Horace Haines. Then he said, "Chief research officer is just a stepping-stone. I intend for you to be CEO of Haines Companies."

She thought her ears had tricked her, or maybe his wiring had overheated.

He smiled. It was faked, but clearly his circuitry knew she needed reassurance.

She played the words back the way she heard them come from his mouth then swallowed hard.

Herman went into the kitchen. "Coffee?" He lifted two delicate hand-painted cups from a cabinet.

He's getting better at being human.

"Where does it go?" The impish question burst from her without a thought.

He paused a moment, as if stumped. "It mixes with chemicals and gives me some supplemental energy. The digestion isn't as efficient as a true biological system." He began to unbutton his shirt. "It comes out—"

Stephanie shoved both palms toward him. "Not necessary to know."

He tidied up then brought the cups, his hands so steady that the coffee inside didn't slosh a bit.

Herman sipped. "We need to start now. I'm not willing to nag Matt anymore."

She squinted her eyes at him. "So how does the human shaman gene benefit Gimish?"

Herman shrugged his shoulders. "Enhances his hero status if it proves beneficial to AGS."

"Aha, so it's to benefit AGS, not us."

Herman raised his eyebrows. "The benefit is mutual, but it's much more important for you Earthlings."

"How so?"

"If Earth fails to provide value, then AGS will stop patrolling this sector of space. You will be left to your fate." He shook his head. "You do not want that."

Stephanie's hand jerked, spilling some coffee onto the saucer. "They're protecting us?"

"I hope so."

Stephanie gulped. "From what?"

Herman shook his head. "This part of space is new to us. For now I'll leave it at that."

She was silent, not for drama, but to gather her thoughts; then she asked, "Will you be contacting Gimish from time to time to report our progress?"

Herman frowned. "I'm afraid Gimish has been dead for several millennia."

She frowned. "You said he left here just weeks ago." She laughed nervously. "I'm sure this has to do with Einstein and relativity, but indulge me with a sophomoric explanation." She felt a sinking in her belly, a fear that he thought her an idiot for not understanding the paradox. Or worse, that his circuits had indeed malfunctioned, and she was not to become CEO of Haines Companies, but rather she was Alice, who must appease the Red Queen.

Herman acted as if nothing was amiss. "He did leave a few weeks ago, but when he gets home, he will be time-transported back to his era. As such, he is both already dead in Nirvania and at the same time traveling back to Nirvania. The important thing is we cannot contact him or my planet."

She had no idea what to do, so she kept asking questions. His answers described a truth that in no way fit her view of reality. The longer they talked, the more willing she was to let her reality step aside for his larger truth.

When she had a grasp of the landscape, she asked, "So what is Matt's role going forward?"

"Being a descendent of Ahmose, Matt has the latent shaman gene. He is the primary source for it."

"Matt is our source of the shaman gene!" Stephanie said in disbelief.

"Yes." Herman shook his head as if having difficulty accepting his own words. He explained further. "That infamous night at the mine, Matt descended into the depths and, without the aid of a flashlight, maneuvered through a maze of tunnels to find Gimish's hideout."

Stephanie nodded her head. "Yes, without a map or guide, he found the Sufi stronghold tucked between the mountains in North Africa. They wanted to stone him because they thought only Satan could have revealed their location to him."

Herman also nodded. "He's done stuff like that many times. Anyway, Gimish tested him to verify his shaman powers and he passed."

Stephanie sipped her coffee. "Please explain the test."

Herman cleared his throat as if to begin a long-winded story.

"The short version, please." Stephanie set her cup down.

"On Nirvania we manufacture an artificial element we simply call Number 268, i.e. the two hundred sixty-eighth element in the Periodic Table. It is made by preparing templates of assorted atoms from the tiniest to the largest, grains of sand to basketballs in comparison. They must be jammed together in a very specific way. When triggered properly, the atoms form one 268 atom.

"Gimish had some barely passable templates that were made in Haines laboratories. He asked Matt to use his power to trigger them. Matt meditated for quite a while, but some templates triggered and formed 268. For Gimish, that proved Matt's shaman powers."

Stephanie frowned and flashed on Emil's pool cue. "Sounds like playing pool but on an atomic level."

Herman chuckled again. "Analogically like our African friend, yeah."

"I assume there must be women who carry the gene," Stephanie said.

"Yes, and Matt has to share his genes with these women to revitalize the shaman power."

Stephanie looked down and bit her lip. "I suppose it can be done without sexual involvement."

"Of course. In any case, we have a few hundred of these shaman gene carriers, but I have only one of you."

Stephanie burst into nervous but happy laughter. "I expect to pinch myself and wake up in my bed."

Herman set his coffee cup down and adjusted his tie. "Pinch away. You will still be here."

She clasped her hands in front of her waist. "We have to discredit Wendell's video of Gimish's spaceship. It's blurred, but not that blurred. It might be difficult to convince people that he filmed something else."

Herman chuckled. "Not as much as you think. The hovercraft is exactly the same shape as the AGS shuttle." He shrugged his shoulders. "We Nirvanians achieved perfect aerodynamics millennia ago. Why would I design an aircraft any other way?"

"What about color and size?" she asked.

"That's where our challenge is," Herman said.

***

101

Obfuscation

Matt sat up in bed and ruffled his hair. In only boxer shorts, he wandered to the dining room window and stared down.

"Steph?"

Silence.

He looked into the kitchen nook. Seeing the empty carafes and the leftover eggs in the bottom of the disposal, he mumbled, "Where's my coffee and stuff?"

Around 8 a.m. he came into the library. Stephanie and Herman were in an isolation booth, working with side-by-side VCRs: one running Wendell's film, which now belonged to Haines Companies, and the other, a film of the new hovercraft.

Matt tapped on the windowpane and waved. Herman ignored him. Stephanie frowned and mimed for him to pick up the phone that connected them to the outside.

He put the receiver to his ear.

"Levin called for you. Take care of him. Herman and I are dealing with Wendell's film of the AGS shuttle you forgot to tell me about. It's kind of a shame, isn't it? Wendell knew the truth before I did."

The phone clicked. He stared down at her, his mouth hanging half open.

She flicked her fingers like a broom and turned her back to him.

At 10 a.m. she ordered the hangar crew to apply a metallic tint to the inside of the hovercraft cockpit glass, making it appear to be one solid shell just like the Nirvanian vehicle. By 1 p.m. everything was ready.

**

Matt's body tensed. He clamped onto the phone like it was a life raft. He made his face sincere, as if Levin could see him through the phone line. "Really? Wow! I was just out there the other day with a Geiger counter and couldn't pick up a thing. I guess that explains it. Two Henderson mines? I can't believe the goddamned county gave me the file for the wrong mine."

He heaved a panicked sigh. "Oh crap, I'm really sorry, David." He fumbled with excuses and explanations that sounded regretful and mixed up.

102

He sighed deeply into the phone so David would hear his remorse. "Well, David, at this point things have to move on. I mean, I don't think the mine is relevant since the UFO will be debunked."

David broke in, fast and vicious. "Rodriquez will not be pleased with this falsehood. I'm sorry about the mess-up with the county office, but ultimately this is on you. I can't lie to the public. My career is on the line. This needs to get fixed before the broadcast."

Matt hem-hawed, but Levin talked over him. "Herman's giving us full access to the hovercraft—that's a win—win for High Five and Haines—but I'll still look like a nincompoop if anyone ever finds out I let this mine thing slide."

"Yes, David, it is too bad. I know Herman hoped this hovercraft exposé would lead to a long-term partnership between Haines and High Five, something like a science series. I'm sure he wants you involved."

David cleared his throat in a way that sounded threatening. "Right now you're long on ideas but short on substance. I hope you can change that, for both our sakes."

"Hold Rodriquez off," Matt said. "I'll talk to Herman and get back to you."

David grunted, still sour and peeved. "Okay, but get back to me before the meeting at the shed."

Levin hung up, thrust his arms into the air, and mouthed a silent, "Nailed it!"

**

Matt rushed back to the library. Heads down, Stephanie and Herman stuffed papers into their briefcases. Stephanie flung the door open and marched out ahead of Herman.

"Not now," Stephanie said and brushed past Matt, then glared at him. "Someone has to cover for all your lying." She marched toward the elevator.

Herman paused beside Matt. "She figured it out. You should have told her up front. I'll talk to you tomorrow." He dashed off like a speed walker.

"Wait!" Matt chased after them. When he caught up, he blurted between breaths, "Levin figured out there are two Henderson mines. He's threatening to tell Rodriquez before you meet. I got him to back off until we work something out."

103

Stephanie slammed to a stop and whipped around. She pushed her face within inches of his. "Well, there you go. Maybe this could have been prevented if you treated me like an equal partner from the start."

Her eyes were squinted and red. She pressed her teeth into her lower lip to stop it from trembling while she stared past him.

They stood in silence, his eyes locked on hers, begging for reprieve; hers focused on the wall, refusing to acknowledge him.

Herman broke the deadlock. "Matt, come with us. We'll talk about it on the way over."

**

The helicopter rotor sounded like a hurricane. David Levin kept saying, "Huh?" after every two or three words. Stephanie raised her voice and spoke more slowly. It didn't help.

Finally, she gave up and shouted into the phone, "We'll be there in a few minutes. I'll talk to you when we land."

Levin yelled back something about urgent and before the meeting.

She hung up.

The rotor's whine deepened to a drone. She shifted forward for a better view. The helicopter hung over a colossal paraboloidal structure of shimmering chrome that stretched for two city blocks.

She felt she was in free fall while they descended from the apex of the building. Eight stories below them, cars looked like toys. Her body kept dropping. The structure expanded, seeming to stretch from horizon to horizon.

Moments later, they were on the ground, the three of them standing before the shining futuristic structure. Stephanie knew, without asking Herman, that its design had been borrowed from Nirvanian architecture.

She shaded her eyes to block the glare from its walls. Suddenly the building groaned and four-story-tall doors parted, allowing them entry to the kingdom of Haines.

She recalled the underground labyrinth hidden below the Shotwell Mine. Herman said it extended beneath the Henderson as well.

The labyrinth, she thought, *the SAM, this hangar, the hovercraft, and everything Haines, all infusions of Nirvanian technology. And I'm to make sure the world never finds out.*

She broke away from that thought. Matt's eyes met hers. She wondered if he was thinking the same thing. They had traveled a common journey, and despite his infantile attempt to hide that truth from her, their common history welded them together.

They entered the structure, their footsteps ringing out, announcing their arrival.

A block away, near the middle of the building, some Haines staff huddled together. The clicks of approaching feet broke their concentration.

The Haines foreman hurried to greet the new arrivals. After a quick obligatory exchange with Herman, he turned to Stephanie. "Well, finally we meet!" He had never heard of her before that morning, however, throughout the day they had spent hours on the phone, batting suggestions back and forth and eventually agreeing on how to make the hovercraft match Wendell's UFO.

"Glad to meet you, Roger Thompson," she replied, delighted to attach a face to the voice. She looked over the setup and nodded. "The hovercraft is positioned perfectly. Now where will we be presenting?"

"In our conference room." Roger's words dripped honey while his hand lay against her lower back, turning her toward a long room with floor-to-ceiling windows.

Good, she thought. *It'll be like performing a magic show for children.*

**

Yellow security tape marked the path to the conference room, allowing the High Five staff to walk tantalizingly close to the hovercraft.

They filed in. The doors were shut. Curtains were closed. Lights were dimmed, and Stephanie began her lecture.

Outside, Haines staff placed spotlights to match the lighting in Wendell's video.

Inside, Stephanie stood near side-by-side screens. One displayed the image of Wendell's UFO; the other, the Haines hovercraft. The boulders and brush in Wendell's film also appeared in the hovercraft photo, giving the appearance that the two machines were the same in size as well as shape. Creating and placing the scaled-down models of the natural objects had been Stephanie's idea.

She pointed out five signatures common to both aircraft: the aerodynamic shape, the size (as it had been made to appear), and three unique aerodynamic features that did not exist on any other known aircraft. When her lecture addressed one of these common features, bright circles highlighted the item on both screens.

Out in the hangar, the four-story gates closed, lights dimmed, and scale-model rocks with soil and weeds clinging as if they had been pulled straight from the desert were placed around the hovercraft.

While Stephanie made her finishing points, the curtains retracted incrementally until the hovercraft, in just the right light, became visible behind the audience.

After a hearty applause, Stephanie made a modest curtsy and said, "Now please look out the windows in back. I believe you will see Mr. Boyd's UFO as he saw it that Wednesday night several weeks ago."

They all turned. Some gasped. Others jumped to their feet and rushed to the window, fumbling with their cameras as if at any moment the craft would accelerate into space and their opportunity would be lost.

It didn't fly away. The conference doors opened, and everyone poured onto the hangar floor, cameras rolling.

**

By 5:30 p.m. things had wound down. Hands were being shaken all around—Roberto and Herman, Roberto and Stephanie—everyone with everyone they could reach out to.

Herman and Roberto were moving away from the crowd when David Levin, his face red and disturbed, rushed forward. Herman smiled and signaled Levin to join them. Roberto, clearly annoyed, ticked his head several times, signaling Levin to move in the opposite direction.

Levin came anyway.

"David, I'm glad you found us." Herman sounded bubbly. "Let's all move toward the far door." Then he winked to Roberto. "We'll be the first in line."

At the far end, the giant doors clanged. A crack of light appeared and widened.

"I need to talk to you," David said, touching Roberto's sleeve.

Roberto gave David a hostile stare.

David's mouth opened, but before he could speak, Herman laid a heavy hand on his shoulder, gripping it firmly. "We've got a lot to talk about. David, would you mind letting me start? I think it'll be worth it to you."

Roberto gave Herman a puzzled look, then glared at David.

Herman pointed to the light beyond the doors. "I told you we'll be first in line. The food is just out there. I knew we might finish late, so I took the liberty of having my chef prepare a Western barbee for us. I hope you'll accept my hospitality.

"It'll give us time to talk about an idea that Stephanie came up with. I think High Five management will like it."

The light poured through the widening doors, revealing tables decked in red and white checked cloths. On the runway beyond, two cooks in crisp white chef hats and scarlet aprons stood before a huge grill.

Roberto thrust his right thumb up. Everyone quickened their steps.

In front of the chefs, Herman announced, "They've got everything here you can imagine, so order whatever you like. If they haven't already made it, they'll cook it for you. For me, I always take Piero's special. It's always a new creation, and it's always good.

"Once you've plated up, I hope you two will be so kind as to sit with Stephanie and me at the executive table there in the corner." Herman winked and added, "By the way, Piero has a couple of bottles of a special wine for us. Or if you like, there's some Czech beer he had flown in from a little brewery in old-town Prague. Whatever you prefer.

"I'll let Stephanie explain her idea, but the Boyd UFO fiasco convinced her that Haines needs to become more transparent to the public. She's got some great ideas. I wouldn't be surprised if she replaces me as CEO someday."

After the main course, Stephanie began. "Mr. Boyd's film of our hovercraft brought home the general lack of information available to the public regarding Haines's activities.

"For instance, most people think we're just a defense contractor. In truth, only twenty-five percent of our business is related to the military. As you saw in the presentation, the hovercraft's emergency evacuation capability is superior to that of helicopters, and its widespread use would increase survival of evacuees by thirty-four percent.

"This is just one example of many societal benefits from our research. Herman says it's a shame that the public is unaware of our work and that of other corporations as well. He wants to fund a substantial science program to increase public awareness of those technological advances."

107

Herman cleared his throat and raised his wineglass. "Don't be modest; you brought the idea up first."

She smiled and tilted her head bashfully. "Infomercials, little short clips that are more advertisement than information, are used by some corporations. The public rightfully rejects them. We want unbiased objective programming."

She stopped and looked from Roberto to David as if considering the viability of her plan. Then she nodded slightly, as if to herself, and moved on at an enthusiastic clip. "We want the public to really understand our work and how it will impact them now and in the future. We want meaty stuff, science and engineering, but it has to be presented in an exciting way, and it has to be understandable to the layman.

"We believe that a Haines-High Five partnership can make this happen."

She paused and raised her glass. "Gentlemen, Haines wants to fund a science segment on High Five News. We provide the money; you decide the content."

She held her glass toward David Levin. "The only string we attach is that Mr. Levin be the moderator. We like his presentation style and his ability to make science understandable to laypeople."

Rodriquez touched his chin with his finger as if in contemplation. It lasted about two seconds before the grin spread across his face. Then he asked Herman, "Do you have a phone? I'd like to call the office and tell them we'll be working late on a proposal."

David's mind drifted into reverie, then he said, "Roberto, I think I should focus on this and forget that mine exposé."

Roberto stared at him in disbelief and said, "A-yeah."

***

Chapter 9: The Chosen

Haines board members stood in small clusters while they sipped Kona coffee and engaged in chitchat during the last minutes before the Haines Trans-Air workshop.

Carr's perfect hair matched his blue-gray pinstripe suit tailored to his athletic body. In an exasperated undertone, he complained loudly, "The binder came last night, late, typically late."

All knew otherwise. Previous meeting binders were always early. If anything, Herman was reliable, even machinelike.

Others, relieved that another had flung the first barb, rushed to Carr like iron filings to a magnet. Each had a reason to target Herman—nothing personal, just working an angle.

Carr and Harlan Phipps had positioned themselves amid a group of neutral board members, those who would flock to the winner after the carnage. With a demonstrative arc of his arm, Carr placed his finger on the binder title and read, "Presented by Stephanie Noble." His eyes peeked over the folder and his cheeks bunched into a besmirching grin. "Wasn't she Horace's personal nurse at the Shotwell? She must do something really well." His grin widened, and he scanned the group, side to side, assuring that they got the undertone of his comment. He winked at Harlan and said slightly louder than a whisper, "You think it's the same for Herman? God knows he needs to loosen up, but it's ballsy of him to push her on us."

Then his face drained flat and mean. He shook his head and proclaimed, "Bad judgment."

109

Another crony burst out, "Maybe if we're lucky, she'll pole dance at the end of the meeting."

Frowns shot from those outside Carr's clique. He covered his mouth in boyish embarrassment. "I hear she's good looking."

Harlan added, "Her sophisticated intercourse must have impressed the old dog. Got to give him credit, at least he got her nailed."

The red-faced cackling ended when a bell signaled the start of the meeting. Still murmuring, they shuffled toward the board chambers.

Carr went to the refreshment station and pretended to fill his coffee while he eyed the seating pattern.

Then he spotted her. He had to stare. The sexy cowgirl had morphed into a corporate executive. There she stood in an elegant chartreuse suit, her hair short, businesslike, yet still flowing as if tossed by a breeze.

Well, he thought, *she's delicious.* He felt his groin stir, like the time he had dinner with her while planning to have her for dessert— but she betrayed him. His fantasy about their relationship collapsed into a cauldron of anger and sexual arousal. A real lump rose in his pants, rubbing against his underwear and propelling him dangerously close to embarrassment.

He lowered his coffee cup to his waist. His mind told him to be discreet while his rage demanded that he dominate her. He looked out the window while wrestling to gain control over his libido, but little leaks in his brain kept flashing on her: the sexuality and the disloyalty.

He shifted his leg under the coffee cup.

She should never have denied me.

His anger grew. He let it fuel in increments while his logic center kept it under control.

Like a petulant child, he eyed her.

Her, responsible for the strategic plan of the greatest technological company in the world? Herman fucked up. Let his dick get control of his brain.

His grin curled back, baring his incisors.

**

Several others moved to the snack area to get pastries. Two rock stars of the corporate world grabbed theirs and looked for seats. Carr slinked in behind them.

110

He sighed deeply, attracting a glance from the real estate magnate. "Ron," he whispered, lifting the binder slightly, "late, not professional."

Ronald Stump nodded his head and adjusted his tie with two irritated jerks. He didn't make eye contact, nor did he speak.

Carr grasped the back of Len Amendola's chair and pulled himself toward the men. "I wish he would respect our opinions enough to give us time to form them."

"We're supposed to work it out today, together, no foregone conclusions. That's why it came late, part of this new decision-analysis process," Len muttered.

Cheeks flushed, Carr glared at the back of Amendola's neck. He chuckled derisively. As if he just noticed, he said, "This is nuts! First Herman, the Shotwell's operations manager, is appointed CEO. Then he picks the Shotwell nurse as corporate planner?"

Ron studied Carr. Two seats left of Len, Doc Watson, a lifetime Horace Haines supporter, spoke up. "We all know that the Shotwell jobs were a façade. Horace kept his top guys close, regardless of where he was. The woman's probably the same deal."

"Sure." Carr snickered.

At the front, Herman and Stephanie huddled, going over details of the morning's agenda, at least one of Herman's minds was. Another, his research unit, listened to Carr.

With a booming, "Okay," Herman stepped to center stage. The chatter stopped.

"We all knew Horace Haines." He paused and lowered his head in a moment of silence. He raised it up again, and with a forlorn grin, he scanned from face to face, without speaking. He cleared his throat. Several in the room exchanged disturbed glances; others glued their attention to him.

He looked down again and shoved his hands into his pants pockets in a very relaxed, homey manner. He looked up again. "Horace—he's the one that could think up the most harebrained ideas you ever heard of."

Several, including Watson, burst into uproarious horse laughs. The nervous ones stared at him blank faced. Some wiggled in their seats.

"And had the practical know-how to turn those ideas into billion-dollar industries while you and I sat by in dumbfounded amazement."

Watson and those who had known Horace nodded their heads.

"We can all agree Horace was a stellar entrepreneur. May I say, *the* stellar entrepreneur." Herman nodded his head as he glanced from face to face, tricking several of Horace's detractors into nodding back in agreement.

Oh, my God, Stephanie thought, *he's been watching Jimmy Stewart movies.*

Indeed, he had.

"Given Horace's achievements, you might be surprised that he considered it quite a coup to have pulled Ms. Noble away from the University of California's Medical School, where she was the assistant director of research. Why such a big deal? Her specialty is an emerging branch of statistics called decision analysis. Its purpose? To find the optimal course of action for any endeavor.

"Big deal, you say.

"Well, let's look at who else uses decision analysis to guide their efforts. There are only a handful at this time: NASA, the World Bank, Israel's government, and..." He frowned and turned to Stephanie for help.

"SAC Air Command," she said. "They hired William Bing about three months ago." Then, with a slight blush of embarrassment, she realized that no one knew who "Bing" was, so she added, "Dr. William Bing, chairman of Princeton's Statistics Department."

Herman laughed. "I understand UCSF is still looking for her replacement."

The room gurgled with delight.

Stephanie glanced at Carr. His face was emotionless, but it did not hide the beast within. She felt her shoulders begin to shake. Her mind went blank. Her eyes became distant as she stepped up to the podium.

***

Not Only a Dream

She found Matt in the library, bent over his worn leather books and so absorbed that he didn't notice her. She seized the opportunity to let off some of the day's tension and slid along the wall behind him like a kitten bent on ambush. She held her breath and gingerly peeked over his shoulder. The book was one that never

112

left the environmentally controlled Stanford archives unless requested by an important person, usually a donor, and only then if the recipient's facilities could maintain the mandatory environmental constraints. When Matt finished, the book would be sealed in a container and returned along with a temperature and humidity chart showing that it had been properly cared for.

His gloved hand slid a dull blade under the page and gently lifted it. She bent her head near his ear and cleared her throat. His body jerked in reflex.

"I-I knew you were there." Without looking up, he marked his place with a strip of chemically neutral paper. He looked into her face. His eyes begged forgiveness. He waited. There was nothing he could say; he had expended all his words a day earlier while she gathered her things to move into an empty apartment, where she would live until her custom flat was ready in the northwest corner.

"We're having a dinner reception at seven tonight. It would be nice if I had an escort. I don't want any of the wives thinking I'm after her man. More so, I don't want their men to believe they have a prayer."

Matt grimaced. "I thought we were through."

Stephanie stroked his head. "No, we're not, unless you want that. I don't want it, but I had to let you know you hurt me."

He started to explain again, "It's a big responsibility. I wasn't sure how to—"

She put her finger over his lips and said, as she had so many times before, "That explains the first day that you didn't tell me. Maybe even the first two days, but that doesn't explain why I had to figure it out myself after weeks. We can go on from here, or not."

"Okay." He cupped her fingers in his hand.

She drifted off to the night they first met, behind the old motel, when they watched the moonlight glistening on the distant mountains. Why couldn't time have frozen right then, with them perfectly in love?

She understood that with his injured feelings he was inclined to continue his research, even though it divided them further, he in the past, she and Herman struggling to gain the future. He claimed that the past needed to be protected in order to secure the future. How the past, which had happened, required action to be preserved was beyond her.

She pointed to the book. "French? About what?"

Her hand slid to his shoulder and toyed with his shirt collar.

His eyes sparkled. He wanted to share his obsession with her.

"It's a reference from the notes of Heinrich Mann's books about Henri the Fourth. It sounds very odd. I suppose I could be misinterpreting, but I'm pretty familiar with the language used here."

Stephanie tilted her head as if in thought. "Yeah, you said eight years of French, between high school and college; it's more than I could tolerate."

"More than eight years, counting the historical documents I've studied on my own. Anyway, I think Herman attempted to kill Henri the Fourth."

Her hand stopped. "You what?" she blurted. "That's crazy—I think?"

Matt pointed to the book. "It sounds like it's describing a supernatural being."

She leaned further over him, running her hand down over his chest. "Then it must have been Gimish, because Herman wasn't a human being until the last hundred years or so. Anyway, if they wanted to kill him, who could have stopped them?"

"Yes, I thought about that. The only answer I can think of is me."

She sighed with exasperation. "I don't think history will change overnight. You can be my escort to the party, then go time traveling in the morning."

He chuckled. "I think I do need to do some more research anyway. For one thing, I should interrogate Herman."

"Interrogate?"

"He can be elusive."

"True." She withdrew her caresses and clamped her hands to the back of Matt's chair.

He shoved the book to the middle of the table. "I don't have decent clothes, at least by your high-flying board's standards."

Stephanie released the chair and put her mouth next to his ear. And yes, her top blouse button had managed to work itself free. "Of course you do. We had a tux tailored for you."

She turned his chin toward the door. A suit bag hung on the knob. "You have about an hour. Come by my apartment when you're ready."

She kissed his cheek then took off with the rear of her skirt pumping like a throbbing heart. She stopped at the door and glanced back over her shoulder. "Don't think you're out of jail yet."

"Well, if it isn't the happy couple?" Marie stepped into the room. As head of security, she and her staff supervised the construction of Stephanie's new apartment, monitoring the movement of everything: workers, tools, and materials delivered to the floor. She personally went over the site with detection equipment at the end of each day. To be blunt, when the apartment was finished, there would be no bugs, except hers.

Sounding annoyed, Matt said, "Where'd you come from?"

She gave him an "are you nuts" look and said, "Just popped up the elevator to check the apartment construction."

Stephanie chimed in, "Yeah, she brought up your suit and inspected my apartment while I hunted you down." Then with her back to Marie, she mouthed to him, "It's cool."

"Great corner window, Stephanie," Marie gushed. "Nice guest bedroom, too. Matt, if you're a nice boy, I bet you'll get to spend the night sometime." She winked at him then smiled appreciatively at Stephanie and reminded her, "Day after tomorrow, target practice with the .40 cal."

She left.

Matt shook his head and whispered, "Incredible."

**

Away from the lovebirds, Marie's face hardened. Her teeth clenched and ground. She stopped by the elevator door, running her palms down each of the sleeves of her rust-colored jacket. She tidied the front, rechecking the buttons for the tenth time. Then she punched her code into the security panel. Her next stop—the sixth-floor reception room, where she would undoubtedly see Carr Ferguson. Just the thought made her hands tremble. She balled her fists to stop it and whispered, "I want to kill him."

**

Suntanned neck poking from his form-fitted tux, Matt arrived at the sixth-floor banquet room looking great. Marie surprised him, pulling him into the women's lounge to gel his hair. The news of a man in the women's room spread among the board wives, and several came to see, then to comment and compliment, or to adjust this or that, showing their currency in style or maybe just as an excuse to touch him.

Finally Marie said, "Enough," and shooed them away. They exited, not saying a word to their mates, but confident they could counter any adulation spoken regarding Stephanie.

Then Marie slapped Matt on the butt and ordered him out. He doubled his fist coupled with an overtly playful snarl, and took a demonstrative step toward her.

Her eyes widened. In reflex she launched forward, shoving with such force that he banged his head into the wall.

"God, Marie! What the hell? I was kidding," Matt said.

He brushed off his tux with loud swipes of his hands.

"I'm sorry." She eyed his hair and made a desperate smoothing motion with her hand. "It's messed now. Let me fix—"

He shrugged her off and walked away.

**

Herman paraded the young couple before his board, letting Stephanie work her intelligence and charm while he rambled about the need for a chief research officer, a theme he worked throughout dinner.

In the wee hours, the last guests excused themselves. Stephanie surveyed the room, a mini combat zone of scattered cloth napkins draped over chairs and huddled among wineglasses in various stages of depletion.

She expelled a long, relieved sigh, then slipped to the kitchen to brew a cappuccino. In six hours, at 7 a.m., she would facilitate the conclusion of the decision-analysis process.

The chrome belly of the coffee machine rumbled to a boil, followed by the hiss of steam. Half in a dream, she turned the handle and bled the brew into her cup.

A dark image shimmered across the coffee maker.

"Matt?" she said and whirled. She gasped and pressed back against the granite counter. Coffee sloshed across the slab and the back of her hand. Reacting to the scald, she released the cup.

Carr Ferguson studied her as if she were a piece of meat in a butcher's market. He gradually positioned himself like a predator preparing to lunge at its prey.

She couldn't move. She locked on his fierce eyes. In her mind she conjured voices of dead women pleading to the same evil beast.

"A hussy should wear either red or black, don't you think?" he said.

116

"What?" She threw her head side to side as if trying to awaken herself from a nightmare. She balanced over her quivering legs, praying she wouldn't collapse to the floor.

"Don't you think a whore should wear black or red panties?"

Stephanie felt her chest constrict. Her throat gulped. She pushed all else out of her conscious and prayed to hear someone nearby.

His face stirred with a victor's elation.

She projected her voice into the room beyond, her words quaked. "I'm not discussing women's underwear with you."

That sounded stupid, she thought.

"But I'm sure you would discuss it with another man." His tone conveyed an accusation of betrayal.

Cooing flirtatiously, he said, "But I wouldn't want that to stand between us." He had changed so fast it chilled her spine.

Had she heard voices near the exit? Had the door opened? She strained her ears. Her right hand found the cup of steaming coffee again. She wrapped her fingers around its handle.

He watched her grip tighten and he morphed back into the wolf. He slid his left foot forward as if to test the prey's reaction.

He's crazy.

"What's going on?" Marie shouted and shoved herself between them.

He leaned back and said as if joking, "Marie, we should be more careful about meeting like this. I wouldn't want Herman to think badly of his girls."

The emotion drained from his face. For just a flash the ghoul studied them side by side.

Marie's face reddened. "You leave."

He smirked. Then as quietly as he had come, he slid away.

Their eyes followed his every step until the conference door closed behind him. Neither spoke, watching and waiting for someone, anyone else to come in.

Stephanie gasped. "What the hell did he mean about you two meeting?"

"Mind games," Marie spat, but she couldn't cover the shudder in her voice. Then she opened up. "I hate him. I want to kill him. He makes voices wail in my brain. He carves my psychic the way a sadist carves a body. He knows it, and he loves it."

**

Thirty minutes later, Stephanie began to feel she owned her body again. Standing before the big corner window, she and Matt floated above the streets, their heads touching. Holding hands, their footsteps echoed through the empty apartment to the guest bedroom. With nothing more than a sleeping bag to protect them from the hard floor, they wrapped themselves in each other's arms and let their tongues explore each other's mouths, then ears and necks and bellies.

Just before she and he passed over the edge into nonsensical surrealism, Stephanie muttered, "When you understand that you and I are the world, the whole world, then I'll forgive you."

She passed into a dream, one where she lay awake but couldn't move. She saw a panther come into the room and circle them. She watched, believing it came for Matt. It circled past him, rubbed its nose on her hand, then lay on the floor beside her.

It wasn't there in the morning. It had been a dream, but it wasn't only a dream.

***

Chapter 10: And Other Dreams

Seventeen days after the night of three helicopters, Jim Runningbird headed for the Black Lava. The distance from his reservation home was exactly 97.6 miles. A fellow tribesman gave him a lift to Moapa, the first sixty-five miles. From there he walked for seven hours, during which his sweat mixed with the dust then ran down his face and neck in dirty trails that dripped onto his collar. At sunset it condensed into a homeless odor. Long after that he reached the Black Lava and told the guard he had come to play pool with the little Arab fellow named Emil.

He didn't need to say more. Most of the security staff had received a billiards ass-whooping from Emil at one time or another.

The stone-faced guard took a minute to study him, then finally asked, "How'd you get here?"

"Walked."

"No doubt. Sit on that bench." The guard pointed to one outside. "I'll call him."

The time was 11 p.m., but Emil shed tears of elation at the sight of the big brown man. They went to the community poolroom, placed an order for burritos and beer, then played the rest of the night. About 7 a.m., staffers began to arrive. Emil begged off several requests for rematches, then took Jim up to his private billiards room, stopping at the kitchen to pick up coffee, tacos, and fry bread.

Early in the afternoon, they took a break and ordered enchiladas.

That did it.

119

The walk, the play, and the food pressed down on Jim's shoulders like a load of rocks. He dropped into an overstuffed chair and, fading into unconsciousness, mumbled, "Ah, Emil, ah, let's go home."

"I am home," Emil said.

"Come on. I'll fix you some eggs and real fry bread. This stuff is shit." Jim's eyelids sputtered in a fight to stay open.

"How far do we have to walk? I don't have a car."

"I'll call Uncle Derek," Jim said.

"When?"

"Today." Jim pushed himself up on weary arms and staggered to the phone.

**

Marie told them that Emil had gone. Guilt ridden by their neglect of him, Stephanie and Matt joined the panicked search. Herman, on the other hand, cancelled Emil's seventh-floor access.

In the fifth-floor security center, Stephanie, Matt, and Marie bent over Bob's shoulder while all studied the video feed from one of the perimeter cameras. Bob, Marie's right-hand man, pointed to the time stamp on the film. At 3:21 p.m., Emil and Jim loaded several six-packs of beer into the back of a pickup driven by another Paiute.

"Both Paiutes," Marie said, pointing at the monitor. "Same broad-shouldered athletic build, same high chiseled features, one in his early thirties, the other in his late forties, father and son?"

"That one is Jim." Matt planted his finger on the screen.

"So how do you know him?" Marie asked.

Stephanie broke in. "He was at the Henderson when we confronted High Five. Good-looking guy."

Marie twisted her face into a puzzle, then with a bemused smile agreed. "Yeah, he is."

The whole clip took only one minute and fifty-three seconds, but it was clear Emil left willingly. That didn't guarantee his safety; the film ended with the Paiute driver popping a beer and swigging it down while fishtailing down the street.

**

At 85 mph, it took one hour to reach Lower Pahranagat Lake at the southern border of the reservation. Everything slowed after that. Derek took the scenic route, stopping at gas stations, cafés,

120

horse corrals, and shanties. At each place, Emil was introduced in Paiute and English to friends and family.

Three a.m., with no beer left, they reached Derek's house. The two Paiutes stumbled into the kitchen to cook fry bread. Emil sat on the kitchen table and watched. Twenty minutes later, plates of fry bread and eggs clattered onto the table, and forks were passed around.

Afterward, they sat silently in the front room, coffee cups dangling from their fists. Dawn light filtered through the window, and they started a new day without ending the previous one.

Jim broke the reverie. "Must of taken some time to get that good at pool. Is pool big in Africa?"

Emil stared glaze-eyed, as if his mind were too tired to think. Finally, he spoke. "Nope, not a big deal in my land. I'd play a few hours at a joint whenever Kalid sent me to town."

"You must have natural talent," Jim said.

Derek stared blankly, unwilling or unable to participate. Then he wandered back into the kitchen. "Man, I got to have more coffee if I'm going to make it today.

"How 'bout you?" He stared at the cupboard as if talking to it. Before they could answer, his arm went limp and the coffee pot clanged against the countertop.

"Shit!" He twisted the pot to see if anything broke. "I've gotta take a nap."

Jim shook his head. "Getting old, Unk Derek. Me and little brother have been up three days straight, and we ain't crying about sleep." He turned to Emil. "Ain't that right, little brother?"

Twice Jim had called him little brother. Emil's face spread into a slow, tired grin.

Derek grabbed the counter edge with both hands. He ogled Jim then Emil, then Jim again, several times, as if uncertain who was where. "I'm shot." He rambled toward the bedroom. Stopping in the doorway, he grabbed the top of the doorframe with both hands. "Only three days? You don't know what I've been through, so don't talk shit."

He fell onto the bed.

Jim winked. "He'll be asleep…" He curled his hand into a fist. The bedsprings creaked, and Jim unrolled his fist, one finger at a time. When all five were up, he formed the fist again, put his thumb up, and said, "Now."

Emil closed his eyes. "I got good at pool when I came to this place." His subconscious had begun to emulate the Indians' linguistic lexicon and cadence.

Jim closed his eyes. "Yeah, I guess Matt and them got busy with that white-man stuff and left you on your own. So you played pool to occupy yourself."

Emil propped his head on his hands and shifted it side to side, stretching his neck. "Nah, I played at the Lava 'cause I was already good."

Jim nestled back into the stuffed chair. "Sounds mystical. I don't think we'll figure it out without Derek." Then he fell asleep, too.

**

"He's really that good?" Kalid said.

"Yeah, I never saw any better," someone, maybe a village elder, said. "He says that he used to play back home."

Emil wanted to tell Kalid that he hadn't frittered away much time in the little pool hall. No more than an hour or two per trip he took to town.

"You say he was in that mine with the others that night?"

Kalid changed into another person while he spoke. "You say Panther Woman has been around those parts lately. Maybe she gave him the power."

"No," Jim said, "he's not seen her."

"Then she didn't give him powers," Derek said.

"Panther Woman showed herself to Stephanie," Jim said. "I saw it."

"Let's stick to Emil right now," Derek said.

"I can hear you talking about me." Emil opened his eyes.

Snoring on the big chair, Jim's head was cranked to the side at an odd angle. Derek's heavy somatic breathing came from the bedroom.

A spidery feeling skittered coldly down the back of Emil's neck. He raised his hand and stared at it. No doubt, he was awake.

Jim's shoulders turned, jutting to the right then twisting to the left. His lips muttered incoherent words; then his eyes opened.

Through a yawn, he said, "You up, little brother?"

"Just now." The hair on Emil's neck still tingled.

122

"Wow, we pulled a long one, didn't we? I wonder what he did." Jim tilted his head toward the bedroom. "He's a shaman. What day do you think it is now?"

Sounding wide awake, Derek shouted from the other room, "Same day, but evening. You got to track time better, nephew."

Jim chuckled.

Bedsprings shrieked. There Derek stood in the doorway, his hands resting against the frame again. He arched his back like a big grizzly. "Emil, you got good at your game after that night in the mine, right?"

Little hairs on Emil's neck vibrated, sending goose pimples across his body.

Derek wrinkled his forehead as if startled by something about Emil. "So you got any idea what magic caused that? You didn't see a panther there, did ya?"

"No panthers. Only Matt saw the panther. I got close once, but it ran off before I saw it."

"Okay." Derek high-stepped in place and slapped each knee when it came up.

"But I ain't answered your other question," Emil said.

"Go on."

"Well, Matt, Stephanie, and I went to that old mine to find Gimish, because Matt said your panther lady pointed him there. I was supposed to use my spirit body to protect Matt from Gimish. Instead, I fell asleep and dreamed I played pool with all sizes of balls. I was winning.

"Turns out Matt didn't need my help. Anyway, I've played pool great ever since that night."

Derek placed his hands against the frame again and froze like Samson pushing on the pillars of the temple. He closed his eyes.

Jim watched.

Emil watched.

After a long silence, Derek opened his eyes and poked his chin at Jim. "When he says 'Gimish' does he mean Flying Man?"

"Yeah, I think so."

"Flying Man?" Emil stuttered in confusion. "If that's Gimish, then Matt said he died a long time ago."

Derek rubbed the middle of his forehead. "Us Indians think differently. Anyway, I might be able to help you."

Emil twisted in his chair. "Help me with what?"

123

"Uncle Derek is a priest in the Native Way Church," Jim said. "Nothing against your beliefs, but out here we have our own angle on things."

Emil's whole body shuddered like a worm on a hook. "I'm sworn to Islam, even in lands that practice other ways. I'll go to hell if I abdicate."

Derek held up his palm as if to calm Emil. "Think of Islam as a cake, and our beliefs as the icing. We don't demand that you give up the cake in order to eat the icing. We allow you to have both."

Emil's eyes panicked. "I don't have to pray to any gods or drink their blood or anything?"

"None of that stuff," Derek assured him.

"What, then?" Emil felt dizzy, like he was on a narrow ledge over a deep crevice.

Derek lowered his hand. "First I got to see if you really can play pool, 'cause if you can't, then this is all bullshit anyway.

"There's a ranch boy at Ceci's who cleaned me for a hundred bucks the other night. I'm sure he's there now hustling people. If you can't beat him, then you aren't special."

"What?" Emil's eyes jumped from one Indian to the other, but his mind was fixed on the pounding within his chest.

"I'll stake you the hundred," Derek said, "and you play him."

"I have money!"

"Fine, but you're playing to win my money back, and I'm not owing you any favors. Once you got my money back, you can play on your own if you want, or we can talk, if you'd rather. I don't care one way or the other."

**

A blue and white plaid cowboy shirt hanging over the jutting shoulders of his tall thin frame, a splotchy-faced guy stood by the pool table. His smart-aleck grin exposed a set of teeth that gaped like a picket fence.

"He's probably been here since I left, maybe on speed or something," Derek warned.

"No problem," Emil replied.

"We have your back, in any case." Derek patted Emil's shoulder.

The cowboy, awkward as a giraffe bending to drink, curled over the table. His long arm drew back, then stroked the cue. A ball Emil couldn't see banged into the pocket and rattled down.

124

The guy didn't look up, but spoke while they approached him. "Don't matter, big Injun, little Injun, or whatever he is, 'cause I know he ain't no Injun." He paused and sank another ball with his well-practiced stroke. Still curled over the table, he dropped the butt of his cue to the floor then cupped his hand over his chin while studying Emil. "Well, you gonna tell me what you are?"

Derek locked eyes with the cowboy. "He's a Sufi, from Africa."

The boy turned away without concern and focused on his shot, which, in spite of his pissy attitude, was a work of art. Like a rusty winch, he straightened up again, but never quite got the hump out of his shoulders. Even so he stood several inches taller than the Indians. His mass, however, was half Jim's.

"Never heard of a Sufi before. Heard of a Zulu, but they're skinny and tall like me, and really black, not light brown like him." He pointed a thumb at Emil.

Derek glared viciously. "He's Sufi if we say he is." The cowboy flicked his chin toward a fellow sitting nearby. The man, stouter then he, swiveled his chair to half face them.

The player bent toward the table. Before shooting, he angled his face toward Derek. "You want to win it all back at once, Captain Jack? Or you want to go a small bet first to see if Shorty here got any action? I know you brought him to win, though. I've been down that road.

"If he loses, and he will, don't try nothin', 'cause my bud has a .357 aimed at your gut."

Jim locked eyes on the partner. "That's fine by me. I'll sit with him. If he tries something, I'll crush his skull with a beer mug, even if he does put a pellet or two in me."

Jim sat and laid his arms on the acrylic-encased knotty pine table. He leaned toward the bodyguard. "I'm buying the beer, but you need to bring both hands up top—now."

The fellow chuckled as if sure he could handle the situation, then put his hands on the glassy top.

Emil was tired. He knew the cowboy was too, except maybe the cowboy might not feel it until he dropped over from a heart attack.

"All," Derek said. "Winner takes all. If you want to play after that, you can set the bet."

The cowboy shrugged. "Fine, I'm breaking."

125

Emil focused his mind on using his pool powers to make the fellow miss.

The cowboy cleaned the table.

Dismayed that his power fizzled, Emil racked the balls for his round.

"Be careful," the skinny cowboy taunted, "you might blast the cue ball into someone's beer."

Emil made an easy run of his own. Several rounds followed with neither missing.

An hour of this and Derek stepped up to the table. "That's it. It's a draw."

The cowboy tried to push past Derek. "We're playing 'til the end."

Derek gripped the cowboy's cue stick. "You ought to be grateful. He's been making his shots on skill; you made a bunch on dumb-assed luck. Clear out while your arms still work."

"Nobody cheats me!" The skinny cowboy yanked his pool cue away and aimed it like a lance toward Derek's chest.

His partner pressed down on the tabletop and slid his chair back. Jim raised his beer mug as if to take a drink. Both of their faces turned stone cold.

***

Thunder Spirit's Bead Maker

The two men stared at each other, their eyes narrowing to slits.

"Enough is enough," the bodyguard said. "I'll get this crazy fucker out of here." He slid from his chair and was beside the cowboy in an instant. The cowboy's face filled with dull-witted surprise. The pool cue whipped from his hands. The butt smacked him on the back of the head. He slumped. His buddy caught him by the back of his belt and dragged him out.

Mouths agape, the Indians watched as if they had seen a hallucination. Derek and Emil flopped into vacant chairs next to Jim.

"Okay," Derek said, "it's clear you have spiritual billiards powers. Now tell me what happened in the mine that night. Go slowly so my brain can soak it in."

Emil opened his mouth and let it hang there as if he were entranced. A moment later, he shook his head and said, "Can we order some food?"

They did.

126

Derek's eyes blinked several times, then stayed closed. He sat like that while Emil dragged through another painful retelling of the night at the mine.

The food came—hamburgers, fries, and coffee—on a platter carried by a woman who wore a square-dancing skirt that was as big as a teepee. It had a fake white apron sewed onto the front. They ate, not bothering with the ketchup, mustard and pickles. Derek chewed with his eyes closed.

Emil bumped Jim's elbow and pointed across the room. In a booth, framed by side boards that matched their pine and lacquer tabletop, Wendell Lee Boyd sat with two long-haired, bra-free girls and a fiery-haired hippie guy.

Derek opened his eyes and gazed at Wendell. "Isn't he the UFO-video fellow?"

The red-haired hippie, his face badly sunburned, pointed toward them and mouthed, "Indians."

Wendell glanced in their direction. Smiling, the two girls ogled the Indians. Emil smiled back, and in an instant, the three hippies were headed over, Wendell dogging along behind them.

The guy smelled like he hadn't bathed in a month and wore a shirt that reminded Jim of Nehru, another kind of Indian, whose picture he had seen in his high school history book.

The blonde girl, Ruthie, was dressed in a free-flowing shift, the collar embroidered with the outline of flower petals and leaves. Not quite as modest as her garment, she wore nothing under it, which, depending on the angle of the light, was clear to everyone.

The other, Lorelei, less delicate in every aspect, wore khaki attire, the shorts of which clung to her ample bottom. This quasi-military outfit was capped by a red and white paisley hanky tied over her head.

"*Yahaite*, I'm Arbie." The boy started to raise his hand in a Hollywood Indian salutation, but caught himself.

"*Yahaite* yourself. You Navajo?" Derek replied.

Arbie thrust his chest out. "No, but I'm a fourth Comanche."

The two Indians' eyes met. Blond Indians wandered into powwows all the time, white boys with obscure Indian lineage, always maternal, grandmother or great-grandmother.

Jim silently mouthed the words in recital while they marched audibly from Arbie's lips, "Yeah, my grandmother was Comanche, cousin to Quanah Parker."

127

Derek gave a thoughtful nod. "Yeah, Quanah himself. Cousin, you say?"

"Yeah," Arbie asserted.

The girls smiled dreamily at Jim and Emil.

Derek tapped his chest, pointed to Jim, and said in Hollywood Indian fashion, "Paiutes," then thrust his chin at Emil and added, "'Cept him. He's Tofu."

Jim squinted at Arbie. "So where are you from?"

"Chicago."

"Chicago? I thought Quanah Parker was from Texas?" Jim said.

"Yeah, but I never been there. My family all moved north long before I was born."

Derek joined in. "Yeah, a lot of people did that. Anyway Tofu is a small tribe down by El Paso. Most people don't even know about 'em. So now you're one of the few white men to hear of it."

"Tofu?" Ruthie gave Emil a bemused smile. "Tofu is Japanese food."

Jim frowned as if distressed. "Maybe, but don't say that in El Paso. Those Tofus are tired of people mistaking them for food."

Wendell, hidden behind the girls, poked his head out like a rodent. "Jim, you know I don't work for Haines no more."

Jim twisted his lips into a smirk. "Herman probably didn't care for you draggin' all those reporters onto his property either."

Arbie scoffed. "That trespassing thing is bullshit made up by Herman and his Haines cronies. So is the stuff about it being Herman's land." The red in his face deepened, and he shoved his words out like pistons. "I bet if you check the county records, you'll see the company deeded the land to him after the High Five incident."

Wendell's eyes went wild with indignation. "Fuckin' High Five turned my tape over to 'em. Them fuckers always finds a way to fuck ya. You know what I mean, man?" His eyes filled with tears.

Jim wrinkled his forehead into a frown. "The other night, High Five News showed that you filmed a Haines experimental aircraft."

Arbie's hands clutched the edge of the table. "It's a cover-up, man. Any fool could see that Wendell filmed a legit UFO." Arbie's blue eyes jumped from face to face. "So what is Haines hiding?"

The Indians were silent.

128

Arbie pounded the table with the palm of his hand. "Haines has a compact with the aliens. The aliens give Haines new technologies. In return Haines lets them drain our resources, even take our people to experiment on."

During Arbie's ramble, Wendell moved himself out from behind the girls. He even put a hand on the corner of the table, asserting his right to be part of the gathering.

Jim broke in. "Horace told me he willed that mine to Herman."

Arbie giggled derisively. "You knew Horace? Horace Haines? Do you even know who you're talking about?"

Jim stared stone faced into Arbie's eyes. "Met him right here at this bar."

Arbie wavered a moment, but didn't have the sense to stop. "So he just walked up to you and said, 'Hi, I'm Horace Haines.'"

"No, he said he was Bard Spruce, and he asked me to work for him. Out at that mine, in fact."

"Bard Spruce?" Arbie smirked and rolled his eyes at the girls.

Wendell cleared his throat and in a deferential voice said, "Ah, Arbie, ah, Bard Spruce—that was Horace all right. You know, disguised up and all. I seen him like that, too."

"Spruce was Haines," Jim said. "He and I worked together like two braceros, side by side, off and on for several months. Mostly working in the ol' Henderson Mine you're so excited about. We replaced timbers, moved rubble, brought boxes and other stuff in." He shrugged his shoulders at Arbie. "Ain't nothing special in there."

Arbie rested his hands on the table in a moment of contemplation. Then he picked up the pitcher and slowly poured beer for everyone. He poured himself the last half glass then looked at Jim. "Wendell told me you were there that night Herman shut down the High Five saucer coverage."

"We were there." Jim angled his thumb toward Emil.

"We're going"—Arbie pointed to the girls and Wendell—"to camp outside that mine until Herman lets us go inside and look for signs of aliens."

"Told ya ain't nothing special in that mine," Jim countered.

Ruthie turned her head down and picked at her fingers. "Arbie, don't you think he would have seen something if it were there? Can't we just stay at Wendell's rather than camp out?"

129

Arbie hung his mouth open in appal. "Ruthie! No offense to Jim, but the aliens have technology to cover their trail. It'll take an expert to find traces of them."

He gave the Indians another try. "Hey, come with us. I'll get TV coverage. You guys would be great standing in front of a mic, demanding that Herman give back your sacred land."

"It is sacred," Derek asserted.

Arbie's eyes lit up. "So let's get it back. I can get coverage. You'll be a Native American hero."

"Don't need to get it back," Derek said. "The spirit guardian of the valley says it's fine the way it is."

Arbie tapped the table with his knuckles. "We're going to camp there. You can thank us later."

Jim's jaws swelled in outrage. "I told you that place is sacred. Don't camp there. We don't want your shit and garbage scattered all over the place."

Arbie glared back. "We bury our garbage."

"Not there you don't. Just stay away. That out there ain't your business."

Derek studied the palms of his hands. When his nephew finished, he gave Arbie a vicious stare, then turned to Jim and Emil and angled his head toward the exit.

The Indians pushed their chairs out and stood. Ruthie wrapped her arm around Arbie's and in her mousey voice said, "Maybe we should…"

Arbie shrugged her off.

In a conciliatory gesture, Wendell called toward the Paiutes. "Hey, us being on the opposite sides in the past don't mean nothin' no more, okay?"

Jim nodded.

**

The three of them crammed into Derek's pickup.

Derek groaned. "I can feel it coming. Sure as the sun rises, that piss ant Arbie is going to bring a bunch of those hippies out to the mine. They'll shit and dump garbage all over the place."

Jim told Emil, "You might tell Matt that Arbie will be going out to the Henderson."

"I don't think Matt cares," Emil said. "He told me Herman put a gate on the mine that's made from space-age technology."

"Yeah," Jim huffed. "Well, I care. I don't want their petrified hippy turds on sacred ground."

Emil paused for a while then spoke as if puzzled. "I think Matt, Stephanie, and I were in the mine when Wendell made his saucer film."

Derek patted Emil's shoulder. "Yeah, I know. I was up on the hill. I saw the whole thing."

Emil gulped. "Well, Wendell's flying saucer was the hovercraft that brought Herman out to the mine, right?" The seat springs squeaked as he shifted his weight.

"Matt and Herman have been holding out on you," Derek said. "I saw you, Matt, and Stephanie go into the mine at sunset. After midnight the saucer-thing landed. A few minutes later, Wendell showed up. I was the only one who saw the whole thing. At least, I was the only human. Panther Woman was there not ten yards from me, sitting up like a big pussycat and watching it too."

Derek pressed one finger against the pickup roof. "That damned thing was a dot, nothing more than a star way the hell up there. It got brighter and brighter and bigger and bigger, coming straight down." Derek brought his hand down and extended his fingers over and over. "It lit the hills and the whole valley in purple.

"It didn't make noise either; just swish and there it was. It did the same when it left. Straight up until it was a tiny speck. Looked just like a star; then disappeared."

Emil and Jim sat still, their attention locked on Derek.

He cleared his throat. "It was a real flying saucer."

Emil moved his legs and arms and twisted in his seat.

Derek shook his head. "I never saw Herman go into the mine. He was there all along."

Emil clamped his hands together and struggled with that idea a moment. "You sure no one slipped past you?"

"Panther Woman would've let me know if anyone showed up."

"Who is this panther lady? How does she always end up in important places?" Emil sounded perplexed.

"She's a shape-shifter that has lived here ever since First Men came. She was their queen. She said she would protect her people as long as they remember her. We remember her."

"Anyway," Derek said, "Arbie, Red Squirrel Boy, is right. Haines Companies is involved with the star people, because their boss, Herman, is a star man."

Jim spoke up. "All that aside, we're not letting Arbie desecrate the valley."

Emil's face saddened. "You make fun of Arbie, calling him Red Squirrel Boy. What name do you call me?"

Jim answered without hesitation. "Thunder Spirit's Bead Maker."

"That sounds better," Emil said.

"It is," Jim replied. "While Derek did all that yakking, it came to me that all those balls you dreamed about in the mine sound like atoms. In your dream you make them stick together to form a big new atom.

"In our way of thinking, you have the power to create the beads that Thunder Spirit uses to build the universe."

Derek patted Emil's shoulder, "Now you must learn how to put that power to good use."

**

Arbie filled his glass with beer. "These Utes are a problem. It's clear they've sold out to Haines Corp." He looked from face to face. "The more we know about the world, the more it's all the same. Even Indians have their traitors."

Wendell reached for the pitcher. "Arbie, you know Carr hates Herman. Well, I tol' him about your plan to force Herman to give the mine to the Indian Nations. Carr's got friends in the Native American Socialists. He says they'll send help."

"Who?" Arbie asked.

Wendell raised his beer in salute. "None other than Billy Manes."

Arbie's face drained. His lips quivered. "The Billy Manes who shot two FBI agents at Broken Arrow?"

Wendell saluted the ceiling with his beer mug. "Payback is a bitch, Herman."

***

132

Chapter 11: Fiends

Matt slid his gloved finger beneath the ossified page. Holding his breath, he peered into the grains of the parchment as if expecting a cataclysmic fault to shear through it. Remorseful, prayer-like, he swore, "If I don't get it this time, I'm done."

He was lying. Even knowing the fragile pages had only so many turns in them before collapsing into dust, he could never be done studying them.

His shoulder aching, he mouthed words in French, scribbled them in English, his pen point digging through the last page of his yellow legal pad and into the cardboard backing.

He slammed the pad aside and took another from a stack at mid-table.

Would his notes have been better organized if he had accepted Herman's word processor? Would his hand be less cramped? His eyes less watered?

Would this old book have suffered less?

"Hello," Herman said from behind him.

Matt leaned his temple against his fist and returned the greeting.

"What's the matter?" Herman asked.

Matt's finger crawled up his cheek, then flipped his lip. "What's the matter with you? Your mouth just went sour."

"Oh. Oh no, I don't have it right yet." Herman walked off, practicing a casual hello over and over.

While one of Herman's brains handled that, another customized parameters to compare Stephanie to an idealized leader. At the moment he was tinkering with the charisma subroutine. He

133

had contrived the model from the characteristics of great humans, Nirvanians, and other beings, real and mythological.

The unfortunate truth was that many humans who registered high charisma were also sociopaths: Hitler, Caesar, Napoleon, Stalin, and the list went on.

Stephanie's charisma wasn't even close, but she had tenacity, and that might be enough.

Herman's curiosity was as endless as his life, so he ran his analysis on Carr Ferguson, too. Carr had more charisma than anyone Herman could pit against him.

Matt faked a cough then said loudly, "Herman, did Gimish attempt to kill Henri IV of France?"

Humans, Herman thought, *are too dense to be allowed any power.* "Matt, I explained that before."

"So your answer is no?"

"Of course we didn't. Henri represented change and tolerance between Catholicism and the reformists. His opponents were intolerant of even minor deviations from their religious dogma. We wanted mankind to move forward, not languish under the constraints of religious tyranny."

"Then I've found something very odd," Matt said. "It sounds like someone from the future, or an alien, tried to kill Henri. Whoever this being was, he didn't belong in the sixteenth century."

Herman's eyebrows arched in a practiced gesture of curiosity.

"Well," Matt said, "It has been translated from French to German and back to French, then English—but I'm looking at references used by Heinrich Mann for his book *Young Henri of Navarre.* This quote describes something rather extraordinary."

Matt explained, "Just days before the Battle of Coutras, the Spanish and the Catholic League had already made several assassination attempts on Henri. History bears out their concern; it is Henri who wrestles control of France away from the Spanish League. After that the Spanish stranglehold on Western Europe begins to crumble: the Dutch revolt and the Armada is destroyed off the coast of England."

"Yes," Herman agreed.

Matt continued, "An assassin, who is ascribed with superhuman power, attacked Henri's entourage just before the Battle of Coutras."

134

Matt rolled his pen between his fingers. "Herman, is it possible that other synthetic beings have come here? Ones that might intend us harm?"

Herman wrinkled his forehead as if in thought. "It's not likely they could have escaped Gimish's attention. Yet—"

Matt broke in, reading from the book: "The demon burst from the brush, shooting red beams from his eyes. Jacques's horse was killed with one swing of Morto's huge hand."

Matt digressed, "Morto is the name given to this monster being."

Herman signaled Matt to go on.

Matt increased his pace. "The steed fell upon Jacques, breaking his leg...Jacques was fortunate for the dust hid him from the assassin's fury...monster stepped over him to attack others.

"Marc...thrown, horse and man into a tree...neck snapped..."

"Okay," Herman huffed. "In those days of religious animosity, both sides exaggerated the evils of the enemy and the purity of their own. Morto was surely just a large man turned by rhetoric into a monster."

"There's more." Matt continued: "He wore a monk's robe, gray and splattered with his victims' blood, some of it old and tar-like. A steel helmet of medieval style enveloped his head, but it showed no seams and was of a form I have never seen before or since. His hands, large as a man's skull, were clad in iron gloves, yet they moved with the dexterity of my own fingers.

"Under his cloak he wore superior armor, for although he was shot from only yards away, the ball deflected off. Despite this heavy accouterment, he leaped like a leopard from one victim to another."

The next page was missing. Thereafter the story continued: "After a fierce battle, the Englishman quelled the beast whom—"

Matt looked up. "At this point, Mann inserted a note about a linguistics issue."

Matt read on, "—we encountered previously on the Night of Saint Bartholomew. The beast's assault reduced our numbers from two dozen to only nine. We hastened Henri away, barely getting him to safety before a regiment of Spanish musketeers closed the road behind us.

"Later in the safety of Coutras, we spoke again of what we had seen. Several claimed he was indeed the Devil, for the fires of Hell belched from the mouths and bellies of his victims. We all

135

remembered the smell of incinerating flesh for its smoke laid thick on the air. There was no doubt that we had encountered 'Morto Sacude,' the Spanish assassin who accompanied the Guises, spreading torment and destruction among the Lord's people."

Thereafter another section was torn away, and the remaining pages were blank except for an ending note written in a different hand: "This is the diary of our fallen comrade and brother Gaston Benoit, ever faithful to the moment of his death, this day at the barricades of Ivry, where our Lord has granted us victory. God bless the soul of my dear friend,

(signed Jules V., Grand Master)"

"Very interesting." Herman sounded bored. Then he frowned. "What does Mann's note say?"

Matt scanned the bottom of the page. "Heinrich says the monster's name comes from the Spanish 'mortifero sacude,' meaning death by vicious shaking or beating."

"Let me read that." Herman peered over Matt's shoulder. "I'm interested in the one there, in the margin. Something about the German version was smeared and he couldn't tell if the word was 'wer' or 'wen.'"

"I don't know German. What difference does it make?"

"Matt, just like in French, one form refers to the subject, the other to an object. Either the Englishman was there at Saint Bartholomew's Day, or the monster was. Because of the smear, we don't know which."

Matt sighed in exasperation. "Okay, so you agree this thing is not human?"

Herman rocked his hand back and forth, indicating uncertainty. "I'll do some checking of my own. Right now, Stephanie and I must model the effect of Jimmy Carter's petroleum policy on our airline business. We have another board meeting in a week, and I don't want Carr embarrassing our new chief research officer. If we're lucky, she'll make a fool of him again and he'll be relegated to the status of a clown forevermore."

Matt thumped his fist on the table. "Herman, I want to go to Paris."

Herman had moved to the window. He stared out. "I'll arrange it with the French National Library."

"No," Matt said. "I mean Paris, the evening of August 24th, 1572, the night of the Saint Bartholomew Massacre."

136

Herman knitted his eyebrows into a frown. "Matt, your book is ambiguous in its suggestion that the beast was there on Saint Bartholomew. Such a trip would be dangerous and offers uncertain value."

"If an attempt on Henri is made, then I need to be there."

Herman sighed then walked back to the table. "Matt, the past has happened. It is impossible to change."

"Herman, my premise is that I went back and made it the way it is now. If this thing is synthetic, then aliens brought it to Earth. Isn't it imperative to find out who and why?"

Herman leaned back and stared up at the ceiling. "Stephanie and I have that meeting. I would like you to hold off until we're finished."

"It can't wait."

"Matt, it doesn't matter when you leave, the past will be the same when you get there."

"Yes, the past will be the same, but I might not be. If I wait, I could get into an accident and die. What then?"

Stephanie entered the library.

Seeing her, Matt stood to leave, then told Herman, "Have period clothes made for me. I'll need a modern firearm as well, preferably a high-caliber semiautomatic pistol."

Herman signaled Stephanie over. He picked up the board agenda then huffed at Matt. "You can't take modern weapons into the past. If they fall into the wrong hands, they will disrupt history."

"I'm not going into the Saint Bartholomew massacre with antiquated weapons I don't know how to use. I do want to live through this, and I'm required to live through it, if my theory is correct."

Herman studied the report in his hands.

Matt hissed then started for the door.

Herman watched him then called out, "Okay, a revolver."

Matt stopped. "Two."

Herman narrowed his eyes and pressed his finger against his temple as if he had a headache. "I think I should go with you, rather than let you take two guns."

"So you do agree with me," Matt taunted.

Herman stared coldly at him.

"What's going on?" Stephanie asked.

Herman ignored her and continued to talk to Matt. "But I can't go with you. I have to operate the SAM. It would be nice if I

137

could train someone else to do that." He turned his gaze to Stephanie.

Her palms went up in protest. "I'll not—"

Herman interrupted her. "Looks like I have to run the SAM. Take two revolvers. Identify this being and get back here. If it is what you think, we'll send a strike force after it later."

Matt smiled and started for the door.

"Matt," Herman called out, "leave nothing behind. If a smart blacksmith finds even one shell casing, he'll reverse engineer modern firearms from it."

Herman turned to Stephanie. "It looks like I'll be gone for two days. You'll need to run the board meeting on your own. It's time you proved yourself to them, anyway."

Stephanie's face hardened. She balled her fists and glared at Matt, then spun around and stalked out the door.

***

Beelzebul's Love

On the eastern outskirts of Las Vegas, a modular building sat on cinder blocks in the middle of a gravel lot. The sign on the door read "CLOSED."

In the back room, Carr briefed his gang. He glanced from one to the next, his eyes twinkling assurance of his bond with each of them. They were skilled craftsmen, the best he could gather for his takeover of Haines Companies. Blood would flow, maybe lots. In the end Herman and his flunkies would run away or die, preferably the latter.

Carr sat on the edge of a desk, a foot or so higher than the others. He bent his front leg in a manner that made him appear relaxed and confident, which he was.

"Wendell."

Wendell stiffened to attention. Carr liked that. It was what he expected from Wendell, knee-jerk compliance. It was a good model for the new guys, a couple of ex-Green Berets who needed to understand there were no ambiguities regarding the alpha predator of this crew.

"Wendell, what did Arbie think about Billy Manes coming to help get the Indian land back from Herman?"

Wendell grinned. "I think it scared the piss out of him."

138

Carr's face went blank and he stared into the eyes of Harry Birch, one of the newbie Green Berets. "It should scare the piss out of him." He pushed his chin toward Birch. "Billy Manes of NAS, who single-handedly killed two FBI agents at Broken Arrow. Got acquitted, with a little legal help from yours truly.

"I've always got an eye out for the top talent." He smiled at Harry, who stiffened but forced a smile back.

"Harry," Carr said in a mocking voice, "you were supposed to get hired onto Marie Rothe's security crew. What the fuck happened?"

Harry's smile faltered. Before he could form a response, Carr continued, "You let me down. That's not good."

Harry did the ol' military stare straight ahead and keep the face blank.

Carr liked that unquestioning military bearing. It meant Harry was scared but would stoically take his medicine. Carr laughed. "Relax, Harry, you'll get a chance to make it up, but first Wendell."

Wendell glanced about in panic, his gaze landing on Laura, aka Kit and enumerable other aliases. No one knew what she would call herself today.

"Wendell, Billy's in town. He's got some contraband I want you to deliver to your hippie buddy."

Wendell started to ask, but Carr cut him off. "Explosives. The next time Herman goes in that mine, I want the hippie to blow the entrance shut."

Wendell protested, "But I don't know nothin' 'bout 'splosives."

As if to a child, Carr said, "Now, Wendell, you want this job, right?"

Wendell's eyes widened and his head bobbed up and down in a frenetic yes.

"Billy will teach you 'bout 'splosives; then you'll teach Arbie. Nothing much to know. Just don't blow yourself up before you finish the job."

Carr laughed heartily. Everyone did.

Wendell shut his mouth, pressing his lips together in a hard line. His head pumped up and down in agreement while Carr talked. "You deliver the stuff to Arbie then wait further orders. Billy will meet you at the bus station in an hour. Don't make him wait."

Wendell pressed his hands down on the top of his desk and waited like a puppy to be released.

Carr frowned then made his face red, something he had trained himself to do. Then he screamed like a lunatic, "Get going!"

Wendell jumped for the exit, careening into an empty chair on the way. It made a lot of obnoxious noise that set nerves on edge.

Perfect, Carr thought.

While picking at his cuticles, Carr yawned and watched the door close behind Wendell. He shook his head. "The boy means well. He's just stupid. I'm afraid he'll end up like his buddy Bobby Hendricks." Then Carr mocked Wendell's redneck lexicon. "Might get himselves blown up with 'splosives."

Kit giggled. She was still Kit, because she hadn't done anyone since Kit, but she had killed a few, Bobby Hendricks among them. Killing and doing were different. She had done Janet Schlest.

Carr laughed with her. The others joined in with unnatural chuckles. They had worked with homicidal maniacs before and several were such themselves.

Carr lifted two eight-by-ten glossy photos from his briefcase. He studied them, then looked at Harry. "Okay, Harry, here's your chance to get back at Marie for violating your constitutional right to work." He passed one photo to Birch. "Kill her."

Birch stared coldly at the picture. "Yeah, that's the one."

"Pass it around." Carr pointed his finger at the other occupants of the room. He lost himself for a moment in the second picture. He handed it to Birch. "This one violated my trust. I trusted her once; then she ratted me out to Herman. Kill her too."

Carr's eyes twinkled. "Harry! Then you and I will be square again." He slapped his knee with mirth. "Lucky for you, I've landed an insider to open the doors for us."

One of Harry's cohorts held the glossy of Stephanie and mumbled, "Too bad."

"Listen up." Carr projected his voice over the room while passing out briefing binders. "Everyone needs to be able to sleepwalk through their job. We don't know when we'll get our chance, but we need to strike when we do."

Over the next five hours, Carr led them through their roles. In the end he put Kit in charge of the assault team.

She grunted and tucked Stephanie's picture in with her stuff. While Harry and his buddy moved toward the exit, she held Marie's photo near her face, tilting it back and forth. Then she cooed in a disturbing birdlike way that froze the men in their tracks. Everyone turned to watch her.

Her eyes glistening, she stared at Marie's image. "There you are, my dove."

She glanced over the picture to Carr and his men. She spread her lips into a jack-o-lantern grin that displayed revoltingly jagged incisors.

"Where do you think she got that purple hair?" she asked.

Harry's buddy said, "She dyed it. A lot of chicks dye their hair odd colors."

"Natural," Laura gushed. "Wouldn't it be a pretty scalp hanging on your belt?" She widened her grin to reveal more jagged teeth. "That's their custom. They take the scalps of their dead for keepsakes."

Harry and his friend stared into each other's faces.

Harry couldn't keep his mouth shut. "We've been all over the world. We've never heard of people that do that."

His friend nodded in agreement.

Kit's mouth curled into an animalistic snarl. Her body lifted up perceptibly as if to charge them and rip into their throats. Both men shifted their bodies sideways to her.

Her eyes were wild. "That's your problem. You're too provincial." She showed them Marie's picture. "This woman is dangerous, very dangerous."

The second Green Beret started to speak. Carr caught his attention and signaled them both to leave.

When the door closed behind them, Kit crossed her arms sullenly. "I need more ammo for my blaster."

The thing she called a blaster looked like an electric toothbrush to Carr, but since she was very useful and fun, he humored her. "I looked many times where you told me. It isn't there."

"You didn't try hard enough," she pouted.

He sighed. "I did. You even went with me once. Remember? You couldn't find it either."

"You gave up too soon." She crossed her legs, causing her skirt to slide up so high on her thigh that his organ half inflated.

"Maybe," he suggested, "after you left it, it flew back to the planet you came from."

Her face turned thoughtful; then she pushed her lower lip out and said, "Spaceship, not planet."

He stroked her hair. She grasped his hand and laid her cheek on it.

"Did you take care of my problem?" he asked.

She gave his hand a slight nip. "I take care of all your problems, love. Don't I?" Her playful bite drew blood. She pressed her mouth to it and sucked.

***

Return of SAM

"The SAM is five hundred meters deeper than before. Does that bother you?" Herman asked Matt as they walked from the jeep to the entrance of the Henderson Mine.

Matt knotted the muscles in his left cheek into a half smirk. "Five hundred pounds or five hundred tons, if it crashes down, both will kill you."

"Not me." Herman turned to speak. "Nor the SAM. It's in a bunker that can withstand an atomic blast, and if the tunnels crumble, I could dig us out."

Herman's powerful hand gave Matt a childlike touch.

Practicing human emotions, Matt thought in disgust, but the hand stayed there, lying gently on his shoulder. Sadness welled up in his chest, blanketing his disdain. *Oh, my god! I'm beginning to believe Herman is human.*

He wanted to push the offending hand away, but could only look into Herman's eyes and wait for him to speak.

"I'm here." Herman dropped his hand and walked on.

Matt took a deep breath and followed.

"The real problem," Herman said, "is the SAM. Its function is to compensate a space traveler for the time he uses to accomplish his mission, which frequently is decades, even centuries, and in the case of Gimish, millennia. When the mission is complete, the SAM device returns the traveler to his era so he can live a normal life with his family and friends."

At the mouth of the mine, Herman pointed to the lock on the new gate. "Looks like a simple combination lock." He grasped it and it clicked open. "But it really senses the touch of those who are authorized. For this one, that is the two of us. An intruder can try combinations all day and never get it to work. He can pound on it, but it will never—"

Herman held his finger to his lips in the hush sign, then took several steps into the mine shaft. He pulled Matt with him. "Let's wait in the shadows for a while."

142

Herman peered out toward the distant ridgeline. "I had to modify the SAM to be bidirectional."

"What?" Matt said with sudden alarm. "The SAM was never intended to retrieve anyone from the past?"

"I said that a few minutes ago." Herman continued to scan the distant hills. "I fixed it."

Matt yanked on Herman's sleeve. "I'm the first to test your fix?"

Herman kept focused on the distance. "It won't be a problem."

"Maybe we should send a goat or something else to test it," Matt suggested.

Herman arched his eyebrows into a frown. "We have no time for such frivolity. I have to get back and help Stephanie. Besides, while we're procrastinating, you might get hit by a car or have a heart attack. Wasn't that your argument for hurrying through this?"

Matt felt his face redden. "Don't be an ass," he snapped.

Herman laughed. "It works. Matt, have you ever known me to make a mistake—on anything scientific or technical, I mean?"

Matt said he couldn't recall such an event, but that didn't mean it never happened.

Herman continued to stare out the mine entrance. "I've developed a rudimentary tracking system that can retrieve a time traveler from a point in x,y,z,t space. You will carry this tracking device. I'm glad you had this theory about intervening in the past. It gives me a chance to test my design."

"That word, 'chance,' is bothersome," Matt said.

"Careless use of language on my part, Matt. I've caused your heartbeat to increase, sorry."

"Will Morto Sacude be able to hear my heart?" Matt asked.

Herman tilted his head in a gesture of uncertainty. "I advise that you avoid attracting his attention."

Herman grasped Matt's bicep and pointed toward the hills. "There it is."

"What?" Matt slid deeper into the shadows.

"Someone coming toward us. I just heard some pebbles knock loose."

"How far away?"

"I'd say approximately 953 meters, straight out from the mine, the third peak away."

"Not a thousand meters, but approximately 953?" Matt said sarcastically.

"I could telemetry it down to centimeters if you wish."

"No need," Matt replied.

"I see him now," Herman said. "He looks like a vagabond, I believe they are called hippies. Red hair. Red skin, like a Norwegian who's been outside too long without wearing sunblock. It appears he can't afford real shoes. He's wearing sandals."

Matt shifted back and forth, attempting to see where Herman pointed.

"He has a hacksaw and a crowbar." Herman slapped his hand against his pant leg and chuckled. Herman lost interest in the man and moved to a flat wall deeper in the tunnel. He emitted several shrill whistles. The wall peeled back, revealing the elevator.

**

Several hours after Matt departed to the sixteenth century, Herman felt the ground shake. On the monitor he watched an avalanche bury the mine entrance. Under the weight of the rubble, the gate bent into a parabola, but it never broke. His sensors picked up chemical traces of nitroglycerin. He surmised that the redheaded hippy had tried to blow the gate open with dynamite.

Arbie had done what Herman wanted ever since High Five came out to the mine; he had blown the mine entrance shut.

***

Chapter 12: Saint Bartholomew

PARIS, August 24, 1572

Matt's throat gagged on the stench of vomit. Disoriented, he searched the abject blackness for any form to focus on. Instead, he sensed his body falling backward. Inches later his back plopped against a stone wall. He took his first breath. The acrid odor rushed into his lungs. His stomach surged again. He pressed a balled fist to his mouth to hold the flow back. His twisting stomach slowly settled.

Far off, the ghostly scream of a child cut through the dark air. Chills raced over Matt's skin. Closer, a woman pleaded. Gruff voices rebuffed her. Now she prayed hysterically. There was a sharp snap. Her voice ended.

Matt tucked his right hand under his coat and grasped one of the revolvers strapped across his chest. He pulled the hammer back. The click echoed off the nearby walls.

The distant child wailed again. "Papa, Papa." Over and over the word heaved out. After each came a dead stillness while the youth gathered his diminishing strength to scream again. Each time the pause grew longer and the heaving more laborious. Matt had arrived in Paris, 1572, the night of the Saint Bartholomew Massacre. Murder ruled the streets.

Weak light from the street revealed that he had landed in a narrow alley. Trying to raise himself, he pushed against the building. His heavy sixteenth-century boots skidded on the slick alley floor. He flopped, legs outstretched in a gelatinous substance. The retching odor intensified. The liquid soaked through his pants and onto his legs.

He groaned.

Heavy footsteps clopped down the street toward him. He dug his fingers into the mortar between stones and struggled up onto his feet. He recognized the form of a crate nearby. He grabbed its edge and balanced himself then tested his footing on the gunk-covered floor. He shook his pants to separate the slime from his leg.

Mumbling voices neared. Light danced and warbled on the alley walls. It brightened. Two figures, bloody clubs dangling from their fists, stood in the alley entrance. One raised a lantern.

Matt hunkered behind the box.

Wearily, the two men spoke of their killing, each offering justifications that they repeated over and over, but their voices showed doubt, like drunks who had begun to sober.

They moved on, their undulating shadows wavering in the wake of the swaying lantern. Gun against his thigh, Matt peered down the street. Far ahead, around a curve, the glow of the lantern washed back and forth and faded with the footsteps.

Against the building, two bodies lay, pale and nude, one like a ballerina, her arms twisted and flung over her head, her blonde hair laid out like a flower arrangement, its softness marred with clotted blood.

His hands trembled. He holstered the gun and walked up the silent lane, looking for the landmarks that Herman had shown him on old maps. Among the bleak buildings, nothing stood out.

The river. The Louvre. They were the keys he needed.

He hurried on, looking for a landmark, any landmark. Light glimmered from a side street. The clamor of voices, loud and boisterous, announced that a large street gang approached. Matt ducked into the shadow of a wall and down another alley. He threaded his way past dull-eyed buildings, where those who lived inside hid and prayed to see morning.

He stopped at every corner and studied the ghost-pale walls for street names. Nothing was posted.

Time was running out.

He began to panic. His chest pushed out short fast breaths.

A low rumble, like thunder, came from his right. Several sharp cracks like twigs breaking followed.

Gunshots. The military will be protecting the king at the Louvre.

He ran toward the sound. The moon broke over the city skyline, painting the buildings and the cobblestones silver. At the same instant the orb's form appeared below him, rippling on the

146

surface of the Seine. Beyond the river, the Louvre glowed in torchlight. Another string of gunshots crackled from within the palace walls.

He thought to swim it, but the undulating reflection of the moon showed a swift current. To his right, Pont Neuf prickled with the silhouettes of soldiers. Between him and it, torches flickered on a blockade.

Rapid feet approached from behind him. Six men, brandishing swords, charged from an alley. They turned right then left.

One pointed to Matt. At the same time, the others spotted him. Swords held ready, they crept toward him.

Blood pounded through Matt's temples. Their plain black attire indicated they were Huguenots. His clothing, however, by design, was ambiguous.

"Brothers?" he said. He reached inside his coat with both hands and cocked his pistols.

"He's a friend," the leader said. The others lowered their swords. The leader approached Matt. "Steady, my friend, we have all suffered losses tonight."

A gaunt man burst from the main group and rushed at Matt. He raised his sword and twisted his face into a snarl. "You bastard! You're one of them. How could you survive alone without a sword?"

Matt backed off while loosening one revolver from its holster.

"Jacques!" The leader positioned himself between the two of them. "He is one of us."

"Barnard, how do you know?" Jacques extended his sword tip closer to Matt.

"Because he's English. The shoes, Jacques, look at the shoes. Only the English wear heels like those. And that stinky filth on his back, he's lain in something awful to hide from the mobs."

"I am English," Matt said.

Jacques's shoulders slumped; his arm dropped. His sword tip dangled inches above the pavement. He shook his head, sending tears onto the stones. "Tonight they turned me into a dog. We've run here, slashed there. We've looked everywhere and have found neither family nor friend."

Matt lowered his gun back into its holster. "I was sent by the queen to protect Henri. I must get to him quickly. Perhaps you can help me."

"They've taken every bridge." Barnard pointed to Pont Neuf. "There is no way to get across. Henri must rely on God. We all must rely on God."

Barnard extended his hand. "I am Barnard Dubois, a lieutenant to Jules V. He expects you. He told me to bring you to him."

"What?" Matt's brain replayed Barnard's words, trying to make sense of them. Matt pointed toward the Louvre. "Henri is in danger."

"I've explained!" Barnard jabbed his finger at the enemy blockades.

The frantic clatter of someone running came from the alley. They all turned and raised their swords.

A square-jawed man in Huguenot clothes burst into the open. Heavy chested with long arms and short legs, he seemed to vault on his knuckles like an ape.

"Jules!" Dubois shouted.

Farther down the alley, a glow reflected on the walls. It brightened. The murmur of taunting voices increased with it. A tenor rose over the others. "We'll catch you, you Huguenot monkey. We'll slash your belly open like a pig."

In front of the barricade near Pont Neuf, another large mob boiled onto the street. With clubs and axes swinging, they marched toward the Huguenots.

Jules signaled his men back into the alley. "Too many on the street. We'll fight our way past the smaller group in this rue."

"I'm sick of it," Jacques said, then twisted his face into a snarl and raised his sword. "Let's show the bastards."

Faces taut, the Huguenots trotted shoulder to shoulder up the narrow passage. Ahead, eight of the roving murderers blocked their path.

"You want to fight, do you?" the tenor derided. His cohorts spread out from wall to wall and drew their swords.

Barnard pushed Jules behind him.

Matt slipped into line next to Jacques and yanked his shoulder. "Stand clear. Let me use my pistols first."

Jacques nodded. "Make them count and be quick."

Matt elbowed for space. "Give me room to aim."

One adversary in a soldier's uniform raised an arquebus to his shoulder. Matt leveled his right revolver. Never having fired the gun before, and not knowing its accuracy, he aimed for the center of the metal breastplate.

The .357 boomed. The recoil flung Matt's hand skyward. The arquebus clattered to the ground, the man's breastplate cratered in, and he flew backward against the wall.

"Good shot," Jacques said. "Now let the swords do their work."

"There's more." Matt fired two more shots into the enemy. Two more adversaries slammed to the ground. One opponent glanced wildly at his fallen companions and ran. The others looked from the dead to the retreating comrade and followed him.

"Quickly!" Dubois ordered. "The other mob has come into the alley behind us!"

Matt glanced back. Torches filtered into the alley along with the angry hum of the mob. Someone said, "There they are." Five eager assassins rushed forward.

"Run!" Jules tugged at Matt's coat. Matt shrugged him off. He targeted pursuers in rapid succession. Each time the gun roared like a cannon. Two attackers were blown off their feet. A third man whirled to escape and stabbed his own leg. He fell screaming and thrashing.

Two more raced back into the crowd, stalling the mob and causing chaos. Matt pulled his second revolver and fired three quick rounds. Three more fell screaming. The front of the mob turned and pushed into those behind them. Full pandemonium broke loose.

Barnard tugged Matt's sleeve. "Come, English. While we can."

Far ahead, the footfalls of the other Huguenots grew faint.

***

All Alone

Emil was gone. He preferred a sofa somewhere on the reservation to the opulence of the Black Lava. Herman and Matt were gone. An urgency in sixteenth-century France had drawn them to the tunnels deep beneath the Henderson Mine. Herman now sat at the SAM's controls, and Matt? Stephanie assumed he no longer existed.

Not in present time. Which is to not exist at all.

Why hadn't Herman insisted that Matt leave after the board meeting?

149

Carr will move when he sees I'm alone. This is a bad time to take that risk.

Would Matt even return?

That thought, like a barking little dog, kept disrupting her concentration.

Not a good time to be distracted either.

The fear of failure made her bones cold. Gastric discomfort, just short of nausea, hovered in the top of her abdomen.

It happened once before.

UCSF: Strategic planning meeting June 10th, 1974.

Her board being comprised of medical professionals, she made the mistake of believing logic would govern their decision making—she recommended they drop the sickle cell anemia project. Before the facts were on the table, the room exploded with outrage. People she considered friends called her hateful names in a verbal stoning.

Helpless and in shock, Stephanie looked to her boss, and then lover, Greg Jacobson for help. He turned and walked out of the room.

That memory sent shivers over her body. She crossed her arms and hugged herself, but the chill didn't leave.

She looked around her apartment, its floor and tables scattered with charts, reports, and memos. She had studied them, sitting, lying, standing, pacing, taking only a few short catnaps since Herman turned his back on her to placate Matt.

She needed to shout at them. Wash the anger out of her soul, but they weren't there, and she couldn't let her rage eat her strength. She needed all of it.

She entered the hall. Her footsteps echoed over the Italian tile, a once elegant sound, now empty-warehouse spooky.

As if spirits peek from inside mirrors, lurk in shadows, even hide within well-lit walls.

She peered at a security camera. *Eyes everywhere. I'm sure Marie has them in my apartment, too.*

The hair on the back of her neck tickled like someone had slipped from a doorway behind her. She hunched her shoulders and looked back.

Nothing, yet eyes everywhere. Why isn't Marie here? She of all people should live on the seventh floor.

Stephanie looked at her watch and hurried to the elevator. She stood before it, her breath too rapid, and pressed the button. The time of the board meeting had come.

**

Downstairs, in her sixth-floor apartment, Marie read the latest security system data. She didn't page through a formatted report like a normal person. Instead, she read raw numbers, row after row, thousands upon thousands, as fast as she could move her eyes over them.

She did it with glee, like a kid playing a video game, like the child who had sat at a little desk in the corner of Herman's office and tinkered with computers and high-tech prototypes given to her as toys. If something stumped her, she would ask Herman and he would lecture encyclopedically on every nuance of the problem without diverting his attention from a missile design, a new jet engine, or whatever he was working on.

She learned fast at five, and now, at twenty-six, she digested the security data at near computer speed. In less than an hour she arched her back against the chair and placed her palms behind her head for a moment. Then she sent her finger plunging, like a descending mortar, onto the escape key, disconnecting her from the system.

Her eidetic memory was perfect for everything that had happened since Herman adopted her, and was amnesia empty for anything before that.

Which is odd, she thought. *Shouldn't a photographic memory start at birth, maybe even before.*

Memories before Herman were walled off by cinder blocks painted in vomit green enamel. Attempts to penetrate those walls precipitated clammy spasms and sweats that sent her under a pile of blankets, where she curled her knees to her chest and remained that way, sometimes for days. The distress was so great she trained herself to avoid any thought of the green wall.

She rolled her chair across the room, pedaling her feet toward the exit of her private security center, one kept off the grid and unknown to staff. "Paranoia," Horace told her, "is a good thing."

Now, her heart raced.

Why?

Board members were arriving at their suites on the fifth floor. All had access to the sixth floor, even psychopathic Carr Ferguson

151

and his nefarious cohorts. The thought of him conjured a glimpse of the green wall and set the demons creeping forward from the back of her subconscious.

Why do I stay on six where he can roam with impunity?

A fantasy formed: Carr wandered out of the boardroom into the sixth-floor hall. She leveled a .45 at his head. He looked up. She fired, painting the walls with pieces of his skull. The feeling was near orgasmic.

Then the green cinder bricks began to stack up between them.

She tossed her head, flinging the vision away. *The goddamned bastards won't let me finish one satisfying daydream.* She meant the green bricks, as if they had minds.

Stomach cramping, she jumped to her feet and forced her attention onto papers, which she arranged, stacked, and moved about in ordered randomness, filling time, letting the demons nod back to sleep.

Finally, she rushed to the kitchen and started a burner under a teapot. She took a tea bag, swinging it like a pendulum, waiting. In exasperation, she filled a cup with water and put it in the microwave. She turned the stove off.

Nothing helped.

Maybe, she thought, *I should walk into the board meeting and press the .45 to his head. Could the green walls protect him then?*

She gasped. The teacup clattered to the countertop.

"Damn it! You self-indulgent bitch." She smacked herself across the cheek, hard. She hurried back to her computer center and reopened the database.

***

Jules's Mission

"Psst, Barnard."

The whispering voice came from behind a low wall. A head popped up. An arm waved. Matt and Dubois vaulted the wall and landed amongst cabbage plants and the rest of Jules's Huguenot band.

Jacques grabbed Matt's sleeve. "What the hell kind of pistols are those? You fired three times from one gun. Then even more times, I don't recall how many altogether. You were still firing when I ran."

"Ahh, Jacques," Jules hissed in an irritated tone, "have you never seen a double-barreled pistol?"

"Yes, but—"

"But what? Two barrels, three barrels? Has anyone made a limit on the number of barrels?"

"But—"

"But, but, but. Be done with it, I say, and be glad for it. His guns saved us tonight. Now other duties call you."

Jules signaled them to gather around him. "Barnard, you and the others go west. Wherever you encounter brothers and sisters, insist they join you. They will want to stay and look for lost family. Don't let them. Their only hope, your only hope, is to build a formidable group and get out of Paris."

"But what of Henri?" Matt asked.

Jules's eyes flashed in the moonlight. "I'm his personal valet. A few hours ago he was safe in the king's chambers. King Charles will hold him hostage to keep us from seeking revenge for this night."

"Barnard, take them and go." Jules waved the others away but held Matt back. "You, English, help me complete my mission, one Henri deemed more important than his own life."

Barnard jumped the garden wall then signaled his men to follow. Their footsteps faded into the night. Jules waited until he could hear them no more then started in the opposite direction.

Matt grasped Jules's arm. "I must go to Henri. I know things you don't know. Henri is not safe with that lunatic King Charles."

"You don't know things I know. I am Henri's alchemist, not his butler. If Henri were in danger, I would know."

"There is—" Matt started.

In the shadowy light, Jules' eyes looked unworldly and frightening. "You think you are here for Henri, but you are here for me. Come along. We have work to do." He hurried off, leaving Matt no choice but to follow.

"By the way," Jules said over his shoulder, "Jacques was right about your guns. You fired them, three times with one and five with the other. You should not have brought those guns with you."

Jules grabbed Matt's shoulder. "Don't use those guns again unless you must, or I'll take them."

"Don't worry about my guns." Matt yanked from Jules's grip.

153

"But I do worry." Jules pointed to the black silhouette of a church steeple. "Our mission is there, the Church of Saint-Germain-des-Prés, the oldest in Paris and very, very important."

He walked briskly toward it. Again Matt trailed after him. They stopped by a large oak tree that stood against a tall stone wall surrounding the church compound.

"Stay there." Jules pointed to a gate. "I'll open it for you in a few minutes." Then he launched himself up the tree trunk, his long arms swinging like the beast he so resembled. He leaped from branch to branch with familiarity that indicated he knew the path well. Then he was over the wall and his feet thudded to the ground on the opposite side. His footsteps crunched to the rear of the church. A door creaked. Silence followed.

Matt settled by the gate and watched the dark street for activity. He glanced up into the dark canopy of the tree. *If a fat ape like Jules could climb, then...*

Above him, an open window yielded a muted sound, a scraping back and forth, perhaps a scuffle. A voice, low and threatening, came from deep within. The words were indistinguishable, but the tone was Jules's. The second, more high-pitched voice, sounded distressed. More scuffling followed, louder and more violent.

Then nothing.

Minutes later, the back door squeaked.

Matt lifted a pistol from under his coat.

One round left.

The gate creaked open. "What are you doing?" Jules asked.

"Waiting." Matt hid the revolver behind his leg.

Jules studied him, then with a demanding wave of his hand, signaled Matt inside. "Come on. We've got work to do."

Jules led Matt through a low threshold into a dimly lit room. Matt drew the hammer back, expecting it to latch quietly, but the snap was sharp.

Jules stopped. The Huguenot stood motionless, listening. His hand drifted to the sash around his waist. His fingers went under it. He faced Matt. "Must be a rat." He continued forward more quietly. Matt followed two steps behind, the gun still against his leg.

They came to another low threshold. Jules stepped through and out of sight. Matt turned his torso and passed sideways through the opening, keeping his gun out of Jules's sight.

A candle sent muted light onto the walls. A heap of fabric lay near an altar. The shimmer of a dark liquid pooled beneath the fabric and spread outward.

"Blood—a priest." Matt spun toward Jules. "You killed a priest." He brought his pistol from behind his leg and angled it toward Jules's abdomen. Matt squatted by the body to check for life.

"Don't judge," Jules said. "You killed more men tonight."

"That was self-defense," Matt said.

Jules snickered. "Well, this was justice." He turned his side to Matt while pressing his right hand into his waist sash. With his left hand he yanked the altar cloth, sending a silver bowl and two cups clanging to the floor.

A knife sparkled in Jules's hand. Matt pointed his revolver at Jules's chest. The Huguenot ignored him and wiped his blade, leaving a streak of red on the altar cloth. He jutted his chin toward the pile on the floor. "A son of a bitch." He threw the stained cloth on top of the heap. A corner uncurled and tumbled down into the pool then wicked burgundy with blood.

Jules held the blade close to his face and tilted it side to side, letting the candlelight wash over it. "I don't want that corrupt bastard's blood rusting it." He stuffed the blade back into the recesses of his waistband.

"You better explain, and quick," Matt said.

Jules slid his thumb under his sash.

"Stop! Stop right there!" Matt wagged the gun barrel side to side, emphasizing the command.

Jules huffed through his nose and held up his open palms. "We played chess every Wednesday at noon. He acted like a friend while planning tonight's slaughter."

"How can you say that?"

Jules shook his head. "This much I know. Thousands of my people died tonight, and this man gave the signal to start it."

Jules's face contorted. The wrinkles deepened in the warbling light. He took two angry steps toward the jumbled cloth as if to inflict more punishment on the dead man.

"Hold it," Matt ordered.

Jules stopped, laid his cheek against his palm, and angled his head to peer at the body. "Put that silly gun down. Soon it will be daylight. If you want to help Henri, help me fulfill his command."

Matt gritted his teeth and kept his gun ready. "I need proof that you are from Henri."

"Damn you. I should have brought Dubois. You're worse than useless." Jules locked eyes with Matt. Matt felt a sudden lethargy. His mind went numb.

Jules's hand slid dreamily to the back of his neck. Matt's pistol became heavy. All the labors of the night, the shock of the murders, the running and the fighting, dragged his arm downward. His eyelids drooped and blinked.

Matt's finger jerked at the swish of Jules's knife cutting through the air. The gun fired—straight into the floorboards between Jules's legs. The knife vibrated in a beam inches from Matt's head.

"That's your sixth shot. I believe you need to reload," Jules said. Sleepily, Matt watched Jules pull his second knife from his waistband.

Matt's fingers closed on a shell in his pocket.

"Just leave it there," Jules ordered. "If I wanted you dead, then"—he wagged the knife at Matt—"this would already be in your heart. Now will you finally be useful and help me finish the job Henri told me to do?"

He took the knife from above Matt's head and returned it to the sheath behind his neck. Taking the candle from the stand, he headed deeper into the building.

"What proof do you have against the priest?" Matt asked.

"The Maria Bell."

Matt knew that from history, but feigned ignorance. "Maria Bell?"

"Yes, a very special bell that sounds like no other." Jules pointed toward the steeple. "I suppose that is why they used it. Its sound always lifted my heart. Now I want to melt it into a silent ingot. I heard it ring just before the slaughter started."

He passed the candle before his chest, allowing Matt to see the splotches of blood on his blouse.

"Since I had to come here for the object we now pursue, I decided to confront Pierre about the bell and the butchery. I hoped he would deny it."

Jules held his arms wide and faced Matt. "The fool bragged about it. He was proud of initiating the murder of tens of thousands of people."

Jules stood there momentarily transfixed; then he flipped his hands palms up. "I had to kill him."

They stared at each other. Matt grimaced, then put the gun away. "Let's get this over with. Why are we here?"

"Such sarcasm." Jules pointed to a squat door, one they would have to stoop to enter. He pushed it open and held his candle within. Undulating light cast over a wall of books.

"Their library," Jules said, "and hidden within, ours."

He entered and set his candle on a table, then took a stepladder from the corner. He climbed it and ran his hand over carvings that framed the top of the bookshelf. Like a blind man reading Braille, he made several passes with his fingertips. His strokes slowed and shortened then stopped. His hand came out with a small wooden dowel between his fingers. He went through the ritual four more times.

"I know how it works," he said, "and it is still hard for me. For someone who doesn't know—it is impossible."

He applied pressure straight up on the ornately carved cap. A narrow gap opened, revealing a cavity. He wiggled his fingers inside, jamming and bunching the skin on the back of his hand against the edge of the wood.

Matt cringed, expecting to see Jules's hand tear open. Still Jules pushed and wiggled his hand deeper into the hole. Tears watered in his eyes.

"Stop," Matt said. "I'll do it."

"No," Jules whimpered between fast breaths. "You don't know it. It would clamp on you like a bear trap."

"It looks like it's doing that to you."

Jules chuckled through tears. "Not even close, believe me, not even close."

A moment later, Jules said, "Hey." He held a black dowel in his hand. He flipped it to Matt. "Did you forget your guns are empty? At least one of them is. You should reload while you can. Morning approaches. We may need them."

"How do you know that?"

"Know what?" Jules pushed his hand into another spot.

"Six," Matt said.

"I could say it was a good guess, or that I'm clairvoyant, but both would be lies." Jules gave Matt an exasperated look. "I counted the chambers in the cylinder. How else would anyone know?" He continued his work. "Why don't you go use one of the pews? You can lay everything out while you reload. That way you can keep track of it all." Then he whispered as if to himself, "It was so stupid to bring those weapons."

Matt's neck hairs tingled.

Jules—alchemist, shaman, or whatever he was—focused on his task, groaning and moaning, but not again looking toward Matt.

Matt carried a candle into the sanctuary and planted it on a pew. He spread his bullets out next to it, then flipped the cylinder open, letting the empty shells roll onto the flat surface. One by one, he placed them into a pouch within his coat pocket.

"Matthew, come!" Jules's yell was high pitched and urgent.

Matt twitched. An empty cartridge went astray. It hit the floor with a metallic clink and rolled like a coin, seemingly forever. Matt tried to follow its sound, but the resonance of the empty room muddled his hearing.

He dropped to his knees and peered where he thought it had gone, but saw nothing.

"Matt, I need you now."

"One minute." Matt's candle set shadows dancing under the pews. No metal reflected the light. He took the candle behind the pew—still nothing.

"Matt, now." Jules sounded desperate. A kicking noise, like feet struggling to find a stable surface, followed.

A disaster, Matt thought. *A shell left behind to be studied and reverse engineered—history scrambled.*

Will Matthew Krause still exist when I return to Nevada? Does Herman now exist to bring me back?

"Matt!"

"Wait a second!"

Matt's skull buzzed. He rushed behind the next pew, then the next and then across the aisle and between the pews one after another.

Finally he stood very still. He chewed his lip until his mouth was on fire with pain.

I'll look in the morning, he thought and hurried to Jules.

**

Jules thrust a large gold-leaved book at Matt.

"Touch it," he said. "*The Pearl of Light,* the most important book in the world."

Matt scoffed. "I thought you were strangling or something."

158

Jules laughed it off. "I have two duties: To protect Henri and to save this book. Now that I have the book, you with pistols that can cut through brigades can take it to a safe place, leaving me to protect Henri."

"You told me Henri is safe," Matt said.

Jules laughed. "You would have been a danger to Henri. King Charles is suspicious of strangers. On the other hand, the loon delights in my enchanting gibberish.

"So, at first light, go. Take a strong horse, if you find one, but always head west until you reach our people. Deliver the book to Monsieur Soisson."

Jules laid the book on a leather pouch. "Carry it in that."

Matt stared at the pouch gloomily.

Jules ignored him. "We have an hour or two before sunrise. Open the book and memorize chapters five and ten."

Matt glanced back at the sanctuary. "I have other things—"

Jules arched his eyebrows. "Tonight, he that knew five and she that knew ten were murdered. If the book is lost, then the knowledge of those chapters will be forever gone." He held his hand toward Matt. "Do that which you deem most important, but look into the book before you decide."

Jules placed his hand on the cover. "They say this knowledge was passed from Ahmose to his disciples. It was first written down by Solomon and kept by him in the Holiest of Holies. It was lost during the Jewish war with Rome. For a thousand years more it was only known through the recitals of those, like the two who died last night, who memorized it. Four hundred years ago, Solomon's written records were recovered by the Knights Templar.

"Now decide. Shall you seek that which can never be found, or shall you save that which must never be lost?"

Matt's brain, intoxicated from the lack of sleep, shouted, *Disaster, disaster, disaster.* His breath became short and quick. His heart pounded loud and labored.

He took the book, putting aside the hunt for the lost shell, and cast his mind and soul onto the chapters.

**

"It's time for you to go."

Jules's voice brought him back.

The rays of dawn glowed dull blue on the stained-glass windows. The stench of burning paper filled the church. The books

159

from the priests' library lay ripped and scattered on the floor. The mysterious bookshelf was gone.

Matt glared at Jules.

Jules shrugged his shoulders. "I had to make it look like a marauder killed Pierre and ransacked the place."

Matt glared. "Made it look like?"

"I destroyed the intricacies of the bookshelf or they would have known poor Victor, Father Pierre's Huguenot servant, had hidden important things from them within it. Now go."

**

Jules watched from the gate. Matt, with the book pouch across his shoulder, walked west; his tired legs, sausages without feeling, pushed forward, one then the other. The streets were quiet except for the flies swarming over the dead.

***

Chapter 13: Assassins

Stephanie entered Herman's sixth-floor office to pick up her handouts.

Stella, the secretary, peeked over stacks of folders that never left her desk. "Call it off," she said, jumping to her feet.

"What?" Stephanie didn't look up but laid her presentation binders one by one into a cardboard box.

"Doc called. He has a family emergency."

"Yikes." Stephanie's hands jerked to a momentary halt. She started again, pressing each binder into place. "I suppose it happens."

"Something's wrong. He sounded distressed."

Stephanie looked into Stella's eyes. They were wild. "Of course he was upset. Family emergencies are agonizing."

"I know, I know that. This was different. I can tell." Unable to explain herself further, Stella kept her frantic gaze on Stephanie.

Stephanie took her purse off her shoulder and laid it on top of the documents. "I need to show the board I can handle tough situations without Herman here."

Stella grimaced. "Yeah, but without Herman and Doc, you'll be deadlocked."

Stephanie gripped the edges of the box and contemplated its contents. She looked at Stella again. "Did Doc leave me anything?"

Alarm spread across Stella's face. "That's it! He didn't! That's how I know something is wrong."

Stephanie lifted the box and held it against her abdomen. "Maybe he'll fax it."

"Can't fax," Stella said. "His proxy has to have an original signature."

"Then maybe he'll send it by courier." The cardboard thumped to Stephanie's heartbeat.

**

Carr's hyenas attacked throughout the morning, disrupting the process and harassing Stephanie at every opportunity. Herman's supporters stood aside and watched.

Mid-afternoon, Stephanie stepped from behind the podium. She crossed her arms and tilted her face toward the panorama of the skyline. Carr tapped his finger on his desk just loud enough to be a subtle irritation. He rolled his eyes and increased the tempo, a tacit jeer at her prolonged silence; then he chuckled low and maliciously. "Ah, for the young anything is possible, in their minds." He looked from face to face, nodding his head as if he were certain of their support.

"Ms. Noble speaks about what can happen." He grinned condescendingly at Stephanie. "But the wise and the experienced focus on what is happening." Then he asked the room at large. "What is happening now?"

He answered for them. "We all know. The highest interest rate of the century and fuel rationing are strangling commerce— particularly the airline business."

His grin fell like a rock. As if incensed by her recklessness, he said, "And you, Stephanie, suggest we go around collecting air routes that others can no longer sustain? How dare you propose such malfeasance with our investors' money." His words imputed criminality.

Ronald Stump cleared his throat and bent his straw blond eyebrows into a concerned frown. Everyone turned to him and waited. He knitted his fingers together then spoke. "Carr, it has been a difficult process that we have gone through, step by step, together. All of these issues have been discussed at length by"—he circled his finger around the room—"all of us. You have chosen to huff and puff with discontent and negativity. Never have you offered a contribution. Why?"

Carr snickered. Two of his cronies glanced from Carr to Stephanie. One, Marvin Lee, said, "You call this planning? I call it an adventurous scheme." Carr's cronies mumbled and nodded in agreement.

Stephanie scanned the room, meeting the eyes of each of her detractors. She walked back to the podium and took her glass of water from the shelf behind it. She held it low so no one could see her hand shaking. She steadied her grip before raising it to her lips, then set it back, careful not to tip it and send it crashing to the floor.

Face full of aggression, Carr stalked her with his eyes.

Don't look at him, she told herself.

It was hard not to. Then her mind saw a movement in the corner of her eye. Without looking, Stephanie knew from the height and the posturing that it was Marie. Stephanie scanned her audience, rotating around the room until she came to Marie standing against the door with a .45 strapped to her waist.

Marie smiled adoringly.

Stephanie twitched a tiny smile back. A rush of strength shot through her. She looked down at her glass, then gave her head a slight, disbelieving shake. *Only Marie could walk into a board meeting with a semiautomatic strapped on her hip like it was normal.*

Stephanie gripped the podium and stared down as if at her notes. Then she raised her eyes through her eyebrows like a boxer to focus on Carr. She forced her face to flush and flared her nostrils. Though inside she felt like formless mush, she stood by will alone, knowing she must take Carr down.

"Mr. Ferguson." Her voice came out loud enough to jolt the participants to attention. "Do you believe the work done by this board today to be adventurous?"

Carr hardened his face into a glower. "I believe you have confused me with Marvin. Marvin used those words just moments ago. Possibly, you need Herman to help keep the members of the board straight in your mind."

Stephanie reached down for her glass, which was empty, but she went through the motions, buying time, letting his words hang naked in the air.

Ronald Stump crossed his arms and faced Carr head-on. "That's not an answer." He barked his words with viciousness. "She asked you if you think we're all a bunch of nincompoops who fritter away our time."

Carr shrugged his shoulders. "I didn't say it."

Marvin's face drained pale.

Stephanie set the glass on the podium with a loud clank. All eyes jumped to her. She shook her head and laughed nervously.

"Yeah, perhaps Marvin said it, but the words came from you, Mr. Ferguson."

She wrinkled her nose, showing her disgust. "After much debate, the board has agreed on this path. No. I'm mistaken, the board, without the help of you, Marvin, or Samuel, agreed to this path.

"Though you suddenly argue against it, throughout the day you have never offered an alternative."

She turned slightly sideways to a less confrontational posture. "Disagreement in this process is healthy. It is essential. We must vet every possible concern. By doing so, we familiarize ourselves with the uncertainties and their potential impacts on our plan, and because we've done so, we are ready if these problems arise."

Everyone sat in silence, letting her words soak in. Carr's face reddening, he glared at her.

Ronald Stump spoke. "It's been a long day. Certainly the proposal is adventurous. I say that in a good way. You know I like bold moves, so long as they are well conceived. I believe buying aircraft while the rest of the industry is in a panic is pure genius. Carter's ship is sinking, and his dogma will soon end. We'll be well positioned when change comes.

"I suggest we adjourn, think it over tonight, and vote tomorrow."

Carr jumped to his feet. "I move we vote now."

Marvin stood beside him. "I second it."

The room began to sway. Stephanie grabbed the podium to steady herself. Though she spoke the words, she did not hear them, "The motion has been made and seconded..."

Next she heard Len Amendola say, "The proposal has carried by one vote."

"Not so fast." Carr stood and held an envelope high. "I have here the proxy from Doc Watson. He was called away, an accident or something involving his family."

Carr fumbled with the envelope, increasing the tension. Marie's fingers played with the flap of her gun holster. Stephanie stared at the envelope, her eyes and ears blank.

Carr pulled a paper free and passed it before his eyes too quickly to read. "The vote is a draw. This plan must be tabled for sixty days." Half crumpling the proxy, he thrust it toward Stephanie.

"Not so fast." Ronald Stump stood. He lifted an envelope from his vest pocket. "I have here the proxy of Herman Rothe. The measure passes by a vote of one."

He extended the unopened letter to Carr. "Would you like to verify?"

Carr locked his jaws. Red faced, he rushed for the door.

Marie blocked him. His eyes followed her hand to the butt of her pistol. She cocked the hammer. His jaw dropped. She released the hammer and slammed her shoulder into him then walked over to Stephanie. When she looked back, Carr had gone.

Stephanie thanked each board member for their effort. When they had left, she flopped into a chair. She let her fingertips touch Marie's. "You were the only one here for me. If you hadn't showed up..." A tear ran down her cheek. She turned away.

Marie laid her hands on Stephanie's shoulders and rotated her thumbs gently into the muscles along Stephanie's spine. "I came to kill Carr, but you won, so I didn't have to."

Stephanie laughed hollowly.

"Do you have to meet with any of them tonight?" Marie asked. "I mean, to answer questions or anything?"

Stephanie slumped back and turned her face toward the ceiling. "They have my phone number if they need me. I'm planning on spending the evening in my room with Piero's hash browns and a Denver omelet made from Mesilla Valley peppers."

"I'm locking down the sixth floor as soon as they're all clear." Marie was suddenly solemn. She twisted her finger around a hair that dangled in front of her right eye and ripped it from its roots. "In fact"—she wound the hair around two fingers—"I'd prefer it if you spent the night in my apartment."

Stephanie straightened. "Why?" Then she thought, *Why not? The seventh floor is a graveyard. It would be good to talk.*

Marie flipped the hair onto the floor. "There's been a security breach. They have access to the whole building, including the seventh floor."

Stephanie gasped. "What the hell happened to 'better than the White House security'?"

Marie pressed her hand against her gut as if she had been slugged. "Someone inside betrayed us. I found clues earlier, but the breach occurred about thirty minutes ago. They're already in the building."

"Who is?"

165

"My guess, whoever Carr sent."

"He wouldn't—" Stephanie started.

"He would," Marie finished. "Bob is tracing all of the camera feeds. We need to hunker down until we know more."

"Can you trust Bob?" Stephanie asked.

"Bob is the only one I can trust." Marie's lips trembled. "It's not because I'm a lesbian that I asked you to my room. It's to keep you alive."

Stephanie lifted Marie's wrist to her lips. She kissed it. "I know."

Marie squared herself. "Come on. We have to get ready."

"What do you mean?"

"You know," Marie said. "They're in the building. We need to be able to defend ourselves."

"We should go to the seventh floor. It's the safest place," Stephanie suggested.

"That's where they'll look for you, and we need to use the security station in my room to look for clues."

"Maybe they've come for someone else," Stephanie said.

Marie stared at her in disbelief. She raised her voice. "They came when you were alone on the seventh floor. That makes you the target. Let's get you safely to my place; then I'll check the seventh floor."

Lightning shot through Stephanie's brain. She heard herself say, "No way you're going up there alone."

***

Morto

Matt glided beneath the roofs' overhangs, hugging the morning shadows. Midmorning, he stumbled upon a pair of dogs yanking at a fly-covered corpse. Street mongrels, they snarled at him while advancing tentatively. He drew a pistol and they ran.

He could take no more. The sun high and hot and his body drained from the toll of the night, he stumbled two blocks further, then fell into the shade behind a barrel and slept.

**

"Matt. Matt, wake up."

Matt squinted through slits. The silhouette of a man on horseback loomed against the sky.

166

"Who are you?" Matt asked.

"Barnard." The rider pointed to himself. "Barnard Dubois. You forget me so fast?"

Matt's mind weaved through levels of awareness, bringing him to an almost cognitive state.

"Get on." Barnard extended a hand.

Feeling disoriented and sick, Matt staggered up. "You have water?"

Barnard handed him a bladder, then raised his finger toward a group of men outside a tavern, who eyed them with hostility.

"I was riding by when I heard them discussing what to do about the protestant who fell behind the barrels. Of course I must help a brother, so I came back and found you. We need to go before they get brave."

Matt climbed into the saddle behind Barnard. They trotted toward the bar. The men, about eight of them, edged into their path. A knife handle jutted from the waistband of their oafish leader.

Barnard angled his horse to the opposite side of the street.

Matt pulled a pistol and held it vertically by his ear and stared straight into the oaf's eyes. The fellow threw his heavy arms wide, blocking his comrades' advance.

"I should shoot him," Matt said. "I'm certain he was involved in the murdering last night."

"Last night is the past," Barnard said. "Today our duty is to get the book to safety. That will be less difficult without a mob chasing us."

A bit farther, Barnard spurred the horse and trotted up a side street.

"For now we ride like this." Barnard patted the horse's neck. "It is a good omen. We look like two Knights Templar sworn to poverty and sharing a horse. However, we will steal another horse when we see a good one."

They were deep in the countryside and still riding tandem when they came to an ancient oak atop a small hill.

"A good place to rest, we can see a long way in every direction yet not be seen." Barnard pointed to the oak's branches. Each as thick as a large tree, they split from the main trunk and stretched outward for five or six meters, then bowed almost to the ground before turning upward again, thus forming a natural shelter near the trunk that would hide them from the sun and prying eyes.

They tied the horse under the limbs then sat with their backs against the tree. Barnard divided bread and fruit from his saddlebag then offered a skin of wine to chase it down.

They ate in silence, each watching the road in opposite directions. Within minutes exhaustion wrestled them to sleep.

**

Beyond the inane chatter of his companions, the soldier heard distant mumbling. He strained to listen but couldn't distinguish the words spoken far off in whispers. He guessed that they came from beyond the distant knoll crowned by the large oak whose branches dipped down near the earth.

Of course they're hiding, whoever they are. So he panned his metallic head from right to left and back, attempting to pinpoint them, but they became silent. He adjusted his radiation sensors from visible light to infrared, then scanned for their body imprints. The setting sun garbled his heat detection.

Morto Sacude's companions rode on, unaware that he had stopped. For practice in the new atmosphere, he adjusted his Doppler to see if he could measure the distance to the whisperers.

A belly laugh from Ricardo Guise ruined that. In disgust, Morto yanked the reins of his draft horse, the only beast large enough to carry him. The horse, wild-eyed as though it knew he wasn't human, resisted with a neigh. Morto thought to rip the bit straight through the bone of its jaws and clean out the back of its spine.

That might be too much for his accomplices. The Guises loved horses above all else.

A damn façade, riding the contrary horse. He could run alongside the mounted riders all day. But he would ride until his human disguise was no longer necessary.

He slapped the horse with the reins and caught up with his royal collaborators.

**

Matt woke to voices whispered inches from his head. Even though woozy, he heard the fear in their tone and held his body still while cracking one eye open.

Two hands pressed against his mouth. He grabbed both by the wrists. Their small femininity caused him to relax his hold. His eyes went from shoulders to neck to breasts, then to the frightened

168

face of a pretty farm girl. As their gazes met, he released her hands. One went flat over his mouth; the other made a "hush" sign across her lips.

His first thought was that her hand tasted like rosemary, sweet and aromatic. Despite her signal, a question formed in his throat and began to resonate through his vocal cords, then stopped. Outside their canopy of limbs and leaves came the clip-clop of horses and the boisterous conversation of riders.

Matt turned toward the horsemen in a gradual, near imperceptible motion. They passed by, visible only as quick flashes of darkness through the thin parts of the foliage. He and she froze, not daring even to breathe, Matt with his back against the tree, the young woman on her knees before him, her hand still against his lips.

A giant on a draft horse yanked away from the others. His head and torso covered with a monk's cape, he held the reins in huge mail gloves. He clamped his armored legs against the horse and stood high in the stirrups. He swung his massive head back and forth like radar scanning the horizon. His scan went beyond the tree toward the downward slope and into the valley below. When he sat back, the saddle moaned under him.

He grunted, then yanked hard on the bit and told the others, "Nothing here. Let's make the inn before dark."

"Good thought," one said, and they went off at a trot.

Holding their breath, they watched the horses fade into the dusk. Dubois brought his face alongside theirs. Still silent, they all stared, listening to the murmur of the riders, who reappeared in the sunlight on another ridge about a quarter mile away.

Dubois whispered, "What—"

The big horse stopped. Its rider turned his face to peer straight at them.

All three froze, eyes wide, hearts churning.

After many long seconds, Morto kneed his horse and galloped to catch up with his companions. The deep bass of his voice mingled with the muted laughter of the others and they disappeared into the haze of evening.

Chills tingled Matt's neck. He knew he had seen Morto Sacude. He lowered the woman's hand, letting her fingers slide softly over his lips; then he raised his own hush sign to the other two. He slipped to the edge of the branches and peered out. He crept back, still without speaking, and signaled they should all go out the opposite side of the canopy.

169

Stooped in the tall grass, Matt mouthed, "Horse?" The girl pointed to the dale below. He signaled her to lead. Backs bent, they marched stealthily through the ripened grain to the dark valley floor.

Deep in the glen, hidden behind a hedgerow were horses, hers and theirs. With a hill and more than a mile between them and the strange being, Matt commented, still keeping his voice low, "We're lucky the horse wandered off while we slept. I think we would be dead if it hadn't."

"I took it," the girl said.

With an agitated motion, Barnard poked his finger toward the distant oak now silhouetted against the darkening sky. "Who was that?"

"Shush!" Matt admonished.

"A demon," the girl said. "The devil has sent this thing to kill us all." She dangled her arms in a loose, hopeless motion. "God help us, but for now, let's go to my cottage. There is food and a warm hearth."

Dubois shook his head. "No, we can't endanger your family."

Stars sparkled in the tears that streaked her cheeks. "You won't endanger them. They were in Paris last night."

Matt closed his eyes. His diaphragm hiccupped uncontrollably. As if in a dream, he took her hand in his. Barnard watched them, then went to ready the horses.

On the way to her cottage she said her name was Annette de Pointers. Her younger sister, mother and father had gone to Paris for the festivities. She had stayed to manage the farm. Matt tried to raise her spirits by understating the disaster of St. Bartholomew night.

Barnard went along, saying, "Your family will surely return home tomorrow or the next day." He lied, giving her a few more hours of hope.

When they were close to her cottage, which lay partially hidden at the intersection of two hedgerows, Matt signaled them to hide. "I'll go first."

"But," Annette protested.

Barnard laid his hand on her shoulder. "Let him check inside. There were many strangers on the road today."

***

170

Trapped

"It's my womb," Marie said of her apartment. "The place where I escape demons with limited success, but I appreciate even a tiny reprieve."

Stephanie rubbed her hand across Marie's Scandinavian table, her fingers sensing its clean lines and rich wood. She spun around slowly, absorbing the softness of the brightly tinted walls draped here and there with tapestries of strange and colorful geometric design.

Marie let Stephanie soak it in for a few moments then opened the refrigerator. "We need to eat or we won't make good choices under pressure. I have some spinach salad and Tuscany chicken." She set it on the table then put a tea kettle on the stove. "Tea with lots of honey will get our blood sugar up. I should get my monitoring station online."

"Won't they know you're online?"

"They don't know about it. Nor can they find it."

"Good." Stephanie wiped her palms on her pants.

Marie set hand-painted china plates on the table. "Let's eat quickly."

Five minutes later, the food was gone except for a few spinach stems. Marie picked one up and nibbled between words. "It's time to arm ourselves and figure out what to do when they come here." She pulled two .45s from beneath the kitchen cabinet and with a, "Bang, bang," held them like a cowboy shooting into the air.

Stephanie's neck muscles tightened.

Marie winked and smiled. "A famous paranoid once told me, 'Always assume that you've been compromised and you'll never be surprised.'"

"Horace," Stephanie said half-questioningly. "How long did you know him?"

Marie laid one gun by Stephanie's hand. "As long as I've known Herman. Sometimes I wondered which one was my real father, or if both were. Never had a mother. At least I don't recall a thing about one, not a thing."

"Too bad," Stephanie said, biting her lip. Then her face lit up. "When did you first realize about Herman..." Her sentence stumbled to a halt. *Could Marie not know?*

Marie pointed to the gun. ".45. A little more kick than the .40 caliber you've trained with, but you can handle it. Same thing, seven rounds to a clip. It'll be over before you need a second one."

Stephanie grimaced. "Sorry, I didn't mean to probe."

171

"Let's go back to my station and see what we can learn." Marie pointed to the gun. "Bring that with you."

Stephanie stood still. "So what are the chances we'll get help before they find us?" She flipped her palms up in an exasperated plea. "A guess, or anything."

Marie played her fingertips along the tabletop, then with the calmness of a mother to a child said, "Stephanie, there will be no help. We're on our own."

"What about Bob?"

"We can't depend on Bob. At best, we have three hours. We need a plan."

Stephanie shoved her fist up under her cheekbone. Her voice was grim. "Plan? That's what I do best. But I need something to work with. What resources do we have? Who opposes us, and what resources do they have?"

Stephanie pushed her cup toward the teapot, signaling the need for a refill.

Marie lifted the pot from the stove and pointed to a plate of cookies. "Brain food, bring it, too."

Stephanie took it all and followed Marie to the back of her apartment.

Marie opened a heavy locked door that stood opposite her bedroom. She glanced back at Stephanie. "I know Herman isn't human, but he's all the family I have. He's always been kind, even when I was awful."

Beyond the door, haphazard arrays of computer sheets hung taped to the walls. Six terminals sat jammed between electronic boxes, the fronts of which blinked with rows of green and red lights. Several phones and stacks of documents covered three tables shoved end to end along one wall.

Stephanie spied a bundle of architectural drawings, open and hanging from a table to the floor. "Black Lava's blueprints, they should be useful."

Marie switched the monitors on, then sat in front of one. "The downside of making this terminal invisible is that I can't actuate alarms, open doors, or cause any action in the building from here. I can only see things.

"I'll query for events of interest." Marie began typing keys at a furious rate. "I assume that our lovely turncoat deleted as much as he could, but tampering always leaves fingerprints."

"Any news from Bob?"

172

Marie's fingers stopped. She took a deep breath. "I'm faster at this than Bob."

"He's had a head start."

Marie began typing again. "He hasn't sent me anything. It would be there." She pointed to a little envelope in the bottom right of the screen. It had a 0 underneath it.

"Could they have," Stephanie paused, trying to find the right words, then blurted out, "gotten him?"

"I don't think so. He's working from home. But..." Marie stared while numbers raced across her screen. Their motion made Stephanie nauseous. She glanced toward another screen that showed Marie's kitchen area. Another showed the sixth-floor hall. The others were flickering from place to place throughout the building. She assumed Marie had set the monitoring up earlier in the day.

"Okay! Here we go!" Marie pointed to a screen at her right. "Look at the loading dock."

Stephanie squinted at the image. "Looks like a service van."

"Yeah, ironically it's a security camera repairman's van. Now look while I move forward."

"A man disappears as soon as he steps out of the van," Stephanie said.

"Someone excised the video that showed him. And here, a few minutes earlier, the van came through the security checkpoint."

The van at the outside gate appeared on another screen. Marie was feeding each important video to a different screen so that they could watch all of them together.

"Now look at the camera in the seventh-floor elevator. 5:30 p.m., ten minutes after your meeting ended, there's a five-sec glitch in the camera output. It happens just when the elevator door opens. Look, it opens about ten inches and closes. The part where someone entered it has been cut out."

"God. If I had gone to my room..." Stephanie's stomach cramped.

Marie laid her palm on top of Stephanie's hand. "But you didn't."

Stephanie jerked. Marie lifted her hand away. In an instant, Stephanie wanted its reassuring warmth back. The cold terror of their predicament chilled her from the inside. Her teeth chattered. She ground them together. She hid her shaky hands under the table. "Whose shift is it?" she asked, her voice quivering.

"It's Tim's." Marie studied her.

Stephanie pressed her lips together, but her whole jaw trembled.

Marie reached out.

Stephanie pulled away. "I'm okay."

Marie's eyes flashed. "Then keep it together."

Stephanie glared back. "I'm fine," she shouted. "Okay, Tim is Carr's agent. I want to call the police. We have two doors between us and—"

Marie talked over her. "Once you call out, they'll know our location. Peter can lock the police out long enough for them to finish their job."

"Peter? I thought…"

Marie shook her head. "Tim's dead."

"What?"

"This started during Peter's shift. My guess is Tim was killed when he showed up for work."

"Why? I mean, why kill him?" Stephanie's voice begged for sanity. "I thought they were friends. Why not tie him up or something?"

"No witness gives Peter a better chance to escape. If he pulls it off, the midnight shift will find Tim dead, and after they scour the building, they'll find us." Marie's voice was flat and academic.

It didn't help. Stephanie jumped up. "I have to go pee." She started for the door.

Marie, already lost in the data files, said without looking up, "Okay, you may not get another chance for a while." She continued working while Stephanie hurried back into the living area.

Beyond the bathroom door, the phone sat on the kitchen counter. Stephanie thought to dial 911, but her bladder demanded relief. She locked the door and sat on the toilet. Her legs shivered. She threw a towel across her lap, hoping to warm them. It didn't help.

When she finished, she ran the tap water steaming hot to warm her hands. She dried them, intent on making the call.

She flung the door open and screamed.

**

"Good God!" Marie thrust her pistol barrel toward the ceiling. "Don't surprise me like that. Come on, we need to lock down."

Stephanie's breath came short and fast. The room wobbled. Marie thrust her hand under Stephanie's armpit and steadied her.

174

"Don't pass out on me either." She walked Stephanie back to the computer room and sat her on a chair while studying her eyes.

"I'm okay," Stephanie moaned. "You just scared the hell out of me."

"No doubt." Marie sat on a table edge. "Based on your usual pattern, they're starting to get suspicious. Once they begin to look for us, it won't take them long to figure out you never left this floor."

"Peter could already know we're here," Stephanie said.

Marie snickered. "That bastard's too lazy. We have some time."

Marie paced across the room. "Look, I don't want to wait around. We're going after them."

Stephanie's mouth dropped. She gulped to catch her breath. "Whoa, let's think this through. Why not get ourselves out of here and send the cops in once we're safe?"

Marie pressed her hand against her forehead. "We won't get out alive."

Stephanie groaned. "Please, indulge me five minutes."

"Five minutes could kill us."

"Making a bad choice will kill us," Stephanie retorted.

Marie jammed her hands against her hips and rolled her eyes at the ceiling. "Okay, give me an alternative."

"Let's get out of here."

Marie tapped her foot while still staring at the ceiling. "There are three ways out: The elevator—they're watching that. The stairs—they have cameras there, and each floor is locked, so once we got into the stairwell, we would be trapped. I have a rope. I suppose we could climb down the dumbwaiter shaft, but I thought of that when I set security up and I put sensors down its length. They'll see our body heat before we get to the bottom."

"Break a window and use the rope," Stephanie said.

"The windows are high tech. An artillery shell couldn't break them, and there are cameras on the outside anyway."

Stephanie shoved her chair back. She glared at Marie. "Okay, tell me your plan." Her hands no longer shook.

"Climb down the dumbwaiter shaft and attack the control center on the fifth floor."

"Fuck!" Stephanie raised her palms toward Marie. "You said the dumbwaiter shaft has sensors, remember?"

"Yes, but the control center is one floor down. I only have to get past one sensor."

"We would have to get by one sensor," Stephanie corrected.

Marie ignored her. "I think I can defeat one sensor."

"How?"

"I have a scuba tank. You lower me until I'm close enough to turn the nozzle on the sensor. Expanding gas cools. It might chill the sensor long enough for me to pass it. You'll have to lower me head first so I can spray the sensor before it registers my body heat."

"Hold a heavy scuba tank while you hang upside down?" Stephanie rolled her eyes.

"Okay," Marie snapped, "it's not great, but—"

Stephanie's eyes widened with sudden realization. "Wait! Matt said something about that." She pinched her forehead between her thumb and forefinger. She snapped her head up. "Yes! Matt said Piero received a new experimental fire extinguisher. It's filled with a refrigerant gas that puts the fire out and freezes the fuel source so it can't reignite. I've seen it. It's small. You can carry it in one hand."

"Okay," Marie said excitedly, "I'll have to call Piero and have him send it up, which means Peter will know I'm here. It won't take him long to figure out you're here too. We need to work fast."

Stephanie rubbed her forehead in little circles. "Okay, so we'll get everything ready before you call Piero."

Fifteen minutes later, Marie wore a rock-climbing harness over a hooded parka. One pocket held a .45. Another had an extra clip. The climbing rope lay coiled by the dumbwaiter door.

Marie signaled thumbs-up then dialed the phone. "Hey, Piero," she said cheerily. "Send me up your new fire extinguisher."

She paused.

"The one by the grill."

She waited again.

"No, I don't have a fire. I need a bunch of stuff off the label for the fire marshal data sheet.

She rolled her eyes.

"No, don't read it to me. You have all night or something? Just send it up. I need to test it to make sure it meets the fire code, anyway."

"Smartass. If you have a fire, use the other one. I'll bring it back tomorrow.

"Yeah, right now."

176

The phone clicked in the distance. Stephanie's body slumped forward and her breath gushed out. Far below the dumbwaiter click-clacked upward.

"Game time," Marie said.

***

Chapter 14: Annette

Matt pushed the door to Annette's cottage with the toe of his boot. He pressed his back against the wall and slipped into the central room. The odor of oak and herbs wafted on the air. Dead silence throbbed in his ears.

An iron kettle sat in a glowing fireplace. A long table with five stools stood in the middle of the room. Bundles of herbs hung from the ceiling. To one side, a ladder led to a loft, which probably Annette and her sister shared. He imagined the loft beds neatly made in anticipation of her family's return.

A single cricket chirped from beneath the table. To his left, a doorway led to another room. Leading with his gun, he peeked inside. Another bed neatly made.

He swallowed and closed his eyes.

A clink came from the central room. He whirled about with his gun leveled. Annette raised the pot from the fire. Barnard stood in the doorway.

Matt hissed and holstered his gun. "You should have waited until I told you to come. I might have shot her—and you."

Annette laid the pot on the table. "I insisted."

"Crazy," Matt huffed in English.

She lifted three mugs off pegs and began to fill them from the pot.

Matt closed his eyes. His head slumped. *Going through the motions as if we were her kin, joylessly, yet sharing with someone.*

She handed Matt his cup. "I fear the worst. A neighbor came by this morning and warned that the danger has spread from

178

Paris. He was in the city with my parents. Though he did not see them among the martyred, neither had he seen them alive."

Matt took her hand again. She stroked her finger along his. "I will keep my hope. The day before the holocaust they were to visit a friend who lived beyond the walls of the city. Maybe they spent the night there."

Her eyes met Matt's. She squeezed his hand. "Thank you for your kind words." She glanced to Barnard. "And you too." Then she settled her gaze on Matt. "There is always hope in our Lord."

She dropped sprigs of herbs into each cup. The scent of mint rose on the air. Matt savored it with a long and slow breath.

"My neighbor warned of the group we encountered tonight. It's said that the giant wears armor so thick no bullet can penetrate it. His hands are so strong and quick that he once destroyed two swordsmen in a blink. He kills all, women and children included, with delight."

"Yes, I'm sure he is the one we saw." Barnard sipped his tea.

She lifted a clay pot from the table. "Around here we've decided to carry what we can into the woods and make our way to Navarre. We'll make our stand there."

Annette handed the pot to Barnard. "Honey?"

"Thanks." He passed it back after putting a dab in his drink. She handed it to Matt before taking some for herself.

Annette continued, "Anyway, today I bundled essentials for the road. Then I hauled other valuables to an ancient vault my ancestors have kept since the days of the Roman occupation. It's well hidden and dry."

Barnard took his bundle of herbs and flipped it toward the fire.

"Don't!" Matt jumped to intercept the toss, but failed. "He'll smell it."

The odor saturated the room and went up the chimney and into the woods. Barnard's and Annette's faces turned ashen.

Annette took her mint twigs and laid them on the hearth. "I'm too tired to worry about him anymore."

Barnard cleared his throat and leaned toward them. "Morto Sacude they call him, the Spanish assassin. It is said that he was sent by Spain's King Phillip to assure the Guises take the French throne. The Guises, traitors the lot of them, are happy to be vassals to Spain, as long as they can be the puppet rulers.

"No doubt Sacude must kill Charles to assure the Guises get their prize."

"Hum," Matt said, "that is ominous."

"True," Barnard agreed.

Matt rested his forearm on his thigh. "Morto is not a man. He's a robot, but where did the Spanish find him?"

Barnard and Annette studied Matt's face. Annette spoke first. "What is 'robot'? Is it the English word for devil? He is a devil. No man can hear a whisper from a quarter mile off. And that helmet of his, it seems no helmet at all, but a truly Satanic head with those red eyes."

Matt took a quick sip of his tea. "Yes. He is a devil."

Dubois's head cycled up and down in rapid emphasis. "Yes, yes. Did you see his iron gloves? They fit tight as skin itself. And though iron, they were as flexible as fingers." He locked eyes with Matt. "You're from the New World. Perhaps he is an Aztec? They say the Spaniards use them to create terror and mayhem. In the heat of battle, they rip men's heads off and cut their hearts out."

"Aztecs?" Matt slugged down a swig of tea. "The Spanish brought them here?"

"They say," Barnard said. "You've heard of them?"

"Of course I've heard of them. Morto Sacude is not one, I assure you."

"Your guns." Barnard's eyes drifted to the lumps under Matt's coat. "They are odd." He let his statement hang on that.

"Let me see one." Annette held her palms out side by side.

"They are different from what you're used to," Matt said. "It's dangerous to handle weapons you aren't familiar with."

"All guns are dangerous, even when you are familiar with them," Annette replied. "Still, my father taught me to shoot."

She thrust her hands closer to him. "Let me have it."

Matt crossed his arms hard against his chest.

Her eyes twinkled and she wiggled her fingers.

Matt groaned and drew the gun. He released the cylinder and drained the bullets into his hand, then laid the pistol in hers.

Her arms dropped under the weight. She turned it over and over then squinted down the sights. She flipped the cylinder out the way he had. "I don't think it's Spanish," she told Barnard. She poked her finger through one of the cylinder bores. "This is where he puts the shot and the powder. There are six of them." She looked at Matt's palm. He had already put the bullets into his pocket.

She extended the pistol to him. "You should reload it. If Morto comes, maybe you will kill him." Her knees pressed gently against his.

Matt ran his fingers through his hair. "I can't kill him, but I know someone in the New World who can. I'll need to go back and get him."

"Back to the New World?" Barnard rolled his face toward the ceiling as if begging God. "That will take three years. We'll all be dead by then."

"I can do it in less than three years," Matt said.

Annette moved to the hearth and sat. Her eyes met Matt's again, and this time she didn't relax her gaze.

Barnard cleared his throat and gathered his things. "I'll sleep in the loft." He started up the ladder.

Annette took Matt's cup. "You sleep in the bedroom. And I'll sleep out here." Her eyes, dancing with tension, said otherwise.

**

Matt wiggled under a stack of wool blankets, curling his legs to warm himself. A tiny rustle came from the doorway. Annette stood there in a long cotton gown. In each hand she held a cup. She extended one to him then sat on the bed, her gown sliding above her knees.

"It's our best wine. Why leave it for vandals?"

He pulled himself up beside her. Lifting the blankets to cover them both, he snuggled against her. They drank in silence. When they finished, she kissed him, then laid her head on his chest and soaked his shirt with tears. He kissed her hair and pulled her close. Exhausted, they fell asleep.

***

Luc and the Highwaymen

The bed wobbled and groaned. Matt's eyes shot open. He stared into a pistol bore. The owner cranked the hammer back.

"Up, heretic! If you run, I'll blow your head off!"

Matt pulled the blanket over his chest in a half-conscious attempt to hide from the Dali-mustached man dressed in a frilly purple suit and holding the other end of the gun.

The man swung his hips in a vicious kick to the ribs.

"Ahhh!" Matt howled.

181

"Shut up, you baby." The man held the pistol by his ear like a club ready to smack Matt's head.

This dream had substance.

The sting from the kick blasted Matt out of his groggy state. He cowered away, gripping the blanket edge like a piece of rope between his hands. He flicked his eyes to the chair where his holsters should be.

They were gone.

Annette?

Gone, too.

Did she betray us? Who has my guns?

"You can't kill us," Dubois shouted from the next room. "We're on a mission from the king!"

The laughter of several men followed. One said, "King? Your King Wren of Navarre? I care not about him! Shit on him!"

"No! Your King Charles." Barnard's voice blubbered with fear. "And, ah, ah, Queen Catherine." Barnard swallowed loudly.

Matt's captor smirked, but his face and his attention moved a bit toward the conversation.

Matt shifted his head and shoulders as if he were drawn to the words beyond the wall as well. At the same time he inched the taut edge of the blanket toward his captor.

The man's eyes snapped back to Matt, then sighted down his gun at Matt's forehead.

Matt dropped the blanket and raised his hands.

Dubois spoke in a timid but assertive voice. "They—the king, that is, and the royal mother—have ordered the killing to stop. They sent us to convince the Huguenots to follow Navarre's lead and to yield to Charles's protection." He paused again, as if awaiting a response. After a few moments of their silence, he added, "Surely you know this?"

There was a grunt then one of the royalists called out to Matt's captor, "Bring that one in."

Matt was grabbed unceremoniously by his ear and yanked toward the door.

"Shit! I'm coming. I'm coming," he squealed. His captor giggled and gave Matt's ear another yank.

Three men in flamboyant plumage and colorful frills stood in a semicircle around Dubois.

Another peered out the window. He held his pistol against his thigh and gave Matt a quick unconcerned glance before returning

182

his attention to the outside. Another leaned against the door with pistols held across his chest.

The leader glared at Matt, then yanked Jules's satchel out from under the table. The flap was open. He held it upside down and shook it. "What was in this? Where did you hide it?" Thick-necked and scar-faced like a junkyard dog, he curled his lips into a threatening snarl. His fingers twitched near his gun holster.

Matt gave Barnard a questioning look. Barnard arched his eyebrows, a tacit indication that he had no idea what was going on.

"A-a-a book," Matt stuttered, dramatizing his fright. "A book for the king. A gift for the king." Timidly, he asked, "Did you take it?"

With a tick of his head, the leader motioned Matt to a stool. The throbbing ear was finally released.

Dubois looked desperately into the eyes of the leader. "The king and the queen will be upset if we are diverted from our mission."

The rough man grunted. "Show me your orders."

"They aren't written. With the Guises about, she," implying Catherine, the real ruler of the country, "didn't want the message intercepted."

The bulldog panted a mocking laugh. His lieutenants joined him. Then his humor twisted into a glower that he directed first at Matt then to Dubois.

The murmur of additional men approached from outside. The guard at the window showed no concern. Matt listened for Annette. In a burst of inspiration, he shouted, "Hey, someone out there, help us."

The leader laughed then wagged his gun at Matt. "You shut up!" He thrust his pistol at Dubois and, in a throaty growl, said, "You have nothing to prove your claim?"

Barnard squirmed in his chair. "Yes! Yes! I have. Let my hands free and I'll show you."

"Forget your hands. Tell us where." The leader jutted his chin to one of his fellows. "Renard, let's get the truth out of this Huguenot pig."

Renard grinned and circled behind Dubois.

Barnard twisted his head to follow Renard then in desperation thrust his head toward the table. "Over there, get my jacket."

"Yes, yes, do it," the bulldog-faced man told Renard then spun his pistol on his finger while sneering at Barnard.

"Hold the jacket by the shoulders," Barnard said.

Renard twisted his lips in disdain, then held the garment before his face, inspecting it.

"Cut open the hem of the left cuff and feel for a hidden pocket."

Renard lifted the wrong sleeve.

"The other left," the boss said. His chest bobbed in a silent chuckle; then he winked at Dubois.

Renard plunged a dagger blade between the threads and with a frustrated twist ripped the cuff open. A coin dropped to the floor then rolled in a spiral until it wobbled and fell flat.

The leader lifted it between his thumb and finger. Frowning, he said, "This proves nothing—yet it could be something." He paused, laid it on his palm and tilted his hand back and forth; then he flipped the coin up and caught it. "We'll take you to the king. If you are true, then you can start your mission all over again. If not, he will behead you and we'll be rewarded for catching imposters who claim to be his envoys."

The door flung open. A tall skinny man entered, wearing boots so big he could put both feet into one. "Luc," he said to the boss, "we can't find nothing out here. Let's torture these two. Maybe they know something."

"James, they're passing through like us," Luc said. "They don't know nothing about this place."

James tilted his head from side to side in consternated thought. "Maybe they lied," was the best he could come up with.

"I know they came from the palace," Luc asserted.

Matt saw a twinkle in Barnard's eye. For the first time since he had been kicked in the ribs, he thought they would live.

**

At the outskirts of a village called Sèvres, the party crossed an arched Roman bridge. Mid-span, Luc halted his band, letting captor and prisoner alike rest in the cool breeze that flowed through the pine forest. The relief from the heat gave impetus to idle conversation, which they all participated in, a trend Dubois had fostered throughout the morning ride.

After they cooled, Luc said, "My friend runs a pub here. We'll rest and eat."

Everyone murmured approval.

Barnard quipped, "Luc, can you cover for us? I'm sure King Charles will make good on it."

Luc turned in his saddle and, with his junkyard smile, drew his finger across his throat. "One way or the other." He kneed his horse and they trudged on.

The hooves played a tired clip-clop on a narrow cobblestone lane that twisted between buildings. After several curves and less than two modern city blocks, a square opened before them. Five horses, one a huge dappled gray draft horse, stood tied to a hitching post.

Dubois kicked Matt's shin.

"Ah shit!" Matt bent his leg back and forth to relieve the pain.

A man wearing the lavender and gray of the Guises stepped out onto the porch. A mug dangled from his hand. He took a swig and spat in their direction. "Well, what have the mongrels dragged in?"

"Doesn't concern you," Luc said. His men spread out, their hands resting on their pistol grips.

"Guises," Dubois hissed toward Luc. The bulldog ignored him. The floor inside the tavern began to creak as if a heavy barrel were being wheeled toward the doorway. It stopped. A giant armored hand thrust through the opening and grasped the door frame. Sacude poked his head out then stepped onto the porch.

Luc held his palm down. His men released their guns, but kept their hands close.

Sacude approached Guise. The porch bent and creaked. He laid his hand on his companion's shoulder and said in a deep unnatural tone, "Thomas, these men's voices are familiar to me."

"Yes," Matt said, drawing a scowl from Luc, "your reputation precedes you, the Spanish ambassador who rides with the Guises. Your work is well known. But I'm certain we never met. Possibly you saw us at a distance on the road not far from here."

The huge chrome face swung around and stared down Sacude's arm like a gun sighting on Matt. No one else moved or spoke.

Luc finally said, "Yes, we were doing the king's work in the neighborhood of Angers yesterday. Maybe, if you were near, you saw us, possibly at such distance that it would be difficult to exchange pleasantries.

185

The monster looked away and said, "Since we are brothers at arms, you will show my commander your letter of mark, no? Otherwise we confiscate your prisoners."

"Prisoners? We escort envoys from the king."

"Huh," Thomas said. "Shabby envoys, and shabbier escorts."

Luc's face reddened. The riders' hands drifted toward their guns.

"They got theirselves robbed," Luc said. "Lost their present to the king, they did."

Thomas swept his mug in an arc toward the inn door. "Come inside. Have some wine and chicken. You can show me the papers there."

Sacude, hand still on Thomas's shoulder, said, "It would be better for them to show them now. I don't want to make a mess where others eat."

Thomas's face tensed. He twisted his shoulder from under Sacude's hand. "Yes. Show your authority now. Then we go eat."

Luc stalled. Within seconds it was clear to everyone that he had nothing to show. Sacude pushed Thomas behind him and stepped forward.

***

For France!

"Show him," Barnard said.

Luc frowned.

"Show him," Barnard said louder, "the commission I gave you for safekeeping."

Luc gave Dubois a sloppy grin. He looked past Sacude to Thomas and said, "Since you insist, Mr. Ambassador, I will show him." He stuffed two thick fingers in his waistband and extracted the coin between them. "Out of the way, Ironman. This is for your captain."

He tossed it to Thomas. Sacude's hand flashed out and grabbed it in midair. He grunted while studying it in his palm then handed it to Thomas.

Tomas rolled it between his fingers, much as Luc had when he first saw it. Then he tossed it back. "It appears Queen Catherine dispatched you, so we won't."

186

The rest of the Guise party wandered out of the inn. Eyeing Luc and his crew, their hands went to pistol butts and sword hilts. Thomas held his arm out, blocking them. "Brothers on the same mission," he droned. He thrust his chin at Luc. "Enjoy your repast, and may our paths cross again when France is free of these heretics."

"Be it so." Luc signaled his men to dismount. The Guises rode off. No one entered the inn until the hoofbeats dissipated into the distance.

Renard started to speak. Matt hissed and held a finger to his lips. Renard's face contorted and reddened. His hand went for his saber. Luc laid his heavy palm on Renard's hand while signaling everyone inside. Renard kicked the ground and followed, breathing heavily on Matt's neck.

Constructed of stones and rough-cut timbers, the inn offered a cool retreat for locals, who laughed and shouted at each other over wine, mutton, and pork.

Two farmers hogged a large table in a dim corner. Luc went right to it and, with a swift swing of his thick arm, signaled them away. One look at Luc's gang with their pistols and sabers and the farmers left, plates and mugs in hand.

Luc draped his arm around Dubois's neck. Barnard choked from the odor.

"Because of your sharp wit, I will buy my heretic compadre this meal, and you will not reimburse it when we reach the king, as you will for the other meals I buy you—" Luc paused, and his men chuckled and waited for him to continue "—because you have no money. We must hurry to Paris, don't you think?" He squeezed Barnard's shoulder. Everyone laughed.

"What a monster," James said, ripping off a bite of meat and dragging it through fat drippings. He stretched over Matt to reach a sauce bowl. "Some say Sacude can hear a whisper for a mile." The edge of his coat raked through Matt's food. While he chewed, pieces of meat dribbled onto the table and into the sauce.

Luc stared sad eyed at James then indignantly pushed the sauce at him. "You eat like a pig. Take this. Go get me another."

"You spilled most of it," James complained, meat still dropping from his mouth.

Matt jerked his plate away from James's line of fire.

"Ehh?" Luc's face bent into his junkyard-dog snarl. "Look at Matt. He had to protect his food from your slobbering."

Juice splattering from his mouth, James apologized.

187

"Make haste," Luc said. "Hurry for more sauce and wine. Leave your damned mutton leg here."

James tossed the leg on the table and stomped to the inner courtyard, where the cooking was done. Luc poked Barnard in the ribs and mimed James, holding his own food to his lips and giggling with his mouth full.

"Renard," Luc barked. "Rub his damned mutton on the seat of his stool."

Everyone chuckled and watched. They covered their snickers when James reentered, wiggling through the crowd with a jug of wine over one shoulder and a new bowl of sauce held out front.

"Luc, it's true," Matt said. "Morto can hear a whisper at least a quarter mile away. We saw him do it."

"Aeh? You saw it?" Luc looked to Barnard, who nodded in confirmation.

"Aeh," Luc grunted then swigged. "Barnard's been righteous so far, and until he lies, I believe him."

"You're lucky," James said, tearing into his mutton, "that we found you." He pointed the mutton in the direction of the Guises' departure. "If he got you first, you'd be dead."

Barnard pulled some meat from a chicken leg, and with his mouth full like Luc, he spoke. "The Spaniard is here to help the Guises win the throne."

Luc rotated the mutton between his hands. He set it down and turned to Dubois. "Barnard, the Guises cavorting with this Spaniard, that's not good for France. We should go together and warn the king."

Dubois laid his hand on Luc's shoulder. "I am grateful for your offer, Luc. Having you, a man of King Charles's faith, with me will help convince him of the Guises' treason." Barnard held his cup high. "We are all French, yes?"

Matt clanged cups with everyone he could reach.

***

Shafted

Marie stood by the dumbwaiter. Sweat slickened Stephanie's palms. She held them toward Marie's face.

Marie smiled and mimed, "No talking."

188

Stephanie wiped her hands on her pants. Marie put her mouth to Stephanie's ear. Her breath was hot. "Watch." She opened the door and wrapped the rope twice around a strut inside the shaft. She showed Stephanie how to pass the rope behind her back to take pressure off her arms.

Marie clipped the rope to her harness then looked into Stephanie's eyes. Suddenly she pulled Stephanie close and kissed her long on the lips.

Stephanie flushed. She felt hot and weak at once. Tears trickled from the corners of her eyes. She didn't fight back. Instead her hand played with Marie's hair.

Marie stepped back. She wiped the tears from Stephanie's cheeks. "If we're going to die, I wanted you to know I love you."

Now Marie blushed.

Stephanie swallowed and nodded her head.

Marie clipped the fire extinguisher to her belt. She wrapped the rope around her left leg then hung herself into the shaft head first.

The rope tightened against Stephanie's hands, then her back. In a few seconds, Marie was out of sight. The rope pulsed against Stephanie's arms with each increment she lowered Marie.

*Too many things can go wrong. The rope slips, the sensors don't freeze, the sensors operate even after they freeze…*Stephanie's breathing came fast and shallow. She felt light-headed. Air from the shaft flowed across her face, reminding her to keep steady.

The rope could fray; the rope could break.

Stay focused.

A light blinked from the dark below. Stephanie gritted her teeth and rolled her back into the rope. The strut creaked. The rope vibrated. Stephanie cringed, expecting to hear the fire extinguisher clang against metal.

The pulse in the rope stopped. Stephanie heard a faint hiss, like air leaking from a tire. It kept hissing.

Her arms burned. She wanted to move, let the rope move, do anything to relieve the strain on her arms. They began to quiver.

Hurry, damn you, Marie.

Two flashes came from the shaft.

Stephanie's heart pounded in her chest. She tried to let the rope slide a little. Her tendons felt like they would rip from her bones.

She locked her jaws and pushed her butt down onto the rope. The strut groaned again.

Loud, too loud.

The rope went slack.

**

A cool breeze flowed up the shaft and over Marie's face.

Good. The ice will last longer.

Blood throbbed in her temples. She felt nauseous. She could feel the rope tremble. Stephanie's arms were giving out.

Marie grabbed the iron frame and let her legs drop below her. She flipped her headlamp on and braced her feet on a narrow edge in the shaft. It creaked and sagged.

Marie looked up. Stephanie was peering down. Marie gave her a thumbs-up then the hush signal.

Marie shifted her weight between two beams. She unzipped the gun pocket.

Muffled voices approached. They stopped just beyond the dumbwaiter door.

"Tim, maybe I should go down to the kitchen to see if she sent a note to the chef."

Tim, so it is Tim, Marie thought.

"Nah, Harry, don't be so paranoid. If she did send a message to the chef, he would call control—that's me."

"That damned blonde is taking her time getting back to her apartment," Harry said.

"She wasn't at the bar. Neither was Stump. She's probably fucking him." Tim chuckled. "She goes to her room late sometimes, but she always sleeps there. That woman is so predictable."

Marie dug into her memory to put a face on Harry.

Ex-Green Beret, applied for a position two weeks ago.

They hadn't taken him because of a possible connection to the heroin trade in Vietnam.

Got that one right, she thought and shifted her weight. The fire extinguisher pinged lightly against a strut.

"What the fuck?" Harry's voice grew louder as he turned toward the dumbwaiter door.

"Could anyone get in there?" Harry was close to the door.

"No-o-o, I told you about the sensors," Tim said; then he was quiet, as if watching something.

190

The dumbwaiter door creaked. Marie hunkered below the portal.

The door flung open. The barrel of a .45 poked into the space above her head.

Tim clapped his hands and giggled. "I told you—nothing there."

"You fucker," Harry said. Marie could tell by the pitch of his voice that he had faced away from the chute. His gun clicked into his holster.

She sprang up. Harry's mouth jerked open. His hand went for the gun. A freezing jet of fluid exploded from the extinguisher into his face. His eyes and nose became instant ice. His mouth froze open. From deep inside his throat, his scream sank to a ragged croak; then his vocal cords froze.

His hands forgot the gun and moved to his face. Before they could get there, Marie slammed the fire extinguisher nozzle into his left eye, shattering it like glass. He fell to the floor and rolled with his hands over his face.

Tim looked at Marie, then ran for the control room. Marie dropped the fire extinguisher and pulled her gun. She fired. Tim accelerated, his toes skating over the tile. His head slammed against the wall then slid down, leaving a thick streak of red.

Marie stepped into the corridor. Harry stopped moving, his hands clutching his neck. She held her gun to his other eye and stared into his open mouth. His tongue, frozen in saliva, blocked his throat. Underneath his icy skin, his face turned blue.

She heard the rope throbbing behind her and turned to see Stephanie's legs swing out of the shaft.

"You should have stayed there," Marie said.

Stephanie's eyes jumped from body to body to Marie. Her mouth fell open, but she didn't speak.

Marie pushed Tim aside and entered the control room. "We need to isolate the seventh floor before they realize they're trapped."

**

On the seventh floor, Marie's gunshot resounded in Kit's earpiece. Down the hall, the two Green Berets, who didn't have earpieces, waited for her command.

Jerry raised his palms questioningly and mouthed, "Primary target?" He scurried back to Kit.

191

He whispered, "That bitch ain't coming. Maybe we should go to the sixth floor and eliminate the secondary target."

"Everything's fine. Get back to your position," she ordered.

Marie and Stephanie's conversation in the control room flowed into Kit's earpiece.

"They've knocked out my security cameras on the seventh floor. I'm locking the doors," Marie said.

"You're not planning to go up there alone, are you?" Stephanie asked.

Oh, please do come up, Kit thought. *I'll string your guts across the floor like I did your mother's.*

"I'm gassing them," Marie said.

"Like Nazis?" Kit smiled at Stephanie's moral outrage.

"No, a sedative," Marie replied. "I want to question those bastards."

That's bad, Kit thought.

Kit signaled her two operatives. They funneled back toward her. Loud reports echoed from the elevator and the door to the stairwell.

"We're locked in," one said.

"No problem. Follow me to the extraction point." Kit pointed to the library.

She stopped in its entrance. "You, rear guard," she told Jerry. He crouched in the doorway and trained his automatic weapon on the elevator. "When we've cleared the exit, I'll come back." Kit signaled the second man to follow her.

She moved between the mahogany tables, looking right and left as if searching for something. She stopped abruptly and pointed to one of the soundproof booths. "There," she said. She led him in and pointed to an air duct. He dropped to his knees and began to unscrew the cover. She shut the door then shot him in the back of the head.

She hurried back to the entrance.

"Ready?" Jerry asked.

She shot him twice.

The sedative gas flowed visibly from the hall air vents. She pulled a device that looked like an electric toothbrush from her coat pocket and ran to the stairwell door. Earlier Jerry had joked about it, asking if she planned to sleep over.

She looked back at the library entrance and shouted, "Looks like you're the one who's sleeping over." Jerry didn't laugh this time.

192

The device's bottom began to pulse orange. The indicator showed two full bursts left.

Two!

That made her furious. She squeezed the handle and let out a high-pitched screech. Twenty-two years ago, Kit exited her escape pod intent on finding the Amazonian woman who had preceded her to Earth. In her haste, she left the plasma weapon's regenerator behind. A week later, when she returned, the spacecraft was gone. She saw its imprint in the sand. Somehow it left.

Perhaps Carr was right. Maybe modules return to the mother ship to shuttle more survivors to safety. She never bothered to learn everything about the Verg spacecraft. It was inferior. That was all she needed to know.

A half burst is enough for Earth metal.

Now the blaster base glowed steadily. She turned the parser to half and fired it at the stairwell door. A whoosh of green smacked into the door. The metal turned molten red and bubbled outward. Then it slowly curled back to its original shape and hardened.

Kit curled her lips, bared her dagger teeth and emitted a hair-raising yowl.

Earth metal cannot stop a half burst.

The gas flowed knee deep over the hall floor. Kit's world began to wobble. For the first time in twenty-two years the terror she felt came from within, not from her victims.

It cannot be Earth metal.

"Nirvanian!" She glared over her shoulder toward the elevator and growled. Head reeling, she leaned against the wall and redialed the blaster to full power. Watching the handle pulse, she slid down the wall until she sat on the floor.

Blurry eyed, she thought the handle glowed solid again. Her hand swaying, she aimed at exactly the center of the door and fired.

**

In the control room, Marie and Stephanie leaned close to the speaker and listened to the faint signal from the remaining seventh-floor microphone.

"Two gunshots," Marie said. To Stephanie it sounded like books falling on the floor.

Moments later, a woman's voice yelled something unintelligible, but it was clearly derisive.

193

"Oh my God." Stephanie pressed her hand to her chest. "That's her. It's Kit."

Both bent closer to the speaker. The sound was diminishing. Suddenly, an animal's roar came low from the belly then rose steadily to a high-pitched wail.

"What on God's Earth was that?" Stephanie said.

Waves of chills rushed from the top of Marie's skull and over her temples. "I don't know," she whispered, "but I've heard it before."

***

Chapter 15: Crimson King

King Charles, a tall skeleton of a man, listened to the report about the Guises and their Spanish companion. He praised Luc and Barnard for their work and called it an example for all his subjects: Catholics and Protestants working together to make France stronger.

Then his face drew long and sad. "I must toss you both into the dungeon. You have defamed the Guises, a royal family.

"Be of faith, however, for I shall see you are well treated in prison. If what you say about the Guises proves true, you will be released and rewarded."

Matt, on the other hand, received splendid treatment. His old clothes were burned and new ones made while he bathed.

Freshly attired, he accompanied Charles to a small banquet room wallpapered in crimson felt. The king sat on a plush velvet throne with scrolled maple arms. Below him, on couches and chairs, sat his entourage: a mixed crowd of boisterous men, rapiers dangling from their waists, and frolicking ladies, their bosoms exposed beyond immodesty.

Charles gripped his armrests. Blue veins bulged from the backs of his pale hands.

Matt swept his black felt hat from his head, dragging its long pink dodo plumage on the floor, and at the same instant slid his right foot back in a deep bow. There he paused, looking like a puppet in his deep blue suit, frilled at every outlet, neck, hands, and feet, with pink lace. He bowed first to the king then to the cronies.

"Oh, those colors charm me so." Charles raised his hands to the sides of his head. "They make my temples buzz. I do believe they have a cosmic quality. My alchemist shall investigate."

195

He put his hands on his knees and leaned forward, a child anticipating a marionette show.

"Here, here, take a seat." He pointed to a plump gold-threaded sofa across from him. "They say you are English from the New World. Is it so?"

"Yes, Your Majesty." Matt sat, his pants wrinkling uncomfortably in the inseam.

"Well, we all want to know about those naked savages." A bony finger extended. "Wine! Wine! Fill Matthew's glass, or rather bring him a glassful, of course."

He leaned toward Matt. "Have some wine. It will make the story more entertaining, I'm sure."

Giggles and snickers emanated throughout the audience.

Charles wagged his finger at Matt's crotch. "The clothes, they are beautiful, but how do they fit?" Without waiting for a response, he turned to the room. "I mean if they cramp you here"—he grabbed his groin—"then who cares how beautiful they are."

Mirth prevailed. Two young ladies plopped down by Matt. "We'll check," they said in unison, and in unison they cupped his crotch.

One lifted his hat to her head, where it wobbled high atop her piled wig. The other threw her leg over his and stroked his genitals with her finger.

"Maybe a bit tight here." She waved to the onlookers while throwing her other leg across his lap. "I could repair it. Just take the pants off and come to my chambers." She grabbed him around the neck and kissed him long on the mouth and in the mouth.

The spectators stomped their feet and applauded. The other woman took the hat from her head and bowed as if she had done something.

Laughter, applause, and wine drinking followed.

Charles reddened and his head vibrated like it might explode. "Henri? Henri?" He glanced about the room in anguish. "Where are you, Henri?"

A short fellow amid several ladies on a nearby couch rose up. Dressed as gaily as Matt, he wore a suit of deep purple with lavender frills, but the suntan of his face and neck and the strength of his shoulders made clear that he was an outdoorsman. He was Henri of Navarre, the future king of France. However, at that point in time, with the violence against the Huguenots, it didn't seem believable that he could survive to complete his destiny.

196

"Yes, Charles, my lord, I am here." Henri bowed like a country bumpkin, followed by snickers from among the courtesans.

"Whatever are you doing over there? Come here this instant. Bring your ladies with you." With a disturbed frown, Charles signaled the waiters. "Bring wine and the pig—all of it—to my chambers." Charles counted on his fingers. "Henri, the Englishman, the wine, the pig..." He shook a finger in negation. "No, not the women. Forget the ladies. Privacy, we must have privacy."

A butler threw open an intricately carved door, and the three of them entered a closet-like room that held a small table and chairs.

They all stood.

Charles turned to Henri and demanded, "Who is this man! Is he an English spy? Why is he really here?" He jabbed his finger against Matt and rotated it back and forth in half circles.

Henri stared blank-eyed at Matt. "I've never seen him before."

Charles's anger transformed into a condescending tone. "But, Henri, he is an Englishman. Englishmen are Protestant, which implies he is here to cavort with Huguenots, maybe to bring you a secret message from their lusty redheaded bitch queen."

Henri mouthed Charles's words while they were spoken as if repeating them would help him understand. Then he shifted his feet as if to guide his mind in one direction or another. Charles watched with amusement.

Henri raised a finger in sudden inspiration. "Maybe he comes with a wedding gift from England to honor my marriage to your sister." He turned expectantly to Matt.

"Gift? Gift, yes, let me think." Schemes rushed ill formed through Matt's mind, then he remembered that historically, a book containing hidden codes had been given to Henri. He took a chance and said, "But didn't my comrades give you a book?"

"Comrades? You mean other Englishmen?" Henri gave Charles a collaborator's wink.

Matt nodded. "Yes, the night of the mayhem, my party came to the Louvre bearing gifts from my lord, the Duke of Lexingtonshire." No such fiefdom existed. "I was ashamedly drunk with a whore in the tavern, so they went without me. Did they bring you a book on hunting?"

"Hunting a whore?" Charles giggled. "A man much to your nature, Henri." Then he burst out as if delighted. "Oh, Henri, we hunt together. You must have this book brought to me—now."

Charles rang a bell. A servant stepped forward and bowed. "Philippe, do have Jules V. bring the hunting book from Henri's library, the one from the English..." He spoke to Matt. "What denomination of lord is he?"

"Duke, the Duke of—"

"From the English duke," Charles shouted to Philippe, who was only six feet away. "That book, that very book."

The servant left. Charles turned the topic to the New World and went on about it for a while.

"What hope have the English against the Spanish over there?" Not waiting for an answer, Charles lamented, "It is a pity we French have no foothold in the colonies. Maybe we English and French should align against the Spaniard."

A voice coughed in the doorway. There was Jules with the book on hunting, which he handed to Henri, who handed it to Charles, who opened and then closed it and turned to Matt. "Now it is solved. Your fellow English got here, delivered their modest gift, and went on their merry way. They must have thought it better for you, being a useless whoring drunk, to be left behind rather than face the dungeon of your duchess."

"Likely." Matt lowered his eyes like an ashamed child.

"Well, we all whore some and drink some. Don't we, Henri?" Charles opened the book and flipped the pages. "A book? Such a present to a prince and princess? Matthew, I do understand why you got drunk. I think I would, too."

Then he said to Henri, "Really, Henri, in all fairness, these puritans have no pizzazz. I don't know what attracts you to their way."

Charles gave Matt a patriarchal gaze. "You have not escaped my wrath. I mean, hanging out with that rascal Dubois and a common highwayman like Luc. I believe I'll behead them both. Maybe you too, for your horrid indiscretion."

Jules spoke up. "Your lordship, Dubois and these men came to warn you of danger. You once told me that the loyalty of commoners needs to be cultivated. 'Like a potato,' I believe were your words."

Charles giggled and patted Jules repetitively on the shoulder. "Oh, my dear, in jest I spoke of their beheading. I only wished to see if you remembered my words of wisdom, and you have." He paused with one eye shut and the other staring at his nose.

The king turned to Matt. "Is there anyplace left over there for France to place a toe?" He meant the New World.

"I know exactly the place." Matt raised his finger demonstratively. "It's just west of Florida. I could go to Genoa and hire some ships and crews to carry Your Majesty's colonists there."

Charles laughed himself red. "I would be a fool to trust you with gold."

Jules coughed. "And that is why the king will only give you a letter of mark, which you can show the Genoese ship captains to bind them to our service."

Charles nodded in affirmation.

"Just the same, we should send someone to steer him straight, perhaps Dubois," Jules whispered.

"And why would I trust Dubois? He is also a Protestant, and I am not held too high in their regard these days."

Jules's head jerked. "But you are high in their regard. You saved Henri from the butchers, and others as well. While Dubois is performing his task, he will surely remember that Henri is your guest."

Charles ran his fingers down Jules's coat sleeve. "You are so very clever." Then to Matt, he said, "Dubois will go with you to help with the details."

"Luc's knowledge of the roadways and byways of our country would be useful," Jules noted. "And a few armed men would insure the safety of your envoy."

Charles gripped his chin between his thumb and forefinger. "I believe Luc and his ruffians would serve that purpose well."

"To the king!" Henri's eyes glowed with adulation. They all raised their glasses in a toast.

Two hours later, Matt, Barnard, and Luc's crew were galloping south from Paris on fresh horses, carrying a writ to commandeer anything they required.

As they rode, Matt told Dubois, "I'll leave you soon and will be gone a long time. I suggest you avoid Charles, but if you must return to him, say I went to Genoa."

Dubois grabbed the reins of Matt's horse. "What are you planning?"

Matt jerked free from Barnard. "I must fetch the man who can defeat Morto, or I fear none of us will live."

Matt spurred his horse and broke away. Barnard and Luc chased him. Later they found his horse feeding in a pasture. Matt was gone. Barnard shook his head at Luc. "I'll kill him for this."

***

The Face of Morto

"Herman, I was right. We've got a big problem." Matt swung his legs over the side of the SAM while he spoke.

Herman spun his chair toward Matt. "More than one. I didn't see your guns' signature amongst the incoming matter. Should I presume that you lost them?"

Matt tossed his cavalier hat with its dodo plumage into the corner. He placed a hand on each knee. "God, my body feels all out of place."

"It takes a while for the neurons to adjust after time travel," Herman said.

Matt stretched his neck and turned it side to side. "Well, Herman, the guns won't really make much difference if Morto continues to exist back then."

"Oh, dear, so he is…"

"Yes, he is, and we need to end him."

Herman moved his palm toward Matt in a calming gesture. "We will take care of it. We will, but there's another issue we have to deal with first."

Matt rolled his eyes. "God forbid I throw a wrench in Stephanie's schedule. If we don't take care of my concern, nothing you and Stephanie do will matter."

"Actually, the problem I speak of involves you and me, not Stephanie." Herman mimicked Matt's nastiness.

"Huh?" Matt swallowed hard. He suddenly realized that like a jealous sibling, he was competing with Stephanie.

Herman cleared his throat. "Remember the red-haired hippy I saw watching us when we entered the mine?"

To Matt it seemed like centuries since Herman spotted the sunburned hippy spying on them. "Yeah, what about him?"

"He dynamited the mine shut."

"What?" Matt leaped from the SAM.

Herman laughed and repeated the calming gesture. "It's not a problem. In fact, it's good."

200

"Us being trapped is good? Maybe for you. You don't breathe air!"

"It's perfect for both of us. Now we leave the mine sealed shut. No more snooping by anyone."

Matt heaved out a tense breath. "I hope you're saying there's another exit?"

Herman chuckled. "Of course, would Horace ever walk into a place with one exit?"

Matt raised his arms and wiggled them to get the circulation going. "Then let's get out of this hole. I'm sick of it."

"Not so fast," Herman said. "It's not completely safe for you, yet. Stay here until I stabilize the material his explosion shifted. Keep the door closed and wait for me regardless of how long I'm gone."

Herman went to the door.

"What if you get buried?" Matt asked.

Herman chuckled. "Have you forgotten that I'm a seraph?"

"I don't think it matters what you are when you're buried under twenty feet of rock."

"It does matter." Herman left, closing the door behind him.

The SAM chamber was soundproof, but, as with all of Horace Haines's hideaways, every possible approach was monitored. The feeds went to a row of screens along one wall.

Matt flopped into the swivel chair and cranked up the sound from the camera just outside the chamber door.

Herman's footfalls clicked into the distance. His image disappeared into the shadows. A long silence followed. Matt didn't see Herman on any of the other monitors.

He waited.

When it seemed too long, he looked around for something to occupy his mind. There was nothing. There were no books to read, no tools to work with, no games to play.

A basketball hoop would be good. Matt looked up. *The ceiling is too low. Of course, Herman can raise it.*

Matt twiddled his thumbs.

Damned Horace, he didn't put one thing for entertainment in here. No wonder Herman has difficulty acting human. Horace was not a good example.

Matt began to pace the room from wall to wall, over and over. He thought about ways to defeat Morto Sacude, but without Herman's input they were all fantasies.

The chamber floor vibrated. Then the microphones picked up the rumble of rocks grinding against themselves. He grabbed the

201

desk and peered at the monitors. The door began to clang and shake. It bowed inward for an instant then rebounded to its normal shape. The sound of crunching rocks elevated to a roar. A brown blur piled up near the chamber door.

I'm blocked in!

Matt ran to the door and yanked it open. Blurred by dust, the shape of a huge man loomed several meters away. He plodded toward Matt, the glint of chrome reflecting off his head.

"Aaaaaaaah," Matt screamed and stumbled backward.

Morto Sacude stood sideways in the doorway. His shiny helmet slowly rotated and aimed a red eye at Matt.

For an instant Matt couldn't move; then he slammed his body against the door. He thrashed his legs to drive it shut. The robot's metal hand shot out and grasped the door edge, locking it open as firmly as if it had been set in concrete. Matt shoved again. It didn't budge.

***

Is Herman a Träger?

"Matt, let me in." Herman's voice came from inside Sacude's helmet.

Matt gasped. "Herman?"

The robot faced Matt squarely. The right half of the face was Herman. The left was shiny metal, like Morto. Its left arm shone like chrome; the right one was flesh.

The seraph trudged into the chamber. "I told you to keep the door shut."

Matt's mouth hung open. He stared at the half-robot, half-human face. "I-I thought I was going to be buried. What the hell happened to your face?"

Herman's human half-face frowned in disgust. His human hand swung toward the door and pointed. In the shadows by the door was a large metallic object that looked somewhat familiar, but Matt couldn't place it.

"It's the elevator," Herman said. "I pulled it down the tunnel so I could put it in the alternate shaft. I caused a rock slide and got half my face skinned away."

Matt grimaced. "You look like the monster robot I saw back in France." Matt studied the device in the corridor. "That's the elevator?"

202

"One thing at a time," Herman said. "So let's start with the elevator; it's easiest. I've reconfigured it because the new shaft is diagonal not vertical. It has seats now. More like an auto." He ticked his head toward the door. "The tunnel's stable now. You can go out and take a closer look."

They both went into the tunnel.

Matt circled the vehicle. Thick rubbery wheels protruded from every side. "It's not even shaped like an elevator anymore. How did you change it so fast?"

"It will be called nanotechnology. Haines Companies is scheduled to patent many key aspects of it in about eighty years." Herman patted the vehicle. "This machine can now go through any shaft, up, down, or sideways." Herman opened the carriage door. It reminded Matt of a stagecoach from old Western movies.

Herman's left arm had some skin on it. Matt blinked and said, "Good God, I went completely hysterical. I thought your flesh was gone all the way to the metal, but it's not. In some spots it looks like slight skin abrasions."

"Your first observation was correct. Twenty-one point five three percent of my skin has regenerated since you first saw the damage."

They sat in the carriage, Herman with hands on his knees. The redness of his eye dimmed as the white of a biological eye grew over it.

The carriage lurched forward. Matt braced against his seat.

"No need to worry, I've programmed its course," Herman said. The carriage rocked and rolled like a mini-tank navigating through a war zone.

Herman brought his hands together and made a steeple with his fingers. "Matt, we can now address our other problem. You say that this robot was rather large and completely metal. That is, it had no skin?"

Matt told the whole story of his adventures in France, Herman stopping him occasionally to clarify the attributes of the Morto Sacude.

Matt finished. "Well, what is he?"

The two-thirds of Herman's face that was again human showed concern. The other third was a bloody pulp with a bit of metal still showing through. "We're here," he informed Matt.

"Where?" Matt asked.

203

"We've entered the alternate exit shaft and are starting upward."

The force of the acceleration pushed Matt back into his seat.

"So what is he?" This time Matt sounded urgent.

"I'm checking your description of Morto against my data bank of automatons. In any case, it's quite clear he's a problem. We're going to need help," Herman said.

"What kind of help? If you can't handle it, who can?"

Herman rolled his eyes, which were almost normal, at Matt. "I will have to go back to France with you to disable the träger, so we'll need someone else to run the SAM."

"You say träger? A seraph is better than a träger, right? I mean he's over four hundred years old."

"Matt, I'm over three thousand years old. But you're right, a träger can't hold a candle to a seraph."

Five minutes later the car halted. Herman pressed a button and they disembarked onto a landing platform. The tunnel they had traversed angled back into darkness.

Herman signaled Matt toward the other end of the platform.

"This exits into an area between two boulders. Hopefully our redheaded saboteur won't be standing there when the rocks part."

Matt snorted. "If he is, I'll take care of it."

**

The rock opened and the desert air hit them like a blast from a metal smelter. Matt's first breath burned through his nostrils to his lungs. He swallowed to bring moisture back into his parched throat. Two feet away a gray skink blinked its eyes at the men. It waddled off to perch in a shady niche beyond their reach.

Matt studied the landscape. The desert shimmered hot, dry, and empty into the distance. He spotted his jeep about a half mile to the east. About a quarter of a mile beyond it, dust hung above the destroyed mine entrance. Other than the skink, which now disappeared into a crack, nothing moved.

"We'll have to install some monitors here," Matt said.

Herman scanned the valley. "I have a better plan. This will be the location of the newly formed Henderson Test Site. We'll bring in the newest Haines mobile command centers and use them as the staging headquarters for our SAM activity.

"We'll set one unit on the front end to serve as the security checkpoint." He pointed to a spot by the road. "An eight-foot

204

cyclone fence will channel all traffic to it, giving us complete control of the valley.

"I'll tell High Five that the explosion made the mine unsafe and I've blocked it off to prevent others from snooping and injuring themselves."

They trudged down the slope toward the jeep.

Herman circled the conversation back to the träger. "By the way, I'm ninety-three percent certain he is a träger. I would like to pin it down to his exact model."

They walked on in silent contemplation. On the valley floor Matt asked, "Can you subdue a träger?"

Herman snorted in disdain. "A träger? They're morons, to be blunt."

"I don't want to denigrate your abilities, Herman, but this thing looked like a military unit. It's seven feet tall and built like Darth Vader on steroids."

Herman continued in his condescending tone. "You said he has no skin, only the metallic exoskeleton. I have regenerative skin. Just so you know, it was cloned from humanoids. However, it regenerates much faster than your own skin. Wouldn't you agree that if half your face got ripped off, it would take longer than mine to repair?"

Matt wrinkled his nose in disgust. "If my face were half ripped off, it would never recover."

"Correct, but if I gave you the elixir, it would. You remember the elixir Gimish used to reduce Ahmose's aging? If I gave you the very same elixir, then your face would mend just as rapidly as mine did. In fact, mine healed fast because within my structure is an artificial gland that dispenses elixir when I need it."

Matt shrugged his shoulders. "So how does that help you fight a monster?"

"Ah," Herman said professorially, "to have cloned humanoid skin is technically superior. Superior technology implies military superiority, doesn't it?"

Matt frowned. "Maybe he doesn't want a skin."

Herman scoffed. "But he does want to be taken for a human. To do so he had to convince others that he wore a metal helmet and iron gloves over his head and hands. The rest of his body he hides under a cloak. Surely, he would forgo this charade if he could grow a human skin."

205

"I'm not convinced," Matt said. "Below your exotic skin, you and he have the same metal structure, except he's bigger and stouter than you."

"All things that shine are not the same," Herman said. He bent his fingers into claws and scraped his face to the metal again. He flung the goo off, then smeared his fingers across his slacks. "Push on my cheek as hard as you can."

"Yuk." Matt raised his forearm to cover his eyes, but he couldn't stop looking at the oily streak on Herman's pants.

In a flash Herman grasped Matt's hand, then pressed Matt's index finger against his metal cheek until the finger hyperextended. Matt screamed.

Herman released the hand. "Now, feel the thickness of the metal," he said. He forced Matt's finger onto the edge of the cheekbone. Grimacing, Matt closed his eyes and rubbed the metal between his thumb and forefinger.

"It's paper thin. You could have explained that without ripping half your face away." Matt cleaned his fingers on his jeans.

"Okay, I'll explain," Herman said. "Morto's skeleton has to be twenty times thicker than mine to achieve the same strength. He's heavier, slower, and dumber."

"You hope." Matt checked both sides of his hand then wiped it again, this time on the butt of his pants.

"After perusing my records of artificial humanoids, I've decided this Morto is a class 2 träger," Herman announced.

"How many kinds of pseudo-humans are there, anyway?" Matt asked.

"In Nirvania's quarter of the galaxy there are 3456," Herman said.

"And you eliminated 3455 with the little info I gave you?"

Herman's eyes twinkled. "About 3000 are too primitive to be what you described." Then he winked. "But the truth is, I have other information that indicates he is a class 2 träger."

"Such as?" Matt asked.

"I can't discuss all the details at this time, but 22.1735 years ago I learned that Vergs were operating in this part of the galaxy. Vergs use class 2 trägers as their assault troops."

Matt stopped in his tracks. "None of that makes any sense to me. What is a Verg?"

Herman explained Vergs to Matt then concluded, "If Morto was here four centuries ago, then why haven't the Vergs already colonized Earth?"

Matt thought a moment. His eyes widened and he did a little hop while clapping his hands. "Of course! We stopped them. My theory of historical intervention is correct."

"Hum." Herman pointed ahead. "Someone has vandalized your jeep."

***

Lost Guns

Matt squinted at his vehicle hidden amid mesquite branches several hundred yards away. The hood was up. He took off running. Herman followed.

The jeep's dust-coated headlights stared with the dull eyes of a mugging victim. Limp battery cables hung down like ripped clothing. Matt stared down into the empty battery tray.

Herman surveyed the area. He pointed to auto tracks that ran next to the jeep. "They parked here." He pointed to the base of a large rock. "There's a battery, but it isn't yours."

"Wrong size." Matt slammed his fist against the fender. "The fool should have jumped his battery instead of taking mine."

"Those fools—more than one." Herman pointed to a flowery garment barely visible under a tumbleweed. "Looks like a woman's blouse. I assume the redheaded hippie had a female companion."

Matt kicked the bramble aside and picked up the garment. It was crumpled and stiff. He pulled on the edges and the wrinkles spread like the bellows of an accordion. A reddish-brown stain covered the center of it. "Someone bled badly. Look, one sleeve is torn off."

Herman took the cloth and studied it. "Maybe they took the sleeve to make a tourniquet."

A rock shard fell from the folds of cloth. Matt picked it up. His eyebrows raised in surprise. He handed it to Herman. "Someone stabbed themselves with a Folsom arrowhead."

Like a jeweler examining a diamond, Herman angled the surface back and forth. "Yes, there are bloodstains on it." He rubbed it on his sleeve, then put it close to his eye again. "Very strange, it has no tool marks."

207

Matt stuck his palm out for it. "Ten thousand years of wind, water, and ice probably polished out the tool marks."

Herman gave Matt a deadpan look. "I already considered those things. This stone point was never worked. It appears to have emerged straight from the ground already made. That is a geological impossibility." Herman pulled his arm back to fling it away.

"No!" Matt jumped to block Herman. "Give it to me!"

Herman shrugged his shoulders and handed it over.

Matt grunted. "Considering you're a genius, sometimes you do the dumbest things."

"I already recorded it in my database. We really don't need it."

Matt winked. "Yes, but shamanism is my expertise, right?"

Ignoring Matt, Herman peered down the road. "It's late and it's forty-five miles to the nearest hamlet. I suggest we get started."

"Wrong." Matt pointed to the western ridge. "It's twenty miles to the nearest Paiute village. The country is rough, full of deep winding canyons, but if you can keep us on track, it'll be a lot faster."

Herman shrugged. "No problem, at the top of the ridge I'll lock in the village's coordinates."

Matt grabbed a bottle of water from under the seat and hiked toward the ridge. Herman followed.

Midway up, the slope steepened.

His shirt wet with sweat, Matt placed his left hand on his hip and panted. He gulped down two big swallows of water then took his time reattaching the bottle to his belt.

"Another five or six hours of up and down." Matt wiped his forehead. "If I don't dehydrate. What a pain in the ass this is."

"After dark, I can carry you," Herman said.

Matt flung his palms up in the air. "Why not now?"

Herman scanned the hills. "After Wendell's UFO video, we don't need one of me charging up this hill with you on my shoulders."

Matt groaned. "Well, do you hear anyone breathing anywhere nearby?"

Herman scanned side to side. "Nope. What does the shaman say?"

Matt smirked at Herman then closed his eyes. "Okay, let me link with the cosmos." He turned gradually until he felt a change. He opened his eyes, facing distant boulders bright yellow in the setting sun. Long blue shadows oozed like spilt wine from their bases. Matt grimaced. "I don't know. Let's get over the crest before you do anything radical."

When they reached the top, Matt pointed to a valley that lay blue-gray between distant buttes. "The village is there." Matt lowered his finger to trace a twisting gulley below them. "While we're weaving around in that, we'll need to stay locked in on the objective."

Herman nodded. "No problem."

They started down, a wake of loose gravel sliding along with them. After snaking through the gullies for thirty minutes, Herman's internal compass showed they had come one mile closer to the village.

Matt wiped away his sweat. "It'll be dark and you can carry me soon. Which direction is the village?"

Herman held his hand out like a spear. Matt studied the landscape then pointed to a hill that loomed beyond the canyon. "Let's use the gulley a while longer then climb that hill. At the top we'll adjust our route again."

At the top they could see more steep gullies cutting across their proposed route.

Matt hung his head. "There's supposed to be a horse trail near here. We should have crossed it by now. Anyway it's time for you to carry me. I'm tired and fresh out of water."

"There's the trail." Herman pointed to a break in the brush several hundred yards away. He gyrated his head side to side, then added, "Two horsemen are approaching on it."

Matt looked beyond Herman's hand. In the distance, two riders worked their way through the brush."

Herman chuckled. "I believe they are Jim and Emil."

Matt squinted.

The riders kept their heads down as if examining the desert floor. They stopped. One dismounted and pointed here and there at the ground. He remounted, and they turned back toward the village.

"Oh shit, they're leaving," Matt said. Behind him, Herman emitted a high-pitched shriek. Matt pressed his hands flat against his head and bent in pain.

"They see us." Herman waved. "They're waving back."

"Did you have to do that?" Matt's ears throbbed so loudly that he couldn't hear his own words.

"Did you have to leave the guns behind?" Herman retorted.

Chapter 16: Herman's Trust

The air, moist and fragrant with cilantro, cumin, and roasted chilies, made Matt's mouth water. Derek, by the stove, filled a large platter with enchiladas, beans, and rice. He carried it to the table, his arms bowing under its weight, then returned to the counter to eat his meal there.

Jim poured red chili sauce on his food and took a bite. While chewing, he told Derek, "Sure enough, we found the tracks you told us about. We were following 'em, with our eyes to the ground. I guess these two figured we were about to go back to town and leave them. Herman let out a yell so high pitched he could have passed for an opera singer." Jim looked at Herman and laughed.

Emil giggled. "I bet you can't do it again." He scooped some beans onto his plate.

Derek studied Herman. "Well, he's kinda big like an opera singer. Herman, can you demonstrate that sound here?" He and Jim exchanged glances.

Herman wrinkled his lips in displeasure. "We were pretty tired already and I didn't much want to walk all the way here in the middle of the night. I don't much want to demonstrate that sound either, here or anywhere."

While chewing, Emil sputtered, "Well, no worry. We heard that opera lady and our heads sprung up to see where the heck the noise came from." He reached for more salsa then turned to Jim. "Am I eating too much of the hot stuff?"

Jim laughed. "No, you're family now. You take all you want, little brother." He pointed to Herman. "He could be a problem, but he's not eating much for a big guy."

Derek paused and studied Herman. "Yeah, you don't eat much for someone who's had no food all day."

Herman made circles around his stomach. "Not doing so well right now."

Jim arched back as if offended. "You saying Injun food ain't good?"

"No, not that. All the crap with the explosion and the jeep being vandalized got me out of sorts."

Jim took a big bite and laughed. "I was just jokin'."

Derek pecked at his food. "Hey, while ago we said there aren't any redheaded fellows around these parts, but we were wrong. Remember that redheaded hippy we saw with Wendell the other night?"

Jim stopped eating. Emil's eyes widened. Emil spoke first. "Yeah, he was saying that flying saucers refuel at your mine and that Haines Companies is hiding it from everyone."

Matt thrust his chin toward Jim. "You say he was with Wendell?"

Jim chuckled. "Yeah, we had quite an event there at Ceci's with those two and their hippy girlfriends."

Derek explained. "I think they all live with Wendell. From the look on his face, he was ready to go pitch a tent in the desert just to get away from them."

"Arbie. That's his name," Emil said between bites.

Jim tapped the table with his fingertips. "Good memory, Emil."

Emil took another bite. "Yeah, and you remember what he wanted to do, right?"

"Yeah," Derek said. "Folks say he already got some outsider Injuns and they're tryin' to recruit locals to help them take the Sacred Silver Valley back from Haines Companies."

"Bunch of urban Indians," Jim said derisively.

Herman took a whole enchilada and a big serving of beans off the serving plate. Jim and Derek stared incredulously while he downed it all. Then Herman stood and carried all the empty plates to the sink and rinsed them.

Derek watched in awe. "Ain't often you get a CEO to wash your dishes."

Herman put down the last dish and turned his back to the sink. He picked up a dish towel, thin and already damp, and wiped his hands. He smiled at Derek then Jim and Emil. "It comes at a price. Your quips about the sound I made and my eating habits tell me that you know I'm different."

Matt blurted a half protest, but Herman raised his palm to stop him. "They know already."

Derek thrust his chin at Herman. "I was there that night, same as Wendell. That was a UFO he filmed, and we all know it."

Matt sighed.

Emil jutted his face toward Matt and frowned. "No thanks to you." He spun toward Herman. "Or you."

Herman crossed his arms and leaned back against the counter. "You'll need to keep this information to yourselves." His words were harsh and his face severe.

For a while everyone sat in silence.

Then Derek's face took an angry blush. "And if we don't?"

"Then your indiscretion could cause the demise of the human race."

Derek crossed his arms and rocked back in his chair. "So you aliens are threatening us."

"No, we're trying to save you. It's other aliens that threaten you."

Jim watched his uncle. Emil glared at Herman.

After a long pause, Jim exhaled a long loud breath. "Well, he probably knows more about what's out there than we do."

"That's right," Herman said. "And I need help if I'm going to protect you."

Jim thrust his thumbs into his waistband. "Okay, I'll go along with that, but I want to know more, a lot more."

"Me too," Emil said.

Derek stood. "I'm going to sit on the porch." He left the room.

Emil rose to follow, but Jim signaled him to stay. Then to Herman, Jim said, "Derek won't be a problem."

Herman dropped his hands to the countertop. "Thanks. I need to use your phone; then we should get back to the mine."

**

212

Jim slammed on the brakes. The dust from their wake overran them, curling through the beams of the headlights and wrapping the pickup in a swirling gray cloud.

The dust dissipated on the night breeze and Herman, who sat in the front passenger seat, pointed to the reflection off the jeep's headlamps. "There it is. You could slide in next to it."

Jim looked about then pointed. "That's a better place." He began to back the pickup into a more open spot.

"Where's this new entrance to the underground tunnels?" Jim peered at the boulders while stepping out of the pickup.

"Straight where you're looking," Matt replied.

"The rocks actually slide back like something from a Flash Gordon movie?" Jim asked.

Matt pointed his thumb to Herman. "The original Flash Gordon."

They both chuckled.

Herman smiled good-naturedly. "Before we go in, I want to get that hippy blouse from under the jeep seat. I'd like to have the blood analyzed."

Jim reached back into the pickup to get a flashlight.

Herman headed to the jeep without waiting. He felt under the seat. "I'm sure I left it here."

Jim shined the light into the jeep cab.

"I don't need that," Herman said.

Jim flashed the light onto nearby brush. "I suppose the cloth could have blown out. Could be halfway to Mexico by now."

Herman shook his head. "Someone had to take it. I had it solidly wedged in."

Matt took a flashlight from the jeep and also began to search the nearby bushes. After a few minutes he called out, "Hey, it's here." He held the blouse up by two fingers.

"Hey, what's that?" Jim shined his light at the ground.

Matt frowned and added his beam to the spot.

Herman was the first to speak. "It's a paw print from a mountain lion."

Jim patted Herman's shoulder. "Herman, that cloth didn't blow out of the jeep. She took it."

"She, who?" Herman asked.

Jim smirked. "Panther Woman, you're not the only supernatural being around."

213

Herman snorted with disdain. "I'm not supernatural. I have nearly twenty thousand years of science built into me."

Jim poked Herman's shoulder. "Such a short time? The spirits have had power since the beginning of time."

Herman rolled his eyes.

Jim blinked the flashlight at the paw print. "Explain that." The light reflected off of something shiny deep in the brush. "What the…"

"Garbage," Herman said.

Jim flung his arms in the air and screamed, "I told that redheaded son of a bitch not to camp here." He flashed the light around, hitting wads of toilet paper and tin cans.

Jim stomped toward Matt. A few feet away he aimed the light like a gun straight into Matt's eyes. "Damned stupid white men!" He shoved past, knocking Matt sideways. Matt's mouth flung open in protest, but he couldn't muster a word. Jim marched to the middle of the road, then stopped. He shined his light back on Matt and Herman. "Are we going to look at your secret entrance or not?"

***

Alien Construction

The sun's rays crawled over the edge of the Earth in early dawn. Matt and Jim sat on a boulder and drank coffee from the chrome cap of a thermos bottle. Herman sat below them, his arms wrapped around his knees. When offered the cup, he refused. "I don't need it. I'm just imitating a human who is cold." He chattered his teeth and shivered to prove it.

Jim pushed the cup at him. "Take it for fellowship, then."

When the sun was high enough to drive the chill off, Matt said, "I need to buy a battery for the jeep."

Jim handed Matt the pickup keys. "I'll stay here and help Herman."

Herman stretched, pushing his arms high and wide. He paced the area of the proposed Henderson Research Station, squatting here and there like a surveyor. Jim watched.

Herman looked up. "We might as well clear out the brush and level this off while we wait for the command modules to be delivered."

"Delivered?"

214

"Yeah, I used Derek's phone last night to order them. They'll be here before noon."

"You'll need some earthmovers to level this," Jim said.

Herman smiled. "Or something else. I'll be back shortly."

Herman entered the door in the boulders. He reemerged ten minutes later carrying a silver stick similar to a flute. "It's the staff Ahmose used to magnify his shaman powers, something neither I nor Gimish ever understood, but even without shaman powers we can do powerful things with it. Move twenty meters over there to avoid flying debris."

Herman didn't become a blur of turbine blades. Rather he moved like a karate master or whirling dervish performing a formal dance. At the end of the first phase, the air smelled of burned mesquite, and every plant that lay in the footprint of the new research station had been turned to smothering ash.

Jim could tell the exact size and position of the two trailers. He started to ask about the rocks and boulders that protruded jaggedly into the marked-out area. Before he could, Herman started kata 2, which involved surgically cutting the stone so the modules would fit them in a perfect match. Sparks flew, the air filled with the odor of ozone, and the rock surfaces took the shape of an abstract sculpture.

"It looks like it will fit as tightly as one of those Inca walls." Jim pointed to a huge slab of sandstone about three meters tall and five wide. "But even you can't move that big block without equipment."

Herman eyed the huge piece. "It's about a hundred tons. You're right, I can't move it myself." He stepped further back, still studying the boulder. "Want to help?"

"I hope you're kidding."

"No." Now Herman's arms flashed like rotor blades. He sent the beam from the staff across the rock in a crisscrossing fashion. When he stopped, the large rock was a grid of half-meter by quarter-meter blocks.

He smiled at Jim. "I liked your idea of the Inca wall. These will fit together to form a nice barrier around the compound."

Herman handed the staff to Jim, then climbed the back of the boulder. He began to heave the cut stones into a sandy area. He worked his way down layer by layer until all the stones were scattered over the sand. Not one had hit and cracked against another.

Jim held the staff up. "Wow, this thing beats Harry Potter's magic wand shameless. I would love to use it sometime."

Herman smiled. "You might."

Eyes wincing into slits against the midday glare, Jim peered over Herman's shoulder. "There's a dust plume coming from the highway."

"Yes, four semis, I heard them pull off the highway about eighty-five seconds ago."

Jim frowned. "Four semis? What did you say they were bringing?"

"Two TR18 command trailers, complete with self-contained air supply, a bulletproof shell, a satellite link, and living quarters for five, along with a tractor to move things around."

"We'll back one up to the SAM entry point in the rock. The other we'll put in front to serve as a security post for our new facility."

**

Hours later, dust swirling in their wake, the trucks headed back to the highway. Herman pivoted to face the southern mountains. He stared at the horizon for a few seconds then said, "One of our hovercrafts is approaching from Vegas."

A minute later, a speck appeared over the Toad Mountains. After two more minutes the hovercraft circled above them.

**

"Doesn't look like anything nefarious is happening down there," Stephanie said into her headset. The pilot circled the hovercraft, giving her and Marie a chance to survey the situation before they landed.

"That's Jim with Herman, right?" Marie said. "You know, the Indian who took Emil from the Black Lava."

"You are so on top of it," Stephanie teased.

"I do have a photographic memory. I would remember him even if I hadn't said he was handsome."

Stephanie punched Marie's shoulder. "You're chipper, considering we could have died yesterday."

"The Black Lava situation is back to normal," Marie said. "Should I be morose about it, and not appreciate a good-looking man?"

Stephanie rolled her eyes. "I didn't think you liked men."

216

Marie grinned. "I didn't think I did either."

The aircraft landed. Dirt swirled around their windows. Marie pushed the door open. "Let's go find out what's going on." She grabbed her riot gun and jumped out. She hit the ground, running like a commando, .45 pistol strapped to her waist, the shotgun swinging with her stride. Stephanie followed, shielding her eyes with the palm of her left hand.

"Hey, Dad," Marie called out.

"Marie? Why are you two here?" Herman shouted.

Jim, who was bent over the tractor's controls, stood up to see the women. "You have a daughter?" he said in complete bewilderment.

The four of them converged.

Marie pointed to the pallets of materials. "So you did order this stuff. When Bob said it was shipping, I worried Carr was making a move here too."

Herman glanced from one woman to the other.

Marie's face became serious. "Security was breached all the way to the seventh floor—"

Herman interrupted, "What? I don't see how that could be, unless we—"

"Were compromised," Marie finished for him then went on to explain. "Tim got turned. He killed Peter then took over the control room in a plot to kill Stephanie on the seventh floor."

"What?" Jim asked.

Marie faced him, her eyes sparking. "I killed Tim and his bodyguard and retook the control center. Then I gassed the assassination team on the seventh floor. Unfortunately, their commander killed her subordinates and escaped. We're certain Kit was in charge."

"The door. Tell them about the door." Stephanie's voice warbled.

Marie rubbed Stephanie's back. Jim watched her hand and she stopped. Their eyes met for a moment.

"It's the damnedest thing," Marie said to Herman. She moved her eyes to Jim then waited.

Jim looked confused. He glanced from Marie to Herman. "If it's top secret, then I'll…"

Herman shook his head. "Marie, he knows. You can speak in front of him."

217

Marie lavished a beaming smile on Jim. "I had enough gas in there to knock out a bull elephant, and Kit still managed to get out."

"Got out?" Herman frowned. "You didn't lock the doors?"

Marie widened her eyes. "She blasted a hole in the seventh-floor stairwell door."

"The seventh-floor stairwell door?" Herman repeated as if expecting her to correct herself.

"Yes, then she blew a two-meter-wide strip out of the parking garage wall."

Jim looked from Stephanie to Marie to Herman and shrugged his shoulders. "I suppose military-strength explosives could do that."

Herman's face became solemn. "All doors on the seventh floor and the walls adjacent to them are made from high-test Nirvanian alloy that I recovered from the hull of Gimish's spaceship. There is literally nothing on this Earth that can penetrate it. In fact, there is very little in the galaxy that can."

Jim's eyes widened. "You're saying she's an alien."

"Worse," Herman said. "She's an alien with technology we've never dealt with before." He turned to the women. "I don't want you going back to the Black Lava until I can go with you."

Marie huffed. "Dad, I'm head of security. I already took care of it." She turned to Stephanie. "Let's go shoot some guns and let the men muscle this equipment around. When they've gotten it assembled, we'll come back and make it work." She glanced at Jim. "Unless you want to come, too."

Jim angled his head toward Herman. "I promised to help him."

Marie smiled. "Okay, your choice."

Jim watched the women walk off side by side. "I don't mean to insult, but how do you have a daughter? I mean, she's a little unusual, but nothing like you."

Herman patted Jim on the shoulder. "She's adopted, and yes, she's not like me." Then Herman winked.

**

Target practice completed, Stephanie and Marie lay against a large south-sloping rock and absorbed the sun.

"It's really cold today," Stephanie said. Their guns, breeches open, lay on Marie's nylon backpack.

218

"A lot of it is the wind." Marie zipped her jacket up tighter. "Pretty, though, we can see a hundred miles from here."

They took in the canyon, its walls ranging from rust to pink. The valley floor meandered through desert willow bunched here and there against boulders. Far beyond, the slope rose and blended with the distant mountains.

"How is Herman your father?" Stephanie asked.

Marie didn't respond for a long while.

Stephanie waited.

"He is my dad, at least as close as I'll ever get to having one." Saying that caused her inner demons to stir; still she forged on. She needed to share with someone. Maybe with a friend she could break through the green wall and find her beginnings.

"He says I'm adopted, but I don't think it was formal. When I was young, I thought he and my mom were married, and one day she would come back for me."

She shook her head. Her eyes watered. "Never happened. When I asked, he always said the same thing. 'Your mom loved you, but she had to go away.'"

Stephanie stroked Marie's hair. "I'm sure it's true. Something monstrous must have forced her to leave you."

Marie wiped her cheek. "You know an eidetic mind shouldn't forget. I've often thought my mother hypnotized me to make me forget bad things that happened."

Marie dragged her fingertips from Stephanie's shoulder to her wrist, then clasped hands with her. "For some reason, since I've known you, I've been able to see more. I think Mother wants you to help drive my demons away."

Her throat tightened. Her hand, damp with sweat, dared to find one of Stephanie's fingers.

"I quit asking Herman." She held the finger tightly like a child would.

Stephanie kissed her on the forehead and then the cheek. "I'm your family now. I'm your sister forever."

Loneliness banished for the moment, Marie trembled. Tears rolled down her face.

"There's more." Marie blubbered the words.

"Hush, you don't need to say more." Stephanie held Marie against her.

"I want to. When I talk—to you, my mind flashes. Reality rises from fog. Just now I remembered the day Mother gave me to

Herman's secretary. It's still hazy. I can't see her face or hear her voice."

"How old were you?"

"Four." Marie wiped her eyes on her sleeve. Her voice began to harden. "Look at me, I'm supposed to be protecting you. Instead you have to comfort me as if I were still four."

She handed Stephanie the .45-caliber pistol. "It's late. Let's go."

**

Herman's precision, along with his superhuman strength, made the test site come together with the ease of an erector set. Jim, on the tractor, raced to keep pace. They had the equipment in place when Herman heard the women cross a ridge two gullies away. He looked up to see their heads bobbing down into the next ravine. At the same time, the sound of an auto came toward them from the highway.

Jim looked up. "Sounds like a car headed this way. Maybe Matt?"

Herman's face concentrated like a human trying to focus. "More than one. None are Matt. Engine pitches not right. The third one might be a pickup, but not ours."

Jim watched the most distant point on the road. "Three vehicles and no one we know. That can't be good. The girls took the guns. Maybe you ought to go get the staff and put it into flamethrower mode."

Herman watched the dust trail approach. "They can't hurt me. Get in the trailer and lock the door. If there's a problem, I can handle it."

Jim shook his head. "If it's that red-haired shit, then you better hide him from me."

"And if they have guns?" Herman asked.

Jim threw the tractor into high gear. He rambled up the road and parked behind the gate they'd set up earlier. He hopped off the machine. Two big Chevys and a pickup raced up and jammed to a stop inches from the fence and Jim.

The doors flung open and ten Indians leaped out. Arbie pried himself out last and limped forward. His pants had a pinkish wet spot on the thigh, like something was oozing from his leg. His face pale and sweaty, he winced with each step.

Jim laid a sledgehammer across his shoulders. Herman picked up a pipe wrench and joined him.

The leader, Billy Manes, rushed forward and stopped with his face inches from Jim's. "Move, motherfuckers. We're claimin' this property in the name of NAS and the Paiute people."

Three of them had pistols protruding from their waistbands. The rest were so clustered together that it was impossible to see how many more guns were among them.

"I'm Paiute," Jim said, "and I represent the tribal council. There ain't no NAS business here. Go back to Dakota."

Billy's eyes flashed electric with anger. "NAS represents all oppressed Native Americans, even Paiutes."

"Paiutes don't need your help. This is sacred ground for our tribe, not yours, nor any other tribe with Aztec blood." Jim bellied up to the fence with the hammer held in the air like it wasn't any heavier than a garden trowel. "You ain't coming through."

"You're a white man's boy." Billy's face knotted with hate and he glared at Herman. "He is a desecration on this land. But we'll cleanse it." He feinted a lunge toward Herman. The pipe wrench whipped off Herman's shoulder and stopped inches from Billy's nose. Billy froze. His eyes flashed with sudden surprise; then he hid it.

Herman eased the pipe back to his shoulder. "That's your one warning."

"You're a couple of fucking cavemen with clubs." Billy pulled back his leather jacket, revealing a .45.

"And if you all want to die, pull that gun." A woman's voice came from Billy's left. He froze except for his head. It swiveled and faced into the barrel of a semiautomatic shotgun. Marie stood only ten yards away and had the NAS gang enfiladed, which meant every piece of shot coming out of the barrel would end up in someone's body. Stephanie stood beside her with two pistols leveled at Billy's head.

"You three showing guns." Marie pointed her shotgun at each of them. "Drop them. If anyone else moves, I shoot and don't stop until you're all laid out flat."

Jim took two of the guns and tossed the third into a cactus.

"One at a time peel off and put your hands on the top of this Chevy here," Marie ordered. "Stephanie, if anyone does anything radical, shoot them all. We're not leaving any witnesses."

221

Billy's eyes narrowed to tiny slits, but he said nothing. Jim collected seven more pistols. Herman took three assault rifles from the trunks of the cars.

With all the guns confiscated, Marie signaled the men away from the cars. A heavy one with a red headband went pale, realizing what she was about to do.

Marie aimed her shotgun at the first car.

"That's my car," the heavy one said.

"You fuckers are gonna get it for this," another said.

Stephanie swung her pistols toward his head. He flinched downward as if dodging a bee.

Marie fired the first shot through the closest windshield. The sound still reverberated when she swung the barrel toward the second car.

She fired again, then accelerated, pulling the trigger over and over until the ten-round drum was empty. Every car window was gone. The metal sides were perforated; the cloth interiors, shredded.

"Have a nice ride home. Don't come back," Marie ordered.

"You bitch!" the heavy one shouted and lunged at her. She rammed the shotgun barrel into his Adam's apple. He grabbed his throat and fell to his knees.

The whole group menaced toward her.

"Everyone get back!" Stephanie ordered, rotating her arms, aiming at one then another.

Jim raised his two pistols. "Get in those cars and go!"

Marie bent over the guy, who was now coughing and spitting up blood. "You want to get me? It's easier to kill you right here than to worry about my back forever." She whipped her voice into a psychotic frenzy that made Stephanie's back ripple with chills. "I think I'll do that." She laid the shotgun barrel against his head. The trigger clicked. The man screamed and fell, burying his head between his arms.

"Oh, I forgot this gun is empty." Marie's face flushed with a wave of crimson that boiled from her neck to her forehead. She dropped the shotgun and pressed her pistol against the back of his skull. "This one isn't, you motherfucker."

Petrified, everyone stared at her finger on the trigger.

***

222

The Green Wall

Stephanie began to tremble. She wanted it to stop before she vomited.

"Never! Never ever fuck with me again! Ever! I'll kill your fucking ass! You hear me!" Marie banged the barrel against his head. Blood gushed from his scalp. "You hear me!" She did it again. He rolled back and forth, moaning sadly as if certain he would die.

Stephanie's mind turned it into a movie, distancing herself from its terror. The man crawled away. His friends helped him into the glass-splattered backseat. A few still had the nerve to angle hate-filled eyes toward Marie. The movie ended with the cars limping into the distance on flat tires, and Marie sighting her pistol at them until they were gone.

**

"Matt's here," Jim announced, peering through the huge observation window of the security trailer.

"Good." Herman stepped out of the office. "Could you give this to Matt? It's the directions for my attorney in Vegas, who I've already called. He's preparing the documents we spoke of."

Jim took the card. "I'll do better than that. I'll call Hector and have him meet Matt at your guy's place."

"Splendid!" Herman grinned like a diplomat.

Jim raised the phone to his ear. "I still can't believe it. We can make a phone call without any wires!"

"Yeah, it's satellite linking technology. We developed it for the military. They paid for the satellite. We inserted our network in beside theirs. We get to ride on their dime."

Marie stepped out of the control center. Manuel Diaz, an illegal Mexican national who had worked as Horace Haines' personal guard, followed her. Thanks to Herman, he now had a green card.

Marie had her arm around his neck. "Manny's a quick study. He got it all down on the first try."

Herman patted Manny on the shoulder. "Remember the cameras will focus on any activity outside so you can check it out. No need to confront anyone. Stay inside where it's safe, and call the Paiute Police if you need support."

"Thank you, Mr. Herman. Marie told me all that stuff already. Thank you for giving me work again." Then Manny lowered his eyes. "I want you to know how sorry I am about your friend Mr. Horace. On the TV, they say he passed on. He was my friend too."

223

Herman nodded. "I know you were loyal to him. That's why you're here now. Anyway, don't worry, he lived a long and interesting life."

Manny's eyes gleamed with excitement. "I read the paper. He surprised me, so many things they say he did."

Herman shook Manny's hand. "Thank you for the kind words. Remember the Paiute Police are responsible for everything outside this enclosure. You are responsible for everything inside."

Marie finalized details with Manny. Everyone else exited to the parking area, which was surrounded by a wall reminiscent of those built by the Incas. On the monitor, Marie saw Stephanie pull Herman aside.

"Manny," Marie said sweetly, "do you mind if I could have some privacy for a phone call?"

"Of course, no problem, Miss Marie." Manny bowed slightly and went back to the bunkroom.

Marie shut the soundproof door to the control center. Herman and Stephanie had separated themselves from the others. Marie directed the distance microphone toward them.

"That was psychotic," Stephanie said.

Herman slumped his shoulders.

Stephanie jutted her head toward him. "She needs medical intervention before she does something you can't buy off."

Herman gazed vacantly into the distance.

Stephanie slammed her hand against his chest. He didn't budge.

"How can you do that? You have all this money and you neglect your own daughter's mental health. You've got to do something." She balled her fist and thumped it against him again.

"Stephanie, when she first showed these tendencies we hired a team to work with her."

"Maybe you better try again."

"Your psychiatrists can't help her," he said. "It's in her genes."

Stephanie knotted her face. "Really?" Then she threw her hands up in disgust. "Oh, what the hell did I expect from a robot?"

Marie flipped the microphone off. She lowered her head onto her arms and sobbed.

**

224

Matt started his jeep. Stephanie spun away from Herman. "Matt," she yelled.

He looked toward her.

She faced Herman again. "She says you know what happened but never told her. Did you withhold that information from the psychiatrists too?"

"They knew enough," Herman said.

"Herman!" She shook her head, tears flinging across her cheeks. Then stomped toward Matt. "Matt, I'm riding with you."

"Stephanie," Herman called out, "we need to discuss the acquisitions plan."

"I'm done with Haines Companies." She slid into the passenger seat. "You can keep your CEO job."

"Stephanie," Matt cautioned.

"Men," she hissed through clenched teeth.

"Okay," Matt whispered and stepped on the gas. The jeep accelerated then slammed to a stop, with the rear wheels spinning up a fountain of sand.

In front, Herman pressed his palms against the jeep. It pushed him slowly backward. The engine strained harder while his feet dug deeper into the earth. Matt threw the gear shift into neutral.

Herman walked around to Stephanie. "I'm afraid this Kit thing will trip her memory. You need to stay close to her."

He walked away.

***

Chapter 17: The Induction

Redlands City, Nevada, tribal capital of the Palo Verde Paiute Reservation, backed up to a cluster of hills that formed a natural amphitheater. That's where they built the high school football field. Like small towns across America, the football stadium served as the focal point for most outdoor events. Tonight it was the venue for the Harvest Festival.

Like a colony of ants, the stadium swarmed with activity: performers, artists, technicians, food preparers and, of course, officials, all bustling to prepare for the evening's performances, which would raise funds for the reservation's medical center.

In the valley far below, buses from Vegas hotels pulled off the highway and wound up the desert road, stirring a pale cloud of dust in the evening shadows.

In a far corner of the staging tent, several members of the tribal council and a delegation from the Black Lava sat in an informal circle of folding chairs. All of them decked out in Western wear, they looked like a group of ranchers drinking coffee and discussing cattle breeds or the weather, but their agenda was much trickier—the transfer of the Henderson Mine back to the Paiute Nation while avoiding the meddlesome fingers of the Department of Indian Affairs.

Eddie Gomez, tribal chairman, a short, wide-chested man, peered at Herman through thick black plastic-rimmed glasses. It was clear from his intensity that he read lips to supplement his hearing

226

aids. He raised his right hand from his knee to point a callused finger at Hector Chaparral, Stanford Law School graduate and the tribal council's youngest member. "Herman, you've heard Hector's plan. Is this something you would like to do?"

Herman, sitting between Stephanie and Marie, pushed his white cowboy hat back on his head and smiled. He made eye contact with each of the council members, Hector, Eddie, Bob Neagle, and the elderly shaman Charles Stagskull accompanied by his understudy, Derek Runningbird.

"My first purpose is to give the land back to the Paiute Nation. I never expected to be inducted into the tribe as a means to make the land transfer, but, frankly, I'm honored." Herman turned to Marie. "It is even more special for my daughter, who, as an orphan, has lost her heritage. Tonight she will acquire a new one with your people."

Marie smiled obligatorily while keeping her eyes away from Stephanie Noble, whom she had avoided for several days.

Across the room, Charlene Springwater, Emil's girlfriend, stood in full native costume, gorgeous and elegant. She engaged in conversation with the people near her while keeping an eye on the negotiating parties.

Stephanie fidgeted. The pink cloth she had tied around her cowgirl hat, which had looked cute at the Black Lava, now felt so wrong, along with her new pink plaid shirt and fresh blue jeans. Without thinking, she plucked at the ribbon like a chicken pecking at an amorphous barnyard blob. Enough plucks and the blob would disappear. The ribbon did not.

Derek frowned and stared at Stephanie, then hastily whispered to Charles. Charles stared straight forward as if digesting what he had heard. Then he turned his head to Derek and asked something in a disbelieving voice.

"Yes," Derek said in English and studied Stephanie again.

Charles gazed at her.

In her peripheral vision, Stephanie saw them and blushed while avoiding eye contact with either of them.

Charles cleared his throat and raised his chin toward Eddie. Eddie rested his elbows on his knees and leaned toward the older shaman.

Stagskull raised his finger toward Stephanie and spoke commandingly.

Stephanie's arms felt cold. She hugged them. *Good, they don't want me here, and I don't want to be here.*

Eddie's mouth fell open. "You want her in the tribe, too?"

Without waiting for Stagskull, Derek nodded his head emphatically. "She must."

Eddie waved him off and leaned closer to Stagskull. "The council agreed on two. The father and the daughter have to be accepted into the tribe so, as Paiutes, they can convey the property back to the tribe without interference from federal law."

He flicked his finger toward Stephanie and explained as if to someone of diminishing capacity, "Miss Stephanie isn't related to him, so there's no reason for her."

The old shaman's eyes twinkled. He tilted away from Derek then cranked his head to peer back at him with an expression of amusement.

Derek bobbed his head with one firm nod.

Charles then spoke to Eddie with vehemence, punctuating each word with a finger jab at Stephanie. It was clear that he prophesized the plagues of Egypt if Stephanie wasn't inducted into the tribe.

For the first time in days, Stephanie and Marie looked at each other, wild-eyed, like deer caught in headlights. Then, Marie turned away.

Stephanie fingered the ribbon that wrapped her hat and mumbled, "I don't think I'm dressed appro—"

Eddie sighed and looked up at Charlene. "Miss Springwater will be dressing Miss Marie in traditional clothes. I'm sure she can put together something for you too."

Glowing with anticipation, Charlene came up to Marie. Eddie spoke to her in Paiute. With a slight glance toward Stephanie, Charlene curtsied and said, "Yes, both of them."

She laid her hand on Marie's shoulder and smiled at Stephanie. "Are you two ready? It takes a while to put a traditional dress together."

Stephanie picked at her ribbon.

Marie stood and smiled at Charlene. "I'm ready. Come along, Stephanie."

Eddie looked at his watch. "I need to get over to the stage and commence the tourist performance. Their show will take about two hours. We'll give them another hour to get out of here then we'll start the real ceremony."

228

He and the councilmen excused themselves, each with a shake of Herman's hand. Hector delayed a moment to say, "We can sign the title transfer as soon as the ceremony is over."

Herman smiled and shook Hector's hand again. "Looking forward to it."

**

Charlene made small talk and got terse responses while she led Marie and Stephanie through the stadium parking lot toward the village.

Stephanie held her hat in hand and continued to pluck at the ribbon. When they entered the lanes between homes, Marie snapped in exasperation, "Leave it alone."

Charlene looked at the hat. "You don't like it?" Then she snatched the hat and put it on. "I like it, the pink especially." She pushed her face at Marie and asked, "How do I look?"

The two warring friends broke into laughter.

"It does look good." Marie laughed and glanced at Stephanie.

Charlene took the hat off in a sweeping bow and said in a heavy Texas accent, "Now y'all come on down to our little festival and have yourselves a good time."

Stephanie pressed her hand against her stomach to suppress her giggles. Before either could launch into the awkward justifications for their behaviors, Charlene intervened, "Okay, we need to get moving. It does take a while to get you decked out. I do like the hat, though." She thrust it back to Stephanie.

"No, you keep it. You having it kind of binds us all together."

Charlene put it back on. "Tonight we are all becoming sisters, really, truly sisters in the eyes of the tribe."

At a nearby house a young woman poked her head out of the door and waved.

"Oh, that's Rose," Charlene explained. "She's going to help us."

"Two of them?" Rose asked, clapping her hands together. "I get the second one."

Charlene laughed. "She was jealous because I got to be in charge."

"Hurry," Rose said. "We haven't much time."

Giggles came from inside the house, and another woman peeked over Rose's shoulder.

229

"Actually," Charlene said, "this is really unusual. It's the first time a white person has come into the tribe since the Hendersons, and they were both men. Everyone wants to be involved. We have lots of help."

**

In geometric formations, the blinding stadium lights hovered against the night sky like alien spacecraft. Below them, the crackling loudspeaker announced the last performance of the evening. A group of young ladies dressed in native costume chattered excitedly while they exited a small residence and headed across the parking lot toward the stadium. They hurried, hoping to make it to the tent before the tourists swarmed the buses.

From the shadows a voice screamed, "You owe me a car, bitch!"

***

Not Left Behind

"Were they talking to us?" Rose asked. The Indian girls scanned the rows of parked cars and buses. Marie bit her lip and looked down. Stephanie locked her teeth and shook her head at Marie.

"They want me," Marie said without raising her head.

"Why?" Charlene focused her attention on the rapid crunch of feet that rushed from behind a lane of cars.

"An incident last week on your tribe's newly acquired property," Stephanie said, still staring at Marie.

Three men emerged from the shadows.

"Give her to us." Billy aimed his finger like a gun barrel at Marie. "The rest of you go on and do your cutesy hoop dances for the whiteys."

"We have a whole village of our people over there." Charlene pointed at the stadium. "You better leave."

The speakers in the stadium began to reverberate with drums and the chanting of people the girls wished were nearer.

Billy swung his hand toward the stadium. "They're busy kissing up to tourists. It's just you and us."

A heavy man with a big patch on the top of his head stepped out. "She wrecked my car." A baseball bat dangled from his fist.

230

More of Billy's henchmen emerged from between tourist buses. Two also had bats.

"Hey, girls." Billy's voice turned friendly. "She's my ex." He pointed to Marie. "I just want to talk to her about some stuff she stole from me. You all go ahead. She'll catch up after we chat."

The men advanced on all sides. Charlene scanned the lot for help. Not another soul was in sight. She bent and grabbed four large pebbles. "Rocks, girls, rocks!"

They each scooped up two or three lime-sized rocks.

"We've got a good women's softball team," Charlene said. "We'll crack a few skulls. After that it's fingernails, teeth, and six-inch hairpins. We don't give sisters up."

Billy menaced forward. "Don't be stupid, girl. She's a whitey, not one of ours. We'll just rough her up enough to teach whitey a lesson."

Stephanie rolled her rock back and forth, painting it with sweat from her palm. It felt awkward. She shifted the rock to her left hand and wiped her right hand on her deerskin skirt.

Her eye caught movement in the dim light between the buses. She peered into the shadows, hoping to see potential help.

Billy's men edged closer.

There the movement was again, the disappointing whiff of engine exhaust from a bus.

The motor is running.

She jumped forward. Her arm swung back and her feet danced in the sidestep stagger of a javelin thrower.

Billy's men stopped. Their eyes focused on the rock that flew from her hand, high in the lamplight and over their heads.

"Some softball team," one said. They all followed the rock's arc, waiting to see what damage it would cause when it descended.

A bus windshield exploded. Inside, the driver snapped out of his stupor, raising his hands, fingers spread, in front of his face.

"What the fuck!" he screamed. He flipped the headlights on. In front of him stood a knot of frightened women surrounded by a band of club-toting ruffians. He held his palm on the horn, blasting it nonstop. Club raised, one thug raced to the bus door and smashed it, then yanked it open. A moment later the horn went quiet.

**

Eddie paused and flipped a page of his script. An annoying bus horn filled the silence and continued unabated.

231

To Eddie's satisfaction, it stopped as suddenly as it had started. Then a desperate scream sent a chill down his spine. The voice belonged to Charlene Springwater.

Jim and Emil looked at each other. They raced from the stands, shouting and waving for others to follow.

Matt saw the commotion, then heard the sound. Derek vaulted from the stands and followed Jim and Emil.

A low mournful cry came from beyond the rows of cars. Jim rounded a bus. In the headlights he saw the women dressed for the festivities. One kneeled holding another's head in her lap.

"What happened?" Jim shouted.

"They came to take Marie," Stephanie said.

"Where is she?" Jim's eyes were frenzied.

Marie looked up, cradling a young Indian woman's head. Face wet with tears, she said, "They hit Rose."

**

The exhibition was over. The buses were gone. A few remaining tourists haggled over craft items. The shopkeepers began to box their wares.

Eddie left the press box, mentally checking his list, putting things in their place, locking cabinets, and powering systems down.

"Eddie Gomez?" a timid voice, one that was new to him, said from the doorway.

Eddie shut the electrical panel then studied the stranger in the doorway. An anemic man, insect eyes magnified behind Coke-bottle glasses, extended a microphone tentatively.

"Eddie Gomez?" he asked again.

"Yes, I'm Eddie, but I'm sorry, the ceremony is over. The press box is closed. If you're a reporter, come back tomorrow night; I'll be sure you have a good seat."

The man's face twisted into an antagonistic scowl. Like an assassin, his hand dropped to his waist and pressed a button on a box cinched there. It clicked. He waddled forward, thrusting the microphone like a bayonet.

His voice transformed into a booming baritone. "This is Jerry Palomino, San Fran's 666 Hipster Hot Radio, here live on the Palo Verde reservation north of Las Vegas, city of corporate sin.

"I'm speaking to Eddie Gomez, Paiute chairman, who stands accused of collusion with Haines Companies to steal tribal mineral rights. Yes, you heard me, Haines, the world's most criminal war contractor.

232

"Mr. Gomez, are you involved in secret Haines Companies manipulations?"

Eddie lurched back as if Jerry were indeed a giant insect. "What the hell are you saying? Get out of here! Now!" With the speed of a karate expert, Palomino jabbed his microphone into Eddie's chest, causing an electronic crackle. Sounding terrified, Jerry shouted, "Gomez has attempted to smash my mic."

Captain Lightfoot stepped into the booth. "Is there a problem?"

"The police are coming with billy clubs swinging," Jerry shouted into his mic. "I must run."

He squirreled out under Lightfoot's arm and bounced through the bleachers. "We will topple you corrupt bastards. You sold the Paiute birthright to corporate pigs. We'll bring you down, oink, oink. Tomorrow night, I'm exposing you on my broadcast from Camp Desert Sunrise."

"You okay, Eddie?" Lightfoot asked.

"Yeah, for now, but trouble's brewing. Rumor is those jokers are lobbying to recall the council. They've got their own slate, a bunch of ex-cons."

Lightfoot watched Jerry hurry across the football field, his distant voice shouting, "Ladies and gents, friends and neighbors, this is Jerry P-a-l-o-m-i-no in the Nevada high country for six-six-six h-i-p-s-t-e-r radio, where we don't report the news, we make the news." His little box clicked off and he vanished into the gray of the parking lot.

"They crossed the line when they attacked Rose. They'd better just leave." Lightfoot tapped the flap of his holster.

***

Panther Woman

Dimly lit by infrequent lampposts, the streets of Palo Verde were empty and quiet, except the medical center, where a group gathered around the bed of Rose Stoneflower. Her face pale and drawn, Rose grasped Stephanie's arm. "I'm sorry. I was supposed to be your guide." She glanced at the heavy cast on her right upper arm. "I can't go to the Toad Mountains wearing this artificial thing."

Not understanding Rose's meaning, Stephanie laid her hand on top of Rose's. "You've done so much already. I can't believe you went through the ceremony with a broken arm."

233

Derek touched Stephanie's shoulder. "It's time."

Rose smiled then released Stephanie's arm. "Blessed be your path."

Stephanie let her fingers linger on Rose's. "I'll visit you in the morning."

Rose waved weakly; then her eyes fluttered and shut.

Outside, diagonally across the street, Charlene held the reins of two horses. She beckoned Stephanie to her.

Derek stepped between them and took Stephanie's hand. "Did you notice that your dress is simpler than the other ladies'?"

Stephanie blushed. "It's okay; I knew they hadn't planned on me being in the ceremony."

Derek chuckled. "It's not that way. Your dress is old school, made from natural materials using natural tools, no metal, no synthetic. Your dress is very special. It's what a young woman wears when she is to receive her blessing from Panther Woman. You are the first to wear the design of the morning people." He pointed to Charlene. "She is your guide."

Stephanie swallowed. Her mouth didn't work.

Board meetings, acquisition plans, things scheduled for tomorrow. Tomorrow? How many days are required to receive a blessing? I'm not prepared. I don't know how to prepare.

The thoughts flew through her mind, circling and reemerging. She glanced at Charlene, whose eyes pulled at her.

Stephanie looked down. "Why me?"

"Two decades ago Panther Woman told me to deliver you to her."

Stephanie frowned. "How could that be? I was a child in Nebraska twenty years ago."

"You were not a child when I saw you. You were a lioness defending her cub. Now go. Panther Woman has called you."

Energy radiated inside Stephanie. She took a step toward Charlene, then turned to Derek. "Tell Herman—"

"He already knows."

**

They rode a moonlit trail that crossed under Highway 375.

Charlene pointed southward to the silvered slopes of Toad Mountain. "We'll get there after sunrise." Charlene then raised her face to the star-splattered universe. In the pale light she and her horse floated on the landscape like ghosts. Goose bumps rippled across Stephanie's skin. She tried to turn Charlene's image back into a person, but the light and shadows shifted, keeping the scene surreal.

Stephanie's temples tingling, she conjectured that Panther Woman had already twisted the world into an alternative reality.

She ran her fingers through the mane of her horse. The hairs slid over her palms like strings of diamonds. She held her arm before her face. The leather fringes on her sleeve shimmered like thin strips of silver. In an instant, she expected the horses to lift them to the stars.

"Modern things like flashlights and guns are forbidden. Everything we have with us"—Charlene's arm drew a circle around them—"was made the old way, with Paleolithic tools."

Stephanie looked up. "The night sky is so magical. Only when darkness blocks our world can we see the immensity beyond and wonder what it holds."

Herman had told her. It wasn't all good.

Charlene raised her hand as if to touch the pale orb. "The Harvest Festival is always at full moon. After each festival, women are sent to seek Panther Woman's blessings. She only blesses women."

"But," Stephanie said, "Matt saw the panther once, and I heard Derek—"

"Derek?" Charlene burst into laughter. "The old shaman, Charles Stagskull, told him not to hunt in the Toad Mountains. He did anyway, because he wanted to win the hand of Lotti Claymaker by giving a big deer to her clan.

"He wounded an enormous one. Of course, it was a spirit deer." Charlene filled her voice with disgust. "Then he tracked it through the winding ravines and accidentally wandered into the spirit canyon. He fell asleep on a flat rock and was awakened by smelly, warm liquid running down his neck. Panther Woman peed on him for violating the sacred valley; then she cursed him. The only way he could counter the spell was to become her shaman."

"It sounds like he was tricked," Stephanie said.

"Tricked or not, men shouldn't go into the canyon. If they do, they always pay dearly. Derek will pay. Matt will too."

Charlene's words lingered in Stephanie's thoughts. Finally Stephanie asked, "How many women have you guided to Panther Woman?"

"You are my first. The time before, I was the seeker."

235

"Oh?" Stephanie's tone begged for more information.

Charlene clicked her tongue against her teeth. "What each receives is not to be shared."

"I'm sorry that I asked. This is so strange for me. I'm grasping to make sense of it."

"Maybe it's better if it doesn't make sense." Charlene arched her hand toward the sky. "Let's enjoy the moonlight and ride in silence."

**

Early rays warmed the rim of the Toad Mountains. Stephanie chewed a slice of dried apple, letting it mix with her saliva until it tasted fresh and sweet. Beside her, Charlene crushed leaves and bark with a stone metate. Then the sun's rays flashed over the mountain and bathed them in light.

Charlene closed her eyes and let the sunlight pour onto her face. "It takes the chill off."

Sighing in contentment, Stephanie imitated her. They indulged in the sun's warmth until Charlene broke it off and pointed across an arroyo to a wind-hollowed cave.

Stephanie could see pectoglyphs carved in the lacquer at the cave's entrance and on boulders below it.

"It is the initiation point for my sister line," Charlene said.

"The cave faces west," Stephanie said.

"Yes, so that the sun will warm you before you enter the dark realm."

"But Derek said I am from the morning people. Wouldn't west facing make me an evening person?"

Charlene looked toward some willows in the arroyo. "First, we'll tie our horses in the shade. They'll have grass and a pool of water there. Once they're set, we'll go to the cave. Tonight when I prepare you, I will speak of the morning people."

**

Stephanie adjusted her grip on a bundle of mesquite branches and pushed herself ten more steep steps up the slope to the cave. She dropped the wood next to Charlene, who daintily placed a handful of pine needles and herbs into a small pot that had begun to boil.

236

Stephanie collapsed onto a woven mat in the shade. "I didn't encounter scorpions or rattlesnakes." Her words came slowly from her dry mouth.

Charlene stirred the leaves. "Of course not, you have been under her protection since we left the village."

Stephanie held out her dust-covered arms. "I'm filthy. It doesn't seem right to go on a quest this way."

"Very soon." Charlene peered to the west. The shadow cast by the setting sun cut across her cheekbones. "All will be ready and we will go to a spring in the canyon above. You will bathe, and I will dress you. Then you will go into the darkness, alone."

Charlene leaned away from her small fire. "The morning people."

"Oh, yes," Stephanie said, "I'd forgotten about that."

Charlene held a finger to her lips, silencing the interruption. "The morning people came from the rising sun, east."

Stephanie turned her finger toward herself and emitted a long musical, "Oh, so I am a morning person."

"Yes and no. The morning people came long, long ago, when mountains of ice still crushed the land. Our people met them here and together they all lived as one people for a time. Then a disease spread among them and most of the morning people died. Panther Woman, their matron, went into the Toad to morn. She secluded herself in the sacred canyon and cried until only her spirit remained. They say when she comes out of the valley again, she will bring all the people of Earth together."

Charlene pulled Stephanie up by her wrists. "But now you must prepare to meet her."

**

Stephanie stood naked in the golden sunset. She closed her eyes and luxuriated in the prickle of the spring water evaporating from her skin. Charlene stood behind her, brushing her hair with a tortoiseshell comb. Then, fingers flying, she weaved eagle feathers into the strands until they formed a crowning arch across Stephanie's head.

"Look!" Charlene held Stephanie's ceremonial dress up.

Stephanie slid her fingers under the downy feathers Charlene had tied along the sleeves' fringes. "It's beautiful."

"It is," Charlene agreed. "Put it on and look at yourself in the pool while there's still light."

With the sun's rays retreating from the canyon, and evening shadows stretching across the land in puddles of purple and blue, Stephanie peered into the water. Blurred by ripples, a tan face formed and changed with every disturbance: blue eyes, high cheekbones, feathers fanning from golden locks, smooth skin, wrinkled skin, braided locks capped with an animal skin, fierce penetrating eyes…

***

Chapter 18: The Blessing

Darkness came. Light from Charlene's fire flickered on the nearby rocks. Charlene lifted the lid of her small pot and tested the liquid with her finger, then took a sip. She contemplated a moment then handed the teapot to Stephanie and said, "You don't have a context for this. I'm going to break the law. I'm going to tell you about my quest."

Charlene stood and shouted up the ravine. "Forgive me, Mother, but she is not one of us. She doesn't know what to expect."

Charlene squatted by the fire. "More, drink more." When Stephanie gulped twice, Charlene laughed. "Leave some for me."

Stephanie handed the pot back.

Charlene took a long drink. "My path began with an enchanted moon, like last night. Everything from the mountain slopes to the tiny mesquite leaves became jewels under it.

"I started right here." Charlene pointed to the rock she sat on. "And I went up this canyon." She pointed to the dark vee in the mountainside. "You will start here and go there. After that your path will become different from any other. Yet, as with everyone, it will lead to the sacred valley.

"My path started with a walk up a gentle floor that seemed never ending until the fox twins appeared before me. I followed them to their burrow, a bore in a rock wall. It was so tiny that I shudder at the memory of it." She held her hand out to prove her point. She pulled it back and, hugging herself, rocked side to side.

Stephanie pulled her knees to her chest. "I understand. You don't have to tell me more."

239

"I do!" Charlene snapped.

Stephanie reached out and stroked her hair. Charlene pushed her hand away, then at the last instant, grasped it and held it.

"I had no choice but to enter that small hole, but the smallness and coldness of it chilled my bones and turned my stomach sick. Without a ray of light, I crawled further and further. The foxes and their reputation for treachery plagued me. My heart drummed into the rock that surrounded me. There was no escape. I could only go deeper. I remembered all my failures to family and tribe, and thought Panther Woman would let me die as a warning to others.

"Already certain I would never escape, I went on, no longer thinking, just going. Then it opened. I could stand. In front of me, the moon shimmered on the rocks. I took four steps, and the world ripped like a wall of water, and I stood in the spirit canyon.

"I can't tell more. Know that you will be tested. Don't fear death; don't give up."

The moon broke over the canyon wall. Charlene squeezed Stephanie's hand. "Go now." She wrapped her arms around herself. Swaying, she began to chant.

**

Under the pale light, the stones on the valley floor became a trail of gems, broken here and there by cacti sculptured from crystal.

Stephanie let herself absorb it and she went on.

The canyon narrowed. Ahead, the glassy cliffs boxed in on all sides. Dreading Charlene's tunnel, she tensed. She glanced from rock to rock, expecting the foxes to appear. A stub on a nearby branch twisted and winked at her.

She flung her hand up to cover her gasp.

Two eyes stared out of the limb.

"Hoot, hoot," the limb whistled.

Stephanie's heart pounded. The skin of her scalp and face tingled.

It's an owl...

She lifted her hand toward him. He fluttered his wings and flew over her shoulder and down the canyon. He skimmed low and into a cottonwood.

She pursued him through the brush, but he disappeared when she got there. The hoot came again, this time from within the cliff wall a few feet away. She pushed her palm forward, reaching for

240

the stone. It touched only air. She stepped forward, extending her hands to feel the space. The light changed and she saw a narrow schism that cut through the rock.

Her heart accelerated.

She turned sideways and forced her way into the narrow slit. Blackness wiped away all sight. She felt in front of her and inched forward, time after time, until her mind lost continuity as if she were in a dream.

Finally, a vertical blue wedge cut the blackness. She jammed her body between the stone surfaces and wiggled toward it.

Around her, black turned to gray blue. Ahead the cliffs danced with violets and blues. Farther on, fiery oranges and reds flickered across them.

A campfire, she thought, first pleased, then frightened. *Poachers, evil men violating the sanctity of the valley.*

She pressed her back against the wall and lowered into a squat. Her hands bracing against the ground, she took rapid panicked breaths.

I must confront them.

They'll kill me. Rape me.

Her fingers wrapped around a rock.

Fist-sized, a hammer.

Her other hand fumbled over the ground.

A root.

She raised it. She dropped the stone and felt the length of the stick. Its end formed a bulky mass that entangled a water-smoothed rock.

A natural club.

She took it in her right hand and tested its weight with a low, easy swing. She crawled toward the campfire, keeping a large boulder between her and it.

Burning logs crackled. Flames reflected on nearby rocks. She took a deep breath. Her head buzzed.

The low hum of voices filled the air. It grew louder. *"Ka too shi maaanaaa."* It vibrated like a giant pipe organ. *"Nama! Na! Nama Na! Nama Na!"*

Shivers ran through her body. Blood roared in her ears. She laid her war club against her left shoulder and stood.

She had arrived.

**

People stood to the right and to the left of a pathway that led to a platform where a woman sat on a throne of pelts. The fur of a lion flowed over her shoulders, its mouth framing her head with two long fangs. Turquoise joclas hung from her neck.

She raised her arms. The hymn silenced.

"Arise," she said, "the mother of the morning people has come."

Paleolithic people stood, those on the left differing from the right.

Stephanie approached and saw that like Charlene, Panther Woman was a mixture of both.

Stephanie kneeled before her.

"Arise. From me you have come, and beside me you shall stand; I, mother of the Earth people, and you, mother of the sky beings. I am the beginning; you, the end."

Panther Woman raised Stephanie to her feet.

Suddenly they were alone. The fire was gone. The moonlight spilled over them. The being led Stephanie to the throne, and they sat side by side.

Through the night, Panther Woman taught her of the two peoples: the morning people who came from the east in leather boats, ever following the ice cap until they came to land; the western people walking, ever following the ice cap over the land bridge. Both worked their way across the continent, generation after generation.

They met near there, each strange to the other, each clearly human and a potential ally in a land of dangers. They intermarried and combined skills to produce new technologies, one of those is called the Folsom point by modern people.

When dawn colored the horizon, the Paleolithic spirit gave Stephanie her blessing: "Through you, mother of children, shall come the blessing to kindred who inhabit the sky. You did not bear the first child to whom you already have given life, but through her they all shall be saved."

Light softened the edge of the canyon wall.

"Be courageous and hunt thy destiny with a vengeance. Know that I will precede you, and your enemies will fall before me, but remember, be wise in all things, for I cannot protect my beloved from her own folly."

Panther Woman withdrew a flint-tipped fang from her headdress. She pulled Stephanie's left arm toward her and cut. The

242

pain scorched Stephanie's flesh and into her neck. The flint slashed five times, carving a bloody star.

Panther Woman's arm carried the same symbol. The sun broke the canyon rim. Stephanie raised her face to the sky and took the first breath of her new life. When she looked back, Panther Woman was gone.

***

Marie's Hope

At 6 p.m., Stephanie poured hydrogen peroxide into her wound and dressed it, then stripped and crawled into bed. Twelve hours later, she rose, threw on sweat clothes and walked out of her bedroom.

"Good morning."

Wearing a silky multicolored robe, Marie stood in the vertex of the two huge picture windows. "It's like I'm floating over the city." She raised her yellow and burgundy sleeve to point at the mountains. "I'm level with the peaks."

"I forgot you were here," Stephanie said.

"You slept for twelve hours straight. That quest must have been something."

"Beyond words."

"There's fresh coffee. I made it rather than have Piero send some up the dumbwaiter. I've become wary since our escapade in it."

"Wow." Stephanie studied Marie's robe. "It's like a priestess's or fantasy princess's."

Marie held her arm up. "Yeah, kind of a Japanese kimono with futuristic symbols. Herman had it made."

A tear dripped from the corner of her eye and streaked her cheek. "It makes me sad and happy at once. When I wear it, I feel protected, at least I imagine I am."

"It's beautiful," Stephanie said.

Marie stood and twirled, fanning it out. The sleeves were adorned with intertwined blue and gold helixes, the lapels displayed interlinked circles, gold alternating with cobalt blue. The back portrayed a woman on horseback, a spear in one hand and shield in the other.

Stephanie stared then shook her head as if awakening. "It's beyond words." She poured herself a cup of coffee and headed for the door. "I need to talk to Herman. I've been gone too long and feel panicked a bit."

"Tell him I fixed all the security issues. Found a few others too." Marie refilled her cup and rushed up beside Stephanie. "I'll walk with you. I'm headed back to my apartment."

They walked in silence awhile. Marie's face radiated a sense of joy. "Hey," she whispered, "what do you think of Jim?"

Stephanie's mind balked. "You're still fixed on him?"

Marie's face filled with joy. "Surprised you, huh? Surprised myself, too."

"I think he likes you." Stephanie turned away and headed for the library.

**

Stephanie found Herman asleep by the stacks, which meant he was really running simulations about this person or that situation. He opened his eyes as she approached and smiled as if he had been waiting for her.

She signaled him to one of the soundproof booths. When he shut the door, she lipped, "Is this room bugged?"

He pointed to the light and the edge of the table and, with a slash motion across his throat, indicated that he had removed them. "She's bugged everything," he said the way a doctor would speak about a difficult patient.

"Why?"

"It's Horace's influence. If I had understood humans better, I would never have let her spend so much time with him during her formative years."

Stephanie's face grew furious. "Speaking of her early years, it's time you told her the truth."

Herman flinched his eyes away.

"Why is it so difficult with you?" she demanded.

Herman held his palms up. "You saw how violent she can be."

Stephanie shook her head at him. "You know more than you're saying. You need to get it in the open so she can see where her anger comes from. Then she could deal with it. Trust her."

Herman's face became sober. "It's not that simple."

At an impasse, they stared at each other.

Stephanie took the lead. "She told me that some woman brought her to your office. Why doesn't she remember more?"

244

Herman sighed. "You need to hear it all, and you'll be the one who explains it to her."

Stephanie scrunched her face in disbelief. "Why me? You're her father!"

Herman turned his fingers toward himself. "Me? I think we need someone with a bit more human sensitivity. Also it needs to be a woman."

Stephanie tossed her head. "Are you saying that because she's a lesbian? If I were a lesbian, would you say I'm unfit to be CEO?"

Herman seemed perplexed. "It's not that she's a lesbian; it's that she is Amazonian."

The words swirled nonsensically in Stephanie's head. "What did you say? Amazonian, like mythology?"

"No, like women who live on the planet Amazonia."

Stephanie raised her eyebrows. "Real live Amazons from the planet Amazonia. Have you short-circuited?"

"I assure you she is. I tested her DNA. I could have told her that long ago. But terrible memories might flow into her mind if I did."

"What things?"

Herman shook his head. "You don't want to know."

Stephanie snarled then chuckled sarcastically. "But you will tell me anyway, because you've appointed me to enlighten her."

Herman nodded. "I'm sorry."

Stephanie crossed her arms and rolled her eyes. "Go on. The quick version, please."

"She escaped to Earth from a Verg slave ship."

Stephanie wailed in exasperation. "Verg? Slave ship? In space? There is no quick version to this story, is there?"

"Correct." Herman explained everything he knew about Marie's escape, which was a lot.

When he finished, Stephanie said, "These Verg are despicable. No wonder she washed her memory of them."

"Yes, they are evil, but more hideous things happened to her and her sister after they landed here, things humans did."

Stephanie's face flushed.

Herman waited. She signaled him to continue. "Her sister was murdered by homicidal pedophiles at the Wild Horse Rest Stop near Las Vegas."

Stephanie laid her hand against her forehead. "Oh God." She refused to accept what he had said. She balled her hands into fists. "How do you know?"

He bristled. "The evidence is extensive and my analysis was thorough."

"Convince me," she demanded.

"At the time, I handled Horace's Vegas land acquisitions. That office stood right here, where the Black Lava is now.

"One month and three days after we opened, a woman showed up, asserting that she had rescued an Amazonian child from a highway rest stop near here. She left Marie and proof of her claim with my secretary."

Stephanie interrupted. "So a woman delivered Marie to the only alien on the planet. That can't be an accident."

"You're right. I have no idea how she found me. Many of the realtors we worked with had difficulty finding our offices."

"What evidence did she leave?" Stephanie asked.

"Marie's Verg slave garments and a note that said: 'Marie and another Amazonian girl dropped to Earth near the Wild Horse Rest Stop. The other girl, whom Marie calls Vicky, was brutally murdered. You can verify this with the highway patrol.

"'In the sack are the slave garments Marie was wearing when I found her. Test them and test her DNA. It will prove my claim.

"'For obvious reasons, you are the only one whom I can entrust her to. Don't try to track me.'

"At first I thought Horace had gotten one of his starlets to pull a prank, but the smock in the sack was made of extraterrestrial material.

"I checked with the highway patrol. Indeed a young Jane Doe, about age thirteen, had been assaulted and murdered at the rest stop. She was described as wearing an old smock of gray material. Of course, they never figured out that the material didn't exist on Earth. And, of course, I checked Marie's DNA.

"I eventually located the escape pod they used to come to Earth. Actually, I found two pods. I hid both in the Henderson Mine. For years, I've assumed the mystery woman was also Amazonian and had commandeered two escape capsules, one for the two girls and one for herself."

Stephanie clinched her fist into a white-knuckled knot. "Terrible. Escape from slavery to have your sister murdered by humans." She flinched as if slapped. "Then have your mother abandon you? What kind of woman would do that?"

Herman cupped his chin in his hand. "For years I expected the woman to return. Now I know why she didn't."

"Why?" Stephanie hissed.

Herman pointed toward the seventh-floor exit. "When I heard Kit did that, I went back to the mine and gave the pods a thorough inspection. I found this."

Herman held a gray disk in the palm of his hand.

"What is it?" Stephanie reached out, but he pulled the object back.

"I believe it is a recharger for the plasma device Kit used to destroy the door."

"God." Stephanie lowered her head and laid both arms on the table.

Herman stood. "Messy, isn't it?" He opened the door to leave.

"Wait," Stephanie said. "What day was the Amazonian teenager murdered?"

"It was March 12, 1951. The highway patrol estimated that she died about 6:30 a.m."

"When did the mystery woman bring Marie to your office?"

"Two days later."

Stephanie frowned. "Maybe the mother came in the first module with the girls?"

Herman shook his head. "The modules are designed for one adult. The mother would have endangered all their lives by coming with the children. An Amazonian would never do that."

"So how—"

"Never mind, it's past," Herman said. "Figure out how to tell Marie." Herman dropped the disk into his pocket. "I'll deal with Kit."

**

Back in her apartment, Marie switched off the hidden microphone that Herman had missed. She stood to a half-crouch and screamed. She took the edge of her desk and flung it on its side, then yanked out drawers one by one and slammed them against the wall.

Emptied of emotion, she sank down. Staring into nothingness, she whispered, "My dear mama, I know you will come for me. I know you will."

***

Return to France

Manny sat in the security trailer, his elbows braced on the control panel to stabilize his powerful binoculars. Across the valley, the camp of hippies and NAS Indians grew daily, and sure as Jim had said, the sacks of garbage so dutifully managed at first were now open and their contents scattering across the landscape.

Manny glanced to his side. "I don't like it, Mr. Herman. They're disrespecting the Paiutes, and the hotshots bully the others, too."

Herman patted Manny's shoulder. "If they jeopardize our stuff, then mobilize the Haines SWAT team; otherwise just keep the Paiute Police informed. They'll deal with it in their own time."

Marie came up behind Herman. "Manny, if you have any problem, use the direct link to Bob, he'll send someone to help, or I'll come out. Just don't open the door to an outsider."

Herman pointed to a Haines SUV pulling into the parking compound surrounded by an Inca wall. "Here comes everyone now."

Marie went outside to meet them on the walkway. As they all entered the command trailer, she pulled Herman aside. "Why is Jim here?"

Herman looked away.

"You're taking him, aren't you?"

"I'll need his help," Herman said.

Marie threw her hands up. "Why? He doesn't have a stake in this."

"We all have a stake in this."

Marie knotted his shirt sleeve in her fingers. "You've only tested that machine once with one person. Now you're going to take three back?"

"I've figured it out. Look, Marie, this träger is the shock force for a Vergish takeover of Earth. By stopping him we stop them."

248

Marie's jaws clenched. She snapped out her words. "Take me, then. I'm an Amazon, right? Whatever the fuck that is, it doesn't belong here."

"Marie, you shouldn't have listened in."

"Oh, it's okay to tell Stephanie that I'm a psycho and that she's my caretaker. I'm just not supposed to listen in."

Herman studied her grip on his sleeve, then looked into her eyes. "I was trying to protect you."

Marie released his shirt and shoved his arm. "From myself, I suppose. You're taking me with you. God knows what I'll do here left on my own."

Herman reached out for her hand. "I need you here—in case I don't come back. You'll need to help Stephanie—"

"Oh, precious Stephanie." Marie snickered derisively.

"And Emil and Charlene and all your sisters and anyone else you can protect. I'm afraid the Vergs are planning another attempt on Earth." He lowered his voice. "They were close by. That's how you got here."

Marie locked her jaws and shook her head in tight little jerks. "Don't take Jim," she said.

Herman didn't respond. She ran back into the bunkroom, locking the door behind her.

"Emil's already down there. You two go ahead," Herman said to Jim and Matt. "I need to talk to Stephanie."

After the others got on the elevator, Herman shut the soundproof door between the security center and the research lab. He approached Stephanie.

"Obviously we'll stop this träger. History bears out that Earth was never invaded by the Vergs."

"That assumes he was a träger," Stephanie interjected.

Herman's face pleaded with her to listen. "In any case, you know how she came here…"

Stephanie frowned. "She? You mean Marie? Can you just use her name? You know, like she's your daughter or something."

"Marie," Herman started anew, "is on the warpath."

"So?"

"So she listened in again. She's probably listening now…"

Stephanie's frown deepened. "I'm sorry, but I'm with her on that. You should have told her long ago."

"May I continue?" Herman raised his voice. "The fact that she most certainly escaped from a Verg slave ship near Earth is quite

249

ominous, particularly when coupled with this sixteenth-century träger. It implies a long-term Vergish effort to subjugate Earth.

"In any case, if the Vergs come while we're in the sixteenth century, you and Marie must save your tribe and any others you can. Use this station as a stronghold..."

Stephanie felt her insides sink. "You think you won't make it back."

"It's possible some of us won't make it back."

Stephanie swallowed. "This is scary."

"Not scarier than the homegrown monsters you have on this planet," Marie said from behind them. She was strapping on a .45 pistol.

Stephanie took a deep breath. "I'm glad you're here."

Marie glared at Herman. "Go on downstairs and brief your assault team. We'll take care of this end." Her face softened and she swallowed. "Bring everyone home, including yourself, Papa."

**

"This looks like a Sunday school classroom." Jim stood in the door of the newly created SAM briefing center.

After seeing boardroom dramas on American TV, Emil knew that the Naugahyde sofa and roller chair did not belong in a real conference room, even for a surreptitious project. He glared at Jim. "It's not finished, *pendejo*. It will have ergonomic chairs, a conference table, and electronic—"

"Okay, okay." Jim's face flushed under his brown skin. "I'll just take my ergonomic chair." He sat in one of the folding chairs. "And watch the fancy presentation on the electronic screen." He raised his hand toward a flipchart that sat atop a wobbly tripod.

Emil hissed and shook his head, then burst into a laugh. "Okay, you come back alive and maybe you can help finish this thing."

"Of course I'm coming back alive. Who would beat you at poker if I didn't?"

Herman entered the room. Matt jumped to his feet and clapped his hands together. "Okay, let's settle down. We've got a lot to go over, and our lives depend on getting it right."

Jim and Emil stared deadpan at Matt.

"First thing," Jim said, "is you are going to cut the happy talk. This is shit any way you cut it. So no bullshit esprit de corps crap."

250

Herman thrust his chin toward Emil. "I've trained Emil to operate the SAM. He will manage the injection and extraction."

Emil took the cue to outline his role. "We have two issues. First, the SAM has limited capacity. The second is time tunnels. They, like mine tunnels, have to be separated by enough distance so they don't collapse and kill the people in them." He glanced to Herman, who nodded.

"Therefore, you'll be dispatched at twelve-hour intervals. Your arrival points are dispersed over a five-kilometer radius to further reduce the possibility of a time tunnel collapse. The same pattern will be used to bring you back."

Herman looked from face to face. "If anyone is interested in the complex analysis of time tunnels, I'll conduct a seminar when we return. Now Matt will tell us about the situation in the region."

"Okay," Matt said. "Our gathering point is a huge oak on a knoll about ten kilometers from Sèvres. From there we will proceed about one kilometer to a cave where I believe my pistols are hidden."

The discussion went on to exhaustion, over four hours, during which Matt insisted that he take another gun. Herman staunchly refused, saying that Jim, a responsible person, would take the staff, Herman having configured it into a laser saber. Herman and Jim would maintain the group's safety until Matt recovered his guns.

Next Herman explained how the SAM would locate them for extraction. "We each will carry a transponder that gives x,y,z,t coordinates of our location in time and space. Immediately after the Battle of Coutras, the SAM will start pulling us out in twelve-hour intervals."

"What if we haven't neutralized Morto Sacude yet?" Matt asked.

"Thanks for asking, Matt," Herman said. "I will place a code in my transponder, which the SAM will read before beginning extraction. If our mission is complete, the code will be all 0s, If we have not finished, then the code will be of the form '#ddmmyyyyladmmsslodmmss,' giving the number of us still living (#), a new date for our departure, and a location in degrees, minutes, and seconds of latitude and longitude."

"What if we're scattered all over the place?" Jim asked.

"The SAM will begin at the coded extraction point and work outward in space and time until it finds us."

Jim turned to Emil. "Little brother, you think it will work?"

251

Emil shrugged his shoulders. "I took a transponder back to the 1850s and shipped it in a railway car. SAM found it 400 miles from its start point."

"You went back?" Jim asked.

"Yeah, to test it. I'm not going to do something I didn't test." Emil shrugged his shoulders like it was no big deal.

Someone knocked. Stephanie peeked in. "We've flown in food from Piero. Come up top and eat with us."

**

Stephanie, Charlene and Marie placed platters of barbequed steaks, fries, and chili beans on the bunkroom table, then dashed back to retrieve a cooler full of wine, beer, and other drinks.

Herman took Stephanie's arm. "Charlene?"

Stephanie grabbed two beers without looking at him. "Emil will be isolated in the SAM control center while you're gone. He should spend some time with her now."

Marie picked up a plate and went straight to Jim and asked, "What would you like?"

Jim took another plate. "What do you want?" They filled each other's plates.

Holding a plate out, Stephanie nudged Matt and said, "Hey, Matt, what do you want?"

His eyes watered. He put his mouth close to her ear and whispered, "You."

Stephanie gulped. "Okay, let's start with dinner. Then you get back safely, and we'll work on that idea."

Against Herman's protest and to Manny's alarm, they all carried their plates outside and sat on the boulders overlooking the valley and Camp Desert Sunrise.

***

Chapter 19: Everyone Gone

Barnard gave Annette the best horse, and now she led by a hundred meters. Over her shoulder, she could see a royalist closing in on Barnard. She feared he would be killed. Even lying flat against the neck of a galloping horse, she felt herself tense at the sound of the pistol. She turned her head to see small puffs of dust as the lead ball skipped up the road and past her. Barnard was still in the saddle and in front of his closest pursuer. The other four soldiers, by the grace of God, had fallen far behind.

Her horse's legs flashed with its stride unbroken by the steep incline of the hill. At the top, the huge oak beckoned her. Her mind drifted to the day she'd found Matt and Barnard sleeping there. She feared that today the old oak would not be able to save Barnard and her, but she would give it a try.

She wheeled around the tree and out of sight. Her pistols were empty. She looked around for anything to use as a weapon. A two-meter-long dead branch dangled from the tree.

A lance.

It dangled by a sliver of bark. She grabbed it with both hands and yanked. Its rough surface tore into her palms. Cursing, she yanked again. It broke free. Crooked and brittle, it would not withstand much force, but it would be enough. She cradled it like a spear and waited with heels ready to dig into her mount's flanks.

Beyond the tree, the frantic rhythm of hooves grew louder.

Barnard peeled off the road and passed her.

She braced her weapon.

"Annette! Get in here!"

Her mouth dropped. Her mind spun. *Matt here? I must be crazy.*

The royalist rounded the tree. The horse's reins in his mouth, he held a sword in one hand and a pistol in the other. Branch aimed at his neck, she spurred her mount. He dodged aside then, with a sadistic grin, swung his pistol barrel toward her.

The blur of a large brown man leaped through the air and knocked him from his horse. The pistol fell to the ground without firing. The brown man bashed the soldier's head with a stone. The royalist quivered then lay still.

Annette grabbed the dead man's pistol then rolled under the branches toward the trunk of the tree. Inside the canopy she came face to face with Matt. He pulled her to her feet.

Barnard and Jim slid in beside them.

More hoofbeats approached. The second pursuer leaped to the ground near his fallen comrade. He thrashed his saber through the dense oak branches, cutting his way to the heart of their refuge.

He leveled his sword at them. Barnard and Matt shielded Annette. A third royalist arrived and was battering his way toward them.

Annette watched from behind Barnard's shoulder. With a grunt she cocked the dead man's gun and shot the second royalist in his throat. He flung backward to the ground.

"Get his sword," she said.

The third man entered their refuge.

"Ahhhhh," Jim yelled and rushed forward, holding the staff at low guard.

"Get the sword." Annette pushed Barnard toward the weapon while keeping an eye on the unequal duel of a rod against a sword.

The Frenchman snickered at Jim.

Beyond the tree, a fourth soldier arrived and called tentatively, "Francis, Michael?" Then came the sharp clicks of two pistol hammers being pulled back.

"Tejon, in here," his compatriot urged.

Tejon emitted a shriek that ended with a loud dry snap. Francis sliced his saber through the air. Jim jumped away. Quickly the soldier stepped forward with a thrust. Annette opened her mouth to scream. Before she could, Jim whirled the staff. A red line etched across the sword, and half of the blade fell smoldering to the ground.

Francis's face stared at his blade in confusion. Jim whipped the staff back, cutting the man's sword arm off at the elbow.

254

Blood shot out. Francis gripped his stub. His eyes rolled back and he plowed forehead first to the ground.

Above them, a heavy object crashed through branches, slowing with each collision until Tejon's broken body plopped onto a thick limb above Annette's head.

The leaves and branches on the outside of the canopy rustled and cracked. Annette raised her reloaded pistol.

"No," Matt shouted and shoved the barrel to the side. "He is our friend."

Herman emerged.

Annette fell on her knees in front of Jim and kissed his hand. "Thank you, thank you. Without you, Barnard and I would be dead."

Herman shook his head in disbelief. "Matt has that strange ability to be at the right place at the right time."

Annette scowled at Matt.

He smiled back. "Oddly, we did arrive just in time to help you."

Annette put her hands on her hips, her elbows jutting outward. "Oh, really? You who gallivanted off, leaving Barnard to explain your disappearance to King Charles?"

Barnard laughed. "It's the past, Annette. Matt, you did put Luc and me in a quandary. Luc worked it out, though. He told the king, 'Matt walked off a cliff and vanished beneath the ocean's waves. Remember what a whoring drunk he was? He missed your sister's wedding because of it.'"

"Charles found that quite humorous."

"And Henri?" Matt asked.

"You said he would escape and he did. Annette and I are camped with his army near Coutras."

"Good, we've come to join him." Herman extended his hand. "My name is Herman McGuiness. This is Manado, the Native American ambassador to Queen Elizabeth. He and I have come to defeat Morto Sacude."

Annette looked up at Tejon's limp body. "Based on this, you might have a chance."

"If Henri is at Coutras, then why are you here?" Matt asked.

"To get your guns." Annette began to rifle through the pockets of the first soldier.

"My guns are still here?"

"I figured them out." Annette gave him a defiant look.

Matt's face went pale.

255

Her eyes laughed at him. "I was going to use them, but Jules V. said I should keep them hidden. They are in my family's secret cave. It has remained undetected for more than two thousand years."

"Let's get them now, then," Herman said.

"It is not so easy." Barnard nodded toward the dead bodies. "These men and others ambushed us about two miles back. The countryside is swarming with soldiers from the Spanish League."

Annette checked Tejon's body. "We should strip these dead. We can wear their uniforms and perhaps slip to Coutras without being detected."

She flung Tejon to the ground and pulled off his jacket. "Barnard, Matt, and I can use their uniforms." She pulled at the soldier's waistband. "Ah, a short dagger, perfect for a woman."

The branches rustled and Jim led the horses under the canopy. Annette studied him and Herman. "We'll never find uniforms big enough for either of you, unless we can steal one from Morto—but his would be big enough for both of you."

She pointed to Jim. "He is very quiet."

"He doesn't speak French," Matt said.

"All help is welcome." She threw Francis's jacket in Matt's face. "Put it on."

She sized Jim up. "Manado is okay like he is. They will either think he is a mulatto or an Aztec. Most likely a mulatto, because he doesn't have the hideous tattoos."

Jim frowned at Matt. "What did she say?"

"She said that we'll pretend you're an Aztec."

Jim's eyes went cold. "I hate those bastards. They sent war parties to capture my people to sacrifice to their gods."

Mat shrugged his shoulders. "Well, you can pretend to be one until we get past the royalist guards."

"What did he say?" Annette asked.

"Aztecs killed his people."

Annette stood up and brushed her hands off. One palm oozed blood from the branch she ripped from the tree. "They follow the Spanish onto the battlefield and execute our wounded. They smash men's skulls and eat the brains. Others chop heads off and bathe in the flowing blood. All of this blood and matter cakes on them until they stink like vultures. Demons from hell." She nodded toward Jim. "Tell him he can take revenge for his people at Coutras."

"Four guards and one prisoner..." She put on Tejon's hat. It flopped down over her eyes. "I need to tighten it up." She retrieved a sewing bundle from her saddlebag. She sat on a low branch and started to cinch the hat down. Focused on her needle, she said, "Barnard and Matt, try on these royalists' clothes. If needed, I'll adjust them too."

With the clothing in hand, Matt moved toward the other side of the tree.

"Why the sudden modesty, Matt?" she called.

Matt took Barnard's arm and whispered, "She's a bit tough."

Barnard put his head close and whispered, "When she learned her family had been killed in Paris, she swore to kill a hundred for her mother, a hundred for her father, and five hundred for her sister. Mom and dad are avenged, but I don't think Elena will ever be."

Matt coughed then said, "Are you telling me she's killed over two hundred men?"

"Not men, soldiers." Dubois curled his nose up in disgust. "She cheats—my wife uses cannons."

"Cannons?" Matt blurted. "Your wife?"

"Yes, yes," Barnard said. "She's the best at aiming, so Henri made her captain of the cannon brigade." .

"How many cannons are there?"

"Three." Barnard smoothed the dead man's jacket down in front. "This fits marginally okay. How about yours? It will have to do, in any case. We don't have time for her to fix them."

"We should go," she called out from the other side of the tree. "Herman will be a prisoner. We are his guards. We'll go down to the farmer who lives in my house, and trade these guys' money and other valuable things for my father's two big Percheron horses. While you are bartering, I'll slip down to the cavern and get the guns and the book."

**

Annette returned from the cavern with the two guns hung across her chest. She pulled her hat down and stood at a distance so the farmer, with whom Barnard dickered over the horses, would not recognize her. When Matt and Jim led the two huge Percherons out, the farmer protested.

Annette pulled one of Matt's guns and pointed it at the man. Making her voice sound deep, she shouted, "Monsieur, you protest so because you are a sympathizer with the heretics. I will take your horses and inform General Joyeuse of your treason."

257

The farmer bowed his head and raked his hands through his hair while pleading, "No, I am loyal. I am loyal. Take my horses for the service of God. They are my gift. They are my gift."

Barnard took the man's hand and stuffed the dead soldiers' money in it. Still pointing the gun, Annette mounted her horse. The others pulled up beside her. "Besides, they're my horses anyway," she said through grinding teeth.

Barnard turned her gun barrel toward the sky. "We're late. Let's not leave a bloody trail for the enemy to follow."

She shoved the gun back into the holster. Matt put his head close to hers. "Besides, they're my guns anyway."

Annette sneered at him. "I think I should keep one to defend my artillerymen."

Without turning, Herman said, "Annette, I'm afraid I must insist that you give them both back to Matt."

She heaved out an exasperated breath and glared at the back of Herman's head. "You kill Morto Sacude; then I will give them back."

Turning to her, Herman smiled and said, "If I don't kill Morto, it won't matter who has the guns."

***

The Road to Coutras

Annette took the holsters from across her chest and handed them to Matt.

"And the book," Matt said.

"Jules told me to bring it. He said you are too careless." Annette smirked; then she touched Matt's elbow. "I wish you could have gone to the cavern with me. There are amazing things in there. Father says—said—it's our family line through time: the Franks, Visigoths, Romans, Gaels, even back to when we made things from stone. Forever my family has lived on that land. I will get it back someday."

She tilted her chin toward Jim. "That stick he carries, it looks like a rich man's cane, yet I saw a flame shoot from it and cut the royalist's sword in half."

"Ah." Matt nodded in confirmation. "It is something used by the natives in America."

"Too bad we don't have more of them," she said.

Herman looked back at her. "This one will have to do."

258

Annette slackened her horse's pace until she was back beside Barnard. She kissed him. They clasped hands and rode like that throughout the day.

**

The third evening, Annette and Barnard led the group deep into the brush to camp.

"We're nearing enemy lines," Barnard explained. "Tonight we'll post guards and sleep without a fire."

Matt took Herman away from the others. "This journey has already taken two days longer than I planned. I'm worried we may not get there before Morto attempts to assassinate Henri."

Herman glanced about to make sure no one could hear him. "My internal map shows we are less than ten kilometers from Henri's camp. We should get there early tomorrow."

"Hell, Herman, they've been leading us down goat trails and back lanes. I'm not sure we'll cover ten kilometers tomorrow."

Herman walked back to Barnard and asked, "When will we start tomorrow?"

"At dawn while enemy eyes still sleep. We'll be there at Coutras by noon."

"Very well then," Herman said, "Jim and I will pull sentry duty tonight."

After the others were asleep, Herman told Jim, "Get some rest. I'm awake all the time anyway, and I hear better than you do."

**

At dawn, Matt stood with his blanket wrapped over his shoulders. "Thank God it's over. I'm soaked from the dew, and every part of my body is bruised by rocks or bitten by insects."

Bundled with Barnard under a low branch, Annette poked her head out. "We're nice and toasty."

She snuggled against Barnard and kissed him. "Honey, we're almost home. Maybe we can be over the lines before those lazy royalists finish their coffee."

Matt shook his arms and legs then danced about, raising his knees high.

A huge hand shot out from under a pine bough and caught Matt's wrist. Before anyone could speak, Herman was crouched in their midst, his eyes wide, and his finger over his mouth. He let go of

259

Matt's arm and pointed to the road, then pumped his hand downward several times, signaling them to take cover.

Watching the road, Barnard and Annette crawled back into their bush. Matt hunkered behind a tree. Beyond the branches and leaves of their hiding places, soldiers, gray in the morning light, marched up the road and over a ridge. The earth shook with their stride.

Between brigades, teams of mules labored against heavy cannons. The column stretched the length of the road and went on and on. With each minute the sun rose higher, melting away the shadows where the Huguenots hid.

At last the column trudged out of sight and the ground stopped vibrating.

"How many?" Matt asked while looking for stragglers.

"Five thousand," Herman replied.

Barnard turned to Herman. "How many cannons?"

"Five," Annette said before Herman could.

"Two more than our entire army has," Barnard noted.

Annette's hands tightened into fists. "Doesn't matter. I aim better than they do."

"Where can we go now?" Jim asked.

Barnard understood the question without knowing the words. "There's a deer trail that follows a brook." He pointed. Herman interpreted for Jim.

Up front with Barnard, Herman cast his head side to side in continuous surveillance. After several miles of a gentle upward grade, they left the stream and headed down through heavy undergrowth.

Herman pulled his horse to a halt. "There's a camp ahead."

"Ours," Barnard said.

They crept forward to avoid startling a sentry. After several hundred meters a voice called out from a distant treetop.

Annette edged her way up to Herman. She threw her royalist hat on the ground and shook her long black hair. "I am Annette Dubois. Be quick! Bring us to Henri or Jules V."

"How do I know you're not an imposter?"

"Ask again and I'll use your skull for a cannonball."

There was a long silence; then the sentry said, "I'm sending a man to verify you."

"Make haste, then," she called out. "We saw a Spanish column about four miles back. We need to deploy skirmishers now!"

Moments later, a young man pushed through the brush. He studied them with jackrabbit nervousness, then shouted, "They're good." He bowed to Annette then reached for the reins of her horse.

She placed her foot against his shoulder and nudged him away. "Well, if you recognize me, then you know I can manage a horse." She extended her hand to him. "Hop up, and rest your legs."

They weaved their way between barricades and trenches occupied by reformists from every part of Europe: Scots, English, Swedes, Dutch, Germans, and Czechs.

When they came into the main camp, Jules rushed forward. He spotted Matt and laughed. "Matt, you're back! I swear you have not aged a bit in fifteen years."

It appeared to Matt that other than a few streaks of gray, Jules had not aged either.

Herman extended his hand. "I am Herman McGuiness. I'm here to help dispose of Morto."

Matt sat up in his saddle and glanced about. "Where is Henri?"

"He's to the north, inspecting the lines," Jules said. "Oh, and, Annette, one of the wheels on Little James broke. We've pulled the wheelwright off the barricades to fix it." Then he called to one of the soldiers, "Albert, take their horses. They haven't eaten today, I'm sure."

Albert reached for Matt's reins, but Matt jerked away. "What did you just say?" he asked Jules.

Jules reacted with dismay. "I said you probably didn't eat today."

"No! That about Henri inspecting the north line, doesn't he inspect the entire line every day?"

"No, he'll inspect the east line tomorrow."

Matt yanked his horse about. Unrestrained profanity spewed from his mouth, ending with, "Herman, let's go! It's today!"

Herman knew exactly what Matt meant. "You said tomorrow, the 19th, is the day Morto will attack Henri."

"I was wrong!" Matt's horse reacted to Matt's panic and tossed its head. "It occurred when Henri was inspecting the north line. It's happening today."

***

261

Money

The rare-coin shop had meager traffic. Most were repeat customers, buyers and sellers alike. The unfamiliar car drew the owner's attention the instant it pulled up. The attractive woman who stepped out surprised him. For the most part, a woman had no interest in coins, other than to hang a gold one around her neck. Tall, in casual jeans, she would be good for ogling and flirtatious conversation, but probably not a sale.

She paused in the doorway, studied the room, then took her sunglasses off. Her eyes allured, then chilled him.

"You have old money," she asked.

He smiled and swept his hand over the counter. "Everything from the Persians to the latest proofs."

She smiled and twirled her finger in the air. "I'm not used to this. I meant bills: ones, fives, tens, twenties, all before 1950." She wiped her hands on her jeans and approached the counter.

He forced a smile. Sometimes survivalists would buy old paper because the government backed each dollar with one ounce of silver.

"Silver certificates?" he asked.

"Is that what money before 1950 is called?" Her voice was tense.

He kept his smile up. It was good business to be amiable to all inquiries. "The certificates go into the '60s."

He bent behind the counter. She leaned forward to watch. That bothered him. He studied her purse through the counter glass. It hung heavy to one corner.

A pistol?

With a woman you never knew. But with a woman, he wouldn't put his sawed-off shotgun on the counter. That would be tasteless.

He raised the cardboard box to the countertop and laid the lid to one side.

Her eyes jumped to the bills. She exhaled a long breath of relief. "How many are from the '50s or before?"

"They're silver certificates. Age doesn't matter. Each dollar is worth $13.45, today's price for one ounce of silver."

Her face became agitated.

"We could sort them," he suggested.

262

She grasped the countertop and looked pensively at the bills. After a moment she said, "I'll take them all. What is the total face value?"

His insides lurched. *Women. How many times do you have to say something?*

"Lady, you have to pay $13.45 for each dollar value."

She narrowed her eyes at him. "You said that before. I asked you for the total face value."

"Oh." He blushed at his own presumptuousness. He took a scribbled piece of notebook paper from the box lid.

He spoke congenially while he examined it. "Got 'em all at an estate auction last year. People were happy to get more than face value.

"Two fifties, eighteen twenties, nineteen tens—"

She cut him off, "The total is good enough."

He laid his forearm on the glass and wiggled a pencil in calculation. It gave him a chance to check out the fit of her jeans. They weren't snug, which he would have liked, but they still were nicely formed.

He held the result up to her. "Eleven hundred seventy-three."

She pulled a wallet from her purse. "13.45 each, right?" She sounded sarcastic.

He swallowed and nodded. If she bought them all, it would be his best sale since he started the business.

"So $15,776.85 total," she said before he could run it on the calculator. "I'll make it $15,800. Give me a good-luck coin to round it out." She thrust her hand into her purse.

Adrenaline shot to his brain. *Gun?* his mind sputtered.

She withdrew a handful of hundreds.

The adrenaline became joy.

"A three-dollar coin?" he asked himself then searched his display. "I have an Indian Head penny from the year of the Little Big Horn. I doubt you would call that lucky."

She laughed. "It's perfect."

He shoved the shoebox to her and laid the coin on top.

**

Back in the car, she stuffed the coin into her jeans pocket. She emptied the bills into her oversized purse. Some would be unusable. She would burn them later.

She pushed her .45-caliber pistol into the holster on a World War Two army surplus belt then stored two extra clips in an ammo pocket next to the first aid pouch on her left side.

She wiped her palms across her blouse then headed up Highway 6 toward the Henderson Mine.

**

When she pulled into the parking compound, Manuel and Emil were talking on the intercom, a habit they had adopted, along with sharing meals.

Emil felt a sense of foreboding when Manuel said who had arrived. Then the door lock snapped, and Manny greeted her. She told Manny she would stay in the research trailer for several days and he was not to tell anyone.

Emil paced the SAM chamber, awaiting her arrival. He had slept sporadically since the mission began. He had occupied his insomniac mind by sketching floor plans for an improved SAM control center, one with murals enlivening the walls, along with assorted rooms for human comfort, including a library and a game room.

Mainly, he kept a nervous ear tuned to the Paiute Police radio dispatches. NAS activity in Redlands City caused concern about Charlene's safety. He wanted to be near her, not in a cavern.

It took a full five minutes for the elevator to descend.

Every minute is forever in this hole, Emil thought.

He watched the door open. She stared at him with the same tense foreboding he felt.

Words burst from his mouth, inanimate obstacles hurled to impede a beast. "No! No! I can't stay here any longer. It's driving me nuts."

She kept her face and voice calm. "It won't take much time. Is the SAM recharged?"

"You have to take over. I need to go to Charlene."

"Emil, she's okay. NAS is just posturing, trying to get news notoriety. That's all."

"Just posturing! What about when Billy attacked all of you in the parking lot?"

"Okay." Her voice was mesmerizing. "I'll have a Haines security officer stay with Charlene until you can go. I'll do it right now."

Emil's heart fluttered. He stumbled into a chair and waited for it to settle.

She pushed the intercom button and had Manuel patch her through to headquarters. She finished before Emil could raise a counterargument.

Gripping the back of the chair, he stood and waved his hand at the room. "White walls, a hard chair, a hard desk, a fridge. No place to heat food, no place to lie down, nothing interesting to do. It's driving me crazy."

"Yeah," she said, "Herman doesn't have the genteel touch Horace had."

His head jerked in surprise. She had him. They both burst into laughter.

In that moment of relief, he pointed to a wall. "See there! I'm going to paint a mural of my village and the mountains. I'm going to make Herman put a billiards room down here, too."

"I'm sure you can have whatever you want." She handed him a small sheet of paper. "Now I need you to do this."

His eyes went to her French Foreign Legion cap with the long flap in back, then to the first aid kit mounted on her olive green military belt that looked like the cloth version of a Peg-Board. His eyes settled on the gun holster on her right hip.

"I can't." He took a breath with each word. Then he gushed out, "The energy level just got high enough to bring them back."

"I don't have to go far, only two decades and a hundred miles, and I weigh less than half what Herman weighs. You should be able to replenish what I use in less than a day."

"They're in a very dangerous place. An extra day there—"

"Emil, you know it doesn't work that way. Days here don't equate to days there. They'll spend exactly the same amount of time there. They'll just get here a day later."

His eyes desperate, Emil blurted, "But it's one more day I can't help Charlene."

"I took care of that." She held two fingers up and extended her arm toward him. Her hand floated there. His eyes locked on her fingers; then she spoke. "Two young girls are sure to die if I don't go."

He gulped and held his hands palm up in a gesture of pleading. "Wait until Herman gets back. He knows the machine better than me. He should do it."

Her two fingers held unwavering. Her lip began to tremble. "Please! I don't know that Herman would let me."

He flung his hands into the air. "Soon everyone I know will be somewhere else." He marched with loud angry steps to the SAM. He moved his index finger against its side in an exacting way. Faint glyph-like figures appeared and disappeared with his hand's movement.

She came quietly to his side. "I'll be there for three days. The energy drain should be minimal. You might be able to bring me back in just a few hours."

"It doesn't work that way," he snapped. "You can't have time tunnels close to each other. I think I should wait a day to bring you back." Then he stared at her defiantly. "Herman would know exactly how long to wait."

He began to thrust his finger hard against the glyphs. "I want to bring Jim back. Now it'll be two days before I can do it."

She laid her hand on his shoulder. "Bring him back before me, if you want to."

Without looking at her face, Emil reached up and squeezed her hand. "I don't know if it's safe—for any of you."

"Herman wouldn't have done it if it wasn't safe."

He put his finger against the side of the SAM again. "How much do you weigh?"

"119 kilograms."

Emil laughed. "You don't weigh 119 kilograms. That's more than Jim weighs. You weigh 119 pounds."

"You're right, but put in 119 kilos for a margin of safety."

He moved his finger about. The SAM canopy opened.

She hugged him then climbed in.

He looked at her lying there, one hand on the gun, the other on her first aid kit, both white knuckled.

"Those coordinates, where are they?" he asked.

"The Wild Horse Rest Stop on Highway 93, 6:00 a.m., March 12th, 1951."

His scalp tingled. He remembered a story Derek told him: A woman materialized in thin air then raced across the sand dunes.

***

266

Search for Henri

"What is happening?" Jules's frantic eyes came to rest on Herman.

Herman's voice was calm but urgent. "We have evidence that Morto plans to kill Henri today. We need to find Henri right now."

"I can find him better than his own generals." Jules yelled to his assistant, "Albert, bring my horse! Hurry!"

"I'm going too," Barnard said.

Annette took Barnard's hand. "Little Jacques, I can't lose a third of my artillery. I have to make sure he gets fixed." She kissed him long and passionately. "Be careful."

A man galloped toward them, leading two saddled horses. Albert was on one in a blink. In another blink, Jules was on the other and waving for them all to follow him.

Annette spurred her horse up beside Jim. With the reins in her teeth, she pulled a pistol from her waistband and gave it to him.

**

After an hour of beating through the brush in sweltering heat, they came to a small clearing. Jules called them together. "How much time do we have?" he asked Matt.

Matt threw his palms up, admitting ignorance. Jules turned to Herman. Herman pointed back to Matt. "It's in the realm of the mystic."

Jules rotated in the saddle, surveying the group. "We need to divide in half so we can cover more ground."

Herman shook his head. "In half, neither party will be strong enough to stop Morto."

Jules wrinkled his forehead. "Then die trying, because to continue like this will be to do no good at all. I will lead one group and Barnard the other."

Herman turned to Jim. "You and Matt go with Barnard."

Jim pulled the staff from a scabbard. "Will this thing cut through a robot's hide?"

"Probably not," Herman said. "If you find him, stay alive until I can get there. We need to work together to stop him." Then to Jules, Herman said, "We need a signal to bring ourselves back together if either group finds Henri."

"Move toward gunfire, pure and simple headed," Jules replied. "But if you hear movement and can't identify friend or foe, use this call." Jules imitated the sound of a woodchuck.

267

Jim repeated the sound. Jules grinned his approval and the two groups separated.

**

Gunshots and shouts of confusion resounded near Dubois's group less than fifteen minutes after the separation. Barnard cupped his hand behind his ear and leaned toward the sound. Several of his men did the same. One shouted, "It's Henri!"

They drew their pistols and advanced at a trot.

"There." Jim pointed to a blue cloud of gun smoke in the trees fifty yards ahead.

The men dismounted. Dubois waved them forward through the woods. Barely visible, hidden in brush and trees, a party of Spanish foot soldiers fired arquebuses at someone farther up the trail. Dubois signaled to attack the Spaniards. Jim grabbed his arm and pointed to another band of ten enemy soldiers who were slipping through the woods to flank Henri's men.

Dubois made a neck-slit motion and pointed at the latter band. At that instant a Spaniard spotted him and shouted out a warning.

The royalists' party turned and fired. A cloud of blue smoke filled in around them. Amid it, the Spanish unlimbered their swords and charged, yelling with manic bravado.

The French raised their pistols. Dubois ordered them to wait for his signal.

Ignoring him, Matt drew both revolvers and laid down a precise and steady fire. Within a minute, he emptied both of his guns, leaving three Spaniards dead and two others on the ground thrashing in pain. Their comrades panicked and turned to run.

Dubois shouted, "Fire!"

Down the line, the Huguenots leveled two pistols each and fired in unison. Acrid smoke filled the air and stung their eyes. It choked in their throats, but they blinked back the pain and drew their swords, ready for the charging Spaniards.

A swarm of rifle balls smacked through branches and shredded leaves around them. One Huguenot fell screaming then trembled and lay still.

Fifty yards away, the smoke of burnt powder filled the air around the first Spanish position.

Matt, his guns reloaded, leaped on his horse. Lying low in the saddle, he charged up the trail, firing into the enemy as he rode.

Seeing themselves surrounded by Huguenots, the Spanish ran into the brush.

"James! Richard!" Dubois called out.

"Barnard? Is that you?" someone shouted from Henri's group.

Dubois waved toward the voices. "Don't shoot! We're coming in."

**

Henri grabbed Matt's shoulders and hugged him. "Charles, may he rest in peace, actually thought you would hire Genoese ships and sail to the New World under his flag."

Henri paused and scratched his head. "I thought you would too. It would have been such an easy way to acquire a nice fleet of merchant ships." Eyes twinkling, he looked from face to face. "Am I the only one to see that?"

Jules smiled sheepishly. "Not many have your pizzazz, sir."

Henri scrutinized Jim. "Well, you got to the New World somehow. Have you brought us an Aztec?"

Matt held his hand toward Jim. "This is Manado. He and my associate, Herman McGuiness, have come to put an end to Morto Sacude."

The woodchuck call came from up the trail.

"It's Jules and a stranger," a sentry shouted from a tree.

Matt looked up to see Herman approaching. "The stranger is the one I spoke of, McGuiness."

"A Scot? I'm glad to have another Calvinist. They come from everywhere, their journeys often as dangerous as battling the papists. Matt, you should have waited for me at camp. You could be eating chicken and drinking wine rather than being shot at by constipated Spaniards. They're afraid to shit lest a piece of their empire fall out their ass and get lost."

Jules and Herman rode up.

Henri tipped his hat to Herman.

With a wave, Herman replied in French, "At your service and a rare pleasure indeed."

Jules glanced about. "Sir, you must get to camp. They say that the Morto plans to lay you dead this day." Jules then ordered Henri's men to prepare for departure.

Clowning surprise, Henri watched his men as they hurriedly brought his horse and surrounded him.

269

"Gracias, I'm sure," he said, "but aren't I the general here and the king-to-be as well?"

Lieutenant Neff, a man whose face was as gashed and scarred as his leather breastplate, said, "And indeed, you are second only to God. However, Jules speaks with God, and at the moment his voice is convincingly anxious, so let's get back for that chicken and wine you just promised."

Henri mounted his horse. "I mentioned chicken, but did I promise it?"

"Same as," Neff said and rode next to him. Another soldier rode on the other side.

"What's the fuss?" Henri complained over his shoulder to Matt. "These Spanish here are just skirmishers. The main body is two days away."

"One day away, sir, at best," Matt said. "We spied a contingent of about five thousand, probably men hardened from fighting Turks in Greece and Italy."

"Ah," Henri said in a muse, "maybe Morto is in Greece. We haven't heard much from him for the last decade."

"We have good reason to believe he is here now," Herman said.

"So you know of him?" Henri asked.

"I know his kind and I know their ways," Herman replied.

Henri frowned. "He is very odd, always in armor. Is he from the New World too?"

"Much of the New World is unexplored, so let's say he is from the unknown world," Herman said.

Henri eyed Herman and then Jim. "Well, Morto is a mighty warrior. You should carry some weapons. One of you has none, and the other, two worthless pistols and a silly stick, pretty, but silly. Do you plan to sit on him and fart in his face?"

Herman smiled. "Guns or swords never worked against him before. My way, the only way, is to muddle his brain into a stupor."

Henri shrugged his shoulders. "God bless you if you can. He kills and kills at will. I'm glad he decided to beat up on the Turks for a while. It gave you time to get back from the New World."

The trail narrowed and skirted between the forest and a steep ravine, forcing them to travel single file along the lip of the gulley. Henri's bodyguards reluctantly moved in front and behind him, leaving him vulnerable to snipers' shots. Here and there, a tree, half of its roots exposed, teetered over the gorge.

270

Ahead, the trail wound into a meadow. Arquebus fire opened on Henri's lead guards as soon as they came to the clearing. Two dropped dead off their horses. A third, his right arm hanging broken, struggled into the brush.

The remaining guards urged the others to retreat. Herman's Percheron, too big to turn on the narrow ledge, clogged the trail.

***

Chapter 20: Morto Sacude

Men screamed. Horses kicked. Spanish lead pounded the trees and whistled through the leaves. Herman stood high in his saddle, shielding the king from the musket balls.

Matt slid from his horse and worked forward. He pushed past horses. Their ears pricked and flicked. They snorted and stamped. He passed Henri then slid under the belly of Herman's Percheron. Before him the remnants of the front guard lay behind logs and tree stumps, pinned down by constant Spanish musket fire. Crouching huddles of Spanish infantry advanced through the haze.

From the rear a voice screamed in terror. A chill ran down Matt's neck, standing his hair on end. He spun around to see Jim's Percheron stagger on the edge of the gulley. Its rear legs slid over the steep embankment. Its head tossing, its front hooves dug frantically to hang on.

A chrome monster with fingers bent like claws reached for Jim. Jim swiped the staff across Morto's eyes. It roared and covered its face with giant hands. Then it doubled its right hand into a fist and shattered the Percheron's skull. The horse and Jim fell into the ravine.

"Herman!" Matt shouted.

Herman, already aware of Morto, jumped free of his horse and charged through the brush like a human tank.

Morto went for the next soldier in his path. The man fired two pistols into the monster's chest. Morto flung the man and his mount against a large oak. The horse fell, kicking the air furiously. The man hung lifeless, his head caught in the Y of a branch.

Matt's hands trembled. *It's happening just as described in the book.* An arquebus ball hit the trail by Matt and bounced past him, then dug deep into the trunk of a tree. Vicious shouts broke out. The Spanish rose up and charged. Arquebus balls cut the air near Matt's head. He cocked his guns and fired over and over.

**

Neff hauled Henri into the space Herman had trampled down when he charged to attack Morto.

At the back of the line, Morto held a third Frenchman high. Sparks popped from the man's eye sockets; smoke belched from his mouth.

The rear guard continued to fire their pistols with rapidity and accuracy. The balls smacked the träger's chest and face, bouncing off him and whizzing away like angry wasps. Morto took the next man's leg and snapped it like a dry twig, then yanked it off. Screaming, the victim placed the barrel of his gun against the monster's head and fired. Morto retaliated, smashing the man's face and sending blood and brains over the last two defenders.

Herman hit Morto full force. With jujutsu fluidity, he ran his arm between the träger's legs and slammed him down. Together they hit the earth with a thud that sent a portion of the gulley bank sliding downward.

**

Below, dirt poured into Jim's mouth, making him cough and bringing him back to consciousness. He blinked his eyes. His hand pushed against the yet warm neck of his horse. In death its body had absorbed the brunt of his fall, keeping him alive. He staggered to his feet. He lifted the shiny end of the staff from a pile of dirt then pulled himself hand over hand up a tree root to the trail.

The two robots rolled across the ground, hurling fists at each other with eye-blurring speed. The force of the impacts crumbled the earth around them.

In samurai fashion, Jim swung the staff over his head and delivered a slash across Morto's face.

"The code, the code," Herman shouted. Undaunted by Jim, Morto fired mailed fists down like pistons onto Herman's chest and head.

Jim's fingers moved deliberately over glyphs on the side of the staff. A deafening siren shrieked. At the same time balls of throbbing light shot from the staff to Morto's eyes.

Morto spun to face Jim and froze.

**

Matt squatted behind a fallen tree. He flipped the cylinder of his revolver out and reloaded for the third time. Beside him, Renee, one of Henri's bodyguards, peeked around the trunk and advised him, "They are still there. They are not coming at us. I think you have killed too many and they will not charge again. But there are still too many for us to force our way past."

Matt jiggled the empty shells in his pocket. He had used a good portion of the bullets he had intended for Coutras, a decisive battle that would determine the course of history. He pressed his shoulders against the tree stump and held the pistol in both hands. With their only escape from Morto Sacude blocked, soon they would all die.

From the rear, Dubois shouted, "Morto Sacude is dead. We can retreat!"

Matt raised both pistols. "On three, get Henri and go. I'll keep their musketeers at bay.

"One, two…" He sighted down the barrel of one gun and began firing. "Three!"

Renee and the others scurried back to Neff. With Henri between them, they rushed to the rear. Two Frenchmen crouched near Jim and drew their pistols, ready to defend him and Herman with their lives.

His guns emptied, Matt hurried back to them while fumbling more ammo into his revolver.

He squatted by Herman and told the Frenchmen to leave. "I'll do the rear guard."

"Okay, okay," one said, "you stand guard while I take care of this." He pointed to Jim.

"He can take care of himself…" Matt's words stuck in his throat and his face paled.

"What?" Jim said.

Herman looked down at Jim's leg. "God, we don't have time for this." He grimaced then told Jim, "Take a deep breath."

"What?" Jim asked.

Herman laid his hand on Jim's leg and yanked.

274

Jim screamed and clamped his thigh between his hands.

Herman held up a bloody branch. "This was sticking out of you."

"I'll tie it off," one Frenchman said. The other stared at Herman's head. Half his scalp and one ear hung to one side. His metal skull flashed through bloody smears.

"Help me stall the enemy!" Matt ordered and dragged the man into the brush.

"Herman!" Jim screamed.

"He has to tie it tight to stop the bleeding," Herman said.

"Not that—Morto!"

***

Restart Circuits

Morto's eyes blinked then moved from side to side. Herman gave an exasperated sigh. "He's got a restart circuit."

Jim raised the staff again.

Herman pushed Jim's arm down. "No! Wait until the last possible moment." Herman pulled a small canister from his vest and took an emerald capsule from it. "Here, swallow this. I need your leg to heal fast."

Morto Sacude moved his head back and forth like a dazed person trying to orient himself.

Herman kneeled next to the träger and thrust his face close to its head. "Don't shut him down until he stands up. Then do it fast. I need as much time as possible on each cycle because his circuitry will learn how to negate the staff's effect."

"How much time do we have?" Jim asked.

"Three tries, maybe fifteen minutes at best."

Herman backed up on his hands and knees, examining Morto's neck from just a few centimeters away. He continued down over the neck and chest, peering as if through a microscope.

"Can I help?" Jim watched over Herman's shoulder.

"Keep the staff ready." Herman continued to scan Morto's body.

The monster's arms pressed against the ground with fingers spread.

"He's getting up," Jim warned.

"I know. Wait until he stands. I want to examine the entire front of his body before you shut him down again."

275

Morto's knees drew to his chest. Herman studied the tops and sides of the robot's legs.

"Now?" Jim pointed the staff at the träger's eyes.

"No! Not yet! We still have twenty more seconds. His pirate masters would need to shut him off without special tools, so there must be a physical switch on the leg since they activate last. It would be covered by a flap or lid."

Herman ran his hands over Morto's legs from the knees to his feet. While he probed an ankle, the big body stood. The head glanced right then left with superhuman quickness.

A knee shot forward, kicking Herman against a tree.

"Now!" Herman shouted.

In a blink the träger sprang through the air and landed with his feet straddling Herman.

The staff blared its noise. Balls of light shot out and splattered against Morto's face. The träger crashed to the ground. Herman stroked his fingers over Morto's face, head, and neck. Again he pushed his eyes close to the träger to view him microscopically.

"I'll connect to his programming center and see if I can disable him that way." Seconds later, Herman rocked back. "It's shielded."

Jim pointed the staff at Morto's face. "Can we melt his brain into molten goop with this?"

"It might make things worse." Herman scanned again with his fingertips.

Up the trail, two Spanish helmets peeked over a stump. Matt rattled off four shots. The Frenchmen followed with one each. One Spaniard fell to the side. A volley of arquebus fire shredded the bushes around Matt and the two Huguenots. A ball bounced down the trail, stirring puffs of dust; then it slammed into Herman's leg.

"Better get behind me," he told Jim.

"They aren't." Jim pointed to Matt and the two men.

"Yes, but I need you to stay alive to finish this."

Morto raised his head and rotated it slowly. Herman held his eye to the giant's ankle. The robot kicked him away.

"He's activating faster," Jim said.

"Jim, staff!" Herman yelled. Again it worked.

Herman started to scan again. "This is it. If he comes around again, I'll fight him as long as I can. You and Matt get Henri away from here."

**

276

Forty-eight hours after injecting them into the past, Emil was to bring them back one by one. Twenty-four of those hours had elapsed, and it felt like twenty-four years to Emil.

Why couldn't Charlene stay down here? It's not like this place is a big secret anymore.

Emil kicked the chair. It spun like a top then careened off the wall then smacked into the side of the SAM. He crouched down, shutting his eyes and covering his ears.

He waited. Nothing happened. He expelled his breath and let his hands fall to the floor.

Herman said it would defend itself.

He tiptoed to the chair and rolled it quietly back to the control desk.

Herman's crazy, talking like that thing is alive.

The machine's luster brightened.

Does it read my mind?

He stammered, "You know, this place is not good for a normal human. It doesn't bother you, but for me, a week down here and I would be nuts. Then you really may have to kill me.

"I didn't mean that.

"There's lots of space down here. Herman made the conference room in a day."

Emil walked to the door and peeked into the adjoining space.

"Herman put lights in there, too. Don't know where the power comes from. It wasn't a problem, though. If he wants me to do this again, then I need..."

He held his fingers up as if to count, then took a pad and sat on the desk's edge.

"I need these things: a kitchen, a bunkroom, an exercise room, a library and workroom. I need someone else, at least one more person, maybe two to split shifts with."

Emil pointed his pencil at the machine. "But Herman won't let anyone else know about you. He's afraid they will blabbermouth. That's why I have no help.

"Just one more person..." His arms dropped. Tears filled his eyes. "Just one more person—please!"

Emil held his wristwatch up to his face. "Twenty-four hours and fifteen minutes. Good God." He dropped his pencil and held his forehead between his hands. "Every minute is infinity."

Upstairs in the research trailer there are bunk beds, food, magazines...

277

"So how's it going, Manny?"

"Fine. Glad you came up, Emil. It's boring as hell up here, except for those crazy Indians and hippies over there in Camp Desert Sunrise."

"At least you have a window. Back there ain't nothing but rock."

Manny looked behind Emil. "So where's everybody?"

"They're in an experiment. When they do that, I just wait until it ends. I came up here to keep from going crazy. Got any food?"

"Ah, some eggs and chilies, I got plenty."

"Hey, maybe a little cheese too?" Emil stood in front of the sink and pulled a cutting board from the cupboard. He began to split and seed the chilies. "Charlene taught me how to make something with chilies, eggs and cheese. I'll make enough for both of us."

Twenty minutes later Emil passed a plate to Manny.

Manny pushed the binoculars to Emil. "Want to watch the hippie camp?"

They set their plates on the counter and passed the binoculars back and forth while describing what they saw to each other.

"Hey!" Manny said with alarm. He held the binoculars to his face. "Looky there." He pointed to a distant blue thing that looked like an ocean cargo crate. "That damn Arbie cut the fence and drove his VW bus through it."

"You going to throw him out?" Emil asked.

"No, man. I don't leave the trailer. I just call the Paiute Police, and sooner or later, they'll take care of it. So far it's been mostly later."

Manny picked up his phone and talked to the tribal dispatch for several minutes. He sounded frustrated.

He said goodbye politely then slammed the phone down. "They got their own problems over on the other side. Some of them NAS guys making trouble at the tribal council. He says the Arbie hippy ain't big enough to bother themselves with."

"Hey, mind if I call Charlene? Make sure she's okay?" Emil asked.

"Go ahead. I'd go crazy if I didn't talk to my family some each day. The calls are all free. No phone company, it goes straight to a satellite."

278

"We could take shifts up here until I have to go back down there," Emil said.

Manny nodded his head. "Why don't you get a nap? When you're done, I'll take one."

Emil took the offer and flopped on a bed in the bunkroom. He couldn't fall asleep. He thought about his old sufi master, Kalid, then about his new studies with Derek. Kalid made him practice specific breath and heart control. Derek just said to dream about his billiards skills. Kalid said to pray to Allah. Derek said pray to whoever you feel like, or no one if you'd rather not.

Emil thought he would practice Kalid's way. He took deep breaths and held them. He focused on slowing his heartbeat.

He didn't know how long it took, but sometime later he found himself in a pitch-black place.

Light came in flickers so small that he almost thought they really weren't there. He decided to knock the little specks of light away with his cue stick then go back to sleep.

He readied his cue, but the little lights stopped. He waited and they started again. Now he realized his pool cue was too big, so he made it become tiny small. Then he made himself small to hold it. The third time the flickers came, he could see that they were jumping at the speed of light from one plate to another. He moved his cue faster than the speed of light and knocked them away before they could reach the second plate.

The room became dark again. He felt elated. He could sleep now. If not him, then something else would.

**

The shots from the enemy musketeers diminished, but the shouts of the wounded did not.

"Go to Henri," Matt told his fellow rear guards. "Leave without us."

Herman looked at Matt. "All of you, leave now! Get Henri back to camp."

"I'm staying." Jim held the staff, ready to try one more time.

"Me too," Matt said. "If we fail here, there will be no safe place."

But this time the photons in Morto's microswitch were deflected off course before they crossed from emitter to absorber. Morto remained asleep.

**

Henri and Matt entered the Huguenot camp late in the day.

Annette raced to meet them. Her eyes begged Henri, then Matt. "Barnard?" she asked.

Henri, face pinched in sorrow, said, "We were ambushed; we beat them back but with great loss. Barnard stayed to help the wounded. Matt and I took the last two horses and hurried here to prepare for the battle."

Annette's eyes burned into Henri's. "Barnard should have come with you."

Henri grimaced. "The guns." He pointed to Matt. "We'll need his guns in the battle."

Annette glared at Matt. "You should have stayed and he should have come. You could have talked him into it. You can talk anyone into anything." She turned and stalked away.

Henri winced and called after her. "Barnard will return. They all will. I'm sure. Annette, you hear me? I'm sure of it."

She kept going and didn't look back.

***

Wild Horse

The woman Emil transported with the SAM stood in a trough between rolling sand dunes. Six feet away, a jackrabbit sat still then twitched his ears toward her. His leg muscles tensed. His heart raced. So did hers.

A breeze rustled nearby sagebrush. No other sound came to her. She lunged. The jackrabbit zigzagged away, his feet flinging little puffs of sand.

Wrong place, she thought.

She churned out knee raises, flying up a sifting dune to its crest. Hand over the bill of her cap, she spun in a circle. Unbroken desert stretched in every direction.

"How can this be?" She spoke out loud, as if someone nearby could explain it to her. No one did. She gasped for air.

Two girls needed help and the clock ticked.

She dizzied. Was that normal with time travel? She needed a steady head to think.

A monstrous growl whirled her around. Her hands fumbled for the holster flap. The blood in her head banged against her temples.

280

A hundred yards away, purple smoke dissipated into the air. The rumble came again, the raspy cough of a diesel engine. A billow of oily exhaust floated up and away. The bright yellow side of a caterpillar tractor blinked through the layers of brush.

She raced to the top of a higher dune. Stretching onto her tiptoes, she made out the roof of the earth mover and two others sitting idle. Beyond them, a wide swath of desert lay ripped open, destroyed vegetation heaped on either side all the way to the horizon.

Her stomach knotted and she bent in pain.

What she saw didn't make sense.

The answer slammed its way through her confusion.

Interstate 15, FUTURE I-15.

She had given Emil the coordinates of the new I-15 Wild Horse Rest Stop. She needed to be at the old Highway 93 Wild Horse Rest Stop—and it had to be nearby.

Twenty-six minutes? Was it enough time? Where to go?

If only she had driven out and studied the area before going to Emil. She bit her lip and fought back the sense of failure.

She gazed down the barren corridor leveled by the bulldozers. Did she see an overpass at the edge of the horizon? Or was it a trick of the morning sun?

Morning sun. East.

She forced the map of the area into her memory. The features shimmered and blurred while she moved her mind along the route of old Highway 93.

North and west.

She cranked her face over her right shoulder.

A *honk, honk, honk* rose then faded with the gusts of wind. She squinted and turned her head, left then right, to home in on the sound. The wind stilled, and the direction of the honks became clear. She stared beyond the dunes, searching for the glint of glass or the geometry of structure.

She jumped forward at a full sprint. Her legs churned through blown sand that sucked her strength and turned her muscles to rubber. She forced knee raises, straight up a steep wall of sand. She shoved herself through the limbs of a mesquite, its thorns cutting her blouse and skin.

She stretched up, blood beading on the backs of her hands and splotching in circles on her shirt. She pressed her palm against a gash in her forearm while scanning the horizon again.

281

In the corner of her right eye, she saw the distant rectangle of a white mile marker, and beside it, the notch in the side of the hill above her—Highway 93.

She wiped her eyes on her sleeve and touched her gun.

The vulture honked again and drew her eyes to a momentary flash of glass.

She sucked in her breath and ran, her mind plotting the fastest route, around high dunes and over the low ones. Her entire being focused on getting there in time.

**

A hundred yards away, she saw the rest stop with two fifties-model cars, Oldsmobile or Chevy, unoccupied, one in the shade of the building, the other in the parking area. She stumbled onto the pavement. Her legs, rubbery from her run, almost dropped her onto the asphalt. She wobbled past the shaded car. Her fingers tugged the holster snap. Her hand gripped the pistol. She stopped at a building corner. A muted sound came from inside.

She brought the gun across her body and chambered a shell. Hands shaking, she raised the gun above her head.

She snaked the gun barrel toward the front of the cinder-block building. A skinny man with hair greased back like a gigolo leaned against the women's restroom door. His back to her, he watched the highway.

She dropped the gun behind her right thigh and stepped out. "Hey." She forced the word out with her gut muscles.

"Huh!" Pressing his back against the door, he whirled. Narrow-faced and beady-eyed like a rat, he studied her skittishly.

His sudden alarm mutated into a disarming laugh. "You scared me. Where the hell did you come from?" His voice was loud as if to alert another.

From beyond the door, a low plaintive sob sent chills over her body.

"The kid peed in her pants. Wife's cleaning her up." He squared himself, blocking the door.

"Out of the way," she demanded, then held her left arm out, showing the long red streaks of dried blood.

"Oh, nasty. She'll be done in a minute." He tapped on the door. "Another young lady wants in." He took a sudden step toward her. "It'll be your turn—"

She sighted the barrel into his eyes.

282

He gasped and thrust his hands out defensively.

"Move," she ordered.

His eyes locked on the gun. He backed off.

"Farther!" she said. "Or I'll kill you here."

He backed faster, yelling as he passed the door, "You have company. She has a gun!" He ran around the building.

She kicked open the door.

Light spilled across the floor and onto Viekki's battered legs. The teenager lay motionless against the green-enameled cinder-block wall.

The Verg slave's smock was shoved above her waist. Blood pooled under her. Her swollen, bruised face hung horribly to the side.

Lightning crashed in the woman's head.

Too late!

Her grip on the gun slackened. She faltered, her knees dipping toward the floor. She braced herself on the edge of the counter. Movement at the back corner of the room yanked her attention to it. Two small feet thrashed from behind the last porcelain toilet bowl.

A man, on his knees, yanked against the stall's locked door and reached for a leg. Time stopped. His face lifted toward the woman.

Outrage gave her body renewed strength.

He moved like a slow-motion movie. His eyes widened in terror. Rising to a half crouch, he rotated toward the back door. His feet churned toward the exit. She fired. The bullet floated through the air then hit him mid-spine. He collapsed to the floor. She fired again.

He lay still. Gun outstretched, she approached the last stall.

"Marie, it's safe." She used the few Amazonian words she had pried out of Herman. "We go."

On hands and knees, Mierri scurried out. Eyes frightened, she urged with words the woman didn't understand.

Outside the building a car started. The woman rushed to the front door. The vehicle accelerated past her. She saw the driver for a fraction of a second. Her heart paused while her mind struggled to understand that she had seen Carr Ferguson, twenty years younger.

She gritted her teeth and sighted down the barrel.

Before she could get Carr in her sights, footsteps tapped rapidly on the sidewalk behind her. She whirled around. The gigolo raced from behind the cinder-block wall toward the other car, the only remaining car. Walking calmly behind him, she leveled the gun.

The first bullet, through his midsection, flung him sideways across the pavement. Hazy eyed, he raised his face toward her. She shot him in the hip for Viekki. Then she shot him in the knee. While he writhed like a headless snake, she finished him off so Marie would never hear his voice again.

She looked back in the building. Marie stood outside, squinting against the harsh sunlight at the woman, the gun, then the body on the ground. Emotionless, she reentered the restroom, shutting the door behind her.

Failure weighed on the woman's heart. She came to save Viekki and to spare the children from the violence. Instead she added to it. Just like the newspapers of the period said, two men, child molesters, were dead. Their victim, a never-to-be-identified Jane Doe, was also dead.

The newspapers also had told her what would happen next. She had twenty minutes. Standing outside the restroom, she gathered her tattered emotions.

She opened the door. Tears flooded her eyes, graciously blurring the scene.

Fingertips curled over the counter, Marie rested her chin on its edge and gazed at her sister's body.

"Marie." The woman turned the child's shoulders away from her sister; then she laid Viekki flat on the countertop. Her jaw trembled. Tears blurred her eyes. Someone would arrive and find the body in fifteen minutes. She tidied Viekki then took the penny from her jeans pocket and pressed it into the teenager's palm.

She lifted Marie. The four-year-old laid her head against the woman's cheek and grasped her neck. The woman recited words that Herman once told her would be said over a dead Amazonian warrior.

Did he know I would do this?

She finished with the Amazonian requiem, "Mothers and sisters, let us live well so we may join her in the Vale of Hatta."

They both laid their hands on Viekki's chest, then presented their fingers to each other's lips.

Marie knows this too damned well.

They had eight minutes.

She carried Marie to the car, stopping to wrench the keys from the dead man's fingers.

284

She floored the gas petal. The car fishtailed onto the highway and headed west toward Vegas.

They spent that day like mother and daughter, window-shopping hand in hand, their communication limited mostly to touch. The woman bought Marie several outfits, like mothers of four-year-olds do.

At night, Marie fell asleep on a real bed, maybe the first ever. The woman sat at the little motel room table, and between gasps of pain and tears, she composed her letter, which she folded and placed in the clothing store sack along with the Verg slave smock. She laid one of the outfits she bought on a chair.

In the morning she dressed Marie in a white dress with pink polka dots. She finished by tying a pink and white striped ribbon in the girl's hair. Hands on the child's shoulders, she studied her work.

She stroked the ribbon thoughtfully; then she thrust her teeth over her lower lip and trimmed off half an inch.

The ribbon pieces drifted down, shifting on the still air. The woman grasped Marie's hand and led her to the door.

They parked in front of a modular office unit, with a placard over the door that read "Horace Haines Land Acquisitions."

She lifted a wide-brimmed hat off the backseat, one that would cover her face, then led Marie to the front door. She kneeled and told the girl, in words the Amazonian did not understand, that someday they would meet again.

An hour later, Stephanie drove back to her hotel room and waited for the SAM to pick her up.

***

Desert Sunrise

Camp Desert Sunrise had become a hellish cesspool for Ruthie Cesnik. Now, Sancho's hand lay on her upper thigh, fingers against her vagina. Ruthie pushed it away once, but he twisted his face into an angry knot and slapped it right back, clamping harder. She winced. She would have purple bruises on her leg. She blinked back tears and said nothing.

Outside her tent door, Arbie pointed his finger at the gulley. His mouth wagged at Billy Manes, who sat on a rock and conversed with two of his lieutenants, Bengo, a pudgy ball of fat, and Tuco, a long, lanky well-tattooed ex-con, both mean as rabid wolves. She knew. She'd had sex with them both, and she had initiated it. At

285

least, she thought she had. But she knew if she hadn't lavished herself on them, they eventually would have taken her anyway. She had thrust herself on Sancho too; by then it wasn't to piss Arbie off, but to keep the other, lower pack animals at bay. If she were lucky, this all might end before Sancho let them fight over her.

The wind blew Billy's conversation to her.

Arbie pontificated, "There's shit all over the arroyo. Your guys used to hide their shit under rocks, now they just leave it there for others to step on. Flies land in it." He batted a buzzing insect away from his mouth.

"Arbie, just do it farther down the gulley," Billy said.

"But we need the support of the locals. They'll turn against us if they see this mess."

Behind them a piece of newspaper lifted out of the gulley and flapped through the air, then wedged itself onto a mesquite branch. Farther off, garbage stuck here and there on cacti and rocks strung out for half a mile.

"We should ask UNESCO to bring out more toilets. We'll say that Haines security wrecked the others." Arbie pointed to the five UNESCO toilets that lay like fallen logs on the other side of the arroyo.

Like a schoolyard bully, Billy stood up and punched Arbie's arm.

Ruthie heard the thud. Arbie's face knotted in pain. Like a sea creature retracting into a shell, he slunk back.

"Let me worry about the locals and the shit." Billy's words, brusque and condescending, asserted his dominance. "We have the locals on our side." He pointed to a small group of derelicts that lay with backs pressed into the shade of a boulder. One took a swig from a whiskey bottle and passed it to another.

Billy laughed. "Hey, Tuco, get Arbie some bags and a shovel."

"Arbie, if you're so concerned, go clean it yourself," Tuco yelled.

Arbie bent his head down like a beaten dog. "No, Billy, I was just saying—"

"No! Arbie, you're so concerned. Go clean it yourself," Billy ordered with his finger aimed toward the gulley.

"I'm not—" Arbie started, but Billy cut him off.

"Tuco, go get the goddamned bags!"

"Billy, Billy." All heads turned to the voice of Jerry Palomino. "I got the film crew. You want to come and lay your shit on them?"

286

"Ain't no garbage bags," Tuco grunted.

Billy, who had started toward Jerry, stopped and faced Arbie. "Don't mention it again. Next time there will be garbage bags."

Arbie grimaced and lowered his head. Billy smirked then marched off with Palomino, both gesticulating excitedly with their hands.

Arbie's eyes, filled with remorse, settled on Ruthie long enough for Sancho to giggle and push his fat paw smack between her legs. She pulled it hard against herself and heaved a sexy moan. Inside, her guts twisted and turned. It was all she could do not to vomit.

Survive a day. That had become her motto.

**

Down the ridge and a good part of a mile beyond, within the Haines security trailer, Manny sat at the console, watching through his binoculars and listening through the distance microphone. In front of his big window, the metal gate installed by Herman and Jim lay bent to the ground along with fifty yards of cyclone fence. The NAS operatives had flipped him off while they drove their pickups over it.

Manuel was relentless. All day long he watched and listened. He even cranked up the distance microphone when he went back to the bunkroom for food or for relief. He napped late at night when the whole Camp Desert Sunrise snored. Even then he slept in his chair with the volume full up.

Through the glasses, he saw fat Sancho drag Ruthie through camp. It was right after Billy humiliated Arbie at the edge of the gulley.

Sancho pushed her off balance, then yanked her along, causing her to stumble; then he bumped her shoulder, making her stumble in the other direction. She hadn't resisted him. He did it, Manny surmised, for pure sadistic pleasure.

Manuel pounded the table and yelled a string of Spanish curse words. *"Pinche! Cavron! Guina Calgato!"* He expelled them with all the air in his lungs, adjusting his pitch in an attempt to make the glass vibrate.

The glass didn't vibrate, and his anger didn't abate.

Manny had watched the whole history of Ruthie and the Indian chiefs. He knew she'd given herself to them to get away from that twerp Arbie. Yet from a distance, he'd seen the landscape and

287

knew from the start the path it would follow: from Tuco to Bengo to Sancho, each one more debasing.

Last night, when the camp went dead, Manny didn't take his usual nap, but loaded a shotgun instead. Despite Herman's directive, he opened the door and descended into the darkness. The shotgun angled across his shoulder, he had hiked toward the camp. Then reality soaked in and he returned to the security station. The sun came up. The hours of the day ticked past. Today, enumerable times while scanning the camp, he had rehashed his aborted foray. Now, tired from lack of sleep, he slipped into a stupor.

Billy Manes's voice yanked him to attention. "The snipers came last night."

"The TV station can't know about them," Palomino warned. "They have to believe the police started it."

"Jerry," Billy said condescendingly, "this is what I do. I make newsworthy scenes. You take care of the cameramen. I'll do the rest."

"Okay, you need to tell me when it's going down."

Manny listened for fifteen minutes then switched on his radio. "This is Manny Diaz, Haines Research Station. Over."

The radio crackled, "Mona, Reservation Police. Manny, what's up? Over."

"I need to talk to Lightfoot. It's urgent."

"They're all in a meeting right now," Mona said.

"It's urgent. They need to know this."

Mona sighed. "You should have called ten minutes ago. They've gone into radio silence."

"They've turned off their radios?" Manny's heartbeat skipped. "Yes."

"Dogs bite. Four of them have long, long teeth." Manny used the code he and Lightfoot had agreed on.

"Shit, Manuel, I'm the only one here. I'll have to lock up and track them down, and I don't have any idea where they are."

"What about the patrol guy? He's due here any minute. Does he have his radio on?"

"Everyone is silent," Mona replied.

"I have to go." Manny hung up. Hands trembling, he pulled on a gun belt and stuffed a .40-caliber pistol into the holster. He grabbed the shotgun and dumped a handful of shells into his jacket pocket then pumped a round into the chamber and stepped into the desert. He left the door ajar on purpose. If he or the Paiute

288

policeman got injured, he didn't want locks impeding their retreat to safety.

**

Behind Camp Desert Sunrise the ridgeline pushed up against the turquoise sky. On the far side of the hills, the Paiute patrol dismounted. They left their horses in a crude corral then split into two groups. Derek led his group up a ravine, where they hid in a stand of willows. The rest of the patrol waited amongst boulders while Lightfoot scanned the ridge with his binoculars.

**

After the initial hoopla of running around and waving guns in the air, the snipers settled into their positions. But that was hours ago. Now, they contorted their backs and hips in every imaginable way to relieve pokes and aches. Their eyes went from watching for the target, to playing peek-a-boo with each other, then to searching for the shade of a bigger rock or a place more comfortable. After that, they sank into the gray haze of mental oblivion.

**

Lightfoot kept low and zigzagged to the willows. He took Derek by the shoulder and pointed to a sniper. Derek worked his way up the hill, using boulders and brush for cover.

Lightfoot dispatched two other men to take out two other snipers.

The evening sun, big and orange, lay against the world and cast its rays across the earth. Derek's target turned his face away from the glare and lay in the shade, gyrating his hips to a hummed tune.

When the sniper finally realized someone was with him, Derek could read the guy's neck tattoo. The man sat up and scanned in the wrong direction. Derek rushed him. The sound of hurried steps whipped the sniper toward Derek, his rifle rising while he turned. Derek's foot drove the gun's barrel into the ground. It broke free from the assassin's hands and clanked down the slope until it stuck in a clump of cactus.

Derek pressed his shotgun against the sniper's forehead. "Don't move. Don't squeak. Lay flat on your belly, hands behind your neck, or you're a carcass."

289

After Derek's fellow tribesmen took down the other two identified snipers, he flashed a mirror at the boulders where Lightfoot's men waited.

Eight policemen unleashed their billy clubs and weaved up the slope at a trot. Led by Lightfoot, they crested the ridge and descended through the deep shadows of a gulley that opened onto the valley near the squatters' camp.

**

The fourth sniper, unaware of his companions' fates, trained his gun toward the Haines Research Station and the road where a Paiute police officer arrived daily to beseech Camp Desert Sunrise to gather their garbage and leave.

The sniper laughed to himself. Today that officer would get a big surprise, maybe a permanent one. In the rifleman's peripheral vision something moved. He squinted into the shadows of a ravine that descended from the ridge to near the camp. He swung his rifle toward the shadows and peered into the scope. His finger moved to the trigger.

***

Chapter 21: Coutras Begins

October 20, 1587

Jim peered over Herman's shoulder and watched pieces of Morto's head flash away under the blur of Herman's hands. Then they reappeared in a heap by the seraph's side. Now a mass of lights pulsed within the träger's inner cranium.

"So that is what your robots' brains look like." Jules leaned toward Herman. He was the only Frenchman left. Barnard had taken the others to hold off the enemy until Herman could get Morto under control.

Herman placed his palm against the opening in Morto's skull. The light inside dulled. "Robot," he said, "is an interesting term. It's Russian, and it won't be invented until 1921."

"Possibly," Jules replied, "but Matt used it. That's where I got it."

Herman's arms whirled again. Morto reassembled. Then Herman commanded, "Morto, awaken."

The träger's eyes brightened.

Herman raised his hand. "Sit up."

The beast raised its torso.

"Stand."

Morto stood.

Leaning on one knee, Jim exhaled as calmly as he could. "Well," he said, "I'm very glad we don't have to carry him." He extended a hand to Jules and pulled him up. "I'm just a dumb Paiute, but I did go to college, and I know 1921 is a long way into the future. It seems the more we learn about things, the crazier they get. Jules, you don't belong here anymore than Morto does."

Jules nodded. "You as well. I daresay we all shall go home when our missions are finished."

"And home for you is?" Jim asked.

"Currently the late 1800s."

Jim and Herman glanced at each other. Even Morto seemed in awe, maybe more than the others, since Herman had cut his mental capacity down to that of a child.

Jim asked first. "Why the 1800s?"

"I've got another project there."

"Such as?" Jim narrowed his eyes into distrusting slits.

"I write books that open the human imagination to a future of unlimited potential."

"So have I heard of you?" Jim asked.

Jules shook Jim's hand. "I've been remiss. My full name is Jules Gabriel Verne. You read some of my books in high school."

"We need to move out!" Dubois yelled from the hilltop.

"Shall we?" Jules bowed with his arm outstretched.

Late that evening, Barnard brought his troops back to the Huguenot stronghold.

**

At daybreak gunfire came from the woods near Coutras. Shouts and frantic activity erupted throughout the Huguenot camp.

Morto stood by Herman while they watched the commotion. A nearby colonial shouted, "Prepare for battle! Joyeuse is here." A band of pikemen lined up behind him.

"Where the hell is Henri?" Jules yelled. The front door of a nearby chateau flung open and Henri emerged, strapping on his sword as he ran. Behind him a young maiden held a blanket to her partially uncovered breasts. "Be well, Henri," she cooed.

"What do we know?" Henri shouted while he ran.

"This morning a large movement was reported less than a mile from here. That gunfire is likely them." Dubois nodded his head toward the musket fire.

Matt rushed out of the same chateau. A second maid stood in the shadows behind the first. Matt studied Morto while strapping his guns on. "Herman, maybe we could use Morto against them for a change."

"Not a good idea," Herman said then turned to Henri. "In Coutras, I will find a fisherman and we will take Morto into very deep water. I'll dispose of him there."

Henri nodded. "Good, go now while we still control the town."

Herman bowed and led Morto away.

Matt chased after him. "But you can't do that. Someday he will be found..."

Herman stopped just long enough to point at Henri. "I know how to handle my business. You take care of yours."

"We came to finish Morto. What else is there to do?" Matt asked.

Henri called out, "Matthew, I need you and your guns with me. Let McGuiness do what he must."

Herman, his face emotionless, nodded toward Henri. "Win this battle. That is what we have yet to do."

A cloud of dust rose at the opposite end of the field. A horse galloped toward them. The rider crouched low over the horse's neck.

"Annette!" Barnard shouted.

She reined the horse to a stop beside him and leaped into his arms.

"Thank God you're safe." She tilted her head toward Matt. "I was going to kill him for leaving you behind."

The roar of arquebus fire cracked the air. Blue-gray smoke rose from the woods two hundred meters away. Henri sent a regiment of pikemen and musketeers to keep the enemy occupied. Then he kneeled amid his generals and spread a map on the ground.

Henri gripped his beard between his thumb and fingers. He looked from one general to the next. "What do we know of the enemy's disposition?"

General Batiste signaled a cavalry officer.

The man saluted. "Sir, our best estimate is that they are twice our strength." He trailed his sword point over the chart on the ground. "However, reconnaissance shows that Joyeuse demonstrates no creativity. He has distributed his force evenly across the battlefield."

Henri smiled grimly. "So we get a break. Look! Our left flank is behind this swamp. A few snipers can keep half of the enemy at bay. The rest of us can go against him on the plain. Any thoughts on this idea?"

He crossed his arms and awaited his generals' comments. Verne, though not a general, was the first to speak. "It seems good. Let the swamp defend our left."

"They can't cross it," Batiste said, "even if we put no soldiers there, but placing a few will bait them on."

Approval came from all around.

Henri pointed to a small hillock. "I will hold my cavalry in the middle. There I can hammer any weaknesses in their line.

"Conde on my right, Soisson on my left. Go now and secure my hillock before the enemy does. Monsieur de Turenne and La Tremuille will secure our right flank beyond Conde." He pointed. "There before the warren."

"Aye, aye," the officers said over and over and shook each other's hands. Annette stood by and waited out their jubilance, which was not jubilance but bravado, each raising the courage of the other. When it slowed, she said, "If only we should be so pleased when it is done."

The group became somber and silent.

Henri broke the lull, joking, "Ann, we don't worry, but place our faith in God and your guns."

"As usual," she countered.

The officers laughed tensely.

She stepped forward and put her toe on the map, where a low ridge protruded like a peninsula into the no-man's-land. "I'll put the cannons there."

"Too dangerous," Henri countered.

She pointed to the actual terrain. "There is plenty of brush to shield our maneuvers from their view. Once positioned, we can get off six or seven rounds before they counter us. By then I'll have destroyed their formation."

Henri tugged at his beard. "You really do want to kill them all, don't you?" His voice held no humor. "It is an advantageous position, but extremely dangerous. I don't have many cannons to lose, and I have only one of you."

He peered at the map, then the terrain. No one spoke. His fingers wove in and out of his beard, then he gazed into her eyes. "Okay, you may place them on the ridge, but only this far." He pointed his sword to the base of the protrusion where his infantry could support her.

She bent her lips into a smile as contrived as one carved on a marionette. "Of course, your lordship. Now I will make ready. It is a long haul, and bulwarks must be placed."

"Luc, take your unit and go with her," Batiste told the reprobate Catholic-turned-Protestant, whose conversion was based entirely on his bond with Barnard and Annette.

Already on her horse, she snapped, "Luc, hurry. Maybe this time you can go fast." She spun her horse and took off.

Luc smiled sheepishly and flapped his hand at her. "I'll catch up before she gets the mules hitched to the guns."

Henri's eyes drifted to follow her. "Luc, don't let her extend beyond where I said."

Then Henri spun toward Matt. "You and Jim ride with me."

"Our pleasure, your lordship," Matt said. Jim nodded without waiting for the translation.

The battalions formed into giant rectangles prickling with pikes, then marched to their positions along the battle line.

Henri rode his chestnut stallion before them and said:

"Who among us has not lost family or friend to the jealous heart of intolerance? You have fought for many decades for the simple right to think, to say what you think, to seek God with your soul.

"Those who persecute us come today in their finery, with their plumes and their linens. Their servants shine their armor to blind us. They fly their silken flags as if their wealth will win for them. Do they think they have caught us in our beds sleeping as they did on St. Bartholomew night? Do they think that they can casually butcher our mothers, sisters, and children again?

"Are they so enamored with power and wealth that they would join with Spain to kill their brothers and cousins? They think that we are weak because our armor is dull and dented and our helmets are rusty. Do they not know that our armor is dented from battle after battle and yet we live? Our helmets are rusty from the rain that poured on us, yet we live. Our gun barrels are as straight and our power is as black. Our swords and pikes are as sharp, and we are more determined than they.

"Today we will turn the tide. Today God has given us the high ground, for God loves thought and the freedom of the soul, and God abhors mindless conformity. If docile agreement were His desire, then we would be cows in a pasture.

295

"Go forth, for today He will turn back on the foulness of tyranny. You and I shall be His sword. God bless you all."

He tipped his hat and rode to join his cuirassiers.

**

Annette had her batteries moving long before the blocks of pikemen formed and long before Henri made his speech. Luc walked beside her, lending his weight to the cannons when the wheels sank into ruts or jammed against stones.

Sweat pouring down his neck, he pointed to the spot Henri had designated. "This is it."

She waved him aside and studied the lay of the battlefield.

"This is where he told us to set the cannons." Luc pointed to the prickly hedgehog of the nearest block of pikemen. "So they can protect us."

Hands on hips, she said nothing.

"So we don't lose the cannons," he added.

She stood as if in a daze, her mind focused on the geometry of the field. "It's not a good angle. A bit further, we will do much better." She coaxed him with a smile.

Head down, Luc kicked a stone. "We hardly have time to build basic breastworks." He waved his hand toward the pikemen. "No breastworks to delay the enemy until our infantry can help us."

She signaled the men forward. They laid their shoulders and backs to the ropes and wheels. Luc shook his head and walked beside her.

"See, I told you. It's beautiful." She pointed to the panorama of open pastureland.

"The breastworks should have been constructed last night," Luc complained.

She pointed to a rock protrusion and told one of her cannon commanders, "Avoid that damned thing."

"The cannons should have been positioned last night," Luc added.

"Last night, we didn't know this would be the place," Annette replied.

"Get off your fanny and start building those goddamned fortifications you're bitching about," an old artilleryman said.

Annette's eyes flared. "Jacques, the Lord's name…"

"Ah, the Lord's already decided whether he's against us or with us. A little spirited language ain't going to change his mind."

296

"Just the same—respect."

"I've no idea where to place the fortifications until I know where the cannons will be," Luc said.

Annette pointed. "Peter there, James there, Paul there." All her cannons were apostles.

Luc huffed at her then yelled to his men. "Cut some timber and start building the fortifications. Do the big gun first."

**

Dressed in simple leather armor, Henri's cuirassiers formed compact squads of a hundred horses each. They stretched out along the ridge at the midpoint of his battle line.

Across the field, the royalists' armor sparkled with gold and silver inlays, more suited for museum displays than for battle.

With a shout of confidence the royalists' light cavalry charged against Tremuille's line of pikes. The horsemen fared badly against the wall of spears until a regiment of Spanish mercenaries joined them. The Huguenot line broke.

Tremuille's men retreated back into the streets of Coutras. The Spanish followed, and after them came roving bands of Aztec priests, shrieking wraiths that assailed the wounded and captured Huguenots. Stinking like a slaughterhouse from dried blood and flesh they never washed off, they chopped through ribcages and crushed skulls, ripping out living hearts and dipping fingers into quivering brains.

General Conde pointed to the massacre and shouted, "Henri! We must act!"

Matt paled. Had he been wrong? Did their presence twist history down an unfavorable path?

**

"Wheel! Wheel!" Annette shouted. Four men pushed and pulled the cannon in a frantic effort. She laid her head against the barrel as it swung. "More! You have to lead the front line more. They're coming fast now. Hurry, lead the line!

"Now!" she shouted and patted the cannon barrel, then rushed to align the next one.

The first cannon roared. Half a mile away, combatants felt the sonic blast pass through their insides as if they were jelly.

The three cannons mounted a deadly barrage that ripped through the light cavalry and then the Spanish ranks. The second and the third volley stalled the enemy advance.

A royalist commander screamed for order and turned rage-filled eyes on Annette's position. He saw an indefensible island in the sea of conflict.

***

Ambush

Manny heard the distant hum of the Paiute Police truck. On the hill, the remaining sniper heard it too. He turned his rifle toward the road.

Hidden behind a sage-capped dune, Manny watched the Paiute patrol truck stop in front of the Haines Research Station. Manny was about to stand when voices a few yards away startled him. Gradually he sank down and peeked through the lower branches of the sage.

A pair of legs were visible in the shade of a gulley less than twenty yards away. Above, between yucca trunks, two faces watched the patrolman. Tuco turned his head. He mumbled inaudible words. Bengo bobbed into view with a pistol held by the side of his head.

Now Manny could hear them joking that the policeman would shit himself when he realized how fucked he was.

Manny sank down until he sat on the sand. His heart raced. *Dios mio, how did they not see me?* He leaned back and let his breath out as quietly as possible.

The police truck motor revved. The vehicle puttered toward them. The officer stopped about thirty yards in front of Manny's hideaway.

Manny's mind went blank.

The officer strolled to the front of his vehicle. Ten yards from Manuel, he raised a megaphone. It crackled and echoed off the nearby hills. "Uninvited squatters: On behalf of the Paiute Nation, this is your last warning. You must take your belongings, clean up your garbage, and leave. You have one hour to comply. This is your last warning."

Bengo and Tuco and their accomplice jumped up. Brandishing their guns, they hurried toward the officer. The policeman lowered the megaphone and unsnapped the flap to his holster.

"Run and show us your tail and maybe we'll let you live," Bengo said.

"Or maybe we'll cut your liver out and eat it while you're still alive!" Tuco threatened.

The policeman wrapped his fingers around his pistol grip.

Manny brought the shotgun to his shoulder.

"The Paiute Nation will no longer endure your insults," the Paiute retorted. "You have thirty minutes to clear out." He pointed to a newspaper plastered on the branches of a mesquite. "You'll need to haul your trash with you."

Tuco slapped Bengo on the shoulder. "You're a fucking idiot. We've got four snipers sighting down on you. When I raise my arm, you're dead. Guess what? The press will blame you for attacking us."

Tuco raised his fist to his chest. "On my signal."

Out of nowhere, the windshield of the pickup shattered. The boom of a distant rifle followed. The sudden shock caused Manny's finger to twitch. The shotgun bucked and roared. As if by an invisible hand, Bengo lifted up, floated backward then crashed to the earth. In the same instant, the other two thugs bent forward and pulled pistols from behind their backs.

A bullet smacked the pickup's radiator. The mountainside echoed with the low rumble of a rifle. Manny saw the officer's leg fly up and twist in the air. The policeman landed on his side next to the wheel of his pickup. His arm stretched out. His service revolver fired over and over, sending the spent cartridges spiraling through the air. The third ambusher arched backward. Blood shot from his chest. His knees buckled and he collapsed.

The officer rolled under his truck. The dusty soles of Bengo's shoes twitched. Tuco's face crimped with astonishment. His pistol raised, he turned toward Manny.

Manny felt his shotgun recoil against his shoulder.

Tuco's arms went wide. His pistol drifted away from his hand. Like Bengo, Tuco floated backward while his shirt shredded into rags.

The black shiny barrel of Manny's shotgun recoiled again and again. Suddenly there was a moment of absolute silence. Then through clogged ears Manny heard the officer groan.

"Hey, it's me," Manny said. "I'm going to help you." His words sounded distant and flat as if someone else had spoken them.

**

The sniper tossed his clip aside and reached for another. A foot pinned his hand to the ground. He tried to twist it away. A knee dropped hard and heavy in the middle of his back.

"Drop the gun." Derek yanked it from the sniper's grip. Moments later, Derek moved on, leaving the sniper handcuffed face down in the dirt.

Below him the police emerged from the shadows with clubs held high. Grunting, "Hutt! Hutt! Hutt!" they charged into Camp Desert Sunrise. Three more pickups loaded with deputies roared past the Haines Research Station on their way to the camp. One stopped long enough for two policemen to jump out and run to the fallen officer.

Dust whirled around the trucks and tents. For Camp Desert Sunrise, the sun was setting.

**

Sancho's fingers crushed down on Ruthie's wrist. He stared in a daze from his tent entrance; then he dragged her into the open.

Dust rose through the camp like a biblical plague. She listened to the screams and curses of the other campers and relished their misery the way they had ignored hers.

The drone of puttering trucks mixed with the occasional crack of a tent collapsing. Sancho yanked her off balance and almost to her knees. A nearby tent crumpled and flopped limply across the hood of a truck. Four big Paiute policemen trudged behind it with hickory clubs held upright. One spotted Sancho.

Sancho released Ruthie and ran.

Yes, retribution and deliverance.

She curled off in the opposite direction. Making herself small and insignificant, she moved across the flow of people until the tidal wave of humanity drifted downhill, leaving her alone.

**

Back where it began, the downed patrolman lay on a blanket in the beam of headlights. Another officer kneeled over him, adjusting the compress Manny had made to stop the bleeding. A third officer, with a clipboard, took Manny's testimony. Manuel answered in a flat distracted voice while keeping his attention on the wounded man. Caught up in the tragedy and mayhem, he forgot about the slightly ajar security trailer door, which now, in the dark of night, emitted a beacon that called out to all human castaways tossed on the storming sea of life.

"Do you feel dizzy or light-headed or tired?" an officer asked his fallen comrade.

"Yeah, a little tired, but I'm doing okay."

"I'd like to get you to the highway where an ambulance can meet us. Are you up for that?"

"I hate to take you away from the mission."

"It's pretty well over. A few minutes ago we had forty-one of the sixty-three vandals in custody."

"Billy and his lieutenants?"

The kneeling officer rocked back on his heels and chuckled. "You and your sidekick here took out most of the lieutenants. I'm sure we'll have Billy before the night is through."

"Probably." The wounded officer chuckled then coughed.

"What you say we put you in the backseat? I'll ride along to monitor you." Not waiting for an answer, he turned to Manny. "Do you mind driving? I'd like to get Henry here—"

"No problem, Officer Hightree," Manny said.

Manny drove fast yet braked gently for dips and bumps. For him, nothing else mattered.

**

Hands on knees, Arbie peered from behind a thick clump of prairie grass. He tried to keep quiet, but his heart pounded and he gasped for oxygen. The sound of people and trucks had diminished to a distant moan. The desert near him had emptied of life.

Is it safe?

Ruthie got away from Sancho.

He'd seen her zigzagging through the crowd on her way to freedom.

He ground his jaws together, punched the sand with his fist, then took a deep breath and ran. Far away a tiny crack of light shone against the black of night. It took him only a second to realize where it was.

**

Derek saw Arbie plow through a stand of prickly pear in his single-minded rush to escape. But Derek had more important concerns. A few hundred yards away, a dark mass slinked through the brush toward two eastern hillocks. Occasionally he could make out the forms of individuals in the pack. The hotshot organizers of the illegal camp were leaving their minions to their fate.

Billy Manes was among them. Billy Manes had insulted Derek's people. And Billy Manes had assaulted their women. That would be avenged.

Moving at a trot, Derek angled toward the retreating mass. The throb of a truck surged through the sand behind him. Its headlights danced against the hillside while it tossed side to side, making its way toward the escapees. It crested a ridge and painted them in its spotlights.

A megaphone clicked and a metallic voice blasted, "Halt! This is the Paiute Tribal Authority! On your knees. Hands over your heads. Immediately!"

In the sweep of the light, Derek saw the NAS men drop and raise their arms in surrender. Billy dropped too, then rolled behind the others and scooted off on all fours through the shadows.

Derek chased after him. He tackled Billy and knocked him into a wall of cactus. Billy ignored the thorns imbedded in his side. He rolled through the briar and bounced to his feet with a pistol outstretched. He caught Derek off guard.

Derek reached for his holster. Billy's gun echoed in Derek's ears.

Derek's gun hand dropped. He swayed to his knees. His chest was on fire. The world blurred into a black-and-white movie, getting blacker with each heartbeat. Liquid dripping from his mouth, he toppled forward. His head lay against the ground. He felt his hair being yanked upward. His neck, rubbery and uncontrollable, arched back. Blood rushed down his forehead and into his eyes. Then he felt nothing.

***

Beautiful Mama

Stephanie pushed the blanket off and sat on the edge of Horace's Naugahyde couch in the SAM chamber. Disoriented, she studied the stark emptiness of her surroundings. Her eyes settled on the SAM and she calmed, understanding where she was.

Emil handed her a plate of scrambled eggs. "You slept ten hours."

She shoveled the food down like a starvation victim. "Did you bring the food and blanket from upstairs?"

302

"Yes."

"I don't know how you stand it down here." She wiped the plate clean.

"I'm going to fix it better." He took the empty plate from her.

"Absolutely." She nodded her head emphatically. "This is ridiculous. Worse than prison. Never been there, but I'm sure."

"I'm going to paint murals, have a kitchen, a bunkroom, a poolroom, an exercise room, a library…"

"Anything you want. Herman has to do it." With sudden animation, she looked about the room. "Where is the gun I brought back?"

"I stashed it down one of the tunnels. It can't be found." His eyes told her that he knew what she had done. She coughed an emotional thanks.

She stood and took the blanket by the edge. "I have to go now. I'll help you fix it up down here after all this settles."

"I don't want to be here anymore," he said.

"Well, at least we can fix it up for the next time, and hope to God there is no next time."

"I'm going to bring Jim back in a couple hours." Emil asserted it as if he expected opposition.

"Great, I'm glad." She folded the blanket. "You want me to take this stuff upstairs?"

"No, maybe Jim will want it."

She hugged Emil then started for the door.

"Hey," he called out. "Be careful outside the compound. The police went into radio silence. They were going to run off those Sunrise squatters. I haven't heard from Manny for a while, so I don't know how it went."

"I'm sure everything went smoothly," she said. "I'll have Manuel patch you into the police when they come online again."

**

Stephanie peered through the glass in the door between the research and security stations. A redheaded stranger hunched over Manuel's desk, rifling through papers.

Odd, I didn't think Herman hired a sub for Manuel.

She released the lock and stepped into the security unit. "Hey, are you Manuel's relief?" she asked.

Arbie turned on his heel and leveled a pistol at her. "Well! Look at this. I just got lucky."

Stephanie froze with her hands half raised. "Who are you? Where's Manuel?" She glanced around the room, expecting to see a body poking out from behind a chair.

He shifted his eyes toward the outside door. She saw it was ajar.

Arbie snickered. "I guess he went home to eat a burrito. Hey, I bet you're the one that convinced everybody that Wendell filmed a hovercraft. Probably turned your Nazi Indian police on us too. Well now you're giving me a tour of this place, bitch."

He snapped the outside door shut. "Let's go back where you came from."

Stephanie stared at the gun and swallowed. "That gun has a hair trigger. Lower it, or I'm not going anywhere."

His face reddened. His arm gyrated. "I saw your Gestapo police kill all my friends at Camp Desert Sunrise." He jabbed his finger toward the front window. "Tonight."

He thrust the gun toward her, then giggled at her wide-eyed cringe. "Open that goddamned door."

"I can't. It has to be done from the inside." She turned sideways, making herself a smaller target.

"You think I'm stupid, don't you?" He drew the words out long. Then he snapped out his demand. "Press the keypad, now."

Stephanie looked into the camera over the door. "Don't let him in, Emil."

"Emil? The little Tofu pool player?" Arbie grabbed Stephanie by the neck and pushed the gun into her ribs.

"Hey, Emil, it's me, Arbie. You owe me a few pitchers of beer, remember? Open the door or I shoot this bitch."

**

Emil wished that Jim were lying on the SAM right now.

In a childish taunt, Arbie shouted, "You listening E-mil?"

Emil flipped the speaker switch. "Okay, point the gun away from her and I'll let you in."

"Now!" Arbie twisted the gun between her ribs and yanked her face toward the camera.

Emil mentally recited the Spanish curse words Manuel had taught him. He took a deep breath. "I'll click the door when you turn the gun away from her."

"You've got three seconds," Arbie threatened. "One…"

Click.

304

Arbie jiggled his head and shoulders in a taunt then pushed Stephanie ahead of him.

Emil saw their images disappear from the first monitor and appear on another one.

"You're about to violate a top-security military facility," Stephanie warned. "That's treason. Consider that."

"Bullshit," Arbie said. "I grew up on military bases; I know what military security looks like."

Stephanie kept her voice calm and logical. "This is civilian research for the military. We provide our own security."

"Not very good security," Arbie said. "Once I tell about this on TV, it won't matter how many laws I broke. You and Herman won't be able to lay a hand on me."

When the elevator swallowed them, Emil hurriedly shut all the monitors down. He scribbled a note and laid it and the remote control light switch on the desk corner. Then he walked back and leaned against the SAM.

**

Arbie shoved Stephanie into the SAM chamber. She stumbled away, separating herself from his careless gun antics. She grabbed the corner of the desk and pretended to steady herself.

Emil raised his hands high. "Calm down. I'm not doing nothing."

Arbie swung the gun toward him. "What's that thing you're leaning on? It looks alien. And by the way, there is no such thing as a Tofu. I looked it up at the library."

Emil frowned. "Maybe you didn't look in the right place?"

"You're small compared to those Indians, and your pool playing is abnormal. You're a hybrid."

Emil jutted his face toward Arbie. Then took a short step toward him. "Then that cowboy, who was very tall, must be a hybrid, because I wasn't good enough to beat him."

Arbie squinted down the gun at Emil. "Maybe so. You could be crossed with the greens. He could be from the Anunnaki."

Stephanie searched the desk for something heavy, sharp, or chemically irritating to use against her captor. She saw a torn piece of paper, odd for Herman or Emil, both fastidious. It bore the note, "SN use." A small object, as alien as anything in the room, lay on the paper.

The remote light control.

305

Suddenly she understood Emil's plan. Cut the lights. Arbie's gun would become useless.

She slid toward the controller.

Arbie's focus stayed on Emil.

She moved closer.

Arbie swung toward her. "Uh-uh, no funny stuff. You two stand where I can see you both at once." Then he turned his eyes toward the SAM and studied it as if mesmerized.

While he stared at the machine, Stephanie looked to Emil. He shifted his eyes toward the controller that lay just inches from her hand.

She slid her fingers toward it.

"I asked you what is this thing?" Arbie kept his eyes on Emil but now pointed his gun at the SAM.

Stephanie wrapped her fingers around the remote and pressed it.

Inky darkness blinded them all.

Arbie screamed, "Assholes!"

Stephanie fell to her hands and knees and inched toward the exit. She heard Emil scuttle behind the SAM.

Arbie's breaths grew loud and panicked. A frighten whine squeaked out after each. His feet shifted over the floor indecisively.

"Wak-wak-wak-wak," Emil screeched, loud and shrill, like a sci-fi film beastie.

"Ahhhhhhh!" Arbie wailed.

Boom! Boom! Boom! Flashes of orange went from his gun straight at the SAM. Stephanie cowered to protect herself from ricochets.

There was none. Each bullet rang dully against the side of the machine then dropped with a clink to the floor.

Silence followed. Then the sound of a short circuit hissed. Tiny green discharges wriggled and popped over the SAM's exterior. The SAM's surface became a spider web of green electrical zigzags. The crackles grew loud as lightning in a thunderstorm.

For an instant, all went silent.

A huge green bolt of electricity arced from the SAM to Arbie. A web of green electric discharges danced over his body.

He fell to the ground. He kicked once; then his arms and legs stilled. The spider web of flashes wrapped his body in a dull green glow. His once-red hair stood straight out like a chartreuse Mohawk.

"Turn the lights on," Emil said.

306

Stephanie found the switch and pressed it again. Light flooded in, forcing their eyes into slits.

They approached Arbie. His body showed no signs of electrical burns. No fluids oozed from his orifices. They saw only Arbie, his eyes and mouth wide open and his body glowing green.

Emil stared down at him. "He doesn't look dead."

Stephanie kneeled, taking care not to bump him. "I think he's paralyzed."

"Should we tie him up?" Emil asked.

Stephanie slid away from Arbie. "I don't think we should touch him as long as he's green."

"Yeah, we'll just leave him here until Herman gets back."

"He could come to while you're busy," she warned.

Emil sighed. "So we should tie him up."

"I don't want to touch him while he's green."

Emil bent toward Arbie.

"No!" Stephanie said. "You can't. You're the only one that can bring them back."

She gave Arbie a quick toe poke. Nothing happen.

"Good," Emil said. "We'll lock him in my new conference room."

"Fine." She took his legs, Emil took his arms, and they dragged him to the new room.

"You think he'll be too cold?" Emil asked and began to bind Arbie with an electrical cord.

"I don't care," Stephanie said.

"Me neither. I hope the SAM didn't run itself down by zapping him. It's almost time to bring Jim back."

They studied the SAM from the doorway.

"Do you think it's safe?" Stephanie asked.

Emil chuckled oddly. "I think it knows who its enemies are." He busied himself getting the monitors back online, as if giving the SAM time to get used to his presence. Finally he approached it. "You know me? Yes, we've been working here together like good ole pals.

"I'm going to touch you to get your energy reading."

SAM behaved normally. Emil began to relax. "No change in energy. My God, can you imagine how much energy it took to do that? Not even a tiny dip in the power level."

"Hello?"

Both of their heads jerked toward the intercom.

"Everything okay down there?"

307

"Manny, are you okay?" Emil asked, but his words were drowned by Stephanie's scream, "You nearly got us killed. You'd better—"

"I have bad news," Manuel started. Stephanie's rage evaporated into foreboding.

"What?" Emil asked.

"I'm sorry."

"What?" Stephanie asked.

"Lots of bad stuff. I'm so sick of it. I tried to help. I went out to help the police—"

Stephanie's rage reemerged. "You let that crackpot—"

Manny broke her off. "Derek's dead."

She swallowed. Emil's lungs emptied with a mournful rush of air.

"Charlene's been kidnapped."

"What?" Stephanie's breathing accelerated.

Emil glared at her. His eyes watered. She reached out for him. He pushed her away.

"Marie is headed to the reservation to join the posse," Manuel said.

Neither answered him.

Emil flopped in front of his control panel. He kept his eyes away from Stephanie.

"Manuel, is Matt's jeep here?" Stephanie asked.

"Yes."

She laid her hand on Emil's shoulder. "I'm going after Charlene. Bring Jim back now. Have him meet Marie at the reservation."

"Go then! You should." Emil's words boiled out in anger. He whipped around to glare at her.

Before he could take it back, she was gone.

He laid his head on his desk and mumbled through tears, "What have I done? I've sent Stephanie to be killed."

***

Chapter 22: Time & Space

In a one-room fisherman's hut on the waterfront in Coutras, Herman sat on a stained butcher table, its corners rounded from the hacks of ten thousand fish mutilations.

Morto sat on the floor, his attention on Herman.

The door creaked. A shadow wavered beyond. Herman lifted his eyes in minimal response to the intrusion.

"You're not surprised," Jules Verne said.

"Obviously not." Herman gazed at Morto.

"What are you going to do with him?" Jules asked. "Clearly, you don't intend to dump him in the ocean, where he would be a time bomb waiting to be discovered."

"I'm taking him back with me," Herman said.

"Aye, but as advanced as you Nirvanians are, you never perfected time travel. He's too heavy for your machine." Jules crossed his arms and frowned.

"It's doable." Herman tapped his fingers on the butcher table. "We'll need four time tunnels to take us all out of here. Spacing them over time on both ends should work."

"That's the way you would do it." Jules's eyes twinkled.

"It's basic physics," Herman retorted. "It doesn't matter who is doing it."

Jules's face spread into a bemused grin. "You can't send him ahead of you, he might collapse your tunnel, stranding you here, and there are many reasons not to leave him behind, even for a few hours.

"There's also the issue of capacity. He's thirty percent heavier than you, and your weight pushes the limit of your device. You'll need to make improvements if you plan to keep doing this sort of thing."

A barrage of gunshots came from outside, followed by screams of pain and desperation. Herman pushed past Verne and peeked into the street. Huguenots poured by him in frantic retreat. Two blocks away, a few brave ones begrudgingly fought to contain the enemy while pleading with their comrades to come back and fight.

Herman eyed Verne askance. "We'll continue this conversation in thirty minutes or so." Herman picked up two oaken fisherman's clubs used to kill sharks and other large fish, then entered the street.

He grabbed two deserters and shoved them back toward the battle line. He followed them with his arms spread wide. From club tip to club tip, he blocked the entire lane.

"Stand for freedom and family," he shouted.

Those trapped between him and the fight had no choice.

Someone shouted, "Gather to the Scotsman."

Seeing that help was coming, the men on the line shouted for victory and surged forward. Pistols blazed back and forth, many enemies aimed at Herman, who stood shoulders above the rest. He pushed to the front, where he swung the clubs so inhumanly fast that some claimed he was the archangel Michael sent to save them. Later tales embellished by saying silver light shown here and there on his arms and face.

**

On the hilltop, Henri's cavalry saw the Huguenots rally in the streets of Coutras. At the same time, Annette sent her sixth volley into the royalist formations. It would be her last because enemy pikemen were converging on her position. Dubois's horse bucked and neighed, animating his concern.

"Damn her," Conde mumbled. "She hung herself out too far this time."

"Henri, we should hit their rear and divert them," a rider urged.

"A goddamned piss," a burly, one-eyed warrior said and spat.

310

Henri ignored them all. His eyes set straight ahead, he studied the hole left by the pikemen. No one came forward to fill it. He drew his sword and pointed. "A hole in their line."

"Yes, yes," Conde said. His horse pushed up beside Henri, its teeth snapping with the lust to tear at enemy flesh.

Henri pointed to the forest behind the hole. "See there, Joyeuse's banners: the French, the Spanish, the families. When we move, they will see their error and try to stop us."

"Let them," Conde said.

"Signal the charge."

Bugles rang out.

"Wedge formation. Advance!"

"Sir," Barnard said, his face turning from Henri to Annette's position and then back to Henri. Jim stood beside him, his horse pawing the ground.

"Go to her. Nip at their rear. Maybe you'll do some good. But we must charge." Henri pointed to the gap in the line. "This can end it."

"But, sir," Barnard started.

"I said go."

Jim grabbed Barnard's arm and together they galloped across the field toward Annette's hillock.

"Sir," Matt said, "I would go with them. My guns could make a difference."

"Your guns shall make their difference here. When victory is assured, I will release you."

He raised his sword. "Forward at a trot!"

Henri's cuirassiers came down the hill in a wedge so tight that a hand could not pass between the knees of adjacent riders. The royalists' cavalry charged at a full gallop. They shouted glorious whoopla and strung their line out like stampeding cattle. Their horses, foaming at the mouth, loped in exhaustion as the warring parties merged. The Huguenot ram knocked them aside or plowed over them. Firing point blank into shining breastplates and helmets, the cuirassiers hurled into the breach and up the hill to overwhelm the king's bodyguard.

Joyeuse laid his sword on the ground. The Huguenot victory bugle sounded.

Matt turned, reins in his teeth, and reloading, he spurred his horse toward Annette's cannons.

**

311

Spanish and royalists retreated from the streets of Coutras. Far off, behind enemy lines, the Huguenot trumpet declared victory. Herman dropped his bloodied clubs and returned to the fisherman's shack.

Herman was neither surprised by nor fully prepared for what he found. Expectedly, Morto was gone. Jules Verne was gone. Unexpectedly the room was gone, except for the old butcher table, which floated in a void of neon blue and looked disturbingly like a primitive sacrificial altar. On it, like cheese in a mousetrap, lay a scroll wrapped in a red ribbon. The ribbon was red when Herman substituted pure white light for the neon blue, which he did mentally. Before the change, the ribbon had been fluorescent pink.

The spooky altar didn't deter Herman. He walked right up to it, pulled the ribbon and unwound the parchment.

Rows of Aramaic mixed with an unknown symbology were printed in fine calligraphy down the length of the page. A line of Aramaic mystical mumbo-jumbo preceded each section of cryptic code. Certain that the mystical mush referred to real physical phenomena, Herman believed he could interpret the unknown language, and if a robot can experience joy, he did, because Verne had as much as promised him the secret to improved time travel.

In the direction of the dock, where a second exit to the shack had been, a halo of pulsing purple light beckoned, and with paper in hand, Herman exited the sixteenth century.

**

Head low against his horse, Jim weaved between Aztec priests who wandered the battlefield, their bodies drenched in blood, their hands coated with grease from human organs. To his left Dubois did the same.

Jim's mind latched onto his grandfather's stories of jaguar priests who raided Paiute villages to drag away victims for their sun god. He had come here hoping to exact revenge, but now, the sheer darkness of the priests chilled his psyche and he sought only to be clear of them and to save Annette.

"Away," he shouted. "Away, you hideous beasts."

One rose up from behind a heap of bodies, with blood dripping from his mouth. The Aztec held human entrails over his head and taunted. Jim's horse widened its eyes and leaped. Jim

312

passed over the priest and slashed the staff downward, cutting the devil's body in half.

Like a pack of hyenas, more priests converged on him. One threw a well-aimed javelin. It dug deep into his horse's broad neck, and his second horse in as many days fell from under him. He somersaulted through the air, landing flat on his back. The staff bounced across the ground.

Woozy, he sat up. The shadow of a raised club loomed over him. He raised his hands in defense, but he was slow and lethargic. A tinny bang rang in his ears. The priest's body flopped over his shoulder and the war club slammed into the ground between his legs.

"Get on." Barnard sounded far off, but his hand grabbed Jim's arm. Another priest screamed and charged them. There was another pistol shot, this time closer and clearer.

The priest fell backward.

"Get on!" Barnard's voice was normal. Jim's mind lurched into real time. He stumbled to his feet.

Another priest charged. Jim yanked the war axe from between his legs and swung it.

Barnard's horse brushed against Jim's back. The Frenchman fired his third pistol point blank into the chest of another priest. He extended his hand to Jim.

Jim whirled the obsidian axe in a vertical arc, slicing deeply into the shoulder of an attacker. More were coming.

"Go to Annette. Now!" Jim said and pushed Barnard away. Then he raced to the staff. He took it in both hands, samurai-like. "Go," he shouted and aimed the whistling blue plasma outward toward the encircling Aztecs.

From behind him came a hair-raising war cry, followed by the steady reports of gunfire. An Aztec flew backward. Another fell sideways.

"Go on!" Matt shouted to Barnard. "I've got Jim." Matt circled Jim while laying down a barrage of pistol fire. Those priests that lived, ran.

Matt pulled Jim onto the horse. Far ahead, Dubois bore down on the enemy's rear. Even further off, the pikemen poured over Luc's hastily fashioned bulwarks.

Matt spurred the horse. The battlefield went silent and faded into gray nothingness.

A moment later, the horse trotted to a stop and stood alone.

**

313

After firing their sixth volley, Annette knew they would be overrun. Luc's soldiers retreated to her. No longer able to manage the big guns, Annette's men joined in the hand-to-hand fighting. With the instincts of brothers and fathers, they circled around her last gun.

Over the chaos, the Huguenot bugle sounded victory. No one heard. The fighting continued.

A wounded gunner lay against the wheel of the caisson.

"Gerome, help," Annette pleaded.

Gerome's lips turned up in a blood-drained smile. He struggled to his feet.

"Shrapnel!" she said.

She and Gerome poured rocks, nails, broken horseshoes, scraps of every kind into the cannon barrel.

"Clear!" she shouted. Those who could, moved from the cannon's path. When she lit the powder, she smelled Barnard's fragrance. She felt his breath on her neck. She turned. He wasn't there.

**

The explosion drew every eye to the ridge. Smoke shrouded the trees, then hung in the air.

Henri dropped his spyglass and bowed his head. "She has won. She is lost."

***

Xilon Star Cluster

When *Quantum* neared the Xilon Star Cluster, Uriel began reviving the biological crew. He sat on a low stool beside Captain Yanitur's cryogenic chamber, which had the shape of a huge metallic loaf of bread. Uriel touched holographic glyphs that hovered just under the bronze sheen of its surface. As he touched them, they changed shapes. He dragged some from one location to another along the chamber shell. When he finished, several began to throb. Sitting perfectly still, he tracked these pulsations for twenty-six minutes; then he traced a closed figure, shaped like a shaggy caterpillar, on the chamber lid. Within his sketchy outline, the metal became clear as glass. He looked through to assess Yanitur's status.

314

He expected no problem. The hibernation had been short. Thus the crew required only hypo-metabolic stasis, a much less dangerous process than full cryogenic suspension.

Color seeped back into Yanitur's skin. His respiration, though minimal, became visible. The vital signs were all moving toward their optimums. Uriel tapped his finger within his caterpillar window, and the glass became metal again. He sat still for another twenty-eight minutes, his eyes locked on the vital signs; then he traced out a big circle that became glass.

Yanitur looked good, so Uriel moved more glyphs and the lid opened.

"Wake up, Captain." Uriel enjoyed his moment of power over his commanding officer.

Yanitur's eyes opened. He struggled up onto elbows and turned his head side to side. "It feels like a massive drunk combined with the flu."

"I understand," Uriel sympathized. The seraph did not understand, and the captain knew it; however, Yanitur was so miserable and vulnerable at the moment that he took comfort in Uriel's disingenuous words.

Over the next hour, Uriel helped Yanitur move about, much like one would steady a baby on his first attempt to walk.

After that Uriel moved on to the next person, who was Kale. By the time he got to the third person, Yanitur and Kale were helping him, and the process moved faster.

After the fifth person had been awakened, Yanitur exited to the bridge.

"Situation?" Yanitur asked Argus.

"Kong says his ship's base is on the fourth planet of Xilon 10." Argus pointed to the Xilon star cluster on his holographic screen.

"How much traffic is there?" Yanitur asked.

"It's heavier than I would expect. Like they're preparing for something."

"Us?"

"Nothing military in their transmissions," Argus replied.

Kale entered from the hibernation deck and saluted Yanitur. "Captain, we'll be at full crew strength in three more hours."

The captain turned to Kong. "Can you get us to the base?"

The chrome robot chuckled mechanically. "Kong got you this far."

315

Kale snapped his head toward the chrome träger. "Bad time for being jocular. Can you get us there or not?"

"Yes, Kong guide you there."

Yanitur made a slow chopping motion with his fingertips pointed toward the front of the ship. "Okay, let's start in."

For two hours they glided toward the cluster while monitoring the nonchalant Verg communications. Then a ship called *Long Knife* ended a broadcast with an odd burst of static.

Before it finished, Kong announced, "Verg know *Quantum* here."

Yanitur and Kale exchanged skeptical glances.

"What tells you that?" Yanitur asked.

"*Long Knife* give ambush orders."

"How many ships do they have available?" Uriel entered the bridge after having completed the revival of the last crewman.

"Kong think more than twenty, less than thirty."

Yanitur laughed. "Are they nuts? Even fifty of them have no chance against an Ajax cruiser."

"Verg not stupid," Kong said, "Maybe they do have chance."

"Look at the topology." Uriel nodded toward the hologram of the star cluster.

"I noticed," Yanitur said. "Maybe against other Verg ships it would provide ambush terrain. Against us, its only value is camouflage."

The last of the humanoids trickled to their command stations.

Kale took the first mate's chair. "Remember that alien ally they talked about."

Yanitur tapped his fingers on his console. "Yeah, but while we slept, our seraphim analyzed the effects of the alien blaster. It has some advantages over ours, but not enough to shift the outcome of a battle."

"Aliens give…" Kong paused as if his logic got stuck in a loop.

Kale smiled during the protracted silence; then Kong finished, "Maybe alien advisor have only lousy shit weapon."

Uriel raised his eyebrows. "He has a point."

Yanitur locked eyes with Kale and then Uriel. He tapped his fingers again and sighed. "Okay, send a pulse message to the nearest AGS station. Give them our plan and our location—and the analysis

316

of the alien technology. If things don't work out for us, they'll need to know what they're up against."

**

Fifteen minutes later the intercom crackled with the voice of Merc, the communications seraph. "Pulse message loaded. Ready to launch on your command, First Officer Kale."

Kale took over. "All crew, strap into nearest restraint station immediately. Pulse launch procedure commencing at 08:16:00. Merc, signal pulse launch warning—now." Kale signaled with a downward thrust of his arm then pushed a white button.

Two long shrill beeps blasted everywhere on the cruiser. An announcement followed.

"Pulse launch in ten seconds! Pulse launch in ten seconds! Strap into nearest restraint. This is an executive order. Strap into nearest restraint." Another round of beeps followed. The countdown began: "Ten, nine, eight..." After "one" the announcement said, "Pulse launch initialized! Pulse launch initialized!"

The ship shuddered, and a blinding light more intense than any hydrogen bomb ever to explode on Earth lit the starboard side of *Quantum*. For an instant, a hundred-yard-wide beam of energy was visible; then it shot off, diminishing to a pinpoint on its way to the Nirvanian arm of the galaxy.

The impulse knocked *Quantum* twenty-five thousand kilometers off course before the retro engines generated enough force to bring the ship back under control.

Kale turned off his intercom and faced Yanitur. "Should we send another?"

"Yes," Yanitur said. "That information is vital."

Uriel shifted in his restraint harness. "Captain, another pulse will severely weaken our combat readiness."

"How fast can this star cluster refill our energy banks?" Yanitur asked.

"Thirty hours," Uriel replied.

Kale scoffed. "Let's hope the Vergs don't smell a lame duck."

The apelike träger nodded. "Kong sitting duck, too."

Uriel locked *Quantum* into a figure-eight orbit around two stars, maximizing the refill rate of the ship's antimatter banks. During the fueling process, they contoured their electromagnetic image to resemble a metallic asteroid.

317

Eighteen hours into the recharge, an alarm sounded, ranging from ear-piercing shrill to foghorn low, over and over, on a three-second cycle.

The intercom announced, "Report to battle stations! Report to battle stations!"

The crew scrambled to their positions.

"Assessment?" Yanitur said in open-channel communication that every crew member could hear.

"Incoming, sir, 800,000,000 kilometers out. Bogey to intercept our trajectory in two hours," Uriel said. "A sheetlike craft. Its leading edge is approximately 1000 kilometers in length."

"Sheetlike?" Kale's voice expressed disbelief.

"At this distance I can only offer a conjecture," Uriel said. "I would guess it's less than 100 meters thick." Then he corrected himself. "Sir, the bogey has transformed into an annular shape that is approximately 300 kilometers in diameter."

"I need a precise reading." Yanitur walked to Uriel's station and watched over the seraph's shoulder. "What is its greatest instantaneous velocity?"

"Sir, .6789 c, currently ninety minutes to intercept," Uriel replied. "Hum, it just increased its diameter to 500 kilometers."

"Argus, what about density changes?" Kale asked.

The armaments seraph disengaged from his weapons link. "Sir, it's like a nebula traveling at near two-thirds the speed of light."

While Argus tracked it, Uriel, Kale, and Yanitur speculated on what kind of weaponry a fast-traveling gas might possess, and how they might defeat it. Uriel stopped mid-sentence and blurted, "Sub-particle uncertainty shielding."

Yanitur's eyes lit up. "Right, that's the way she said it would work."

Kale wobbled his head in a dizzying fashion. "Who? What?"

Yanitur pointed to Uriel. "Go ahead, you explain. I never quite understood it."

Uriel faced Kale. "It was Admiral Sharon's pet project at the academy. She did lab research on the concept and taught the theory in class. AGS became disenchanted with the continual setbacks and they defunded her studies."

Yanitur patted Uriel's shoulder and took over. "Shortly thereafter she resigned and went back to Amazonia to take command of their navy. At the time, her move was viewed as a face-saving step."

318

Just then Argus announced, "Sir, the object has divided in two." Before anyone could comment, he corrected, "No. It exploded into fifty particles."

"Amazonian razors," Uriel said.

Yanitur burst into laughter. "I guess Sharon got her theory to work."

"They've got company," Argus said.

After he spoke, the screen widened to show a much nearer and heavier fleet rounding the horizon of a nearby star. This fleet moved to intercept the Amazonians.

"Contact the razors!" Yanitur ordered.

Kale broadcasted through all communication channels. "Amazonian fleet, this is AGS Ajax cruiser. Captain Yanitur requests naval protocol closed-channel communication, over." He didn't wait for a response. "Razor squadron, you face Verg warships, approximately forty-three. Ajax cruiser *Quantum* requests coordinated assault. Respond over closed-channel communication, over."

The Amazonians didn't answer. Minutes later, the Amazonian and the Verg fleets collided, but the clash lasted seconds. The Vergs fired a broadside, missing all of the razors. The razors flew through the Verg fleet, then past *Quantum* and into the Xilon star cluster.

***

Outlaw Band

Stephanie pulled a box of hollow-point ammo from the cabinet next to Manuel's desk. She took two more of "00" shells and tossed them all into a heavy canvas shoulder bag. "Turn it up," she said while slamming the ammunition cabinet shut.

"What?" Manny let out an exasperated sigh. It was the third time she had been rude to him since he'd left the door open, which she claimed allowed a crazy person to attack her and Emil.

Manuel pushed back his chair and watched her while she pulled a Saiga shotgun from the rack and ejected a shell into her shaky hand. She held the cartridge close to her face and said, "00," then reloaded the shell.

"Should I quit?" he asked.

She tossed the gun on the counter and whirled toward him. Her face was terrified. Her lower jaws quivered when she spoke. "No! Hell no! We can't lose anyone right now."

"Of course, I mean when it's all over, I'll quit."

She turned her back to him and grabbed the counter with both hands. Her fingers were white from her grip. Her arms shook.

"I made the mistake," Manny said. "I'll go after them. You stay here."

"No," she said again and strapped on the pistol belt. "It's personal, very personal."

She turned toward him and forced an off-kilter smile. "But thanks anyway. I mean that."

"I can't let you go out there like this." He pointed to her quivering hand. She held it out between them. Both watched it shake.

"It looks bad." She sounded detached and analytical. "But after I'm out there, driving the jeep awhile, it will get better. I know. I've done this before."

He shook his head in disagreement.

"It will." She tossed a secure-band radio on top of the ammo then lifted the shotgun. She signaled him. He hesitated in a dissatisfied silence then pressed the button.

The door lock clicked.

She swung it open.

The caress of the night air was welcomed by them both. She stepped outside. "Emil already knows. Go ahead and turn up the radio so he can hear any news about Charlene." Then she added, "And don't resign."

The keys were in Matt's jeep. She plugged the radio in and laid the shotgun across the back bench. She drove south toward an old jeep trail, two ruts that rambled through the brush but headed on an intercept to the path Charlene's kidnappers were reported to have taken.

Darkness edged in, reducing her world to the jeep interior and the tiny strip of desert in her headlights. She welcomed the isolation.

**

Eddie lay on a cot in the tribal medical center. Marie squatted beside him.

"I tried to stop them," he said. "But that fellow slugged me in the face with his pistol. I think my cheekbone is broken." The whole left side of his face was a red pulp ringed by dark purple.

320

"It's NAS. They all wore ski masks, but I think it was Billy that hit me." He began to cry. "Demons from hell, they were. Two councilmen shot dead, another beaten near to death. They ambushed us."

Eddie's left eye had turned into a golf-ball-sized lump. To save his sight, he needed an ambulance, and he needed one now.

Marie looked around the room for a phone. Both front doors flung open, banging against the walls. Jim entered, taking long fast strides. He came right at her.

She peered into his eyes and swallowed. Did he know?

"What happened?" He looked from her to Eddie.

"Jim?" Eddie drifted into wooziness.

"NAS retaliated for dismantling Camp Desert Sunrise." Marie couldn't look him in the face.

Jim frowned. "Why didn't the tribe wait until I got back?"

Marie bit her lip and hung her head. She couldn't respond. She'd only heard parts of it. Someone who knew more should tell him.

The doors opened again, this time more gently, even reverently. Two police officers entered and walked toward Jim in coordinated step, like a funeral procession.

Sadness pressed down in her chest, squeezing the air from her lungs and making it difficult to fill them again. Her eyes couldn't pull free from the officers.

Jim's face contorted.

A spasm rose into Marie's throat. She bit her lip, but the quake inside her wouldn't stop.

"Jim." Captain Lightfoot's voice needed no more words.

Jim's face drew blank and cold. He hung his head.

Lightfoot handed him the old Winchester. "Derek was ambushed. We've lost him."

Jim's arm fell to his side. His grip barely clung to the rifle. A tear dripped down the side of his nose. He wiped it away with the back of his sleeve.

Now Lightfoot turned his face down. His lips moved without words. Then he faced Jim again. "We're going after them." He swallowed, but kept his eyes on Jim. "They finished him the old-fashioned way."

Jim's fist squeezed the rifle stock. His jaws clamped. His eyes bored into Lightfoot. "Why…" he started but let his appeal for sanity dissipate with his breath.

321

Marie reached out. He looked at her hand as if it were from another universe, then gently closed his fingers around hers.

Lightfoot's eyes flared. "We're not going to let this stand. We've formed a posse. We leave in an hour."

The sound of horse hooves on the sidewalk came from the street. Old Charles Stagskull stood outside the window, holding the reins of two jet-black horses, Jim's and Derek's.

Jim looked in Marie's eyes. She nodded. He faced Lightfoot. "We're going now. We'll mark the way for you."

Lightfoot clasped Jim's shoulder. "Please wait. I don't want..."

Jim cupped Lightfoot's shoulder and then chambered the Winchester with a snap that echoed through the room. Everyone went quiet and looked up. Jim started for the door.

Marie pointed to the walkie-talkie on Lightfoot's hip. "Call Manuel and ask him to dispatch the hovercraft. It's Eddie's best chance to save his eye."

Then she followed Jim.

**

Charles handed Jim the reins and pointed toward the distant line of mountains. "They're on dirt bikes, generally headed for Webb Gap. Lots of caves thereabouts. You know Robber's Roost? It's likely their hangout."

"Billy with them?" Jim asked.

Charles nodded. "They wore masks, but he's the one stomped Eddie." The old shaman thought a moment, then gazed at the mountains. "Take them all; then you'll be sure."

Jim rammed the Winchester into its sheath and mounted.

Marie pulled a Dragunov sniper rifle with a night-vision scope from her car trunk and got on the other horse.

Jim kept his eyes straight ahead. "We're not bringing back any prisoners."

"We're bringing Charlene back alive," Marie reminded him then said no more.

He pushed out front, headed into the empty silhouette of the mountain range.

**

Jim shined his big Mag light at the ground. "Charles is right. They're headed toward Robber's Roost. See the tire print?"

322

"Any chance of these horses catching dirt bikes?" Marie asked.

For the first time since they left the village, he looked at her. "Manes's gang doesn't know this country. They'll listen for motors. When they don't hear any, they'll relax and slow down."

Ten minutes later, Jim and Marie crossed into an arroyo. Jim pointed back and forth across the sandy bottom. "The trail goes from one side to the other, then down the middle for a long ways before it intersects a road. We'll stay on the north side. It's faster."

They were making good time when Jim stopped and flashed his light ahead. The opposite gulley bank was churned with dirt-bike tracks.

Jim groaned. "They've turned away from the Roost."

Shining the light back and forth over the ground, he spurred his horse up onto a mesa covered by fractured rock and low greasewood.

"It's like pavement up here," Marie said. "It'll take hours to figure out their path. We don't have that time. Charlene doesn't have it."

She stood high in her saddle, scanning for lights, sound, or anything that could help. She gasped and grabbed his shirt sleeve. "Did you see that? Something moved over there." She snatched his light and scanned the brush. Branches swayed as if recently disturbed.

"There!" She pointed.

Jim looked at the ground.

"There," she hissed through her teeth.

"I know," he said, still looking down. "It's her."

"What?" Marie snapped.

"Panther Woman. Follow her. She won't show me anything. You're here to rescue Charlene. I'm here to kill."

She could hear the tears in his voice. She wanted to touch his hand, but didn't. Not now.

Marie projected the beam ahead. "There's another arroyo on our right. I think I saw movement on the rim. She's paralleling the gully. Look! Motorcycle tread marks."

"Now she goes!" Marie trotted her horse down to the bottom of the ravine. She shined the light ahead. It caught a sparkle among the rocks. Jim drew his pistol. Marie steadied the light on it. A red dirt bike, its front wheel twisted, lay against a boulder.

323

Jim pulled up beside her and pointed to a liquid sheen on a rock. "Blood. Someone hit a hole and flipped."

"The blood's still wet in the middle," Marie said.

"It can't be more than thirty minutes old." Jim took the light and turned it off. "We're catching up. We need to keep hidden."

A breeze from the southeast brought the distant buzz of dirt bikes. A pale glow lit the foothills for a few minutes, then faded.

"How far?" Marie asked.

"One, one and a half miles," Jim said. "They're headed toward the 93 Overlook."

"93? Like Highway 93?" Tingles rushed down her neck and across her arms. She spurred her horse back onto the long flat mesa. The edge of the moon broke over the horizon, painting the ground blue. "It's hard-pack gravel. The creosote is thin. Is it safe to pick up our pace?" she asked.

"Look." He pointed to a long looming hillside. For an instant headlights brushed a gray streak across it. More streaks followed.

Marie swung her arm toward the northeast. "Look there!" Another light illuminated high on the slopes above a long canyon. "Someone is on an intercept with the bikes."

"We need to take Billy before the two groups join," Jim said.

**

Ninety minutes earlier

Stephanie gripped the steering wheel and grunted in anger. The jeep trail had failed to materialize. Minutes later she began to panic. She saw nothing familiar in the whitewash of her headlights.

Lost. Of course, in the morning she could find her way, but then it would be too late for Charlene.

She took a deep breath.

Calm down. It's close—somewhere.

She studied the scattered clumps of mesquite that stood before her. Easing into low, she snaked between them. As one bush faded into gray behind her, another rose up like a specter in the beam of her lights.

She stopped again and searched the brush with her spotlight. There where the beam faded into dark, ruts cut through the scrub brush.

She drove onto them and picked up speed. A mile later she rounded a curve and slammed on the brakes. A mound of turquoise cloth lay in the trail about twenty meters ahead. A human raised an arm to block the glare of her beams.

"Help me," Ruthie pleaded in a dry hiss.

Stephanie flipped the flap of her gun holster open while grinding into reverse. Sending a spray of gravel and sand, the jeep plowed backward.

"Are you alone?" Stephanie shouted and turned the spotlight on Ruthie. "Hey! Answer me! Are you alone!" She shined the light over the brush on either side of the trail.

"Help me. Water," Ruthie sobbed.

"Come here." Stephanie kept her voice strong and authoritative. She tuned her ears to the brush, checking for the presence of others, then lifted her canteen from the floorboards. "Take this and walk downhill to the research station. I'm going on."

"Don't leave me. No, no." Ruthie fell into the fetal position and rocked back and forth on the ground.

Stephanie thrust the canteen through the side of the jeep. "Do as I said. Take the water. You damned well can't go with me."

"Don't leave me." Ruthie struggled to her feet and laid her hands on the hood of the vehicle. Her dress hung in shreds. Streaks of mud-filled gashes crisscrossed the skin on her legs and arms.

Stephanie tucked the gun under her left thigh and plopped the canteen on the passenger's seat. "Get in."

Ruthie stared at her. "Arbie and Wendell left me."

"Get in now. I'm leaving." Stephanie raced the engine for emphasize.

Ruthie gurgled hysterically and clambered into the passenger seat.

Stephanie accelerated then glanced at Ruthie. "I need you to calm down."

Ruthie breathed heavily. Her sobbing diminished in gulps. She swigged down the water, then stared straight ahead.

"Wendell? How's Wendell involved in this?" Stephanie asked.

"Why are you so mean?" Ruthie began to sniffle.

Stephanie slammed on the brakes hard enough to throw Ruthie against the dashboard. She yanked the canteen from Ruthie's fingers then pushed Ruthie toward the exit. "Get out."

"What?" Ruthie's lips curled downward. "I can't. Please don't. Please."

325

Stephanie jammed the canteen back into Ruthie's hands. "You will answer my questions, and when I tell you to do something, you'll do it. You understand me?"

Ruthie slobbered, getting more and more hysterical.

Stephanie put her hand over the canteen top. "Stop that, or you're out of here." Stephanie jerked her thumb toward the side of the trail.

"Okay. Okay." Ruth's sucked her sleeve into her mouth to plug off her sobs.

Stephanie took a plastic bag from under the backseat. "Here's a blanket. You're probably hypothermic." She helped Ruthie rip the blanket out of its sack.

Ruthie wiped her eyes.

Stephanie put the jeep into gear. "We understand each other, right?"

Ruthie nodded.

"Start with Wendell. What does he have to do with this?"

Ruthie meandered in a barely comprehensible fashion. "He took Lorelei hostage and made Wendell deliver the dirt bikes to Billy Manes."

"Who took Lorelei hostage?" Stephanie asked.

"Carr, Carr Ferguson."

Stephanie's shoulders quavered.

***

Chapter 23: Convergence

Ruthie explained, "Carr's a bigwig at Haines who wants to get rid of Herman and the floozy Stephanie. Arbie tricked him into funding Desert Sunrise."

"Have you ever met Carr?"

Ruthie fidgeted with her cuticles. "Yeah, once. He's scary. His girlfriend is even scarier."

"Where did you see them?"

"At the hideout."

"Where is the hideout?"

"Somewhere in the mountains. Ninety-nine Overlook or something like that. They like to share girls, Carr and his girlfriend do. Lorelei's kind of into it, too. She might not be a hostage. Maybe she wanted to be with them."

Stephanie's teeth chattered. She glanced covetously at the blanket. She blinked her eyes and fought off the urge to demand a corner of it. Then she gassed the engine and shifted gears.

"Your Camp Sunrise buddies are dangerous," Stephanie said. "If we come across them, you have to do what I tell you. You got that?"

"Okay," Ruthie whined.

"Stop gurgling," Stephanie snapped. "I need you to be in control of yourself."

"OKAY," Ruthie screamed shrilly. She fidgeted more with her fingers. "I hate them all. I don't want to be around them. Arbie's a psycho."

Absolutely, Stephanie thought, then asked, "Why do you say that?"

"He blew up the mine."

"Yeah, that's crazy. People could have been killed," Stephanie said.

"A rock from the explosion cut his leg. Lorelei tore her blouse apart to make a tourniquet. Later he said delirious things. One time, he said a lion chased him. Then another time, he said an Indian woman speared him."

Stephanie stared at Ruthie through the dim gray of the cab. "He told the doctors that?"

"No. He didn't want them to think he's crazy."

Stephanie made her voice sympathetic. "Yeah, well, the doctors need to know when people talk crazy."

"Yeah," Ruthie said thoughtfully. "They gave him penicillin. He threw it away."

"That's even crazier," Stephanie said.

Ruthie thought about it awhile then sighed. "I don't think I want to see him ever again."

Stephanie scoffed under her breath. "I'm sure you won't."

The road rose upward, steep and washed. Stephanie dropped into four-wheel drive. The jeep dipped and swayed, its tires throwing out loose stones and dirt. Ruthie clenched the roll bar with both hands.

At the top, the road leveled and went straight across a plateau. Stephanie picked up speed. "Ruthie, listen to me. Billy and his gang kidnapped one of my sisters. They've taken her somewhere near here, probably to that hangout you mentioned. I'm going there to negotiate her release. Can you help me find the place?"

"In the dark?" Ruthie jutted her chin over the dashboard and stared at the road in terror. "I don't want to go there."

Stephanie slammed on the brakes. "Then get out."

"No," Ruthie blubbered. "I'll die if you leave me."

"I don't want you with me if you aren't going to help."

"Okay, I'll sit quietly in the jeep. Will you take a gun when you talk to them?"

"Of course." Stephanie's voice didn't tremble.

Ruthie clamped her hands between her thighs and stopped asking questions.

The black void of the mountain filled the space ahead.

328

The insect-like drone of dirt bikes projected up the hillside. Stephanie gunned the jeep to the top of the ridge then cut the engine and lights. A dull glow painted the slopes nearby. Ruthie looked toward the bikes, then back to Stephanie. Even in the dark the whites of her eyes shone. Her shoulders shook.

"If you can't keep quiet, then stuff the corner of that blanket into your mouth." Stephanie slid her feet to the ground and pulled the shotgun off the backseat.

**

Jim and Marie gained ground by galloping across the mesa. The bikers were now less than half a mile ahead. At the same time, the occasional flash of headlights showed that the mystery vehicle was also getting closer.

"Where's that car coming from?" Marie pointed where she had last seen its beams.

"Don't know," Jim answered. "It could be a Paiute Police vehicle, maybe Lightfoot's posse, or it could be more of Billy's hoodlums."

"Wouldn't Lightfoot be behind us?" Marie said.

"Most likely."

"Then we have to assume it's more of Billy's thugs."

The high whine of the bikes dropped to an idle. Distant voices floated on the air. The tone and cadence implied surprise and excitement.

Farther off, the driver gunned the engine, projecting its sound down through the gullies.

Jim stiffened in his saddle. "That's Matt's jeep. I recognize its motor."

Marie twisted in her saddle toward Jim. "Shit! I think the bikers are setting an ambush. We have to warn him."

"Yes."

Like angry bees, the bike motors roared. The majority went north toward the jeep. Two or three headed south.

Marie pointed to the smaller group. "They're the ones with Charlene. The jeep scared them. They're moving faster."

The jeep's lights came into full view. The engine suddenly stopped, and the headlights went black. Jim spurred his horse. "I'll take the jeep. You get to Charlene before they reach the road."

**

329

Shotgun held across her chest, Stephanie stood and listened. Like a loyal puppy, Ruthie held her blanket tightly and waited for a command.

The motorbike beams crisscrossed through the dusty air. Their engine pitch heightened and grew louder. A bright column of light struck a bush a few hundred yards away.

"Bring the spotlight here," Stephanie ordered. Like a spring released from tension, Ruthie leaped into action. Her hands banged around the cab. Her thrashing took seconds that seemed like years; then she stood beside Stephanie and thrust the lamp out, as if it would solve everything.

"Keep it. Follow me."

She pulled Ruthie toward a cluster of boulders and cacti.

Ruthie began to cry. Stephanie dug her fingernails into Ruthie's wrist. "You need to stop that—NOW! Bite the blanket."

Stephanie pushed Ruthie down behind a small boulder.

Is it smarter to stay and control her, or get far from her?

Ruthie gnawed on the corner of the blanket. Stephanie decided to stay.

Stephanie grasped Ruthie's arm and squeezed hard. "Stay down. I'll be back." Stephanie raced to the jeep.

The bikes sounded close. Their lights bobbed up and down, bouncing off the brush and boulders. Stephanie flung herself across the seat of the jeep. Her hands fumbled for the radio. Her fingers found the power switch. With her thumb, she spun it to full volume. A beam swiped across the windshield.

The bike motors roared. The horizon lit like a football field. The windshield sparkled in their headlights. Stephanie bent low and ran to the boulders. She flung herself next to Ruthie.

Tears ran down Ruthie's cheeks. The corner of the blanket was soaked. She stared with horror into Stephanie's face. Stephanie smiled like a mother comforting a child. That came easy now.

The crackle and background conversation of police radio filled the air. The roar of the motors dropped to idles. Their headlights panned over the jeep, then went dark.

Stephanie stared into Ruthie's eyes. Ruthie's jaws, still biting the blanket, began to tremble. Stephanie angled her head to the side in tacit reprimand. Ruthie nodded and covered her mouth with her hand. Moonlight glistened in tears on her cheeks.

Dry branches cracked far out in front of them, then near the jeep, then to their side. Ruthie's eyes widened. Stephanie mouthed, "Don't move." Ruthie froze.

Stephanie rotated her head until she faced the nearest movement. She saw a man crouch beside a bush then slip forward to another bush and crouch again, moving closer and closer to the rear of the jeep. She saw another slightly behind her left shoulder and froze while this one crawled past them, not more than ten yards away. Ruthie didn't see him.

Stephanie peered at the area behind the jeep, trying to locate the first man. He was gone. Where he had been, a darker form lay in the road. It was a man, prone and motionless.

A sudden motion drew her eyes to the front of the jeep. Two figures dashed out of the bushes and fired into the passenger cab. The person who'd crawled past her earlier screamed, "You fuckers! You almost shot me!"

"Dumb fuck," one called back. "Remember, we're all supposed to stay on this side of the road."

"Fuck you!" he yelled and stood up. "They're gone. Let's blow this damned piece of shit up and get to the hangout. They'll never catch us on foot."

"Okay," one said and aimed his pistol at the radiator.

Two others emerged from the brush and searched the terrain with flashlights. The beams panned over the rocks where the women hid, then moved to other clumps of brush and boulders.

"They prob'ly run down there," one man said, pointing to a gulley.

"Hey!" one shouted. A beam zeroed in on a corner of Ruthie's blue dress that stuck out from behind the rock.

***

Plasma Tornado

The Amazonian razors were gone before *Quantum*'s crew could verbalize what their brains knew. With the razors vanishing behind the horizon of Xilon 1, the closed channel crackled with a female voice. "Captain Yanitur, detain Verg fleet in support of allied assault on the Xilon 10 Verg port."

The voice sent Yanitur into an enraged silence. He clenched his jaws and shook his head at Kale.

331

Yanitur's face reddened and he snapped, "Admiral Sharon, my cruiser is NOT at full power. I request immediate support. Please respond."

The Amazonian commander's voice crackled with interference from cosmic radiation. "Captain Yanitur, provide your power status."

"Admiral Sharon, we are at sixty-three percent," Uriel responded.

Yanitur snapped the microphone switch off and hissed, "Ex-admiral."

"Reserves?" crackled Sharon's voice.

"Zero," Uriel replied.

"Good God, Robert, I taught you better than that." Broken and distant, the ex-admiral's voice expressed amusement then diminished into a static hiss that sounded like, "I'm...support..."

"Captain? The Verg fleet has moved into battle array." Kale's voice elevated with urgency.

Yanitur stared into space where the razors just vanished. "Fire at will." His disgust was clear.

Despite the power limitation, *Quantum* destroyed five of the Verg ships in the opening salvo. While this was happening, a massive dirigible of a freighter lumbered into position behind the Verg battle line. With a sudden flurry of discharges, a cyclone of energy dropped from its belly and maneuvered past the Verg fleet toward *Quantum*. Once beyond the Vergs, the twisting column split into five parts that bent like tentacles to encircle the Ajax cruiser.

"Uriel," Argus shouted.

In a blur Uriel crossed the bridge and linked into *Quantum*'s defense network. Argus continued the attack, destroying one more frigate. Uriel manned the defenses and fired a scattergun blast of plasma slugs at each of the attacking tentacles. Before Uriel's missiles converged on the five targets, each tentacle split into five smaller streams of energy. Uriel's projectiles eliminated eight of them.

Argus abandoned his attack to assist on defense. He twisted his face into a snarl. "If we don't finish this thing, I'll have no power left to stop the frigates."

As if they heard his complaint, the frigates advanced within range of their antiquated weapons.

"Taking evasive actions," Yanitur announced. He jammed on the controls, and the ship lurched straight at one of the suns.

Uriel and Argus each launched a round of plasma flack.

332

"Launch scouts," Yanitur ordered. Five small fighter craft vaulted from the belly of the Ajax and shot toward the frigates. One slammed into an energy cyclone. Both exploded and disappeared.

The seraphim's second barrage smashed all but two of the remaining fingers.

Thank God seraphim learn fast, Yanitur thought.

"We're running low on energy," Uriel announced.

One finger shot past *Quantum* and sank with bursts of violet and orange into the surface of the nearest sun. The remaining energy cyclone cut into *Quantum's* hull.

"Identify and isolate damage," Yanitur ordered.

"Isolating damaged sector." Kale marked off the damaged area with a swipe of his finger on his screen then punched buttons that directed repair robots to the area. "I'm going down there," he yelled to Yanitur and disconnected from his station without waiting for approval.

Argus returned to attack mode, attempting to destroy the massive ship that floated behind the enemy line. He failed to penetrate the Verg shielding. "Power too low to punch through," he said.

The bay doors under the big ship's belly opened again.

Yanitur pulled down on a lever. "Shunting all power to thrusters." He swerved through the gravity of the nearby sun, whipping *Quantum* on a tangent toward the other star.

The battle had taken one minute, and his ship had sustained major damage. Fifteen frigates were destroyed. Approximately thirty others were advancing. His four remaining scouts were yielding ground.

Sharon abandoned us.

Worse, she had abandoned him.

At that moment, five oval flashes of light shot past *Quantum* and zoomed between the Verg frigates to converge on the massive freighter. In a flash it exploded. A wall of orange and white rushed outward, spinning the frigates end over end and dragging them with it.

"I take it back," Yanitur whispered.

"Razors." Uriel clenched his fist.

Pushed by the force of the blast, the Verg frigates struggled to right themselves and wobbled in their attempts to escape. The Amazonian razors butchered them like rats.

"Captain, one of the razors is down," Scout Commander Rathmus said over the closed channel.

"Retrieve her." Yanitur wiped his hand across his forehead.

"Scout squadron en route," Rathmus replied.

"Kale, damage report," Yanitur said.

Below deck, Kale spoke over the nearest intercom. "Sir, we have major damage. Bio-Regen One is destroyed. Android tech Sheila, repairable; android tech Fatima, severe damage—"

Uriel broke in, "Naomi?"

Kale paused. "I'm sorry, Uriel. She's injured. Janus has moved her to incubation for triage."

"I'm sorry, Uriel," Yanitur said.

"We don't know her conditon," Uriel snapped.

Yanitur watched Uriel. Did the seraph log into Janus's database and learn the extent of Naomi's injuries, or was his emotional programming pumping him up with bravado?

Emotionalized seraphs are a bad idea, Yanitur thought. Uriel was the only one on *Quantum* that had emotional programming—a test model. Unfortunately, Uriel was also the intellectual center of the ship, the very most important artificial being on board.

No, the most important being, period. We knew amorous situations would develop between humans and seraphim, but why my bioengineer and my intellectual seraph?

Kale's voice came over Yanitur's headset. "I'm standing in front of a meter-wide hole in our hull. The damage would have been much worse, but Fatima took a direct hit and absorbed most of its energy."

Kale paused. "It looks like she sensed its radiation and stepped between the pulse and Naomi. Fatima's frame is melted beyond recognition. Needless to say, her insides are fried."

Yanitur turned away from Uriel. "Kale, our ETA at the Verg station is eighteen hours. I need that breach repaired ASAP."

"Sir, at full throttle, we'll only have time to put a makeshift patch in place. It'll be good for a gentle atmospheric descent, but not military maneuvers."

"Get it done." Yanitur continued to study Uriel's demeanor.

"I'll need two marines who are cross-programmed in metallurgy," Kale said.

"We're on battle alert," Throdin barked from the flight deck. His marines had deployed there to defend against a possible Verg boarding.

"Release two to Kale," Yanitur ordered. "Prepare your remaining marines for a ground assault at 17.39 hours. You'll target a Verg transport center."

"Yes, sir." Throdin sounded pleased, but it wasn't emotion, just a situational subroutine in his language program.

Twelve hours away from the Verg outpost, the humans settled, one by one, into their battle stations for a couple of hours of shut-eye.

Kale returned to the bridge and gave Uriel and Yanitur a detailed damage report. He finished by saying, "Fatima is a complete loss."

Uriel averted his eyes. "I'll rebuild her. Captain, I request permission to visit the incubator stations."

Yanitur dismissed Uriel then turned to Kale. "We've made them immortal. Fatima's skin DNA is preserved here and in Nirvania, and her memory is archived in both places as well. At most she'll lose a few days of experience."

Kale rubbed his forehead. "Hell, humans lose more than that from a big drunk."

"So, how can it possibly work with an immortal?" Yanitur meant the affair between Uriel and Naomi.

Kale raised his eyebrows and gyrated his head. "Intellectually, Uriel has to know it will end, but he doesn't understand loss emotionally yet."

Yanitur gazed at Uriel's empty chair. "He may soon."

***

Live by the Gun

The men trained their lights on the boulders where Stephanie and Ruthie hid. A volcanic boom shook the earth. A ball of flames rolled skyward. Within it a dirt bike tumbled end over end, then its gas tank exploded. A wave of hot blinding gas rushed outward.

Stephanie leaped up. Squinting into the light, she leveled the shotgun. A secondary explosion erupted. At the same moment, Stephanie emptied two shotgun blasts into the men.

Ruthie screamed into her blanket and kicked her feet.

The guy near Stephanie swung his pistol wildly, his eyes blinking against the blinding light. She fired again. He threw his arms into the air and flew backward.

Another man jumped behind the rear fender of the jeep. A muzzle flashed from brush further up the trail. The report of a Winchester rifle followed. The man staggered and fell.

"Matt," Jim called out, "that's all of them. We have to get going. Marie needs our help."

"Jim," Stephanie yelled back, "it's me. Where is Marie?" She yanked Ruthie to her feet and they ran to the jeep.

"She's following the ones who have Charlene. Let's go!"

Stephanie and Jim hopped into the jeep.

Ruthie stared at the occupied seats.

Jim grabbed her and lifted her over the fender and onto the rear bench. "Who the hell is this?" he asked.

**

Marie spurred her horse hard. Triangulating on the three dirt bikes, she raced at a full charge to close on them before they reached the road.

She crashed through the brush onto the trail less than a hundred yards behind them. They lollygagged along without concern.

In the moonlight she recognized Billy and Wendell. Charlene sat behind a third rider. She pulled the Dragunov and followed, waiting for a clear shot.

The trail wound back around the hillside, bringing the motorbikes closer to her. She raised her rifle to her eye. An explosion roared behind her. A fireball of red and orange filled the sky, backlighting her silhouette.

She yanked her horse off the road and jumped down into the brush. The three kidnappers stopped and swung their bikes around to gaze at the ball of flames.

"Wahoo!" Billy shouted. "We blew up the fuckin' police. Nothing better than crispy critter cops, don't ya think, Wendell? You don't like cops either, do ya? Ya want Lorelei back..."

"We already made a deal," Wendell said.

The third guy made a stupid trilling noise that sounded like Arab women encouraging their men in battle. He did it over and over.

"Shut up!" Billy snapped.

"I don't hear no bikes," the third guy said.

"They'll be here in a bit," Billy said.

They all watched. The whoosh of the fire covered the silence of their voices. Its fuel quickly exhausting itself, the fireball diminished to a whirling gray cloud with flashes of orange. Through its hiss came the low purr of the approaching jeep.

"Let's git!" Billy snapped.

Marie leveled the Dragunov. The blurring images of the riders' heads zipped past her view. She jumped back on her horse and raced after them. Her ears focused on the receding motors, she watched the ever-dimming glow of taillights vanish over the top of the next ridge. The jeep motor purred far behind her. She patted the horse's neck and rode with her hair flowing silver in the moonlight.

I was born for this, she thought.

**

Billy didn't get gooseflesh often. He had it now. He had seen an image backlit by the fireball. *Like a ghost rider.* He blinked and it disappeared.

No one else mentioned it. He didn't mention it either. *What's worse, being spooked or telling others you're spooked?*

"I'll check the road. Make sure it's safe," Billy yelled and leaped out in front, putting thirty yards between him and the other two. He glanced back over his shoulder to see beyond the glare of their headlights.

If there's something there, it'll take them first.

He couldn't help it; his mind blossomed with thoughts of skin-walkers, witches, devil babies, and other demon beasts his grandmother had terrorized him with in his childhood. It made his skin crawl like centipedes.

He gunned the engine and pulled farther ahead.

She's pretty. He hated giving Charlene to Carr, who he knew would kill her when he and Kit were done playing.

He glanced over his shoulder again, this time at the bike with Charlene handcuffed to the driver.

Stupid to kidnap her, like hitting a hornets' nest with a stick.

He turned his mouth into a snarl. He let the beast in him roar. No one could hear it over the motors.

Carr gave him twenty grand for Lorelei and offered another eighty for the Paiute cutie.

Not enough. Billy needed two hundred grand and an airplane ticket to Mexico. That would set him up in tequila-ville for life.

The dull light of the hangout reflected off the rocks ahead.

Billy decided to ask Carr for another hundred thousand.

No harm in asking, he thought.

The horse tiring, the bikes grew more distant. She hadn't heard their engines since they crested the last ridge. If they descended to Highway 93, she would never catch them. Knowing that the horse was in danger of collapse, she bit her lip then spurred him on. His loyal body responded and took powerful strides up the hill.

Maybe she could fire shots over the bikers and scare them into hunkering down long enough for Matt and Jim to join her.

The horse staggered to the hilltop and coughed out his breath. Ahead, a dull red glow emitted from behind a boulder. Rifle in hand, she leaped to the ground. For a second, she caressed the horse's muzzle, then led him into the brush and let the reins drop.

Behind her the jeep purred. She guessed it was ten minutes away.

Too long.

She stacked three rocks in the middle of the road; then, bending low and zigzagging between bushes, she hurried toward the light. Heavy movement in the brush brought her to a halt. She crept forward, putting a clump of greasewood between her and the noise. A man stepped out from behind a boulder. He zipped his pants. "Hey, Billy, ain't nothing up here," he shouted down the slope.

Billy's voice called back, "Wayne, search real careful. Something been clawing at my ass all night."

A faint cry with the timbre of Charlene's voice knifed through the air and cut into Marie's gut. Billy's muffled voice said, "I ain't touching you, bitch—he don't take damaged goods."

Wayne chuckled to himself then said goofily, "Spoooky, spoooooooky." He snickered to himself then started downhill toward the light. Marie pulled a knife and slipped quietly after him. A few feet away, she dislodged a pebble. It bounced off a rock. He spun around with his hand jammed into the back of his belt.

She punched her fist, knife protruding from the side of it, into his Adam's apple. His yell came out as gurgles. His windpipe filled with blood. He stumbled and collapsed into her arms.

Marie picked up her rifle and sneaked down through the boulders. There in the base of a cliff, a hangout entrance glowed with pale light from within. She kneeled among the bikes and listened while she surveyed the entrance and the landscape nearby.

Agitated voices echoed up through the shaft. She pressed against the rock surface and crept closer. The voices became clearer.

"Carr, you promised me 'n Lorelei could go once'd ya got the Injun girl. I done my part. So where's Lorelei?" Wendell said.

Billy laughed snidely. "They aren't trucks. It's In-di-an, or more correctly, if you can remember something so complicated, it's Na-tive A-mer-i-can."

Carr belly-laughed. "Wendell, forget Lorelei. She's a dumb Okie, and she do love to play."

"She ain't no Okie!"

"Okay, Arkan-sawer, then."

"Don't matter, she and I be leavin'. So where is she?"

"She was a pain in the ass. I had to tie her up in the back of the cave just to get her to shut her fucking mouth."

"You left her back there with Kit? Goddamn you."

"Kit left hours ago. Lorelei's in back. Go untie her if you're in such a hurry."

A shot reverberated within the cavern.

Wendell groaned. He spoke, but his voice was garbled.

"I forgot to tell you. Kit left after she and I did Lorelei, you double-crossing hillbilly."

The hammer on a gun clicked back.

"What do you think, Billy? Should I finish off this ungrateful bastard?"

"Fine with me." Billy's voice sounded shaken.

"I mean," Carr went on, "given you came in here demanding double what we agreed for the Paiute girl, you have some interest in what I do to ungrateful bastards, don't you?"

Billy chuckled, but it came out stilted. "We're fine, Carr. Shit, I was just asking. It doesn't hurt to ask, right?"

A protracted silence followed.

Billy spoke again. He sounded apologetic and scared. "I brought you the Paiute girl like I promised. At great risk, too."

"You did, and it's appreciated." Carr's voice had a threatening edge to it.

Wendell's groans became diminished and infrequent.

"I think I'll leave him," Carr said. "Let him suffer for his ingratitude."

"I'll make you a deal," Billy said. "You give me the gun and an extra hundred grand and I'll put my fingerprints all over it. They'll

339

think I did the killing. You'll get off scot-free. You can keep your big exec job at Haines."

"Smart thinking," Carr said. Five gunshots fired in rapid succession.

"What the fuck!" Billy shouted. "One of those bullets could have ricocheted and killed us."

Carr laughed manically. "I fired down the shaft. Bullets can't bounce back 180 degrees. You think I would hand you a loaded gun?"

Billy laughed. The tension in his voice relaxed some.

"You get the Paiute bitch to the load zone. I'll pay you then," Carr said.

"That's a deal," Billy said. "Let's move. My guys should be here any minute now. Where's your chopper?"

Their footsteps shuffled closer. Charlene's muffled sobs grew louder.

Marie hid behind a boulder.

Billy emerged from the entrance, pushing Charlene in front of him. She stumbled and wobbled as if drunk.

"Johnnie," Billy called out. He faced away from Marie. "The boss wants you to take her to his bird."

Marie's heart jumped when a voice responded from behind her. "Yeah, okay."

Johnnie came through the darkness at a casual gait.

"What the hell are you doing over there?" Billy said. "You're supposed to be up here guarding the cave with Wayne."

"I heard a noise, so I took a look."

"Where's Wayne, anyway?" Johnnie asked.

"He ain't back from up there yet?" Billy and Johnnie both peered uphill into the darkness.

"Spooky," Billy said. He shoved Charlene toward Johnnie. "Take Carr's plaything. I want to get paid and shake this place. You got an extra gun?"

"No."

"Give me yours, then. You don't need one down there at the chopper. I might need it here."

Johnnie pulled his pistol from the back of his belt and handed it over. "Like you say, let's get paid and go."

Johnnie pushed Charlene. She tripped and fell. She tried to rise up, but collapsed on her side.

Marie had a clear view of Billy. She lifted her rifle and fired.

340

Her shot broke Billy's left clavicle and flung him through the air. He landed head downward over a rock. His pistol dropped from his hand and clattered into a crevice.

Johnnie dove into cover. Marie fired five shots at him in quick succession. He screamed. His body thudded to the ground.

Marie ran to Charlene and took her arm.

Charlene's mouth opened. Her eyes were dilated and unfocused.

A click came from within the tunnel.

Marie pulled her pistol and turned. Her ears heard a distant hollow clap. Her body lost balance as if pushed by an invisible hand. She tumbled backward and fell over Charlene.

***

Chapter 24: Xilon Ten Verg Station

Mark 16.88 hours, 36.6 minutes prior to the Verg station assault launch

His demeanor somber, Uriel returned to his station. He had just sat through a grizzly three-hour operation where Naomi's arms were removed below the elbows and replaced with prosthetics. In that regard their bodies shared robotic technology. The rest of her injuries were internal. An IV delivered emerald elixir through a shunt in her shoulder while she rested in a drug-induced sleep. Janus projected a seventy-five percent probability of full rejuvenation of her internal organs.

Seconds after Uriel's return, Yanitur's headset beeped.

"Captain Yanitur of AGS cruiser *Quantum*, this is Admiral Sharon of the Amazonian Frontier Navy. I currently have a strike force of forty-six light cavalry razors—"

"That's a lot of words to state the obvious," Yanitur said.

"Captain, refrain from interrupting."

"Admiral Sharon, you are no longer my admiral."

"Captain Yanitur, under the Pacification Compact between our two governments, the superior officer takes command in a joint operation. As such, I am in command of our mission against the Xilon 10 Verg outpost."

"Admiral Sharon, *Quantum* is exempt from the Pacification Compact. I have a primary directive order that cannot be overridden."

"I am aware of your orders, Captain Yanitur, and I am also aware that you have already disengaged from your primary mission. Therefore, you are available for my use." Her stress on "you are available for my use" made a clear reference to when he served as her student assistant at the naval academy, and caused a tinge of arousal in his lower abdomen.

"Robert, cut the BS. We both know we must strike fast to preserve their data regarding the new Verg ally. I hope you learned that much *under* me."

There it was again, an innuendo regarding their intertwinement at the academy.

Yanitur felt his face flush. "Admiral, what is the status at Xilon 10?"

She paused then cleared her throat and spoke in calm, measured words. "Our first sortie eliminated their fighter ships on the ground. We've positioned a two-kilometer-radius electromagnetic net over them, blocking all outside communication.

"Robert, we have besieged them. As soon as your heavy guns breach their wall, I'll launch a ground assault. You need to act with dispatch if we are going to preserve that data."

"I have eight combat marine seraphim," Yanitur offered.

Her voice took a collaborative tone. "I appreciate the value they offer, but we are in position to attack now. Seconds matter. Robert, please hurry." She finished on a request rather than an order.

Why? A warm feeling flowed through his body to his brain. Did she still love him? Did she ever love him? Could she love a man?

"I have a hole in my ship. If their artillery hits it, we'll sustain major damage," he said.

"I have been informed of your situation. Two razors will shield your damage during the assault. The others will escort you to the target. Twenty minutes to contact, Captain."

Two razors shot out to lead *Quantum* to Xilon 10. The other two positioned themselves less than a meter from the gash in Quantum's fuselage. Inside, the seraphim marines, their chrome bodies reflecting the sparks from their welders, saluted with a friendly pump of their left fists. The Amazonians, their golden helmets glistening within the canopies of their fighters, returned the salute.

**

Sixty seconds to assault

Kale toggled the intercom. "Assemble ground force!"

Uriel gave Yanitur a look of concern.

Yanitur smiled slyly. "Our marines should be on standby for backup if necessary."

On the flight deck, Throdin checked the data flow from each of his four all-terrain landing craft. He finished with a visual survey then said into his headset, "Ground force is all go."

Yanitur glanced to each of his officers on the bridge. Everyone had donned their radiation-deflective combat armor. Everyone sounded off with a "Sir!" meaning that their system responsibilities were in order.

"Begin attack sequence," Yanitur ordered.

Uriel cut in, "We have breached planet four's atmosphere. Ten seconds to horizon.

"Ten, nine, eight...

"Commence attack. We are visible. We are visible," Uriel declared.

The cruiser screamed downward. The biological crew members groaned under the g-forces.

"Leveling for assault," Uriel announced.

Their trajectory settled and the g-forces lifted.

Argus fired an antimatter torpedo. It arced over the horizon. A second later it blasted away the Faraday net that the Amazonians had stretched over the outpost. Quantum's radios flooded with panicked transmissions from within the Verg fortress.

"Chatter," Merc said. "Uprising in the slave quarters. They've dispatched infantry to quell them. Their artillery is concentrated on us."

Yanitur wrinkled his forehead into a defiant frown. "Launch ground forces."

"That's against the admiral's order," Uriel said.

"The slave rebellion bought us some clock. The Vergs are holding our people prisoner down there, too. I'm not losing them this time." Yanitur looked from Kale to Uriel.

Uriel raised his thumb. Kale followed.

Yanitur spoke into the flight-deck intercom. "Throdin, launch your marines!"

"Yes, sir!" Throdin snapped. "Ground force launch in ten, nine, eight..."

"Landing craft breaching in order: Ship one away, ship three away, four away, two away, closing transport bay doors in five, four, three…"

The four transports shot ahead of the Ajax and vanished over the horizon.

"Target priority one on my mark," Yanitur ordered. "Mark."

Uriel pulled hard on the throttle. *Quantum* roared forward. The transports reappeared as dots on the horizon, then grew larger, then shot backward underneath them, disappearing into the rear horizon.

The Verg transmission tower appeared as a distant needle. It rapidly grew larger until it extended far above into the planet's cloud cover.

"Torpedo bays one through five armed," Uriel announced.

"Argus, comm tower, at will," Yanitur ordered.

Argus linked to the antimatter torpedoes. "Launching." Five rapid flashes of bright violet leaped from *Quantum*. The air on the bridge filled with the smell of ozone. A blink later, the Verg communication tower's base shredded like straw. Its top lifted up in a sideways twisting motion, then it split into three pieces and collapsed across the rocky landscape.

Quantum settled over the Verg landing strip. Below, the pirates' war fleet lay smoldering where the razors destroyed them on the Amazonian foray.

Energy pulses screamed from the fortress walls and exploded against *Quantum*'s upper hull.

Argus returned fire, concentrating a thousand pulses per minute of sonic cannon fire at the center of the wall. Above his target the fortification began to fleck away. Suddenly the wall shuddered and slid to the ground, leaving a jagged hole. Argus pounded its edges, widening it.

The four assault vehicles whooshed under *Quantum*. The marines leaped out. Using the landing craft as shields, they advanced toward the opening. At the same time, Amazonian warriors swarmed out of hiding. Linking their personal shields into a phalanx, they trotted forward.

Heavy plasma cannons on the parapets cranked their barrels down at the troops. Uriel spun the Ajax on edge to shield the soldiers.

"Torpedo bays one, three, and four armed," the deck sergeant announced.

345

"At will, prioritize and eliminate," Yanitur ordered.

"At will," Argus acknowledged and launched the torpedoes. With huge groans the fortress parapets dissolved one by one and slid to the ground like liquid.

Along the wall, white flares shot into the air. The fortress gates swung open. Vergs poured out, running with their hands held high then falling at the feet of the marines. A dozen old-style trägers, chrome arms raised, followed their Verg masters.

***

Wendell Lee's Ticket

For Marie, the world turned sepia then drifted down a long dark tunnel. Blood spread over her blouse. She coughed. Blood bubbled from her mouth.

Carr emerged from the mine. He shook his head as if saddened. "Tsk-tsk, what a clusterfuck."

"Johnnie," he called out, then smiled down at Marie and Charlene. "Come help me load these pussies."

A muted groan came from downslope.

Carr's face turned quizzical. Marie's eyes fluttered like moths. Her hand fumbled with the button on her shirt pocket. Then fell limp. It rose again; this time two fingers hooked over the lip of the pocket and pulled weakly. Her mouth opened. More blood bubbled out.

"Oh dear," Carr taunted. "Do we need a hankie?" He bent over her and unbuttoned the pocket. "Let me help."

Over his shoulder, he shouted, "Johnnie, don't need your assistance. This one's dead."

He yanked Charlene by her handcuffs, then watched Billy's legs kick in the air. He dropped her then sauntered to Billy. He aimed at the back of Billy's head. "Sorry, ol' buddy." He enunciated 'buddy' an odd way, as if he were performing comedy on stage. "Rule one: No witnesses." He fired. Billy's legs jerked twice, then flopped motionless. "Saves me a bundle of money too."

**

When Carr dropped Charlene, her vision spun and blurred. Sound reduced to the slow throb of her eardrums. Her entire being focused on a bristle of fur that slid against her back then the hot breath that blew across her face. A nudge forced her toward Marie.

346

A panther's eyes bored into hers. Her awareness cleared. Carr was facing away from her, taunting Billy's body. The puma laid its head on Marie and tugged at her shirt pocket with its teeth, then stared at Charlene.

Now Charlene understood. Biting her lips to stifle her screams, she twisted her left hand from the cuffs, stripping the skin off the back of her hand when she did. She stuffed her trembling fingers into Marie's blouse pocket. She could feel nothing other than the fire of her exposed tendons.

A woman's hand extended from where the panther had been. It guided Charlene's fingers back into the pocket. Her eyes immobile, Marie gazed into space.

This time Charlene's fingers touched a hard object. The woman helped her grasp and withdraw it. Charlene's enervated hand dropped the pillbox in the sand. She saw the woman now, squatting by her, a lion's skull cap on her head, its furry legs tangling over her arms. The woman lifted a tiny pillbox and opened it. Six emerald gel caps sat in two rows. Using her good hand, Charlene reached for one then pushed it between Marie's lips.

Carr looked back at the women. Marie was still. The other girl, drugged and delirious, appeared to wipe blood from Marie's mouth. He shook his head and said, "Marie's dead. Kit's going to be pissed she didn't get her chance at her. She's obsessed with that one."

He ambled toward Charlene.

**

Bent low, the old cavalry Winchester held in his left hand, Jim moved down the hill. He could hear Carr mocking Billy, but could not see either. Billy didn't reply.

Then Carr said, "This one's dead…"

Electricity shot through Jim's limbs. He jumped down the slope, crashing straight through the briar, knocking stones loose in a cascade that rumbled down in front of him. He pushed through a large bush. The scene opened before him. Marie lay motionless, her turquoise and white cowgirl shirt glistening bright red. Charlene struggled to hold Marie's head up.

Gun in hand, Carr stared bemused at the women.

Jim jammed to a stop. Sliding over loose gravel, he fell backwards. The rifle slammed against a rock, crushing his finger between the trigger and the stone.

The rifle boomed.

Carr fired back, then sprinted down slope and vanished in the brush.

**

Trotting down the road with the Saiga held across her body, Stephanie saw Carr run. Nearby a helicopter engine started. The rotors wound to a high pitch. Charlene looked to the sky and screamed.

Stephanie dropped her gun and raced toward the women. Jim got to Marie first. When Stephanie arrived, he was kneeling beside Marie, cradling her head.

Stephanie looked into Marie's cold white face. Time became syrup slowing Stephanie's mind and body. Tears dropped from Jim's eyes, wetting Marie's cheeks.

Charlene chanted low in mournful tones.

Stephanie saw Charlene's hand skinned open, exposing rare meat, tendons and bones. Charlene sang on. Her other hand, the handcuff dangling from it, clasped Marie's.

Charlene extended her torn hand; its bloody palm opened to reveal a small box. Jim saw it.

With sudden hope, he urged, "Come on, baby. Hang in there. You can do it."

Stephanie stared at the box. There were six small depressions, two rows of three. Each held an emerald capsule, except one was empty. Stephanie lifted the box from Charlene's hand and closed it. She pressed her fingers against Marie's carotid artery.

Time exploded forward.

"She's alive!" Stephanie jumped to her feet. She waved uphill and shouted, "Ruthie, drive here. Hurry."

"I don't know how," Ruthie wailed.

"You do it, goddamn it."

"I'll run," Jim said and sprinted up the slope.

Suddenly the engine coughed then raced. The jeep wheels lurched forward, herky-jerky, then somewhat steadily the jeep came and ground to a stop twenty yards away.

Jim pulled the radio from the backseat.

Stephanie waved her arms. "No! No! Get the first aid kit under the seat. No time to call."

In seconds, Jim was beside her. He held a metal box with a big white cross on it in one hand, the radio in the other. "Band-Aids?" he huffed.

"Blood transfusion." Stephanie opened it and pulled plastic tubing from a sealed bag. Moments later she had IV needles attached at each end. She tossed a pair of shears to Jim. "Cut open her pant leg. I need a big vein."

"You sure you should do this?" Jim slit the pants open without waiting for an answer.

"Her brain isn't getting enough blood." Stephanie's hands worked while she talked. She swabbed her own forearm with alcohol and began to hunt for a vein. "Let's hope our blood is compatible."

"I'm a universal donor," Ruthie said from behind them.

"You're dehydrated."

"I've been drinking."

"You sure?"

"I'm sure." Ruthie kneeled and pushed her inner arm forward.

Stephanie blinked back a tear then mumbled, "Thank you." She pulled Ruthie's arm over against her knee and held it firmly. "Little stick." Blood flowed toward a pump ball. She pumped it partway through the tubing. Needle held high, Stephanie bent over Marie, searching for a receiving vein. Near the knee she found one. A bit of red washed back.

Stephanie began to pump. "Call Manny, send the hovercraft."

Moments later, Jim said, "They just left the hospital."

"Do they have the coordinates?" Stephanie asked.

"They can use the radio signal," Jim said.

Stephanie squeezed off her tenth pump. "I hope her wound has clotted, or else…"

Without opening her eyes, Marie whispered, "It nicked the aorta. I've sealed it."

A helicopter engine roared, bending the bushes from the force of the rotor. With lights flashing, it rose level with them and then over their heads.

"Carr!" Charlene shouted, pointing up.

A spotlight washed over them from the circling chopper. A man extended from inside and aimed a rifle downward. He fired. The bullet thudded in the sand one meter from Jim.

The helicopter steadied. Jim pulled his pistol and fired while backing toward Derek's Winchester. Another shot from the chopper ricocheted off a rock near his head.

A manic scream came from the mine entrance. A burst of automatic fire flashed at the helicopter. The sniper ducked back inside and the aircraft accelerated upward. Another burst of automatic fire chased it.

Wendell stumbled into the open, the automatic rifle wagging back and forth after the chopper. "Carr, you bastard, you murdered Lorelei."

He emptied his clip, then collapsed into the dust. The helicopter circled wide one more time, then swooped toward them.

Jim lifted the Winchester and whispered, "Be magical one last time for Uncle Derek." He closed his eyes and fired. The helicopter wobbled side to side. Fire burst from its engine. The tail rotor rose high, and the chopper nose-dived down the mountain slope toward Highway 93. Seconds later, a rumbling explosion sent a fireball upward, turning everything around them orange.

"Help Wendell," Ruthie begged.

"You've given all the blood you can give." Stephanie began to take the IV unit down.

"I helped you." Ruthie's eyes pleaded for mercy. "They made him do it. Carr said Wendell would go to jail or worse if he didn't."

"He did help fight the helicopter," Jim said.

Stephanie went to Wendell. She rolled him over and checked his pulse. "He's alive." She ripped his shirt open. "Gut shot. He won't bleed to death."

A luminous dot appeared on the horizon. With it came the distant roar of jet engines. It grew, its boomerang shape more and more discernable with its approach.

"Five minutes?" Jim said. "Can a helicopter get from Vegas to here in five minutes?"

Stephanie's eyes filled with hope. "That one can. It's the Haines hovercraft."

**

Wendell squinted into the bright lights of the Haines Companies Emergency Evacuation Hovercraft. "What is it?" he moaned.

350

Ruthie squeezed his hand and repeated Stephanie's words while emergency responders loaded him into the fuselage beside Marie. Stephanie and Charlene sat between them.

Wendell groaned. "It's what I filmed." His lips twisted into a painful smile. "It is my ticket after all."

***

Lost in Time

Emil ran his finger over Herman's notes. Nothing explained this. He took a deep breath and closed his eyes for a moment. Then he fast-pedaled his roller chair back to the SAM.

How could it be?

He'd gone over everything he knew or could imagine.

How could I lose Matt?

It wasn't possible—unless time tunnels?

He visualized ground falling away and Matt tumbling into Allah knows what: *Another century? Into two different centuries?*

He pushed that thought aside and took more deep breaths to control his panic. Unfortunately, it wasn't quite that easy, in spite of his training as a shaman. He closed his eyes and conjured up Herman lecturing him.

"It's simple," Herman had said, "just like steering a car, brakes, lights, a gas pedal."

"Yeah, simple until something goes wrong." Emil threw his head back and exhaled at the ceiling.

I shouldn't have agreed to this.

"Where did Matt go!" He screamed it as loud as he could. Panic paralyzed all ability to think.

Staring at the glyphs, he told himself, "Walk through it again. Go slowly. Think through every step. You've left something out. Find it." He punched his finger over the symbols, reviewing his earlier actions and rethinking the process.

Matt's marker was first in the queue. I skipped it to get Jim. That should be okay. If someone were injured, you should be able to skip over others and take him first.

But I wanted Jim to help Marie find Charlene.

That was selfish.

It was okay. It shouldn't have mattered. What did the stupid machine do with Matt when I told it to skip him?

He pressed his finger against the SAM and asked for Matt's marker.

The symbol for "operation complete" flashed again.

"How can it be complete!" Emil screamed and slammed his palm against the side of the machine. The instant he did it, he remembered Arbie and the green lightning.

Emil raised his palms in surrender. "I'm sorry. God, don't do anything or I'll lose Matt and Herman forever. Please, I didn't mean to hit you."

He balled his hands into fists and pressed them against his eyes.

"Don't worry," a tiny voice said.

It came from the stone wall just three meters away.

He peered into the pores of the rock.

Something flickered.

He leaned forward and squinted at it. A pinpoint of purple light shined from inside the stone.

He gasped.

The purple light grew bigger.

The buzz of a high-pitched tuning fork stabbed painfully in his ears. He pressed his hands against the sides of his head. The vibration continued unabated inside his skull.

He opened his mouth to relieve the pressure on his brain. He was sure it would hemorrhage and he would die. Then the resonance dropped to a mild drone. He closed his mouth and shook his head, testing for any sensation of damage.

"It's okay." The voice sounded closer.

The speck of purple light had become a bright oval portal. Deep within it, three gray-blue human figures approached through a long winding tunnel.

"My God." He fell to his knees and pressed his head to the floor. "It's Mohammad with Michael and Gabriel," he said.

"No, it's me, Herman."

"We've killed Matt," Emil said, rising quickly to his feet.

"It's not your fault," Herman said.

"Matt's okay. I stowed him at an interim location," a second man said.

"Where is he?"

"My 1890s apartment in Paris," the man replied.

Herman stepped out of the purple halo and onto the SAM chamber floor. He held his hand toward the other man. "Emil, this is Mr. Jules Verne."

Emil giggled and blushed. "How odd, as a child I read books by a man with the same name."

"By candlelight when your parents thought you were sleeping. Yes, I'm that Jules Verne."

"Jules is here to help me refine the workings of the SAM. Matt and Jim were close together, so it grabbed both of them at once. If I and Jim had been together, the load might have been too much."

"It would have been too much," Jules corrected.

"We can talk about that later." Herman sounded a bit peeved. "Now please pardon Jules and me. You can teach Morto to do clean-up work while you wait."

Morto stepped out of the tunnel.

Emil backpedaled several steps. "Is he safe?"

Jules and Herman had the side of the SAM off and were poking rods at the colored streams of light that wound through it like jumbled spaghetti.

Herman said, "Yeah, I reprogrammed him to be benign. I thought we could use him to get some of your projects done."

Yeah, just like you reprogrammed the SAM for two-way travel, Emil thought.

"I'm kind of nervous," Emil said. "I can't think of anything for him right now. Can he just play quietly?"

"Just tell him to sit in the corner. He can be dormant for days, years, even centuries."

Emil considered possible out-of-the-way places for Morto then remembered that Herman didn't know about Arbie. He decided to store Morto with Arbie until everything settled down.

He took Morto into the debriefing room and said, "Sit here, and make sure this guy doesn't leave."

Morto dutifully sat cross-legged inches away from the dull green human.

When Emil returned, the SAM was back together. Jules Verne and the glowing purple tunnel were gone.

"He really wasn't Jules Verne, was he?" Emil said.

Herman shrugged his shoulders. "I think he was, but he's probably more than just Jules Verne. By the way, he said your

353

parents knew all along where you hid your books. How he knows that stuff is beyond me."

The radio crackled.

"Paiute HQ, we have 10 ida 5, kidnap victim rescued. Charlene Springwater is en route to Haines Medical via Haines hovercraft. ETA five minutes."

Emil jumped into the air and yelled a reverberating, "Yes!"

The next transmission sent his exuberance plummeting.

"We have 11 ida 8, tribesman down, female." Now Emil recognized Jim's voice. It broke and wavered. "It's Marie Rothe, 10 ida 45c, I'm afraid..." He couldn't finish.

Captain Lightfoot's voice came in over the radio. "Jim, hang on, we received your 10 ida 20 from the Haines hovey. Our ETA is ten minutes. 10 ida 5."

"The hovey picked her up a few minutes ago." Jim's words plodded on as if he didn't hear anything said to him.

"That's good." Lightfoot was working Jim now, trying to raise his spirits. "Five at most, she'll be in surgery. They're landing now."

"Too long," Jim muttered, "too long, I think."

"Hold on, I'm getting a transmission from headquarters. Jim, Stephanie just told HQ that Marie is stable. Look for our lights. We'll be with you in a few minutes."

Herman stood behind Emil. Both stared at the radio. Herman pressed the speaker button.

"Paiute HQ, this is Herman Rothe. Can you patch me through to Stephanie?"

"You are patched now," HQ replied.

"Thank God you're back." Stephanie's voice sounded frantic. "You've got to come to the hospital ASAP."

"I can't get there fast enough. You'll have to handle this for me. Do you know—does she have a small medicine tin in her pocket?"

"Yes, I saw it. One capsule is gone."

"Only one and she is stable?" Herman asked.

"Marie spoke like she was in a trance and said she closed a wound to her artery. The bleeding did reduce."

"That sounds good. Take another capsule and squeeze the fluid under her tongue."

"What capsules?" the EMP broke in.

354

Herman hardened his voice at the interruption. "It's an experimental regenerative drug we're testing. Apparently it worked. I think she should take a second dose. Stephanie, understand?"

From aboard the hovey came a heated exchange regarding who was in charge. The EMP declared he would not remove Marie's oxygen mask. Stephanie asserted her authority as an RN. The EMP insisted that he was in charge until they were inside the emergency room. Amid the wailing of the jets, Stephanie told the EMP, "This says I'm in charge.

The EMP shouted, "You crazy bitch!"

Ten to fifteen seconds later Stephanie said, "Done, but I might need a lawyer when we disembark."

"Stay with her. I'm calling Dr. Brown to meet you there. He'll make up some reason why you had to give her medication, diabetes or something else. I'll get there when I can."

Herman patted Emil's shoulder. "You did a good job here. We'll be able to bring Matt back tomorrow noon."

"But I almost lost Matt. In fact, I'm not sure I didn't." Emil turned his shoulder away from Herman's touch.

"But you didn't lose him. Like I said, you couldn't have known about this problem."

For a while they both were silent; then Emil remembered. "You know that Arbie guy, the one with the red hair?"

"Arbie? The fool who blew up the mine with Matt and me inside?"

"Yeah, him. He's here."

Herman glanced at all the monitors. "Where? I don't see him."

"Here." Emil pointed to the conference room. "In there."

Herman frowned.

"In the conference room where I put Morto."

"What? Why did you bring him in here?" Herman punched out his words, elevating his voice with each one.

"I didn't—we didn't; he got in on his own."

"That's not possible. How—"

Emil interrupted before Herman could finish. "He was stung by the SAM. He's all green now. Is he dead, because he doesn't look quite dead—but not alive either."

Emil moved toward the conference room, beckoning Herman to follow.

***

Chapter 25: Aliens Among Us

Arbie's chartreuse luster had faded to a moldy green color. His body lay slumped on the floor in the same position it had been the night before. Only his eyes looked alive, and they were wide and frightened.

Herman untied Arbie's hands then lifted the redhead's arm and dropped it. It fell limp as a string.

"He's just paralyzed." Herman pointed to a wet spot on Arbie's left thigh. "What's that?"

"Never noticed it before," Emil said. "We didn't spend much time with him. Everything was crazy with the police and the squatters."

"I think he has an infection, and a serious one." Herman pressed the wet spot hard with his index finger. Arbie's eyes looked pained.

"Good thing he's stunned. He'd go nuts if he could see Morto," Emil said.

"Oh, he can see Morto and he can hear us. You might say his fantasy about aliens has become a personal nightmare."

Pink puss oozed through Arbie's jeans where Herman poked his leg.

Emil studied it. "Oh my. Think we did it?"

Herman shook his head. "No, it's been going on for a long time. I think he injured himself when he blew up the mine."

"He should go to the hospital," Emil said.

"Yes, but we'll need to detox him first. Morto can do that." Herman emitted a long drone of high-pitched whistles and clicks.

The metal monster nodded then retrieved a long thin needle, which he inserted into Arbie's belly button. His eyes shot red beams over Arbie's body while he emitted ear-piercing tones.

Arbie's eyes began to move in tiny terrified jerks. Morto extracted the needle and raised a scalpel close to Arbie's face. In a flash, the monster's arm whipped down, splitting Arbie's pant leg down its length, exposing the leg without scratching the skin.

"Now that the paralyzing agent is neutralized, Morto will dress his leg wound." Herman tilted his head toward the door. "We'll let Morto work."

Arbie groaned and turned his head back and forth. Morto jammed his huge chrome face close to Arbie's and said in a high-pitched metallic voice, "Hold still. I have to lance your wound and drain the poison."

He jammed a funnel-shaped device straight into the wound. Puss and purple blood burst out in globs. Arbie's scream reverberated through the chamber.

Morto held the discharge up to the light. "I have microscopic vision. I can see your cells. Yes, your body is absorbing the alien DNA quite nicely."

Arbie screamed and began to hyperventilate.

Herman rushed into the room. "What's the matter?"

"The robot is hybridizing me." Arbie huffed as if he were choking.

Herman frowned. "But, Arbie, we have an alliance with the aliens. We've agreed to let them experiment on you." Then Herman emitted a bunch of squeaks and whistles.

Morto squeaked and whistled back.

Whimpering, Arbie scrunched into a fetal ball and shuddered.

"Why are you doing this?" Emil asked.

"We could have left him green," Herman said. "Now let's go talk to Manny."

"Don't fire him," Emil pleaded.

"I have to. He endangered you and Stephanie, and exposed our secret."

"A Paiute policeman was wounded. Manny had to help. You're a member of the tribe now. You understand. He only did what you would have done."

"I understand the helping, but leaving the door open," Herman said.

"He wanted to get the man inside quickly. He had to leave the door unlocked to do that."

The radio crackled and Manny spoke.

"Emil, Mr. Herman? Are you there?"

"Yes," Herman replied abruptly.

"I'm patching through a private phone call from Miss Stephanie. She has an update on Miss Marie."

"Herman?" Stephanie said.

"Yeah, I'm here. Emil's here. Manny patched you in from upstairs."

"Okay, they just did a scan on Marie. They can't believe the bullet missed her aorta. The damage is less than we first thought. They've given her some antibiotics…"

Stephanie broke into sobs. She gasped several times then began to regain her composure.

"I did something really stupid. I gave her a blood transfusion. Ruthie was a universal donor…Marie had lost so much blood—I didn't have any choice…"

Stephanie choked up again.

Herman broke in, "Stephanie, it's okay. The universal donor works for her, too. I'll explain at a better time."

Stephanie's panting subsided. She sniffled then said, "She's stable. I think the trial drug helped. They're taking her to surgery in one hour to remove the bullet. It's against the back of her rib cage."

"Is she breathing okay?"

"Yes, it appears to have missed her lung. They can't believe it missed all the vitals."

"Block the surgery. No surgery." Herman sounded alarmed. "They are more dangerous to her than the bullet. They may reopen the wound. Is Brown there yet?"

"He just arrived."

"Tell him to find a reason to block the surgery. He should release her from the hospital as soon as she can walk out."

"I understand."

Herman paused as if searching for words then simply said, "Thanks for saving my daughter's life."

**

Stephanie sat by Marie's hospital bed. Marie blinked then whispered, "It was fun when I was winning." She coughed out a laugh.

358

She reached out and took Stephanie's hand. Her grip was weak and her hand cold. She opened her mouth but had to stop and swallow. She wetted her lips; still the words came out ragged and hoarse. "There's something."

She pointed to the pocket of Stephanie's pants. "Give it." She opened her palm.

Stephanie's face wrinkled in confusion. She looked down, wondering what Marie wanted. Stephanie stood and turned her leg side to side, still not understanding.

Marie pointed.

Stephanie frowned at a cloth fragment caught on the edge of her pocket. She held it up. A chill raced down her back. She bit her lip while dropping the fragment of shiny pink and white ribbon into Marie's hand.

Marie's fingers closed over it. She smiled. "I remember everything now. The pants you were wearing when you gave me to Herman's secretary. The ribbon you tied in my hair before we left the motel."

Tears rolled down Stephanie's cheeks.

"You did it today, didn't you?" Marie said.

Stephanie's chest lurched. "I'm sorry…"

Marie put Stephanie's hand against her cheek.

Stephanie's chest heaved, over and over.

**

When Herman approached, Manny stood up and cleared his throat. "Mr. Herman, I have caused great danger and I—"

"How?" Herman asked. He held the sedated Arbie in his arms.

"Him," Manny said. "I let him in and he almost killed Emil and Miss Stephanie."

Herman frowned. "Manuel, you've been working too hard. Remember, we found Arbie, dehydrated and delirious, in a gulley this morning. We brought him into the security trailer to hydrate him and clean his wound. He's never gone into the research trailer."

Herman looked from Emil to Manny. "Can we all agree on that?"

"Yeah." Manuel pointed at Arbie. "But he'll claim he got in."

Herman chuckled. "He'll say a lot of things, but the fact is, he didn't take his antibiotics and the infection got to his brain. I'm afraid he has become flat-out crazy."

Through the window they saw Matt's jeep pull up. Jim stepped out of the driver's seat. Emil's eyes filled with tears. He gulped and hurried out the door.

Emil threw his arms around Jim. He cried, "Uncle Derek," over and over.

Jim patted Emil's back and said, "He was happy to make you family. Now we're our family, you and I."

**

Arbie lay strapped to a gurney in the middle of the hovercraft cargo area. Jim and Emil sat on one side of him. Herman sat on the other side, speaking to the hospital staff over the phone.

"Yes, we had to strap him to a gurney. We had to sedate him too. Yes, he's been violent. He's been making strange nonsensical claims. Very adamant about it all.

"Oh, Ruthie reported he engaged in similar behavior? She said he threw away his antibiotics? Well, he has been very erratic. His leg's a mess. I bet the infection got to his brain."

The hovercraft began to lift off. Herman hung up then said under his breath, "I guarantee the infection got to his brain."

Arbie studied Herman in a curious distracted way. He turned and gazed at Emil and Jim while mumbling, "Hybrids, hybrids." Then he closed his eyes and began to sing himself to sleep.

The hovercraft rose like a jet-propelled elevator.

Emil's hands clamped on his armrests. "This thing is almost as scary as Morto."

"Wow," Jim said. "You think Morto is scary now? You should have been there before Herman neutralized him. I thought we were goners. Every time we put Morto down, he would start all over again." Jim told the whole story of their encounter with Morto. He finished by saying, "According to Herman, Morto had some kind of a micro restart switch."

"Yeah," Herman said to both of them. "It's ingenious. An exciter emits a string of photons. If any of the photons impinge on a receiver plate, then the circuit is complete and the system, in our case Morto, restarts. The entire string of photons has to be blocked to keep the system shut down. Usually something has to be physically slid between the exciter and the receiver."

360

"We were down to our last chance," Jim told Emil.

Now they were jetting toward Vegas at 400 mph.

"What did you do to stop it, anyway?" Jim asked Herman.

Herman shook his head. "I have no idea."

"Luck, I guess," Jim said.

Emil wrinkled the eyebrow above his left eye. "Mr. Herman, you told me once that a photon is a speck of light."

"Yes, the smallest unit of light," Herman said.

"What would it look like if you were the size of an atom?"

"A very teeny tiny flash, I suppose."

"Like a tiny white ball?" Emil said.

"It might look that way," Herman said.

Jim's lips curled into a big smile. "Emil, have you been playing pool in your dreams again?"

"Well, I did fall asleep at the desk while you were gone, and I dreamed I had a teeny tiny pool stick and I was knocking tiny balls off course. They were coming really fast and I was hitting them really fast. I knocked them all off target."

Jim flipped his palms up in the air. "There you have it, as good an explanation as any."

Herman fidgeted and put his elbow on his knee like *The Thinker*. The hovercraft was landing on the hospital heliport when he spoke again. "You know, Emil was dreaming a few days ago. We were wrestling with Morto four hundred years ago. What you're saying is that Emil can change history by dreaming."

"I don't think it was me," Emil said. He sounded neither convincing nor convinced.

***

Admiral Sharon

Quantum set down outside the crumbled Verg wall. Captain Yanitur and Kale entered the fortress.

"Who is in charge here?" Yanitur asked the nearest Verg.

A pirate said, "They are," and faced a group of Amazonians.

"How did the Amazonians get inside so fast?" Yanitur asked.

Kale looked about. "Only a few dozen here with our marines. How many did she say she had?"

Yanitur reddened. He couldn't look Kale in the face. "She never told me."

361

"Oh." Kale shook his head.

"Oh, yes," Yanitur said. "She used us for a diversion."

Kale twisted his face in disgust. "She must have had sapper tunnels set; then when we created the commotion, they broke through."

A loud splintering sound drew their attention upward. A body slammed through a window, sending a shower of broken glass toward them. A rope, tied to the victim's neck, uncoiled while he fell, squirming and kicking. The rope yanked taut. His body halted with a hollow snap and vibrated then went limp.

Kale stepped back and gasped.

Another window crashed outward. Another body hurled down and snapped to a stop at the end of a rope.

"You," Yanitur screamed to the nearest Amazonian. "Where is Sharon?"

The Amazon curtsied and lifted her hand toward the entrance to the building. "Accompany me," she said.

Another body crashed out a window and jolted dead.

"Shit!" Yanitur hissed, then raced after his Amazonian escort. He half turned and shouted back, "Kale, take charge down here. Have Throdin bring me a couple of marines."

The Amazonian's eyes laughed with amusement when Throdin hurried up with two seraphim soldiers. "Captain," she said, "be assured we have the Vergs under control." She pointed to the three hanged men.

"That is my concern. I would like to interrogate some of their officers while they are still alive." He blocked her path.

Her face still smiled, but her eyes demanded an explanation.

"Who are you?" Yanitur demanded.

She curtsied again. "I am Captain Alexia." Her face remained frozen in a false smile that chilled him.

Yanitur stepped aside and bowed his head slightly. "Captain Alexia, I'm sure you are aware that summary executions violate the Galactic Societies Accord."

Alexia let the smile fall away. "And I'm sure you are aware that Amazonian law requires death to anyone who violates our citizens. In any case, Admiral Sharon requests that you leave your seraphim warriors here."

Yanitur eyed a crystal hanging from Alexia's left ear. "Tell Sharon I happily oblige. Would she be so kind as to desist from killing more prisoners until I can interrogate them?"

362

In a bored tone, Alexia said to no one, *"Kiereki Sjarien, AGS nikki..."* The rest was beyond Yanitur's knowledge of Amazonian.

Yanitur ordered Throdin and the marines to halt. Then to Alexia, he said, "I will have my intellectual seraph join the meeting."

Alexia flashed a bemused smile. It seemed genuine, and equally disturbing. "Not necessary, Captain. As you know, Sharon is proficient in your language."

"Just the same—" Yanitur started.

The Amazonian raised her hand, halting him, then cocked her head to the side. "Sharon says it has been a long time since she last saw Uriel. Please have him come. But we'll go in now. He can catch up with us."

The elevator ascended. The doors slid back, revealing an expansive spaceport operation center. Trägers, already converted to serve the Amazonians, trudged about, heaping Verg bodies into a pile in one corner of the room. Five Amazonians lay dead, their bodies covered by full-length rainbow-colored veils embroidered with symbols of rank and personal history. On the floor in another corner, about thirty Vergs sat cross-legged, their fingers laced behind their heads, which they bowed until their elbows rested on their knees. One groaned. An Amazonian jabbed him with her spear. Several Vergs bled from these wounds.

Her dark hair in a traditional warrior's Mohawk, Sharon wore a cloak over a breastplate of black armor. An armor skirt covered her otherwise bare legs to mid-thigh.

One glance at her shapely legs sent Yanitur's pulse racing while his mind flooded with memories of their time together at the academy.

Her chartreuse eyes studied Yanitur quizzically.

His knees weakened at her gaze.

On her right and left, synthetic beings, not of seraph class but superior to trägers, stood at attention along with her two Amazonian bodyguards.

Her guards punched their left fists out in a karate-like salute to Yanitur and Alexia while saying, *"Reeshie,"* meaning "sister" in Amazonian.

Alexia returned the gesture.

He did not.

Alexia's face wrinkled with displeasure. Sharon's bodyguards held their salutes and waited.

The elevator doors opened again. Uriel entered. He thrust his fist toward the guards and greeted them. Yanitur glared at Uriel, then extended his fist limply.

Sharon stood, thrust her fist out like a battering ram and said, "*Reeshie*, welcome Uriel and Yanitur. Captain, I recall that I assigned Uriel to you when you were my understudy at the academy."

Yanitur clicked his heels together and saluted her with hand snapped across his chest in AGS naval fashion. "Yes, Admiral Sharon. I'm surprised that you remember such a lowly ensign as myself."

She saluted him AGS style in return. None of her guards did. The AGS association was between the two of them. Then she said, "You know eidetic memories are common among my people, still—you really think I could forget you?"

Yanitur felt his face blush.

"Admiral—" he began.

She cut him off. "I was the governor of the colony these slime attacked."

One Verg rose to a crouch. Immediately, a spear tip was thrust into his shoulder. He cursed the Amazonian guard. Showing no emotion, she jabbed him more forcefully, drawing a stream of blood.

Between wails, he shouted, "We didn't attack the colony. We rescued the survivors."

Face flushed with anger, Sharon narrowed her eyes at him. "Rescued them into slavery and prostitution? I have five dead. I need seven of you in compensation. If you can offer me no better information, you shall be the next one."

Yanitur interrupted, "Naval code requires—"

"I have claimed this station for Amazonia. Our laws apply."

Yanitur's stared at her in disbelief. "This was a joint assault."

"Your attack was a diversion. We had already infiltrated their facility and compromised their trägers." She pointed to the robots that, having stacked the Verg bodies, awaited further instruction.

Yanitur's jaws tightened. He glanced at Uriel then back to her. "Our colony was also obliterated. I need to question these men before I go examine the destruction myself. Let me interview the rest before you continue with this outrage."

Sharon walked around the desk and sat on its corner. Yanitur held his gaze on her face, not daring to even glimpse at her legs. The effort made his abdomen cramp.

"We captured the command center before they could destroy their data. You don't need to waste your time with these barbarians. However, if you insist, then take them all onto your ship along with your citizens who are among their slaves. We shall reestablish our lost Amazonian colony—here."

Yanitur locked his jaws and glared at her. "That's an absurd demand. My investigation of our settlements will benefit both of us." He pointed his finger from her to himself, back and forth several times. "On such a venture I cannot be encumbered with a shipload of refugees and prisoners."

Her eyes sparkled with amusement.

He studied the Verg prisoners. "You've questioned them. Which will best enlighten me about the region around our colonies?"

She crossed her legs. They pulled his eyes like magnets. He swallowed and looked up into her eyes.

They laughed at him. "The big-mouthed one who just talked and the old man with the gray beard," she said, the words flowing from her mouth like music.

"Well then, please leave them alive." Yanitur turned to leave. Uriel nudged Yanitur's elbow slightly back toward her.

Yanitur wanted to push past Uriel, but the memories of his times with her boiled inside him, and that overruled all else.

He cleared his throat and faced her with a smile. "It would be our pleasure to have you and your staff join us on *Quantum* for dinner this evening."

"With appetite," she replied, her green eyes locking on his and sending a shudder of lust from his scalp to his crotch.

They saluted. He exited, mad at her, mad at Uriel, and smoldering with desire.

**

Yanitur kissed her shoulder then her neck. Light and timid, like a youngster sneaking a touch, his fingertips slid from her knee to her buttocks.

Sharon watched him over her shoulder, narrowing her green eyes into passionate slits.

Do they say go or stop, or is she teasing me?

His lust subdued his indecision in quick order. She would let him know soon enough, either way.

His hand glided over her hip and between her legs.

She fell back and lifted a faceted crystal from her bag by the couch and held it between her fingers. He glanced at it, wondering, then dragged his fingers up the inside of her thigh until they lay in the lips of her vulva. She gasped then clamped her hand on his wrist and wrestled it up onto her abdomen.

He raked his teeth over her earlobe, then sucked it between his lips. "What's this?" he whispered. He ran his other hand down her forearm to the crystal.

She groaned and pulled his hand to her breast. "A holo-gener," she said between breaths. She extended it toward him. "When you hold it thus," she demonstrated, "it puts you in a holographic world."

Her smile taunted. Her eyes twinkled in the candlelight. "Here." She pressed it between his fingers.

Its signal slammed through his brain and set him on fire.

"Oh," he panted. "Oh my God!" He stared at his chest. He had breasts. His erect nipples tingled with excitement.

She laughed and pushed him onto his back. Now she straddled him. Breathing heavily through her nose, she pressed her lips against his and thrust her tongue in his mouth then withdrew it, then sucked his lower lip between hers.

He trembled. His breath rushed out in pants.

"You know we are lesbians," she teased, then slid her lips down his chest and put his engorged nipple between her teeth.

He arched his back, moaning over and over.

"The crystal fools your brain into thinking you are my wife, Katiri. At that moment he saw Katiri's face reflecting as if in a mirror. It chilled him to his soul, transforming his sexual pleasure into the terrifying memory of Katiri lying dead in the corridor with two mangled Verg pirates nearby and an empty escape chute further on.

Yanitur trembled. Sharon worked him like a harp, shivers of pleasure mixed with the shudder of terror. Yanitur tried to hold his explosion back, but could not. He gritted his teeth and grunted out his euphoria in rapid breaths. She wailed with him and dug her nails into his chest. Lights exploded in his head. Sound banged in his ears. He begged for more, but it ended.

She fell beside him and took the crystal from his limp fingers.

Moments later, she explained while stroking his chest. "Katiri and our children, Viekki and Meirri, came to the colony with the first group. When my fleet arrived, they were gone, everyone was gone, only charred structures and the dead remained."

Tears dripped down her cheeks. "They're not here among these slaves. I suppose the Vergs divided our people into lots, each ship taking some. The first pirate I questioned said they had not.

"I hanged him for smothering my hope."

She took Yanitur's hand. "That pulse weapon that burned a hole in your ship, we've never seen it before. The Vergs sure didn't invent it.

"When you go to the colonies, be careful. Someone we never met is out there."

His mind saw Katiri's scalp and ear stored in a cryogenic vault aboard *Quantum*. Sharon should be told, but he didn't.

***

Chapter 26: Not the End

Up at sunrise, Marie tiptoed down the winding staircase. She paused a moment on the first-floor landing and gazed southeast over the Seine to Ponte Neuf and Notre Dame, then she continued to the lobby.

Alain, the hotel desk clerk, looked up and smiled. "I recognized your footsteps." He pushed a small package toward her then brushed his dark hair back in nervous excitement. His eyes lavished her with a quiet flirtation that had gone on since her arrival.

Box under her arm, she thanked him and headed for the breakfast nook.

"They're not set yet," Alain called out.

She made a disappointed pout.

He relented. "You can grab a croissant and coffee off the cart. If they say anything, have them talk to me." He blushed then smiled.

She turned her pout into a smile and sealed it with a quick wink.

What a flirt I've become. She laughed at herself.

She slid into a corner table with her back to the wall. One of the hotel staff pointed to the coffee pot and made a sipping motion with his hand. She smiled and nodded back. Everyone was friendly early in the morning. Setting the box aside, she took her cup to the hospitality table and filled it. The hostess brought her a plate with a croissant and a pat of butter.

Marie said, "*Merci beaucoup,*" and, of course, smiled. She sipped her coffee until the staff forgot about her; then laid the box on a chair hidden by the blue and white checkered tablecloth and opened it.

Fifteen minutes later Jim walked in. He took a baguette and coffee from the hospitality table and sat next to her. Dejectedly, he dipped the stone-hard bread into the coffee. "So much for French cooking. We have to go to the market today or I'm going to starve."

He frowned down at the empty box then lifted it onto the table. He read the label. "Haines Paris—Security, I didn't know Haines had an office in Paris."

"Everywhere." Marie sipped her coffee. "We're everywhere."

"So?" He thrust his chin at the box.

Marie raised the butt of a small revolver from her pocket.

"Naughty, naughty." He wagged his finger. "I hear they frown on guns over here."

"Permit came with it." She produced a card from her wallet as proof.

Stephanie and Matt entered. Everyone greeted each other in French. Matt wrapped his arm around Stephanie's waist. She didn't move away, but she didn't snuggle either.

"So who got mail?" Matt pointed to the box.

Jim rolled his eyes toward Marie.

"Don't be so judgmental." Marie slapped his hand. Then she lifted the revolver for them all to see.

Stephanie put her hands on her hips. "Good God, Marie, you are incorrigible. I hoped we could relax and relish our victories: Carr is dead, Billy Manes is dead, Arbie has been institutionalized, Morto has been neutralized, Wendell has seen Jesus, and despite our meddling, history didn't change."

Jim tried to take a bite from the soggy part of his baguette. It dribbled down his chin. He got it over the plate before it could plop on his pants. "Crap," he said and wiped his mouth. "Anyway, I was thinking about history. I mean, if we did change history, wouldn't the old history just vanish from our minds and we would never know we had changed it."

"On that note"—Matt pointed at the rock-hard baguette—"why don't we skip the free breakfast and grab something at the little pastry shop around the corner?"

Jim was in the doorway and beckoning before they could debate the proposal.

Herman could have shipped the ancient French books back to the National Bibliotheque in environmentally controlled containers.

Instead, the four of them decided to escort the volumes and spend a week in Paris at Haines Companies' expense.

Matt took the books to the library while the others toured the Louvre. At noon they would all meet for lunch at the Procope Restaurant.

Cherie, a tall, well-portioned blonde of Norman descent, escorted Matt to the archives, where he personally returned the volumes to the shelf. Charmed, more from Herman's donations than by Matt, she suggested they peruse for other titles of interest to him.

Patronizing at first, she warmed when Matt conversed in detail about the sixteenth century. Based on his interest, she pulled several books and prepared them for review at a large table.

Matt donned gloves and handled the manuscripts with care. Occasionally, he stopped to read a passage aloud, which they would discuss, each exhibiting special knowledge on the topic.

Cherie stood and pointed down between the stacks. "I almost forgot, Mr. Rothe said you would want to look at some items in this aisle."

Matt chuckled. "Herman? I'm surprised."

"Yes, he did." She winked then slipped between the rows to a wall covered with artwork from the period. She stood on her tiptoes, her fingers just reaching the bottom of a thin volume. She sighed. "I need a ladder."

"I think I can reach it." Matt pressed against her. He ran his fingertips up the length of her arm and grasped the book.

She blushed and slid her fingers over his palm to take the volume from him.

He placed his hand in the small of her back and pointed to a small picture on the wall. "It looks like a field drawing. I think from Coutras!"

At that point, they were playfully slinging arcane information back and forth in something of an odd courting ritual.

"Why Coutras?" Cherie probed.

Pretending to be uncertain, Matt frowned and moved closer to study the details. He pointed to the right upper quadrant. "This hill looks distinct to the field of Coutras. If I'm right, it's where the woman, I believe her name was Annette Dubois, deployed the cannons. He paused, his eyes watering as if he had developed a personal bond to this historical figure.

His voice shaking, he continued. "Here, in the foreground, appears to be Henri. His heavy cavalry is starting forward, the

370

famous charge, perhaps? It would be a memorable moment for a soldier artist to record."

Cherie shifted her feet and slid her arm under his to point at details. "It is as you described. The hill is an astute observation. Not many would be aware of that."

Her face now delectably close to his, she said in a wispy breath, "Even so-called experts don't know it."

Then she pulled away from his arm, as if to regain her professional demeanor. Matt restrained her slightly. She relaxed. "Anyway, it was drawn by an unknown artist. As you suggested, he probably participated in the battle. These two figures at Henri's right are enigmas.

"This one is Matthew Crowley, our best guess from the little we could gather."

She touched his wrist. "A Matthew like you, also alleged to have been from the New World."

"Wait," Matt said, touching her hand back. "Who wrote about him?"

Cherie bent her face close to his, as if to share a secret, or something else. "Annette Dubois." She raised the thin book toward him. "In her diary that I"—she cleared her throat—"that we just took from the shelf."

She pointed to the figures in the drawing again. "Crowley and the dark man Manado, who claimed to be the Native American ambassador to Queen Elizabeth, disappeared after the battle. There is no further record of them anywhere. Nor is there any record of them before the battle, other than Annette's notes, that is. She claims to have met Crowley shortly after St. Bartholomew Day."

Matt smiled as if amused and pointed to Manado. "He does look Native American."

"Yes, or Moorish or mulatto, but not the Manado who really was a Native American ambassador to Queen Elizabeth. In short, I think they lied about who they were."

Matt pursed his lips and frowned. "Do you think Annette lied about them? Maybe they didn't exist at all."

Cherie sat and swung her leg sharply to cross it. "Why would she do that?" With finality in her voice, she said, "Why would the artist draw them if he didn't see them?"

She smiled again and pushed the volume toward Matt. "Monsieur Krause, *The Memoirs of Annette Dubois*, from her childhood to her death in Paris sixty years later."

371

Matt gasped.

She tilted her head as if to ask why.

"I thought she died at Coutras."

"No, she didn't." Cherie opened the book. "Rather than read through this, you might go to the Saint-Germain-des-Prés and talk to the curator. He is descended from Dubois.

"He lent Annette's memoirs to the library. Sadly, because it is a lent volume, it cannot leave the building. But you can come back here and read it as many times as you want. I'm working days all this week."

She looked at her watch. "Oh, it's about lunchtime."

**

Matt arrived at the Procope Restaurant an hour and a half late.

"Hey, Matt, what happened?" Jim asked while they finished their desserts.

"Sorry, guys, I got caught up in a tour of the sixteenth-century section of the library. They have lots of interesting stuff in there." Matt's eyes lit with excitement.

Stephanie slid over to give Matt room.

Matt sat beside her. "Guess what, Jim. They have a field drawing of Coutras. You're in it."

Jim choked on his pastry. "Yikes, that's bad."

Matt laughed and rocked back in his chair. "Don't worry. It's in an obscure cubby. Even if you stood next to it, no one could figure it out, although the artist drew the tattoo on the back of your hand."

Stephanie put half of her chocolate éclair on a saucer and passed it to Matt.

He let it sit. "Annette Dubois did not die at Coutras."

Jim raised his eyebrows. "No way anyone lived through that explosion." He frowned with quick concern. "What about Barnard?"

Matt knotted his cheek. "I don't think he survived."

Marie gave them an odd look. "Guys, you're talking about people who died four centuries ago."

Matt sighed. "Yeah, but they were our friends. It would be nice to know that their story ended well."

"We've got stories of our own to worry about." Stephanie's forehead wrinkled with curiosity while she glanced from the untouched éclair to Matt.

"Anyway," began Matt, "the curator at St. Germain Church is descended from the Duboises. She said he might be able to tell us more about what happened to them."

"She?" The word thudded from Stephanie's mouth.

"Annette?" Matt asked in faked confusion.

"No. The 'she said' she. That one."

Matt shrugged his shoulders. "The docent who showed me around was a she."

Stephanie scooted the éclair back to herself and took a bite. "Gee, I guess I'm hungrier than I thought."

Matt huffed. Marie rolled her eyes at him. Jim shook his head minutely.

Stephanie finished the pastry then stood. "Let's all go over to St. Germain Church, the oldest church in Paris. Who knows what the hell we might learn."

***

Artifacts

They worked their way through the maze of streets in the Latin Quarter to the church. It now stood on a tiny island of soil, its historical grounds lobed away to make traffic lanes, its extensive gardens and dormitories replaced by younger structures, juveniles with little respect for their elder.

The group joined a guided tour that ended near the tiny enclave where Jules had retrieved *The Pearl of Light* before he burned the bookshelf it had been hidden within.

To Matt's surprise the docent announced, "Please, if you will glance through the half door, which has been opened to allow us to see inside. To your right is a magnificent bookcase created and hand-carved by Master Carpenter Victor Ives in the late 1500s."

"I thought it burned the night of Saint Bartholomew," Matt said from the rear of the group.

The guide laughed condescendingly. "This student of history forgot to turn the page and finish his reading assignment."

Everyone chuckled; some eyed Matt askance. The guide continued. "But he is correct about the destruction of Ives's first bookcase. However, Henri IV commissioned Ives to recreate his famous carving, which he did totally from memory. Look at it. You must agree, we are very fortunate Monsieur Ives survived that

373

infamous night. He was a Huguenot. He lived only because the holy brothers took him to safety. Headmaster Pierre LeBlanc lost his life defending Ives from the very mobs that broke in and burned the original bookshelf."

The tour filed past the door, each taking an obligatory glance; then they all proceeded outside and on to the next stop on their itinerary.

Matt approached the guide, who offered a good-natured apology; then he flipped the latch to the bottom half of the door. "Staff is restoring artifacts inside, so the whole tour cannot come in, but one serious student, such as yourself, is welcome."

A solitary occupant sat at a desk and worked at the tedious task of repairing an old document. He didn't lift an eye to acknowledge Matt. Matt, with hands clasped behind his back, leaned toward Ives's bookshelf and peered into the crevices, hoping to determine whether this, as its predecessor, was equipped with a hidden enclave.

Perhaps, after all settled, the "Pearl" returned to its original hiding place, he thought.

Unable to discern a hidden cache, he informed the guide, "I was told by Cherie Roux at the national library that I could find a descendent of Barnard and Annette Dubois here."

The restorer at the table laid aside his work and stood. "I am Eugene Lucas, the curator here and of the Dubois family line. You must be Matthew Crowley. Cherie called and said you might drop by."

Startled, Matt corrected Lucas. "I'm Matt Krause." He spelled his last name to make it clear. "German or Czech, I'm not sure, but definitely not the historic character you just named."

They both fidgeted and laughed. Matt's eyes came to rest on a small brass candleholder on the curator's desk.

Waves tingled over his skin and down his arms. Words stumbling, he asked, "What is that, if it's okay for me to ask?"

Lucas raised the tiny candleholder toward Matt. "A bombastic forgery, magnificent and unbelievable, it'll take some time to explain." His tone begged Matt to stay and listen.

Matt raised his hand then held back, waiting for permission to touch the object.

Lucas pushed it forward. "Take it. It's not more than thirty, maybe sixty years old."

Matt faked a puzzled frown, but his heart was pounding. He examined the small brass candleholder from all angles, then handed it back. His face still questioning, he offered a weak comment, "It's tiny."

"It has been in our museum for years. At one time, it was categorized as having been made by a monk around 1600. Recently, however, I noticed some corrosion and decided to clean and seal it with a protective coat. When I cleaned the bottom"—he pointed— "there under the stem, I saw something shocking."

He handed a magnifying glass to Matt and used a pen point to indicate the exact spot. "Look very carefully."

Matt looked through the lens, but he already knew what he would find. "Yes, I see that the corrosion worked all the way through the base, and—"

He stared into Lucas's eyes. "The stem is from a .357 casing. That is a modern pistol, I believe."

Lucas nodded disdainfully. "Once I saw that, I tried to determine when the candleholder came into our inventory. Unfortunately our archives were destroyed by the Nazis, so the earliest reference I could find was about 1947. However, that reference claimed that it was made in the seventeenth century."

"Impossible," Matt said.

Lucas nodded. "Yes, impossible, I assume a soldier stationed here during World War II made it as a prank."

"Must be," Matt agreed.

Lucas's eyes sparkled. "There is one problem, though. I have been able to carbon date the paraffin melted inside the holder and that wax is from the 1600s. Whoever faked this went to great pains to make it appear authentic."

"Someone in the occupational forces had too much time on their hands," Matt suggested.

The conversation stalled awkwardly. Finally Matt blurted his main purpose for being there. "At the library, they said Annette Dubois lived a long life in Paris. I thought she and Bernard were both killed at Coutras."

Lucas eyed him. "I've never read any authority that suggested that."

"Please edify me," Matt said.

Lucas laughed. "The period was complicated. Religious wars are full of hyperbole, sightings of giant metal demons, angels sparkling like chrome through holes in their skin. They even suggest that the Spanish used Aztec Indians to terrorize their opponents on the battlefield. Of course, all that is nonsense.

"But in the case of Annette Dubois we have a laudable circumstance. The battle had ended. Uninformed, a brigand of pikemen marched forward to attack her position. She fired her last volley, a mixture of anything they could cram down the cannon barrel. It stalled the attack long enough for a contingency of mixed cavalry, the defeated royalists and the victorious Huguenots, to carry a white flag between the two forces. Both sides laid down their arms, ending the conflict.

"This action is often considered to be the beginning of reconciliation. Dubois speaks to it at great length in the last chapter of her memoirs."

"I'm afraid I have more reading to do." Matt held the candleholder out to Lucas.

Lucas pushed it back. "It's a fake. Keep it as a souvenir of your trip, and a reminder: don't jump to conclusions until you've studied a situation thoroughly."

Matt accepted with a gracious bow, then excused himself. "My friends insist on getting to the top of the Eiffel Tower before sunset."

**

Lucas stood at his window. Cherie entered and stood beside him. "What do you think about the American?" she asked.

Lucas jutted his jaw toward the street. They watched Matt join his friends, among them a large brown man. Cherie pointed to the tattoo on the back of Jim's hand. "Look! Get a camera. Quick!"

The camera flashed from within the church. Matt didn't notice. He was too focused on his friends. They all seemed upset.

Possibly a stolen purse or lost coat, he thought.

"What's up?" he asked.

"We're going back tonight," Stephanie said.

Matt's eyes darted in confusion. "What?"

Marie answered, "They've analyzed the remains from the helicopter crash. Carr's body isn't there. He's still alive."

THE END

376

Author's Biography

Blake grew up just south of Las Cruces, New Mexico, where he spent his spare time exploring the desert in his World War Two surplus jeep. Sometimes he listened to old-timers' tales of Geronimo, Pancho Villa, and Billy the Kid.

Today he weaves his love and respect for the desert along with bits of what he's heard and seen into his stories.

A licensed Professional Engineer in the State of California with Masters Degrees in Energy Conversion and Urban Planning as well as experience as a college math instructor, Blake's writings include a dash of science and technology along with other interesting topics ranging from aliens to the Kaballah.

You can read more about Blake and his writing at his website: www.shamangene.com/BLOG.

Blake is a member of California Writers Club and the Indie Author News.

Other Books by the Author

An ancient alien's story of our past.
The search for his remains.
A race to save our world.
Hunted by human psychics, a castaway alien seeks refuge with
a Bedouin shaman.
3000 years later, Matt Krause is hired to figure out what
happened to the alien called Gimish.
A Far Traveler is the first book in the Shaman Gene series.
A Far Traveler is the 2013 Global Ebook Silver Medal Winner
in Science Fiction.
Available as an e-book or paperback.